A Season for

Ally Sinclair grew up on the North Yorkshire coast and now lives with her husband in Worcestershire, at least until she can persuade him to give into her yearning to live somewhere nearer the sea. No kids, no pets. She sometimes manages to keep a pot plant alive. Briefly.

She has been writing professionally since 2013, and is also published as Alison May and, in collaboration, as Juliet Bell. Ally is a former Chair of the Romantic Novelists' Association, and currently works as an associate lecturer for the Open University.

ALLY SINCLAIR

A Season for Love

CANELO US

San Diego, California

Canelo US

An imprint of Printers Row Publishing Group
9717 Pacific Heights Blvd, San Diego, CA 92121
www.canelobooksus.com

Printers Row Publishing Group is a division of Readerlink Distribution
Services, LLC. Canelo US is a registered trademark of Readerlink
Distribution Services, LLC.

First published in the United Kingdom in 2023 by Hera Books.

Published in partnership with Canelo.

Correspondence regarding the content of this book should be sent to Canelo
US, Editorial Department, at the above address. Author inquiries should be
sent to Canelo, Unit 9, 5th Floor, Cargo Works, 1–2 Hatfields, London SE1
9PG, United Kingdom, www.canelo.co.

Publisher: Peter Norton • Associate Publisher: Ana Parker
Art Director: Charles McStravick
Senior Developmental Editor: April Graham
Editor: Julie Chapa
Production Team: Beno Chan, Julie Greene

Design: Brianna Lewis

Library of Congress Control Number: 2023930983

ISBN: 978-1-6672-0590-8

Printed in India

27 26 25 24 23   1 2 3 4 5

For the Naughty Kitchen. All the caseum, all the love.

Prologue

Once upon a time…

This was it.

Two years after they'd started planning for Emma's mother and stepfather to retire and hand the business over to Emma, one year after her stepfather had collapsed with a heart attack while jet-washing the blockwork driveway, and six months after her stepbrother had turned up on the family doorstep, newly separated and unemployed, Emma's mother decided that it was time for her to take the first steps into her new life.

The taxi was outside. The apartment in Torre Del Mar, forty minutes' drive from the airport at Malaga, had been rented for a year to give Emma's mum time to look for somewhere permanent. Emma would stay in the family house in Richmond until her mum was ready to sell, and, given the four bedrooms available, there was really no way she could morally object to her step-bro, Josh, having moved back in as well.

None of which was her mother's main concern as she stopped on the kerb and clutched Emma's hands. 'Now you'll email me your full proposal as soon as possible, won't you?'

Emma nodded. The plan for the next phase in the development of Love's Love, her parents', and soon to be her, business.

'With proper costings. No back of an envelope nonsense.'

'Of course.' Emma wouldn't dream of putting in a poorly costed business plan. Her mother had raised her better than that. Everyone had agreed that Love's Love couldn't continue to stagger on as a traditional dating agency. The world had changed. They'd kept up as far as having a website and letting people register online, but her mother, Emma senior, was a matchmaker of the old school. She liked to look people in the eye and find out what made them tick. She had a database of clients, but most of her matches were made by knowledge and an instinct for how two people would spark when put together. It was an instinct Emma liked to think she'd inherited.

'It's time for me to move on.'

Emma nodded.

'People don't want a widowed matchmaker. They don't want the ghost at the feast. They want to see a picture of how perfect their lives will be when they find The One.' Her mother frowned. 'I didn't mean…'

'I know.'

'I mean you've got plenty of time to find someone. You're young.'

Not that young, Emma thought. 'And I'm focused on the business at the moment.'

'Quite right. Well, you can dip into Trev's life insurance if you need to.'

'I won't.' Emma was adamant. That money was for her mum's retirement. Trevor would be turning in his grave at the idea of it being invested in the business.

The cabbie cleared his throat. 'Could be forty-five minutes to terminal five this time in the morning, love.'

Emma's mother nodded. 'Average driving time at this hour on a week day is thirty-eight minutes.'

If it were possible to roll one's eyes loudly, the cab driver would have managed it. 'If you say so.'

Mrs Love released Emma's hands and moved to hug her step-son. Emma pretended not to be listening to the whispered instructions to keep an eye on his sister and make sure she ate properly and not to let her work all hours. Emma bit her tongue on that one. Her mother had never been off duty for a moment in her life.

Then it was Emma's turn. Her mum was actually leaving. Emma put on her smile. No place for glum faces in the business of love, she told herself. 'Have a good trip. Let us know when you land.'

'I will.' She wrapped Emma in a hug. 'I know that you can do this. My little girl won't let me down.'

–

Emma stood on the pavement and watched the taxi all the way to the end of the street. Once it was out of view she stayed a moment longer watching the empty space being filled by other cars, other people, other lives going on as normal.

'Come on, Stilts.'

Emma had been 4 ft 8 as a thirteen-year-old, when she and her mum had moved in with Josh and Trevor, and her much anticipated growth spurt had taken her all the way to the heady heights of 5 ft 1. 'Stilts' had been the fifteen-year-old Josh's idea of high comedy. And it had stuck.

She followed him back into the house.

'Do you want to do anything with the house?' he asked.

'What do you mean?'

'Nothing major. Maybe paint a bit before it goes on the market?'

'Why?' The décor was perfectly neutral – cream, pale oatmeal and light grey throughout – and there was not a spot of clutter anywhere. Her mum's love of organisation had found its perfect partner in Trevor's ex-military precision and everything always had a place. It was perfect.

'No reason. Just something to do.'

She frowned at him. 'We have plenty to do.'

'Right. So come on then. What's the grand plan to save Love's Love?'

She didn't answer.

'There is a plan, isn't there, Stilts?'

'Of course. I'm going to go and work on it now.'

She left him lounging in front of the telly and went into the dining room that had served as the business office ever since they'd lived here. Emma opened her laptop. She hadn't lied when she said there was a plan. There was a plan, well, not so much a plan as an idea.

Josh, of course, was all in favour of going fully app-based – the new Tinder was his vision for the future, but Emma was sceptical. They'd be starting from nothing in a crowded market. Even with Josh's IT expertise they'd be lost in the noise from other more established apps. They needed to find a point of difference, a new way to bring dating into the twenty-first century, something that set them apart from everything else that was out there. Matchmaking, Emma's mother had always said, wasn't about data and formulas; it was about connection. They needed to find a way to make real connections.

Emma scanned the bookshelves that lined the room. Her love of reading was another inheritance from her mother, who, in typically efficient style, had loaded everything she could ever imagine wanting to read onto her e-reader and left her physical library behind for Emma's enjoyment. Austen. Heyer. The Brontës. Nora Roberts, Jilly Cooper, Sophie Kinsella. Reading those stories, and listening to her mother – those were the two places that Emma had learned her trade. Her job was to bring people together in a world that was conspiring to keep them apart. Even her own industry, which was supposed to create bonds between people, seemed determined to have people boxed in behind their screens. If Emma was going to ensure that the business her mother had started from nothing would survive she needed to smash that mould. There had to be something more – a world where people could go back to meeting, talking, flirting face to face. No filters. No refreshing an app waiting for a reply. Nothing virtual. Online dating encouraged people to make snap judgements and to hide their true selves. If she could only find a way to persuade people, who were genuinely looking for love, to come together in person and give them the

4

time and space to get to know one another, she might be able to create something great. It was the beginning of an idea.

An idea born out of a different era, the era of Austen, a time when young ladies and young gentlemen of good breeding would engage in a social season with the express intention of finding a suitable spouse. Things would need to be updated, of course. 'Good breeding' sounded questionable enough when applied to cockerpoos, and Emma had no interest in simply running a social club for toffs. And Love's Love had always been an inclusive agency. That wouldn't change. It was going to be a huge financial risk, and an almost unimaginable amount of work.

She put her fingers to the keyboard and started to type:

It is a truth universally acknowledged that any twenty-first-century singleton in possession of good sense is in want of some genuine human contact.

Chapter One

Tom Knight knew he ought to get out of bed. That had been true an hour ago, and two hours ago, and three and four and five hours ago. He dreaded coming to bed at night, knowing that sleep was going to elude him, but in the daytime he couldn't drag himself out. He was supposed to be doing better by now. He knew that. He got told it often enough. *Give it a year.* That had been so many people's advice. Live through one year of birthdays and Christmas time and all the tiny anniversaries you never even thought about when someone was alive. Live through all of that and then you can start to move on.

It had been two years now.

A sharp rap at the door forced his hand. He pulled jeans on over his boxers and padded out to the hallway.

Another impatient knock.

He opened the door to his downstairs neighbour. Glenda? Gwenda? Glinda? Was Glinda even a name? He knew she'd introduced herself when he moved in. She thrust an armful of unopened post at him. 'If you don't empty your box it all just piles up on the floor,' she told him. 'And that's not fair on the rest of us.'

'Sorry.'

'We don't have anyone in to clean that entryway you know. I do it, and I don't mind doing it, but it's not on to have your mail cluttering the whole place up.'

He mumbled another apology as he closed the door. The post was a combination of bills and circulars, which he dropped on the kitchen worktop without opening. One handwritten envelope stood out. Lilac coloured, neatly addressed in tiny copperplate script. He carried it back to bed. Inside was a short note and a newspaper clipping.

He read the note first.

I thought this might suit you.

The newspaper cutting was headlined:

Jane Austen style dating comes to London.

Tom screwed it up, threw it in the general direction of the bin and went back to scrolling through nothing on his phone. It rang in his hand.

'Hi Mum.'

'Did you get my note?'

He feigned ignorance, but she was never going to let him get away with that. 'It's on the website as well. I'll ask Hilly to send you the link.'

'I don't think dating is what I need right now.'

'So you did get it then?'

'Maybe.'

His mother was quiet for a moment, planning her next move, he assumed.

'It would do you good to get out more.'

He couldn't agree.

'I know you don't think you're ready.'

Correct.

'But you can't hide forever. And I'm not getting any younger. It would do me the world of good to know you were meeting people again.'

'I meet people.'

'Where?'

'I just had a lovely chat with my new neighbour.'

'Hmm. I just think it would be good for you. And you never know. You might meet a chap, or a young lady, who's just perfect for you.'

Tom pulled the duvet up around him. 'I'm not ready to replace Jack.'

'Nobody would ever think you would. And nobody could replace him. But you're young. Life goes on, whether you join in or not. Just think about it.'

'I don't know.'

'For me?'

He could picture his mother sitting by her window, books in a pile alongside her, blanket over her knees, glasses perched on the end of her nose. Him being like this was breaking her heart as well as his own.

'I only want to see you happy,' she continued.

'I'm happy now,' Tom protested.

His mother didn't dignify that lie with a response.

'I'm happy enough,' he tried. 'You don't need to fix things for me.'

'Thomas, I'm your mother. I will always try to fix things for you.'

'You don't need to.'

He could picture her pursing her lips in just the same way she used to when he hadn't learned his practice pieces or when he'd tried to steal biscuits from the kitchen right before dinner. 'Well, if you'll be happy at my funeral, knowing that you could have done just this one thing to cheer your old mother in her final days.'

Tom knew when he was beaten. It was time to fold. 'All right. What do you want from me?'

'Just that you'll try. Be open to meeting someone.'

'I'll think about it,' he promised.

—

Annie (Miss Keer, English Literature and Language) finally made it to the staff room, ten minutes from the end of her 'free' period, and had barely sat down, when Lydia (Miss Hyland, PE) thrust her phone under Annie's nose. 'What am I looking at?'

Lydia turned the screen back to herself and read aloud. 'You are invited to participate in the upcoming social season.'

'I don't understand.'

'It's like in one of those books Jane won't let us read.' Forming a book club had been one of Lydia's many, and various, past attempts to get them to do something during the school holidays since the three of them had formed their unlikely friendship group. Unlikely, because Jane was thoughtful, studious and contained, and Lydia was wild and impulsive. Annie saw herself as the point at the middle of the scales, holding the two sides in balance.

Across the staff room, Jane (Miss Woods, History and Religious Studies) put her copy of *Candide*, which she was rereading in the original French to stretch her language skills, down in front of her. 'I'll let you read Jane Austen. In fact, I'll let you read whatever you want. I'm just not paying for good red wine unless you're going to make a bit of an effort.'

'And a bit of an effort means nothing that we might actually enjoy.' Lydia pushed the phone across the table to Annie. 'We should do it.'

Annie stared at the Facebook advert in front of her:

Are you sick of swiping right, of remote relationships, and of 21st century dating altogether?

Then we request the honour of your company at a series of glittering social events. You are invited to make a debut in society and meet single people of good character and good standing with a view to forming real attachments and finding lasting love.

Was she sick of swiping right? She hadn't been on many dates recently. She thought back. Not for a couple of years. Closer to three or four even. But when she had been out on dates it had been all right. She'd got to try lots of things she wouldn't have otherwise. She'd had skiing lessons with George, and tried dining in the pitch dark, for reasons she'd never fully understood, with Frankie.

'So what do you think?' Lydia interrupted her thoughts.

'I'm not sure. If you want to do it…'

Jane had come over to them. 'What are you looking at?' She peered at the screen. 'Oh, for goodness' sake. It looks horrendous.'

Maybe Jane was right.

'Bollocks.' Lydia scrolled down the page. 'Eight events over eight weeks, and most of it's during the summer, so you have time.'

That did sound like it might be fun.

Lydia raised an eyebrow. 'Come on.' She turned to Jane. 'You too. It's time you got back out there.'

Jane shook her head. 'I've only been single a week.'

'You've only been divorced a week. You've been single for months. When did he move out?'

'Before Christmas.'

'And when did you last have sex with him?'

'Lyds!' Annie shook her head. 'You can't ask that.'

Jane came over to the table and grabbed the phone from Lydia's hand. 'It's seven hundred quid.'

'But for eight events, and there's a 20 per cent early sign-up discount. And another fifty quid off for keyworkers. Health, emergency services and school workers it says. Come on. It's cheaper than the holiday none of us can afford would be.'

Jane shook her head. 'I'm not paying five hundred quid for a few parties with strangers.'

It was a lot of money.

'Why are you so keen anyway?' Jane continued.

Lydia shrugged. 'Summat to do, isn't it?' She turned back to Annie. 'Come on. Do it for her. She needs to get back out

10

dating and meeting people. Imagine how miserable summer will be for her stuck in that flat all on her own.'

Annie thought about it. Jane's divorce was only a week old and summer would presumably be her first time alone in the flat for more than a few days. Maybe the three of them getting out together would be a good thing. It would be helping Jane. 'All right…'

'You're right.' Jane spoke at the same time. They looked at each other and then at Lydia.

'Which one of us do you think will be miserable on her own?' Jane demanded.

Lydia shrugged. 'Doesn't matter, you've both agreed.'

'I have not…'

'And anyway,' Lydia smiled. 'I signed us all up this morning. You both owe my credit card five hundred quid.'

Chapter Two

Miss Emma Love
requests the honour of your company
at a drinks reception to mark the launching
of the social season

Annie perched on the corner of the bed while Lydia stripped down to her bra and knickers for the fourth time and pulled another three potential outfits from her wardrobe. This was how things always worked out. Lydia would plan a grand adventure for them and then be horrendously late on the day, so Jane had come up with The System for keeping their friend on track. One of them would say that it was just as easy for her to walk to Lydia's flat and have the other pick them both up there in an Uber. When it was Annie's turn on Lydia watch, she'd arrive half an hour ahead of time, text Jane an update on how late things were running and spend the next thirty minutes trying to organise her friend to pay attention to one part of the getting ready process at a time.

'Maybe if I curl my hair, this would work?' Lydia held up a strapless tube dress.

Annie remembered her directions from Jane. *Be tough with her. We do not want to be late.* 'You only just straightened your hair. The dress is great with straight hair.'

Lydia shook her head. 'No. This is plain and straight up and down. It needs big hair to add impact.'

Annie shook her head determinedly, sticking to her guns like she'd promised Jane she would. 'Then you'll have to wear something else.' She glanced at her watch. It was time. 'What was the first thing you tried on?'

Lydia pulled a silver sequinned dress styled to look like a long-line tuxedo jacket from the discard pile. 'This?'

Annie nodded. 'It's perfect.' Her own dress was a fifties style swing dress with layers of lace petticoat underneath. It was too much, she was sure, but Lydia had convinced her to buy it, with an assurance she was currently failing to apply to her own outfit.

Ten minutes later the silver dress was on, teamed with black tights, biker boots and a metric tonne of mascara, and they were jumping into the back of Jane's Uber.

'The Season was the dating app of its day…' Jane, of course, had printed out the information pack they'd all been sent and was reading it out from her seat in the front of the car. Annie listened carefully. 'Eligible ladies and gentlemen would have an opportunity to mingle, appropriately chaperoned of course, and matches would be made that would last a lifetime. Our Season offers the same experience. A chance to meet, to mingle, and to make the perfect match! What a load of tosh.'

'Don't be so miserable. It'll be fun,' Lydia argued.

Annie let the two of them debate the point. She hoped it might be more than fun. The dream of meeting The One wasn't a dream she wanted to share with the others, but the thought of finding someone and being certain of your affections was almost beyond Annie's imagination.

The car came to a halt outside an elegant Portland stone building. Right then. This was it. The drinks reception for the commencement of the social season was to be held, according to the board just inside the entrance, in the Brandon Library on the first floor.

Annie picked up a glass of champagne from a white-shirted waiter by the door and made her way into the room. Dark wood shelves lined three walls from floor to ceiling, surrounding the guests with walls of leather-bound volumes. Annie's bookworm heart sang a little. The fourth wall was taken up with long windows which sent the late afternoon light streaming into the room, illuminating the cheerfully coloured dresses of the guests. It was the sort of room where one could not imagine all being anything other than well with the world.

She heard Jane sigh behind her. 'Why do I let you drag me to these things?'

'You'll love it,' was Lydia's confident response.

Annie let her friends go past her into the throng of the party. She hung back. Lydia was doing this for fun and larks. Jane was here under duress. Annie couldn't be sure which, if either of them, had the right idea.

Eight events. Eight chances to be brave, to make contact with someone who might think she was the person they wanted. Eight chances to meet someone new to make her… the thought stalled. To make her happy? That would imply she wasn't content at the moment.

The crowd in front of her thinned a little, revealing a tall slim man in a dark blue suit, standing half-turned away from her. Annie's breath caught in her throat. She was seeing things. There was no way he'd be at something like this. He smiled, his head dipped towards the woman he was talking to. The crease at the edge of his smile. The line of his jaw. The shape of his shoulders. Of course Annie wasn't seeing things. She could no more mistake him than she could her own reflection.

-

The first time Annie Keer met Joshua Love, he had the best bucket at the pre-school sand table. She relieved him of said bucket by dint of what her Reception class teacher would later call her 'rather determined personality'. From then onward they were inseparable. Arrangements for what would surely have been the wedding of that season commenced in due course, and the couple went so far as to discuss where they would live and what shape their lives together might take.

They would marry on the beach, live with our heroine's mother because she always let you have chips with your tea, and Master Love would be an astronaut and also professional footballer, while Miss Keer confidently stated her intention to forge a diverse career as ballerina, lift operator and occasional princess. They were five and a half years old.

Sadly, beyond that first hopeful bloom of love, our story takes an unhappy turn. The love affair remained without formal contract being arranged and was, of course, unconsummated. The young sweethearts were torn apart, aged fifteen, by the hero's father's new marriage and relocation to a very fine property in Richmond. And so ended Miss Keer and Master Love's first attachment.

–

The man turned. Joshua Love. What was he doing here? Well, it was obvious what he was doing here – the same as everyone else was doing here presumably. And, of course, he was single now. Something sparked inside Annie and was instantly extinguished.

Jane. She needed to warn Jane. She and Lydia had been right alongside her a moment ago. Where had they gone?

Annie saw her, at the far side of the room, next to a bar set up to serve cocktails. Lydia was leaning on the counter, deep in conversation with the bartender. She rushed over, jostling through bodies on her way. 'Jane!'

'What's wrong?'

'Have you seen…' Annie stopped herself. Of course she hadn't seen. She wouldn't be standing here calmly if she had. If she'd seen him, Jane would, of course, be all over the place. 'Josh is here.'

'Right.' Jane's face was impassive.

'Are you ok?'

Jane nodded. 'Where is he?'

Annie pointed her friend in the right direction and watched her make her way across the room. Poor Jane. Her first social event post divorce, and who did she walk into but her ex-husband?

'Hi.' Hi? Not the most expressive greeting Jane could have come up with, and wholly inadequate to the task she was putting it to, but then what greeting was there that encapsulated, 'Well, this is an odd situation to run into your ex for the first time since you moved out, and also I see that you're dating again, or at least looking for someone to date, but I suppose I can't really complain about that, seeing as I ended our marriage and my presence here would seem to imply that I'm open to dating as well, although, as you probably understand, that's complicated'? It was too much to get into an opening gambit really.

If anything, he looked more surprised to see Jane than she was to see him. She had, at least, had the time it took to walk across the room to prepare herself.

'Hi. I didn't know you'd signed up for this.'

'Well, likewise.'

He frowned for a second. She remembered that frown – it was more born of confusion than displeasure. It was the face he did when he thought he'd put something down in front of him and then couldn't find it. Or when he came into a room and instantly forgot what he'd come in for. 'Oh no. I'm working. It's my sister's company. Well, Mum's company really but Emma's in charge now.'

'You're not at InterFinance any more?' That was more disconcerting than the idea of him dating in a way. She'd understood, of course, that once they were no longer married Josh would probably find someone new. He was handsome, if you liked that kind of thing, and kind and fun. And she didn't want to be married to him any more, so it was a natural next step to conclude that maybe somebody else would. But in her mind the rest of his life was cast in stone. She'd left him. She was the one moving on. Her life had changed. His, she'd somehow assumed, would remain otherwise the same.

'Got made redundant.' He shrugged. 'It's fine. I was bored there anyway and I took voluntary so they paid me off. So

I'm staying with Emma, helping out with this, sort of thinking about what I want to do next. Fresh start. It's all good.'

'Right.'

He did the frown again. 'What's up?'

She couldn't answer that without sounding like a crazy person. She was supposed to be the one moving on, not him. 'Nothing.'

'So, you're on the lookout for love then?'

This was going to be too awkward, wasn't it? 'I mean I don't have to be. If I'd known you were involved I wouldn't have let Lydia talk me into it.'

He laughed. 'So this was Lyd's idea?'

'Who else?'

'I can't imagine Lyd looking for her one true love.'

Neither could Jane. 'I think it's more about wanting something to do over the summer. I'll just tell her it's not for me though.'

Josh shook his head. 'No. It's fine. Seriously. I want you to be happy. And Emma will kill me if she thinks I'm putting clients off. Please stay.'

Jane nodded weakly.

'And I'm glad you've told Lydia about... you know.'

Her face must have given her away. He frowned again.

'You have told Lydia?'

'I'm going to.'

'Ideally before you find someone to cop off with. It's all about making a real-life connection at these events, you know? She's going to notice...'

'I know. I'll tell them.'

'Ok.' He moved to turn away and then stopped. 'Tell them? Who else is here?'

'Just Annie. Lydia signed us all up.' Jane smiled despite the weirdness of the occasion. 'It's sweet. I think Annie really believes in all this stuff. You know, finding your one true love and all that.'

He nodded. 'Good. Well, I'd better…' He gestured vaguely towards nothing in particular. 'Do have a good evening though.'

–

Annie watched the former couple converse, trying to hit the fine balance between hearing what they were saying and not appearing to be trying to hear what they were saying. It didn't work. The room was too crowded and the babble of chatter around her too great.

The conversation apparently over, Josh turned away from Jane and walked straight towards Annie. He stopped dead, and raised a hand in greeting. Annie offered a feeble wave back. Jane's ex. That was all he was to her. She took a step towards him. Before she could get a word out, he turned away and strode towards the podium at the front of the room.

Annie watched as he leaned down to whisper in the ear of the woman beside him. She looked familiar but Annie couldn't place her. She giggled at whatever Josh said to her before sticking her tongue out at him. It wasn't romantic. It wasn't sexy but it was one of the most intimate gestures Annie had ever seen.

–

'I'm going to be sick.'

Josh patted her cheerfully on the back. 'Nah, you're not.'

'I am,' Emma insisted.

He peered at her. 'You're not pale. You're not sweaty. You're fine. It's just nerves.'

Typical Josh. She knew how she felt for goodness' sake. 'I think I know when I'm going to puke.'

'Do you want me to do it for you?'

Absolutely yes. Of course she did. She wanted anyone else in the world to step up and stand in front of that microphone and address this room full of people. But he'd forget something or say something wrong, and she'd made the sound engineer check three times already that the microphone was at precisely the right height for her, which would be somewhere around Josh's ribcage. She was going to have to do it herself.

She made her way onto the stage and gave a small nod to the sound woman to bring the music up for a moment and then down. 'Welcome, everyone, to our drinks reception to launch this very special twenty-first-century social season,' she started. 'This will be a matchmaking experience like nothing you've done before. Obviously, this evening we're very much still in the modern day but by the end of the Season we'll be embracing the Regency era fully – in our dress, our refreshments and even in the dances.'

She let the murmur of conversation die down before she continued. 'Dating in the twenty-first century is a pretty dismal affair a lot of the time. Swiping left or right. Instant judgement on one selfie. Dick pics.'

That raised a laugh of recognition. Emma's confidence grew a little. 'In the early nineteenth century things were rather different. Eligible young ladies and gentlemen would enjoy the social season with the aim of making a perfect match. Honestly, the whole thing was a marriage market. Don't worry – we're not expecting you all to be married or engaged by the end of the Season, but we do want to take the idea of finding a match back in time to something more human, to something with a community around it to support you. That's our goal with this social season. We're offering a chance to meet, to converse, to do things the old-fashioned way.'

This was the tricky bit to sell. 'The Season was about court-ship. It was about allowing yourself the time to get to know a person's mind, to the point where both of you were certain of your intentions.' She cleared her throat. 'Ideally before anyone gets naked.'

There was a ripple of nervous laughter around the room. Emma continued. 'This process is about getting to know each other, not just getting laid, so that means we want you to woo your intended. Talk. Listen. Send gifts or flowers. Be attentive rather than simply horny. Our first ball is in two weeks' time. That won't be a proper Regency ball – we know you don't know the dances yet – but we will be asking you to have a go at a waltz or at least a slow paired-up shuffle rather than attacking the dance floor like a drunk uncle at a wedding.'

She ran through the rest of the programme – the garden party, casino night, formal dinner, a Regency dance lesson (Josh's idea), a chaperoned lunch, which they were all encouraged to invite family along to, and finally, 'Our final event will be a fully costumed Regency ball to be held at Somerset House.' She could hear the crack in her own voice and hoped nobody else would pick up on it. Somerset House could easily use up all the money she was bringing in, but it was beautiful and it elevated the whole season, and by then she'd have enough people signed up to cover all the costs. Probably. Hopefully. She took a deep breath and continued with her speech. 'By which time I hope that you will all have made a wonderful match!'

Emma left the microphone and made her way to where Josh was leaning on a pillar at the side of the stage. 'You were good.'

'How many more sign-ups so far?' she asked.

'Thirty-two so far on the door.' That was good. 'Still sixty-five to thirty-five, women to men though.' That was less good, but not unexpected.

'Right. Well, what are you still standing around here for?'

Josh shook his head. 'You've literally only just stopped talking.'

Not the point at all. 'You need to start schmoozing any men who haven't committed yet.'

'Isn't that what most of the women in the room are here for?'

Humour. Great. Just what she didn't have time for. 'Yeah. Yeah. You're very funny. Go charm some potential clients.'

'Emma?'

'What?'

'Did you know Jane was coming tonight?'

She couldn't meet his eye. She shouldn't lie. She didn't have to offer the whole and complete truth though. 'Not entirely.'

'What does that mean?'

'She's gone back to her maiden name, so I wasn't completely sure.'

'But you had her first name and address and phone number on file?'

So clearly, technically, she had known Jane was coming. She'd been hoping the surname thing gave her plausible deniability. Not telling him was a crappy sister move. 'I'm sorry. I should have told you.'

'Yes.'

'Are you ok? I wasn't sure how you'd feel about seeing her.' She imagined he wouldn't feel great, but actually she'd never had a relationship end badly enough to feel awkward about seeing them afterwards. All her exes were still on her friends list. She was godmother to two of their babies and had been invited to three of their now-wives hen dos. She'd never broken up with anyone without making sure they were absolutely fine and dandy afterwards.

Josh's face was set in the same taut expression of suppressed tension that he'd been wearing for the last year. 'I'll manage. Did you know the others were coming too?'

'Others?'

'Lydia. And Annie.'

Emma shook her head. 'Do I know them?'

'They were her bridesmaids. And Annie was… I knew her years back. At school before Dad met your mum.'

Emma was definitely aware that there had been bridesmaids at the wedding. She had an image of unforgivably dull long grey dresses, but if she recalled correctly, she'd been quite preoccupied trying to engineer an accidental-on-purpose meeting between cousin Jen and nice Phil from Josh's work, who she knew would be perfect for one another. And she'd been right. They'd just had twins in fact.

'Is it going to be a problem?'

Josh shook his head.

'Good, 'cos you're here to work. They're here to meet eligible men.'

'I'm an eligible man.'

Emma swallowed at least a proportion of her irritation, aware that she wasn't out of the sibling doghouse for not warning him about his ex-wife being here yet. 'Well, technically I suppose, in the right light to a sympathetic observer you could be considered eligible, but you're not an eligible man who's coughed up hundreds of pounds to be here so you don't count, and right now we need a few more of them to commit. So go. Get to work.'

Josh shook his head but he didn't argue. Instead he threw her a brisk mock salute. 'Ok Stilts. You're the boss.'

–

Annie collected another glass of champagne from one of the impossibly pristine waiters. Lydia had disappeared into the fray. Jane been cornered by what looked like a group of city boys. At some point Annie would go and rescue her, or, perhaps more accurately, rescue them, but for now she was alone. Alone in a room full of people.

'Well, hello there.' The man approaching her looked nice enough. Shorter than… No. And his hairline was starting to recede a tiny bit, rather than his hair falling full and dark across his brow like… No. And his suit was slightly too big for him, not slimly tailored like… No.

She took a breath. 'Hi.'

'I'm Col. Colin. Colin Williams.' He extended a hand.

'Annie. Nice to meet you.' A silence threatened to linger.

22

'I'm sorry. I never know quite how to start things off in these situations.'

Annie tried to rally. Flirting. That was, presumably, what she was supposed to do in this situation. She could do flirting. She remembered flirting. She used to date so she must have flirted she supposed. You just had to sort of go along with whatever the other person was saying. She dropped her gaze and glanced back up at her companion in what she hoped was a Princess Di way rather than a having-a-stroke way. 'And what is this situation?'

He looked around. 'Honestly, I'm not quite sure. Chap at work signed us all up. Duggers has just been dumped by his missus so we thought it might do him good.'

'Right. So you're here for Duggers' benefit? Not for you at all.'

He broke into a smile. 'I wouldn't quite say that.'

She smiled back at him. See – she could do this. She could engage with a young gentleman. 'Good.'

'So you're signed up for this whole thing then, are you?'

Annie nodded.

'Jolly good. What enticed you along?'

I'm terrified I'll never meet anyone I feel sure of and am destined to die alone. No. Probably not the best response. 'Just never met the right person, you know. Thought it couldn't hurt.' That was better.

'I thought I'd met The One once. Rosie, her name was. It didn't work out.'

'What happened?'

He looked away. 'My brother happened. Unfortunately. Bit of a to-do it caused.'

'I don't understand.'

'Well, they happened. To each other. If you get my drift.'

Annie feared she absolutely got his drift. 'You mean?'

Col nodded. 'He was in the army, off on tour, so he hadn't met her before the wedding. Came home as a surprise for the

23

big day but of course, first night on leave he goes out on the town rather than come straight back to digs, doesn't he? Meets up with a group of lasses on a hen do. Boinks her down the back of the Tesco Express. She only tells him afterwards that she's the bride.'

Annie felt her jaw fall open in horror.

'He tells me all this on the morning of the wedding as a great jape. I still don't put two and two together until he mentions the little flower tattoo this girl had on her shoulder. A rose, like her name.'

'Oh my God. I'm so sorry.'

Colin took a swig of his drink. 'Better to know before the wedding though, isn't it? You have to look on the bright side. See it as a lucky escape.'

'How long ago?'

'The first.'

'The first? Of this month?'

'Yep,' he continued. 'Best thing to do is to hop right back on the horse though, don't you think?'

Annie's heart went out to him. She nodded gamely. 'I suppose there's no point dwelling on things.'

'No. Stiff upper lip and all that.' His bottom lip quivered slightly as he said it.

She grasped around for a change of subject. 'So what do you do for work?'

'Oh. Clerk at Fountain Lane. Barristers' Chambers.' He rallied a little. 'And damn good at it I am too. Used to be in the Logistics Corps you see. Know how to get things done. What about you?'

'I'm a teacher. English. Secondary.'

She waited for the jokey comment about long holidays and early finishes.

'Good for you. Tough job. Teachers and nurses. They're the people the country needs. That's a proper vocation.'

Annie couldn't reply. Was it a vocation? She remembered when she'd been looking at university places. English was a sensible choice, and she did love to read and, like her careers adviser said, it meant she could always go on to train as a teacher, which would mean she could get work anywhere, and there were courses close to home so she could be around to help her mum and she wouldn't be adding her rent as another financial burden. And teaching was a steady wage so she'd been able to get her mortgage. She must like some parts of it, surely? 'I enjoy the books, and sometimes you get a student who really loves what they're reading. That's wonderful.'

'Annie?' The voice behind her made her turn. 'Sorry. Am I interrupting?'

Joshua Love. 'Er, I was just talking to…' She turned back and gestured but Col, Colin, Colin Williams was already taking a step back.

'I'll be off then. Not the done thing to monopolise the young ladies at these things. 'Nuff said.'

'Oh no. You don't have to…' But he already had.

'So… you're all here then?' Josh pulled a face.

'Yeah. It's a bit weird, isn't it?' For a second she almost reached out to touch his arm, to console him in some way. She didn't. 'You talked to Jane?'

He nodded.

'And?'

He was silent for a second. 'And it is what it is.'

'I understand.' There must still be feelings. You didn't just end a marriage, walk away and turn years of emotion off.

'So she has told you?' Josh asked.

'Told me what?'

'Nothing.' He frowned for a second.

Jane hadn't told Annie, or anyone, as far as Annie knew, very much at all about the break-up, but she hadn't been herself for months. There were some days when she didn't seem like she could even be bothered to tell them what they were doing wrong at work.

'Anyway, I came to say hi to you. How are you doing, Annie?'

'I'm well.'

'And your mum and Duncan?'

'The same.' Josh was one of the few people in the world who wouldn't need more of an explanation of Dunc's condition than that.

'Well, it's good to see you.' He started to move away and then turned back. 'Maybe we could catch up properly sometimes?'

'Maybe.' It was polite of him to suggest it.

—

The evening was going to plan. People were mingling. People were chatting. The surroundings and the overdressed waiters were creating a pleasing sense of grandeur and most people had made an effort with their outfits, but it was still definitely a twentieth-century night out. Something was missing. Emma pursed her lips. She needed to put her finger on what that missing ingredient was. If people didn't fall in love with the idea of the social season, and then, hopefully, fall in love with each other, her whole grand plan to reinvent the family business was dead before it had really begun.

'Are you in charge here?' The man asking the question had not dressed up for the event. He was wearing a tight-fitting T-shirt over narrow legged jeans and had a scruffy back pack slung over one shoulder.

Emma put on her most professional, least actually friendly, smile. 'I'm the organiser.'

'Cool. Where do I sign up?'

'For the Season?' She was aware that the disbelief was apparent in her voice.

'No. To be a blood donor. Obviously for the Season.'

Emma didn't let her smile slip. They needed more men, even grumpy, inappropriately dressed men. She picked up her own tablet. 'If you could fill in the form here, and card details at the end for the payment.'

She watched as he rattled through the form, long slim fingers dancing over the screen. While he was occupied she pulled a leaflet from her tablet sleeve. It ran through all the same information as her welcome talk, but she suspected that, if he'd managed to arrive on time at all, this guy wouldn't have been paying attention to the details. She handed it over to him as he passed the tablet back to her. 'This is all the information you'll need, Mr...' She glanced at the screen. 'Mr Knight.'

'Tom.'

'Sorry?'

'Call me Tom.'

'Thank you, Tom. Well, you've got all the details.' She started to turn away.

'And you are?'

'Emma. Emma Love.' She waited for the raised eyebrow.

'Love?'

So predictable. 'Yes. And no. And it's called nominative determinism.'

'What?'

Emma had had this conversation a million times before. 'Yes, it is my real name. No, I didn't make it up when I started working as a matchmaker. Actually, my mother was already a matchmaker before she married Mr Love. And the thing you read about or heard about or saw on *QI* is nominative determinism. It's the idea that our choices in life might in some way be determined by our names, so if your name is Baker you're more likely to be, well, a baker.'

'And Miss Love is more likely to be a matchmaker?' He was smiling and there was a warmth in his dark brown eyes that hadn't been there a moment ago.

'Exactly.'

'Well now I feel bad for never having killed a dragon. I must be a let-down to my people.'

She must have looked blank because he felt the need to explain. 'Knight. You know, like suits of armour and rescuing fair maidens.'

So the newcomer thought he was funny. She filed that in her mental notes. She'd have to look out for a potential partner with a patient soul.

'So I'll let you mingle, Mr Knight.'

She turned away and scanned the room. She couldn't see Josh. He'd better not have run off to have it out with his ex. But no, Jane was right there, talking to a group of young men in suits and ties who looked like they'd got lost on their way home from jobs in the city. Excellent. Seven hundred quid would be pocket change to them. Her challenge would be to get beneath the surface and see who each of them was as an individual and then find each and every one of them their perfect soul mate. Her knuckles were white from the tension of her grip on her tablet. She had eight weeks. Eight weeks, a budget that was balanced on a knife edge, and nearly two hundred people. She wasn't her mother. What if she wasn't up to the task?

–

Lydia grabbed another glass of fizz from one of the many circulating waiters. Annie had been getting chatted up by a well turned-out balding man. Jane was fighting off the attention of a whole group of boys who looked like their gym-honed quads might burst out of their trousers at a moment's notice. And Lydia was… Lydia was on the sidelines, which was not where she belonged at a party. She belonged in the middle of everything, dancing on tables, making jokes, being the centre of everyone's attention.

'What's up with you?' Jane had extricated herself from her group of admirers.

'Nothing.'

Jane didn't reply, but she did give Lydia one of her special teacher hard looks, guaranteed to stop a riot amongst a Year

Nine bottom set within four seconds. Lydia was made of sterner stuff. 'I'm fine.'

'I bloody hope so. This was your idea after all.' Jane paused. 'Actually, why did you want to do this?'

Lydia shrugged. 'Summat to do, isn't it?'

'Something that isn't a whole summer at home on your own, you mean?'

'Speak for yourself,' Lydia shot back. But of course Jane was speaking for all of them. That was very much how they'd started being friends – not just Lydia and Jane, but Annie as well. Lydia had joined the school in the summer term, nearly three years out of training and moving on because it was time for a new career challenge. A new career challenge that didn't involve seeing the maths teacher at her former school every day and, more to the point, didn't involve seeing the maths teacher's wife who worked in the school office. It had all got terribly awkward.

Annie and Jane had been thrust towards Lydia by the Head, presumably thinking that they were all young and female and would therefore definitely 'get along'. And they'd exchanged polite nods in the staff room and Lydia had tried to look delighted every time Annie made her a cup of coffee or offered to come and help her get set up in the gym. They'd been colleagues, acquaintances but not friends, until the Wednesday of the first half term break, when after four days of alternating sitting in her flat with trips to the gym and the mini-supermarket down the road, Lydia had convinced herself that she had important work to do that could only be done on site. She didn't, of course, but she couldn't sit still a moment longer.

She'd walked into the staff room to find Annie already there and they'd greeted each other with an awkward exchange of 'Sorrys' and exclamations that they didn't think there would be anybody else there. Ten minutes later Jane had turned up and they'd repeated the whole performance again as a trio. Truth was, whether they acknowledged it or not, that all three of them were lonely. Their colleagues had families and vacation plans and craved the school holidays with the same intensity that Lydia dreaded them.

For whatever reason, and they never discussed the reasons, Annie and Jane were in the same boat. By chance and serendipity Lydia had found her people, and now they really were her people, the select set of friends who formed her chosen family. Jane was smart and strong and Annie approached everything with such infectious hope and positivity that even Lydia was encouraged, at least occasionally, to see the best in the world around her.

'What are you two talking about?' Annie appeared out of the throng of the party.

'We weren't,' Jane answered. 'This one was staring into the middle distance like a bad soap actor at the start of a flashback sequence. Seriously,' she turned to Lydia, 'where did you go?'

Lydia shook her head. 'Doesn't matter. So how are you two getting on? Any matches made? Any imminent betrothals?'

'No.' Annie answered almost too quickly. 'I mean it's early, isn't it? And we're not really expecting that are we? It's just fun, isn't it? Really?'

Annie's total belief – however much she denied it – in finding her one true love was almost endearing. Almost.

'What about you?' Jane switched the attention back to Lydia.

She pulled a face in response. 'I'm not sure I'm a one true love sort of girl.'

'Why not?' Annie looked horrified.

Lydia could answer that. She wouldn't, of course, but she knew that love and forever and all those promises were an illusion, and she wasn't about to be tricked like that. 'There aren't even that many fit guys here.'

'Yeah. Right. I thought that. Not fit enough,' Jane agreed.

Actually… another tightly-shirted waiter glided past them. Lydia swapped her empty glass for a full one and watched the

30

waiter's equally tightly-clad arse walk away. She grinned. 'Don't wait for me to get a cab, ladies.'

Jane turned to see what had caught Lydia's attention. 'You're going to shag a waiter?'

'What's wrong with that?'

'I just don't think it's really in the spirit of all this. You know, lasting relationships, making a real connection.'

'I'm totally planning to make a connection,' Lydia countered. Everything that woman had said at the start of the evening had set Lydia on edge. She needed to do something to get all that bollocks about finding The One out of her head. She needed to feel something right now, in the moment, to get her out of her own thoughts.

'There was a whole thing about not getting down to it until you'd got to know them,' Annie chipped in.

Lydia shrugged. 'I know he's a waiter. I know he's got a nice arse. Totally soul mates.' She left her friends shaking their heads, jiggled her cleavage up a notch and tapped the hot waiter on the shoulder.

He turned. 'My name's Will. I'm actually a barman, not a waiter. I can't see my own arse so I'll take your word for that. And I'm working.'

So he'd heard all that, but he was playing, not actually brushing her off. 'You can't be working forever?'

'Well, I've got a break in half an hour if you can wait that long for your soul mate.'

The phrase 'soul mate' dripped with sarcasm. Hot Barman was definitely Lydia's type.

Chapter Three

Emma sat down at the kitchen table and unfolded her laptop. She had a spreadsheet with a page for each event. She opened up the sheet for the upcoming ball. Normally the neat little rows and colour coding of tasks pending, in progress, and completed soothed her, but today it wasn't working. It was all so much. She had eight events, each one with costs and risks associated with it. She should have started smaller. She could have hosted a speed-dating night, or a singles mixer – a one-off to test the waters. What had made her think she was up to this? She wasn't her mother. Nobody was.

Emma forced a deep breath into her lungs. She wasn't her mother but she had, at least, seen the queen of matchmaking at work. She could channel her wisdom better than anybody, and she'd come this far. All she could do now was fight to make the Season work. She stared at her rows of notes and figures. It wasn't just the money that was worrying her. Something still wasn't right. A social season was more than a series of events. It was a little community all of its own, with its own hierarchies and rivalries and friendships. She needed another element, something that would create more of a sense of community, of...

'Emma!'

Josh held his phone in front of her.

'What?'

'I want to show you something.'

She didn't have time for whatever funny thing he'd seen on Twitter. 'Can it wait?'

'It's just that…'

Couldn't he see that she had work to do? The second event was only a few days away and there was something missing, some ineffable quality that she needed to work out how to conjure up.

'It's about work.'

Very reluctantly, she turned away from her screen. 'What?'

He was still waving his phone in her direction. 'So it's an app…'

They'd been through this. Emma was resolute. 'No apps!'

'Hear me out.'

'Seriously Josh, no apps; the whole idea is contrary to what the Season was about. This is about doing things in real life.'

'Fine.' He stomped out of the room.

She knew she'd snapped at him, but what was he thinking? She turned back to her screen, but her train of thought was lost. Maybe she needed a break. Just a short one.

She clicked her way to her favourites tab and opened her most frequently visited site, Poker Parade, and logged in as user *QueenOfHearts*. She'd had that username since uni. One time someone in the chat had offered her £2500 to sign it over to them. She should have taken it, but the fact that someone had offered that amount without prompting had made her think it might one day be worth more. And she liked it. She liked the joke on the family surname and business.

She'd played on other sites in the past but this one remained her favourite. It allowed you to play for virtual chips within the site without putting real cash in unless you needed to buy a top-up. And you could set up private tables accessed with a user code so you could play directly with friends. She'd done that a lot when she was at college playing against other students. Not so much now. Josh played occasionally for fun, but none of her Richmond friends did, and the uni mates she'd started off playing against had drifted away over the years.

Emma had strict rules for when and how she played. She played for virtual chip tokens within the site, never for cash.

She never put more than a fiver of her own money in per month and if she lost all her chips she couldn't play again that month. Of course, she didn't lose all her chips, and rarely needed to buy a top-up, because she also had strict rules for when she bet and when she folded. She didn't take unnecessary risks and she only played poker. She didn't bet on sport or politics. She didn't play roulette or blackjack. There was too much luck involved. Poker was about maths and skill. If you had the right strategy the risk of losing it all could be managed.

She joined an open public table and waited for the next hand.

Chapter Four

'Are you coming to Cynthia's birthday drinks?' Lydia stuck her head around Annie's classroom door as the last child straggled out at the end of the day.

'I can't.' Maybe she should. No. She'd promised Mum. 'The card and the present are behind the laminator in the staff room though. Jane should be picking them up.' The card had been right round the staff room on three different lunchtimes and the envelope for donations towards a gift had netted £37, two mini bulldog clips and a Tic Tac. Annie had put the bulldog clips back into the stationery store and made the collection up to £50 so the present wouldn't look too stingy. She checked her watch. Normally she'd be persuaded to go along for just one drink but she needed to get to the supermarket and then across to Mum's before five. There wasn't time. 'Say sorry to Cynthia for me.'

Lydia rolled her eyes. 'She won't notice if you're there or not. Stuck-up old bag.'

'That's unkind.'

'It's true though. Come on. You don't like her any more than I do.'

'I think she must have had a hard life or something.'

'Bloody hell, mate. You'd see the good in Jack the Ripper.'

Annie ducked the accusation with protestations of running late and ran to her car. An annoying drive through end-of-school-day traffic and a fraught run around the supermarket trying to make sense of the heavily autocorrected list her mother had sent followed. *Cheery tornadoes* were replaced with cherry tomatoes with some confidence. The substitution of braising steak for *baring streak* was with slightly less assurance.

She pressed the buzzer at the front door of her mum's building at ten past five.

'Hi. Who is it?' Her mother's voice crackled over the speaker.

'It's me. I've got your shopping.'

'I'll send Hilly down.'

Hilly, the carer, appeared at the front door and helped Annie up the stairs.

'How are they?'

'Duncan's fine.'

'And Mum?'

'Oh… you know.'

She followed Hilly into the small kitchen of her mum's flat. The biggest room – presumably intended by the builder to function as a lounge-diner – was set aside for Duncan, as there was space to get round either side of the bed, and for his hoist and the chair and the commode and a narrow bed for her mum to sleep in the same room.

'Be a dear. Unpack it would you?' Annie's mum shouted through from Duncan's room, but Annie was already on the case. Then she popped the kettle on and made tea for everyone before she dragged a stool through from the kitchen for herself so her mum could have the comfy chair. Before she settled, she leaned over the bed. 'Hello, you.'

Her brother didn't acknowledge her, but that was fine. It didn't mean he didn't know she was there. Duncan was with them. He was locked inside himself some of the time. Sometimes he would smile. And sometimes he used his tongue to select pictures from his board to tell them how he felt or what he wanted. He struggled with that more and more though.

Annie perched on her stool.

'So tell us what you've been up to?' As she spoke, Annie's mum leaned over and wiped a line of drool from Duncan's chin. 'Duncan wants to hear all your stories.'

'Oh well, same old. They're doing *Much Ado About Nothing* as the Year Ten play next term, so I've said I'll help with that.' It wasn't a set text for English so it didn't really help her but Mrs Atkins, who taught performing arts, had convinced her that helping the students get to grips with Shakespeare in any way at all would be worth her time.

Her mum frowned. 'Is that the one with Emma Thompson with all those red curls? The one where they all get in the bath outdoors in the nuddy?'

'I don't think that bit's in our version, but yeah. That's the play.'

Her mother nodded. 'Quite right. You can't have teenagers getting nuddy. People'll write in.' She stroked her son's face. 'Well, if you've helped I shall have to come and watch it. When will it be?'

'Not until after half term. November time.'

'Well, I'll definitely come along if I can.'

'That would be lovely.' She didn't expect her mum to make it. It was difficult for her to get out. Duncan needed her. Annie understood.

'What else are you doing, darling?' She turned back to Duncan. 'He likes to hear about your adventures.'

Annie didn't have adventures. It was entirely a question of perspective though, she supposed. From Lydia's point of view she was a dull old homebody. From Duncan's she was living a life of unimaginable variety.

She hadn't been planning to tell her mum about the Season, but what else was there? 'I've signed up for this sort of dating thing.'

'Ooooh!' Her mother rolled her eyes like a shocked tourist on a seaside postcard. 'Dating! Dating, she says, Duncan.'

'It's called the Season.' So what was it? 'It's like a whole series of events and there's a whole set of rules and etiquette that you're supposed to follow. Like in a Jane Austen novel or something.'

'Like the thing with the ridiculous sexy Duke? We didn't care for that. Too many bottoms.' She pursed her lips. 'Nowt wrong with a bottom but you can take these things too far.'

They fell silent for a moment. 'It'd be nice for you to meet someone though.'

Nice. Yes. That was exactly what it would be, Annie supposed.

'Now let me tell you our news. Mrs Compton at number seven has got the hump about the planters out the front, hasn't she, Duncan? Reckons downstairs have been pulling up her bulbs. And downstairs reckon the planters are nearest their window so it's up to them. It were a right to-do. We opened the window all the way so we could hear properly.'

As she left her mum's, Annie's phone rang. *Unknown number.*
'Hello?'
Nothing.
'Hello?'
They rang off. That was weird.

–

'Who are you ringing?'

Josh dropped the house phone onto the base unit. 'Nobody.'
'Ok.' Emma glanced at her brother's outfit. 'Going out?'
'Yeah. Just a drink with some people I used to work with.'

She forced a smile. 'Have fun then.' She'd been picturing Josh staying in tonight. Living with her stepbrother wasn't ideal, obviously, but it did have the benefit of meaning there was company around if she wanted it. But apparently not tonight. So Emma had the house to herself. Her calendar said that this evening was an evening off. Studies showed that productivity decreased significantly when people worked too many hours, regardless of the nature of the work they were undertaking. So Emma scheduled at least one day, and two evenings, off each week, and when at her desk set a timer to remind her to take a break after precisely fifty-two minutes of endeavour.

Balance in all things was vital.

She'd thought that Josh would be around and they might find something on Netflix and get a takeaway and chill out. Instead, she sat alone on the sofa her mother had chosen in the tastefully decorated living room and picked up her phone. She wondered which friends she might text and ask if they were free for a drink or maybe a movie. Her mind was blank. It sounded pathetic but her mum was her best friend and her boss and her mum. If she'd been here they'd have gone shopping together and played the game where they held up a dress or an outfit and asked the other what sort of partner the woman who wore that look would go for.

She did have other friends. She'd been a bridesmaid two weeks ago in fact – which didn't help her current loose end; Jen and Alex were still on their honeymoon. Miles and Milly had just had a new baby. They wouldn't want her turning up. Sal was all loved up with Sophie – she'd barely replied to a message for weeks. Emma had had a hand in all those matches. But constantly matching her friends up did leave her rather short of single mates to call for a last-minute weeknight glass of sauvignon.

She pulled her computer onto her lap. She'd play a couple of hands and then maybe go for a run if it was still light, or she could go to the gym. It wasn't her gym day. Tuesday and Thursday before she started work and Sunday morning every week were gym days. It was in her calendar, but she could mix things up. Maybe.

She opened the poker site and clicked on the first open table. There were four players already dealt in the hand that was starting. She clicked 'join next hand' and waited, watching the action. The betting started with two blinds – bets that had to be made regardless of the cards that were dealt. The blinds rotated around the table so every player would be obliged to bet when their turn came. A player with the username SirWalt was sitting at the small blind. His automatic bet was twenty-five thousand tokens. The big blind player was ViperBoy, who automatically put in a fifty-thousand-token bet. That was what other players would have to at least match to stay in the hand. The next player folded. The fourth, LondonCowboy, bet fifty. That meant SirWalt would have to chuck in another twenty-five to stay in the hand. He did that and then added another five hundred thousand.

Emma shook her head. Stupid bet. If he was bluffing it was silly to over extend so far so early in the hand, and if he had something a bet that big would scare the other players away. ViperBoy folded, as Emma almost certainly would have done in his seat.

LondonCowboy saw SirWalt's bet though. Interesting. The rest of the cards were community cards, dealt face up on the table, in three rounds with an opportunity to bet or fold between each round. The first set of cards, dealt three together, were known as the river. Two jacks and a three. So if either player was sitting on a pair of threes that was an instant full house. But obviously they both knew that, so they'd be considering what the chances were of their opponent having hit that hand. Of course, it was also possible that either player had three jacks now, or even four of a kind.

SirWalt bet all his chips. He was all in. Did he have the full house? Emma guessed not. If he did his earlier bet had been made on a pair of threes which would have been crazy. LondonCowboy had more chips behind so didn't have to go all in to see Walt's bet, and see Walt's bet he did.

The next community card – known as the turn – was a five. Emma couldn't imagine that helped anyone very much, but there was an outside chance that it could turn trip jacks and a five in the hand into a higher full house. The final community card – the river – was a four. That made the straight – five cards in number order – possible if a player had a two and a six in hand. That seemed unlikely though. Nobody in their right mind would have bet like either of these two at the start if they were holding a two and a six.

The two players' concealed cards showed on screen. LondonCowboy had a jack in the hole. Three jacks. Decent hand. A winning hand a lot of the time. Knowing you had one of the remaining jacks in your hand reduced the chances of your opponent having one and making the full house. Not a winning hand today though. Emma shook her head in disbelief at SirWalt's cards. A two and a six. He'd bluffed the bluffiest of bluffs and made a straight.

A volley of congratulatory messages popped up on screen from the other players.

> Lucky bastard

typed Emma.

The response started with a shrug emoji.

> Everyone needs a bit of luck

he replied.

Emma shook her head. Luck would only get you so far. Taking all the lovely chips SirWalt had just won from him was going to be a real pleasure.

Chapter Five

Annie was already putting a bottle of wine and three glasses down on a table in the corner of the Pot and Kettle when Jane arrived. Someone was missing though. 'I thought you were bringing Lyds?'

'I thought you were.' Annie stopped halfway through taking her jacket off. 'Should I go round there?'

Jane shook her head. 'Nah. It's just a couple of drinks with us. She won't have a full getting ready meltdown just for us.' Jane took a big slug of wine. It felt good. It felt like what she needed. Dutch courage. Tonight was the night she was going to tell her friends the truth. It should be easier than telling Josh. She wasn't putting a bomb under either of their lives and they'd both be supportive. Rationally she knew that. It was just…

'Sorry I'm late.' Lydia had stopped by the bar on her way in and placed another bottle of white on the table. 'I…'

'…couldn't decide what to wear.' Jane finished the sentence for her.

Lydia nodded. 'I hate all my clothes. I need to go shopping. I need to find something a bit more…' She tailed off. 'I dunno.'

Jane took another gulp of wine.

Annie picked up the conversation, telling Lydia that all her clothes were lovely and she always looked great, and then the chat turned to the Season. Jane let her attention wander. She definitely had to tell them tonight. Didn't she? Did she? They didn't know at the moment and they were perfectly happy. And she was fine. She was signed up for an extortionately expensive dating programme in which she couldn't actually date anybody but, apart from that, she was fine. Maybe she could just be single forever.

'Jane!' Lydia's voice jabbed through her thoughts. She was holding the second bottle of wine over Jane's glass. They hadn't drunk that much already, had they? Jane nodded for a refill.

A group of men, about their age, had gathered at the bar. Lydia looked over and then checked her watch. 'I have to get up at six tomorrow. Such a waste.'

'Why the early start?' Jane asked.

'Netball match in the wilds of Essex somewhere. Minibus from school at seven thirty.'

'Term's over. Doesn't that mean sport...' Jane was not an expert in anything sport related. 'Doesn't that mean sport stops too?'

Lydia shook her head. 'Two more matches. We've already won the league, so tomorrow is academic really. Then in a couple of weeks we play this sort of "champions of champions" thing against some fancy school in west London.'

'You're supposed to be on holiday though.'

'It's good for the girls,' Lydia pointed out.

She was right. For a lot of All Saints pupils, school was the only structure in their lives. Six weeks was a long time to be cut loose.

Lydia looked back towards the group at the bar. 'Seriously though, do you think I have time to hit that and still be in bed by ten?'

'Lydia!' Annie's ability to still be shocked by Lydia was quite endearing in its own way. 'I thought we'd signed up for the Season to find real lasting connections. We're supposed to be looking for love.'

This was the moment. This was an opportunity to pipe up with a casual, 'Yeah, about the whole looking for love thing...' The words were there in Jane's head but she didn't manage to release them into the world.

'That blond one keeps looking over here,' Lydia commented.

Jane looked up. The blond guy in the group at the bar did, indeed, keep looking over here. He wasn't her type. Obviously. On many many levels. She took another large gulp of wine. 'We're going to need another bottle,' she announced.

–

> What's the most you've ever lost in a hand?

The question from SirWalt popped up in the table chat. Emma shook her head. Never more than she could afford obviously. Actually, that wasn't quite true. She laughed as she typed.

> All my free evenings for a term.

> ?

was his only reply.

> I was fourteen. My stepbrother was sixteen. He hustled me into betting that I'd do all his chores for the next three months, and take his turns at walking the dog. I had two pairs and he had trip kings.

> Painful.

SirWalt replied straight away.

> What about you?

44

she countered.

> £40k.

> In actual cash????

> Yep. You know how it goes sometimes

Emma did not know. This was why she never played for cash. Even with her cautious approach the risk was too high.

She'd enjoyed playing today though. Players had come and gone but she and SirWalt had stayed at the table right through.

Her stomach growled, and she checked the clock. Late afternoon. She hadn't had lunch. She hadn't called her mum, like she'd promised she would each weekend.

> I have to go I'm afraid.

> Me too. Play again sometime?

Emma smiled slightly. She'd had fun.

> Sure.

He dropped a code that allowed her to get back to the same table again in the future into the chat and signed off.

She was still grinning as she opened up WhatsApp and went to video call her mum. 'What are you looking so pleased with yourself for?' Her mother was tanned and about five years younger than the woman who'd stepped into the taxi a few months ago. 'Is business going well?'

'Er… yeah.' She ran through the figures for sign-ups so far.

'And you're involving Josh?'

'Yes, Mum.'

Emma opened her main event spreadsheet on her laptop in front of her, readying herself for the volley of questions about prices and contracts that she knew was coming.

'That's great, dear. I can't chat I'm afraid. Judy who lives downstairs has invited me out for tapas.'

'Oh. Right. Ok. I'll call you next week then.'

'If you like, darling.'

The screen went blank. Right. It was good that her mother trusted her to run things without needing chapter and verse. Definitely good. She clearly knew that Emma could manage quite well on her own. She looked at the spreadsheet for a second before clicking close. It was fine. Everything was going to be fine.

Chapter Six

Miss Emma Love
requests the honour of your company at
the inaugural Ball of the Season.

Emma weaved her way through the crowd coming up from the tube, dragging her trusty tartan shopping trolley behind her. It wasn't stylish. It wasn't glamorous, but whilst a bijou little wheelie case might have been more aesthetically pleasing, this did a far better job of fitting in everything she could conceivably need.

She pulled it awkwardly up the three steps to the door of the very grand venue she'd booked for the evening's ball.

'Let me help you with that.' The young man coming out of the door towards her leaned forward to take the weight of the trolley.

'I'm fine. Thank you very much.' Emma kept her hand firmly on the handle as her gaze met the dark brown eyes of the man trying, entirely unnecessarily, to assist her. He was familiar.

She stepped to one side, to make room to look at him properly. Oh.

He grinned. 'Miss Love!'

'Mr Knight.' She never forgot a client's name. It was a point of professional pride.

'You're early.'

She narrowed her eyes. 'So are you.'

A moment of confusion fluttered across his face. 'Oh. I was here this afternoon for something else. A work thing.'

'Very good. So if you don't mind…' She nodded towards the doorway he was currently blocking.

'Until tonight, Miss Love.'

–

In the wood-panelled foyer she paused for a second to check the board listing the day's events. A conference on the ethics of animal research. A meeting of the management committee of the South and South East Historical Poetry Society. A recital of Baroque and Renaissance chamber music. He could be an academic, she supposed. She'd lay money, metaphorically of course, against him being either a poet or a chamber music aficionado.

It was a mystery that would have to wait for another day. Right now she had a ball to get ready for, and she'd arrived early to ensure that the livery hall that was hosting this, and several of the other events, was properly ready, and not just ready but Emma ready.

'Miss Love.' The venue's events manager, Harriet, appeared. There was nothing as obvious as a reception desk here. It was the sort of place where if you needed anything the intention was that someone would be on hand to provide it long before you had to go looking. That didn't mean things would be up to Emma's standards of course. Not bringing her trusty trolley of event essentials remained an unacceptable risk.

She trundled it along after her, refusing Harriet's offer of assistance. The ballroom was on the first floor so they made their way to the lift, where a tall man with flecks of premature grey in his dark brown hair, was also waiting.

He nodded at Harriet. 'Good to see you.'

Was there a slight flush in Harriet's cheek? Emma's match-maker senses tingled.

'Nice to see you too. Are you here for anything I can help you with?'

48

'I'm seeing Elliot. Maybe we'll be able to catch up when I've finished.'

'Oh, I've got an event… I'm…' Harriet was flustered.

Emma interrupted. 'She'll be in the ballroom. Do come and find us, Mr…'

'Martin. Robbie Martin.'

That was a name Emma already knew. It was common enough. The Robbie Martin on her list might not be this Robbie Martin. They left him in the lift and Emma set about finding out. 'So who's he then?'

'Robbie. He works for the company that does our PR. He manages the account here.'

'And you like him?'

Harriet definitely flushed red this time. 'He's a very nice man. I mean generally. To everyone. Everyone likes him. He's a good chap.'

'I see.' Her pursuit of this particular bout of true love was arrested by the doors to the ballroom being swept open in front of her. The room was still being dressed but already she could see that it was going to be impressive. The space was exquisite, with a high ceiling with painted roses around the chandeliers and ornate columns punctuating the panelled walls.

Harriet started pointing out the tasks currently in progress. 'Tim over there is our sound guy. He's setting all that up. The musicians are due here at six for their sound check. Marius is here already from the caterers. Marius!'

A tall dark-haired man appeared at Emma's side.

Harriet nodded at him. 'Everything in hand?'

'Of course. Waiting staff will be in position from six thirty with complementary drinks for any early arrivals in the down-stairs lounge. We will open the doors here promptly at seven, with champagne. We have our cocktail bar in the corner here and champagne waiters throughout the evening. Canapés will come out from a quarter past seven.'

'And right through the evening?' Emma knew her tone was tense, but she'd been to too many parties where the food ran out twenty minutes in and the guests continued to drink with nothing to soak up the alcohol. That was not the atmosphere she was aiming for.

A flash of irritation danced across Marius's face. 'Of course, Miss Love.'

Emma was delighted that he was annoyed. People who got offended by the suggestion that they might have overlooked a tiny professional detail were very much her sort of people.

'Excellent.' She looked around. 'Now is there signage downstairs so people know exactly where to come?' She didn't want people thinking they were in the wrong place or loitering around in the foyer feeling unloved.

'Not yet, but I can...'

'No need.' Emma unzipped her shopping trolley and pulled out elegantly produced signage of every type you could ever imagine requiring, all printed on thick creamy textured card with gilt borders. She rifled through the pile and pulled out the combinations of wording and arrows she thought they would need.

'That's very organised.' Was that a hint of a laugh behind Harriet's compliment?

Emma didn't care. She was very organised. After being able to spot two people who belonged together at a hundred paces, it was her second greatest quality.

She scanned the rest of the room. There was a raised podium for the musicians, chairs arranged in twos and fours – no threes, nobody wants to be a gooseberry – around the outside of the room and in the back half near to the cocktail bar, with the floor itself clear for dancing.

'And the waiters know to stay around the edges? The main floor is for dancing.'

'Of course.'

'And the musicians know to only play pieces in waltz time. Three three.'

'Erm...' Harriet hesitated. 'I'll check.'

'Please. It mustn't feel like a wedding disco.'

Harriet nodded and scuttled away, pulling her mobile from her pocket.

Emma needed this evening to go perfectly. She had far too many people who'd only paid for the first two events and hadn't signed up for the whole Season yet. She needed full fees from everyone if she was going to have a hope of covering the costs of the final Regency ball, and she still couldn't shake the feeling that something was missing. It was a series of events – well thought out, beautifully executed events of course – but just a series of events. A social season was more than that. She swallowed back a wave of nausea. She didn't need to fall back on the bail-out her mother had offered from Trevor's life insurance. She was going to do this all on her own.

–

Annie arrived alone to the second event of the social season. Lydia and Jane would mock but, standing in the doorway to the ballroom for the very first time, Annie was content to take a moment to allow her breath to be swept away. The drinks reception had been lovely, but this was something else. The pillars around the room were adorned with flowers. The lighting was soft and music floated across the room to her ear. It was the sort of ambience that made Annie want to stand a little straighter and, in her ideal imagined world, waft a fan coquettishly in front of her face.

She smoothed her long red dress. Red wasn't entirely her colour, but Lydia had thrust the bag into her hands the last time she'd seen her and told her that if she turned up in anything else it would be quite unacceptable.

Putting the damn thing on had been an exercise in wishing that Lyds and Jane were there to help. There was a complicated set of interlaced straps that were now finally lying flat between her shoulder blades and she'd eventually found a strapless bra in the back of the drawer that was prepared to stay up. She felt more scaffolded than undergarmented but even she had been forced to admit that when she looked in the mirror the effect was not unpleasant. Was it really her though? Or did she look like a pale imitation dress up version of Lydia?

Either way, about to cross the threshold into the ballroom, she was glad she'd made the effort. Full length gowns were definitely the order of the evening and gave the room a distinctly timeless feel.

'Hi.'

Annie didn't need to turn to know who it was. She'd spent the whole week conjuring his voice to mind. 'Hi, Josh.'

'Shall we?' He held out an arm for her take and she let him lead her into the ball.

A waiter swung by them with a tray of champagne in low, wide glasses, not the long flutes Annie was more used to. Josh took two and passed one to her. 'I ought to eke this out. I'm supposed to be working.'

She smiled. 'Well one won't hurt.'

'Sure. Bit of Dutch courage before the fray.'

She didn't ask what he needed to get his courage up for. She didn't need to. Jane was coming with Lydia. That had to be playing on his mind. She raised her champagne glass. 'Not a flute,' she offered. *Not a flute? Not a flute?* What sort of conversational opening was *Not a flute*?

He shook his head. 'No. Not sure what these ones are called though.'

'That's a coupe, don't you know?' Col, Colin, Colin Williams appeared at her other elbow. Annie would never acknowledge a flare of irritation at the appearance of a third wheel, and he was hardly a third wheel, was he? That implied that she and Josh were on the way to making a working bicycle, when they were clearly nothing more than old friends. And her old friend was, she suspected, still very much in love with her new friend.

'Supposed to be modelled on Marie Antoinette's knockers, you know. Well one of them at least.' Colin was a font of glassware trivia, but that bit did ring a very vague bell.

'I thought it was Madame de Pompadour?'

'Wasn't it the Empress Josephine?' Josh offered his boob attribution at the same time.

They all laughed, then stopped and stared for a second at their bosomy glasses. It was hard to know where to take the conversation next.

'Would you mind...' Josh broke the silence. 'Would you mind if I stole Annie away for a minute?'

Colin nodded curtly. 'No. Not at all. Discretion the better part of valour and all that.'

'Right.' Josh murmured. 'Well, thanks. Annie, can we?' He nodded towards the door to the hallway and led her into the cool quiet of the rather grand stairwell. 'You don't mind, do you?'

Of course she didn't mind. She'd never minded with Josh. He'd been... well, he'd been her best friend. And then. Annie closed down the thought. She'd had her chances and she'd failed to take them. She was thankful he was prepared to speak to her at all.

'Right. Ok then. It's just...' He took a sharp breath in. 'It's a bit awkward because of, well everything and I'm supposed to be here for work not to get together with someone and, well actually, Emma probably won't mind that. We don't have enough straight men. Or gay men actually, but that's not really relevant. Plenty of gay women though, weirdly. Bisexual actually mostly, so I think she's hoping that most of them hit it off with another woman. You know, even the maths up that way.' He paused.

Annie could feel herself smiling. Josh was always like this. Monosyllabic a lot of the time but couldn't stop talking when he was nervous. 'Josh!'

'Sorry. Yeah. I should get to the point. I was just saying I know it's awkward with Jane, and with me working for Emma rather than being a dater.'

With Jane. Of course, with Jane. 'You should talk to her.'

'To Emma?'

'To Jane!' Men were idiots sometimes.

'Right. You want me to talk to her?'

'It's not about what I want, is it? You and Jane, you know you had a really good thing. If you can make it work you should definitely try.' And she believed that. If Jane could make him happy that would be wonderful. 'Was there something else?'

He opened his mouth as if to carry on but then shook his head. 'No. Well yes, actually, there's a work thing I wondered if you could help me with.'

'If I can.'

'It's just Emma won't go for it and you were always so good with words...' He explained his big idea.

–

Emma watched the room from her vantage point next to the cocktail bar. She had to acknowledge that it was going well. The money she'd spent had been worth every tightly budgeted penny.

'Everything ok?' Harriet appeared at her elbow. She'd changed into a full-length black gown for the evening. Emma appreciated that. Plain black, modest neckline, cap sleeves – still professional, not distracting from the revellers – but nothing that would suggest that Harriet was anything as prosaic as staff.

Emma nodded.

'I need to get your ok to open the extra bottles of champagne?'

They had twelve bottles in reserve, not yet paid for, but available for Emma to authorise on the night. 'They've drunk the first lot already?'

Harriet nodded. 'I did say the extra would probably be needed. You've got a lot of people here.'

That was true. She had and they did. 'Of course. Just ask the waiters not to auto fill. Tipsy is fine. Legless is not the tone we're going for.'

Harriet nodded. 'Will do.'

'Oh!'

Harriet's exclamation provided a distraction from the columns of expenditure that were scrolling through Emma's head. 'Oh?'

'Mr Martin is here. I didn't know he'd signed up for your...' She waved a hand towards the room. 'For this.'

Emma followed her companion's gaze. Mr Martin. The man from the lift earlier. She repressed a grin of triumph. Hadn't she spotted Harriet's interest straight away? She scrolled down her tablet screen. So it was the same Robert Martin. She should never doubt her own memory for names. She tapped the screen off. 'Obviously I can't disclose client details.'

'I understand.'

'It is probably true to say that everyone here tonight is looking to find love though.'

'I thought he had a girlfriend.'

'Split up seven months ago.' Emma bit her tongue. 'I mean, I imagine that would be the sort of amount of time that someone who came along this evening might have been single. I obviously couldn't say for sure though.' Of course she knew for sure. She was rigorous about ensuring that everyone who had signed up was genuinely single. It was one of her mother's golden rules. There was a sort of person – usually a sort of man, in Emma's experience – who used dating agencies as a handy way in to meeting people who might be lonely enough, or hopeful enough, to overlook the indented line around the third finger of the left hand indicating a hastily removed wedding ring. Emma's mother never tolerated that, and neither would Emma. These days she checked social media profiles personally for recent pictures of significant others. Robert Martin looked a little different out of his suited and booted work look, but she was absolutely sure he hadn't posted anything with the late twenties redhead who used to be a mainstay of his photos for at least half a year.

'Right.'

'Perhaps you should go and say hello.'

'I'm working.'

'And surely making guests feel welcome is part of your job?' Emma smiled. 'Everything is in hand. I'll come and find you if there's a problem.'

Harriet hesitated. 'What will I say?'

'What do you want to say?'

'I don't know.'

Yes, you do, thought Emma. She could see it a mile off. Harriet was smitten. 'Then tell him it's lovely to see him and take things from there.'

She watched Harriet approach Mr Martin. He turned his body and tilted his head towards her immediately, angling himself away from the room and wholly towards Harriet, giving her his undivided attention. Human contact. With the right person. That was what people craved.

Emma pulled her gaze away. In a room full of people there was a private moment developing. Watching, even from afar, felt like an intrusion.

'Can't I get a beer?' And standing watching love unfold was an unacceptable luxury when Emma was supposed to be well and truly on the clock. She turned her attention to the altercation developing at the bar.

'It's a cocktail bar, mate.' The barman shrugged apologetically. 'Champagne and cocktails is what I've got.'

'Oh come on. You must have a beer somewhere.'

Emma leaned over the bar. 'It's fine.'

'But it's a cocktail bar.'

She raised one eyebrow at the barman. 'I saw you earlier. I know you've got a stash back there.'

'And?'

'And give the nice man one and I won't complain to the caterer that the bar staff were drinking on the job?'

He grinned. 'That sounds very fair.' He reached a bottle from under the bar and placed it in front of the disgruntled customer. 'Your beer, sir.'

'Wait.' Emma still wasn't quite satisfied. The customer was, of course, always right, but Emma was going for a particular atmosphere this evening and bottled beer was not it. She turned her full attention to the beer-deprived guest for the first time. Who else would it be? 'Mr Knight.'

'I told you to call me Tom.'

'This is a ball, Mr Knight. We have champagne, and punch, and cocktails. We have fruit juice and mocktails.'

He was making no attempt to hide his amusement at her speech. 'And now you have beer.'

'One beer. And then you really must enter into the spirit of the thing.' She turned back to the bartender. 'You understand. After this I'm cutting him off.'

Tom Knight folded his arms.

'Seriously, nobody likes a grump.'

He raised both eyebrows. 'One beer is all I ask for.'

He made to move away into the gaggle of people standing making small talk at the edge of the dance floor. Emma followed. A client was a client and an unhappy client was bad for the whole business. That was what her mother used to say. Perhaps, with hindsight, some sort of footnote excluding particularly annoying clients from this rule would have been helpful, but none had been provided.

She overtook him within eight paces and turned to block his path. 'Why are you here, if you're not in the mood for an elegant soiree?'

He took a swig from his beer. 'To find the love of my life, of course.'

'Why don't I believe you?'

'Maybe you're an irredeemable sceptic?'

'I'm a professional matchmaker. It's my job to believe in love.'

'Then I'm afraid I have no idea.'

She took a breath and tried a different approach. 'If you're genuinely here to find love, then let me help you.'

'You think I need your guidance?' His expression hardened.

'Given that so far I've only seen you exchange more than three words with myself and the bartender, yes. Yes I do.'

His face remained tense. 'All right then, Miss Love. What would you advise?'

'Well in my experience, compatibility can be predicted based on temperament, interests and past experiences.'

He stepped closer to her. 'That sounds rather impersonal.'

'Well, that's only half the equation. The other part is...' What was the other part?

'Passion?' he suggested. 'That moment when you're next to someone and you know absolutely that you never want to move from their side?'

'Quite.' Emma stepped back. Of course passion was the other part. She knew that. It was just hard to think with him so close.

'And you can offer me that?'

'Well, the idea of the Season is that you have the chance to find it by making a direct connection with somebody.'

He looked around the room. The tension in his face had eased, but a sadness had replaced it. 'I fear I might be beyond your help, Miss Love.'

–

Annie eventually caught up with Jane and Lydia hovering by the bar. Lydia was already swaying slightly, apparently full of champagne cheer. Jane was clutching an orange juice and looking more than a little weary.

'I think Josh is looking for you.'

Jane pulled a face. 'What for?'

'I'm not sure, but it seems like he's still into you.'

'What exactly did he say to you?' Jane's brow was furrowed.

'Not much. I told him to talk to you directly.'

'So he didn't actually say that he wants to get back together?'

Annie resisted the urge to roll her eyes. It was entirely clear what Josh wanted. She had no idea why Jane was being so utterly blind about it. 'What else could it be?'

'I'm not sure, but… hold on.' Annie watched as her friend marched to the bar and exchanged her fruit juice for something bright pink that came in a long glass. Jane downed it in one long draw. 'Right. I can't be doing with this. If the mountain won't come to Mohammed.'

Jane stormed off into the throng. That was that then.

–

Col, Colin, Colin Williams was making a beeline in Annie's direction across the dance floor. 'Might I have the pleasure of this dance?'

'Of course.'

She followed Colin onto the floor and they managed to fumble their way into a rough approximation of a ballroom hold. 'Do you waltz?' he asked.

'Not up until now.'

'Well just hang on then. I'll lead.' And off they went with a surprising amount of gusto on Colin's part and only a very passing allegiance to the tempo of the music. 'I had lessons, you know, before the wedding.'

'Right.'

'So at least that came in handy.'

Annie was finding conversation difficult with the rate of Colin's gyrations. It was a blessing when the music slowed sufficiently that even Colin was forced to moderate his pace and Annie could catch her breath. Once his initial frenzy had calmed, Colin was a surprisingly confident lead, whispering instructions to his novice partner. 'One, two, three, back, across, together, back, across, together…'

Annie settled into the rhythm. One, two, three. One, two, three. One, two, three. The floor was about half full with couples. The elegance of the twirling bodies, men in black tie, women in flowing colourful dresses, moving across the floor, turning, turning, turning was intoxicating. Then she saw Josh and Jane at the other side of the floor, moving in rhythm, in time with Annie and her own partner. The flow of the music and the turn of the dance changed the count in Annie's head. *One, two, three. One, two, Josh. One, two, three. One, two, Josh.* Every second turn she found him again in her line of sight. On the sixth turn she realised he was gazing back at her. Half a turn, half a turn and then for a second her eyes locked with his. Half a turn, half a turn, Josh. Half a turn, half a turn, Josh.

She found her breath catching in her throat as her eyes met his.

Half a turn, half a turn… she wasn't even sure why she kept seeking him out.

Half a turn, half a turn… they were old friends. That was all.

Half a turn, half a turn… any other hopes were a long time ago.

Half a turn, half a turn…

And he was there, but he was out of reach. All she could expect were those moments where her breath might catch in her throat and she might live for a second as the person she became in the full beam of his attention. Those moments where she caught a glimpse of what might have been.

Half a turn, half a turn, Josh.

Half a turn, half a turn, Josh.

And then she couldn't see him.

She let Colin twirl her again. She scanned the floor. There was a glimpse of Jane's long silver dress. They turned again. Annie searched the floor. He wasn't there.

She caught a flash of a tall, slender back walking away towards the exit. And then they turned again. Half a turn, half a turn… and… he was gone.

'You didn't have to come after me.' Jane stopped in the hallway and turned back towards her ex-husband.

'I kinda did.'

Jane stared at the floor. He really didn't. All she wanted was to forget the last ten minutes of her life. 'Seriously, it was a misunderstanding. It's not a big deal.'

'You dragged me onto the dance floor and then accused me of still being in love with you, and wanting to get back together.'

Yes. That was fair. She had done that. 'But you're not. And you don't. So it's fine.'

'And, you're ok? Not having second thoughts?'

She tried to gauge his expression. Concerned. But, it seemed clear from his reaction on the dance floor, more concerned that she was having second thoughts than that she wasn't.

'No. Not at all. I just thought you…'

He shook his head.

'No. Clearly.'

'What made you think?' He waved his hand back towards the ballroom, indicating presumably, all of the craziness she'd just sprung on him.

'Maybe I got the wrong end of the stick.' That wasn't right. She had definitely grasped the stick Annie had thrust at her. 'No. Sorry. It was Annie. She was really keen on us getting back together. I thought she must have got that from you.'

His expression changed for a second before he seemed to rally. 'No. Misunderstanding, I guess. We're cool though? You know, as cool as we can be in the circumstances.'

'I am sorry.' She had said it a hundred times already, but somehow it wasn't enough.

He shook his head. 'You don't need to be. Be proud of who you are.'

'But I never wanted to hurt you. I tried so hard to love you, you know, like that.'

He was looking at the floor. 'I know.'

'Part of me still wishes I could have. If it was going to be anyone, I really wish it could have been you.'

'But it shouldn't be that much effort, should it?'

She shook her head.

The layer of awkwardness between them had cracked a little but hadn't entirely gone away.

'I guess we should…' He nodded back towards the party.

'Yeah. I'll be back in in a minute.'

Jane watched him disappear back into the throng. She hung back in the doorway. Annie was dancing with that nice Colin chap who'd taken a shine to her at the drinks do. Lydia was propping up the bar. Jane scanned the rest of the room. There were many attractive, and presumably very personable once you got talking to them, people here, but how did you get talking to them? Jane wasn't just out of practice. She was a total novice. Well, not a total novice. She'd attracted Josh. And… her mind jumped back to the pub a few days before. The group of men at the bar. The blond one who kept looking her way. That had ended, well it had ended conclusively for Jane. One-night stands with blond men from bars were never for her. Never again anyway.

–

'Where were you going?' Emma caught Josh's arm as he came back into the party. Typical of him to skive off halfway through the night. 'Mum said you had to help, you know.'

And then she saw the look on his face. It was the look he'd had when he'd walked in to their mum and dad's house and announced that he was getting a divorce and asked if it was ok if he stayed there for a little while. It was the look of defeat. 'Shit. What happened?'

She thought back through the evening. 'I saw you dancing with Jane. Did she say something?'

He shook his head. 'No. Yes. Not exactly.'

She took his arm and led him firmly across the ballroom and through a door marked *Private* that led to the room they were using as a staff cloakroom.

'What's wrong?'

He shook his head. 'Nothing. Just a bit of an emotional night.' He took a breath and put a smile on. 'It's going well though.'

'Of course.'

'The venue's amazing. Expensive?'

'Within budget.'

He held his hands up as if to acknowledge that he was going to steer clear. 'All right. You're the boss.'

'Is that why you're all grumpy?'

'What?'

'Cos you're working for me.'

He laughed. 'No. Your idea was good. And I'm a nerd, not a matchmaker or an event planner or an entrepreneur or any of the other things you'd have to be to pull something like this off on your own. You deserve this.'

The compliment was worse than him giving her a hard time. 'Oh, you know, it's the first time. Lots to improve.'

'But it's going well, isn't it? And we're ok financially?'

'Mmmmm.' And they were. They would be. She just needed to shave a few costs here and there and sign up a few more people. Ten more. Twenty ideally. Thirty. Thirty would be great. And that wasn't impossible. They were only partway through the second event and registration was open right through event three.

'Stilts!'

'What?'

'You were miles away. And you were doing the hair thing.'

'I don't do the hair thing.' She totally did the hair thing. Her mother did it too when she was stressed out and she thought nobody was watching. Just twisting the hair at the side of the face around and around her forefinger.

'Stilts. Come on. Let me help.'

'You can't help.'

To his credit he didn't bite her head off at that. 'Try me.'

'It's just, I mean the money's tight but it'll be ok.' Hopefully. 'It's more, there's something missing.'

'What do you mean?'

'A social season was more than just a series of parties. It was a community. People's families were involved and there was gossip and everyone knew everyone else and… I don't know. Maybe you can't recreate that over a few weeks.'

He grinned. 'What if rather than recreate, we reinvent?'

'What?'

'Just listen to me this time. Ok?'

'Ok.' She didn't have anything to lose.

'I have an idea.'

–

Jane knew she really ought to tell Lydia and Annie that she was sneaking off, but they would only try to persuade her to stay, so she opted for sending a text from the stupidly expensive Uber she'd ordered and then switching her phone to silent. Forty minutes later she was finally pulling off her not-suitable-for-walking shoes, hoiking her waist-cinching knickers down and bundling herself into her pjs. Ten minutes after that she was installed on the sofa with a hot chocolate, a packet of Maltesers, a ridiculous crime drama where it seemed entirely clear to Jane within the first ten minutes that the victim had been his own twin brother all along, and a worry that she was leaning into the stereotype of the thirty-something single divorcée rather too heavily.

Her landline interrupted her cliché of a perfect night. She checked the clock. Too late for a cold call, and the only other person who rang her landline wouldn't be calling at this time, would she? Jane answered the call.

'Jane, love, there you are.'

'Nana? Are you ok?'

'Oh yes. I'm all right. It's your mam.'

Jane exhaled deeply. What was her mother up to now? The last time her nan had called her with an update, Jane's mum had been in hospital with an infection after getting a tattoo from some guy she'd met in a field at a festival. 'What's she done?'

'It's not so much what she's done, as… well I suppose it is what she's done, in a way.' Her nan chuckled on the other end of the phone. 'She's pregnant.'

'What?' Jane's mother was a month off her fiftieth birthday. 'She can't be.'

'Apparently she can. We start the change late in this family. I was nearly sixty before the hot flushes came on. So think on. You could have another thirty years.'

Jane didn't want to think about the impending, or not, nature of the menopause. 'Right. Well, there's a thing. Do the others know?'

'I rang Ali and Shan. Mani is off goodness knows where. I sent them one of those thingies you set up for me. With the green box.'

'A WhatsApp.'

'That's the chicken.'

'Ok.' Jane's siblings were scattered to the seven winds. Mani was last heard of trekking in the Balinese jungle. Ali taught English to children in Uganda. And Shan ran a surprisingly profitable Etsy business selling handmade tiles from a cottage on a Hebridean island. Fey, the youngest of the five – well, five so far – still lived with their parents in the commune outside Salisbury. And Jane was a secondary school History teacher in Leytonstone. Some apples fell further from the tree.

'So I thought maybe you might give her a little ring?' Jane's nan was always the peacemaker, always the one that everybody was still talking to when fights erupted left, right, centre, and all around.

'I don't know.'

'I know she'd love to hear from you. You're her eldest. I know it would mean a lot. First children are always special, you know.'

'You've only got one child, Nana.'

'And she's very special to me.'

She let her nan remind her of the number of the one and only phone at the farmhouse, and promised to definitely, almost certainly, call really very soon.

Chapter Seven

'You have to go now.' Lydia prodded the prostrate body next to her with her foot. 'Come on. Morning. Time to move along.'

She was determined to keep her voice level and dispassionate, but underneath her heart was racing. Men, even hot barmen, did not stay the night in Lydia's apartment. She had curated the perfect space to disincline them from getting comfortable. Firstly, it was a studio. Bed, one, and only one, armchair, kitchenette against the far wall, door to the tiny shower room next to the bed. And that was it. There was no space to get comfy, nowhere that a couple could sit for a romantic dinner or any of that nonsense. Her bed was a small double – six inches narrower than the standard. It was intended to suggest that once the necessary business had been concluded guests should not get settled. Her windowsill was occupied by a row of tiny teddy bears, presided over from the central position by a particularly creepy-looking vintage doll that seemed to stare at anyone in the bed. If pressed, she was quite prepared to pretend that it was a treasured childhood possession, and not some piece of tat she'd bought at a car boot to add to her perfect antidote to male comfort of a room.

'Seriously, it's morning. Why are you still here?'

The barman – yes, she was sure he had a name, but she had no reason whatsoever to bother herself with remembering it – raised his head from the pillow. 'Knackered. Piss off and let me sleep.'

That was too much. 'You can't sleep here. It's tomorrow. I need to get up and get on with stuff.'

'And I am not stopping you.'

Lydia grabbed her robe from the floor (her bright pink Hello Kitty robe – seriously, how many clues did this guy need that this was not a testosterone friendly space?) and got out of bed, pausing only to yank the duvet off her apparently immoveable guest. She ignored his yelling about the cold and marched over to the kitchenette where she filled the mini one-cup sized kettle and took her one mug from the draining board and dropped in a tea bag.

'So where are you rushing off to?'

Her accidental house guest was pulling on his shirt as he sat up in bed.

'None of your business.'

'So I don't even get coffee?'

'There's a Costa on the way to the bus stop.'

'Wham bam, thank you, Will, then.'

Lydia pledged to forget that name as quickly as possible. 'Thank you for a lovely night.'

'And now my services are no longer required?'

'Exactly.'

'Well, I won't hang around where I'm not wanted then.' He wandered back over to the bed and picked his trousers up from the floor. 'Have you seen my shoes?'

She replayed the previous evening in her mind. Shoes must have come off before trousers, and they'd landed at the foot of the bed. She traced a line from the bed to the door. 'By the fridge,' she pointed.

'Thank you.' Finally he was fully dressed. 'Until the next time then.'

'There isn't going to be a next time.'

He nodded. 'Yeah. That's what you said the last time.'

'I mean it.'

He opened her front door. 'So I'll see you at the grand dinner?'

'Yeah. I mean I'll be there. So maybe.'

He grinned. 'It's a date.'

'It's not a date,' she yelled after him.

She glanced at the clock. 9.27 a.m. 9.27 on Sunday morning. She carried her cup of tea over to the bed and found her phone. Even when falling through the front door in a scramble of lust and limbs, she knew there was no way she'd have forgotten to plug her phone in. Not on a Saturday night. She'd never risk being out of battery on a Sunday morning.

9.29 a.m. She laid the phone in front of her on the bed.

9.30. Her stomach clenched. She waited as the seconds moved by. Then it rang. She counted the rings. One. Two. Three. Then she waited a second to see if they hung up. This time they didn't. One the fifth ring she answered the phone.

'You're ok to talk?'

'He's spark out, pet. Not going to hear a peep out of him before lunchtime, I don't think.'

Lydia knew what that meant. It meant a night at the pub after the football. 'Won or lost?'

'Won.'

'That's good.'

'Yeah. He was all right when he came in. He's been all right generally recently.'

Lydia counted back the weeks in her head. Four weeks in a row she thought she'd been able to talk. But three weeks before that had been three rings and then a hang up. That was their system. No call meant something was wrong. Three rings and hanging up meant the caller was safe but she couldn't talk right now. And then on the good weeks they could actually talk.

'He says he might take me away somewhere soon. Y'know, for my birthday.'

'Your birthday was in April.'

'I know but we didn't do anything then and he feels so bad about it, so we might go somewhere nice.'

'That'll be good then.'

'Yeah. Anyway I'd best be off. Don't want to go over my free minutes.'

Lydia wanted to say that she could call, that she could afford it and that it would be fine. But she didn't, because it wouldn't. If he was in one of his dark moods a simple phone call could be the thing that set him off. Especially a phone call from Lydia.

'So I'll talk to you next week.'

'Yeah. I hope so.'

'Bye darling.'

'Bye Mum,' Lydia whispered, but the line was already dead.

She took a deep breath. Time to get on with the day. The claims of things to do and places to be weren't simply to get rid of Hot Barman. She did have somewhere to be. It was the very last match of the season for the senior netball team. Two weeks later than they would normally play but they had made it to the finals for the first time ever, and that involved a trip to Westhall Abbey Ladies' College in a minibus full of sixteen-year-olds.

She showered, dressed and necked the rest of her now cold tea in about fifteen minutes flat, and was waiting in the street before Annie pulled up to collect her. PE teacher Lydia had much less trouble getting ready than night out Lydia. PE teacher Lydia was gym leggings, a school polo shirt and hoodie, hair in a pony tail, keys, phone, purse and water bottle in a rucksack and out the door. It was a costume she knew how to wear.

–

Meet at school at 10.00. That's what the instructions had said. The minibus finally pulled away at 10.25. At least the delay had been entirely built into Lydia's timings. This was not her first team trip.

Annie was squeezed into the folding seat next to the driver, responsible for keeping order on the journey, while Lydia dealt with navigating the school's dilapidated minibus around the streets of the capital and not killing them all in the process. 'Thanks for chaperoning this.'

'It's ok.'

'No. It's not. You've done nearly all our away matches this year. And last year.'

'It's fine.'

Lydia couldn't resist the urge to tease a little bit. 'But think of all the other things you could be doing. It's weekend. You could be hooking up with some hot piece of ass…' She grinned.

'Shut up!'

'I'm only joking.'

'In front of a bus full of teenage girls. Thanks a lot.'

Lydia glanced in the mirror to check on proceedings behind her. 'They're not listening to us.'

Most of the girls were deeply engrossed in their phone screens.

'But still.'

'But nothing. It's just a joke.' Lydia shouldn't tease. Out of the three of them, Annie was definitely the only one taking the Season nonsense seriously. She wasn't the hot piece of ass type. She was more the 'baking a nice hot pie for her perfect soul mate' type.

Lydia was distracted from her mental dissection of Annie's dating character by her phone vibrating from its position on the shelf between the driver and passenger seats. 'Can you check who that is?'

Annie picked up the phone. 'It's Jane. Shall I answer?'

'Yeah.'

Annie answered the call and relayed the fact that Jane wanted to borrow Lydia's car. That was fine. 'Tell her it's fine and then tell her to get her own fucking car.'

Jane drove Lydia's ageing Clio nearly as often as Lydia did and was, therefore, the keeper of the spare car key. Annie passed on the first half of the message and hung up. 'Don't say eff in front of the students.'

'They're not listening.'

'They're always listening if you say something you shouldn't.'

That was a fair point. Lydia was still living down having been overheard opining that their deputy headteacher looked like he'd be a good ride during her first term on the staff.

'We're here,' she said, somewhat prematurely, as they turned off the road. Westhall Abbey Ladies' College turned out to be some distance away from the street. Annie's mouth was wide open. 'How posh is this school?'

Lydia shrugged. 'Do you think they're playing us as some kind of outreach programme?'

She pulled the minibus to a halt outside what really did look more like a stately home than any school Lydia had ever visited before.

'Is this where we're playing, Miss?'

'I think so.'

There was a gaggle of conversation behind her, the gist of which seemed to be a general intent to mess up some posh bitches. Marvellous. That was probably the sort of thing Lydia was supposed to discourage but, frankly, given that it was a school with a mile-long driveway she could scarcely imagine the sorts of resources the sports teams had. A bit of strategically implemented violence might be their best shot at victory.

A woman in a navy pleated gym skirt and a perfectly pressed Westhall Abbey polo shirt jogged across the expanse of gravel towards them. Lydia took a deep breath and jumped out of the minibus to greet her. 'Miss Hyland? And the All Saints Community Academy?' She was staring uncertainly at the side of the minibus.

Lydia stuck her chin out, ignoring the fact that the school logo had half peeled away and was revealing the faded paintwork of the evangelical church who'd been the minibus's previous owner. 'Yes. I'm Ms Hyland. Lydia.'

'Miss Callaghan.' She didn't offer a first name. 'It's lovely to have you here.' She raised one fist in a mock wave of excitement. 'Big day all around? Championship finals?'

'Yeah.' Lydia was still taking in her surroundings. 'This is a private school, yeah?'

'Well, we say public school, but fee-paying certainly.'

She was confused. 'So why do you play in the normal league? Don't you have your own?'

'Yes. Well…' The previously perfectly perky Miss Callaghan seemed momentarily tongue-tied. 'We did. That is to say, the girls did, with their previous games mistress.'

'So what changed?'

Miss Callaghan smiled brightly. 'I think it's important to be able to mix across all…' She glanced again at the rust bucket Lydia's team had arrived in. 'Well, with all sorts of people. Don't you agree?'

Something previously calm and warm in Lydia's gut turned to cold hard ice. 'Absolutely,' she replied.

'Jolly good. Come along then. I'll show you to the away team changing rooms.'

'We're already changed.' The All Saints girls were now jostling their way out of the minibus, entirely oblivious to Annie's exhortations to be patient and get out one at a time. The minibus emptied more in a lumpen flop of bodies than a measured flow.

'So you are. Well, I'll show you over there anyway.'

Lydia thought of herself as a fit person. She taught PE for a living, frequently went for a run before work and lifted weights at the gym on a weekend. She still thought the walk to the PE block – sorry, on-campus sports centre – was a ridiculously long one. She was starting to suspect Miss Callaghan was taking the piss when they crossed what Lydia firmly believed was the same hockey pitch for the third time, and were finally allowed inside, through sliding double doors next to a sign bearing the legend;

Westhall Abbey Sports Centre. Fidelite, Virtus, Mansuetudo

Latin was not Lydia's strong point but she guessed fidelity, virtue and… 'What's mansuetudo mean?'

73

Miss Callaghan smiled. 'Gentleness. As our founders thought was becoming for young ladies. Does your school have a motto?'

'A place to learn,' deadpanned Lydia.

'They thought about "A great place to learn",' offered Annie.

'But that seemed like overstating things a bit,' added Lydia.

'Right. Well, it's to the point, isn't it?' their host smiled.

Lydia's attention was already elsewhere. This wasn't a school PE block like anything she'd ever worked in. This place would put most fancy hotel gyms to shame. 'You have a pool?'

'We have two actually. Indoor and outdoor. The outdoor is only twenty-five metres though so more of a leisure pool.'

Only twenty-five metres. Of course. The hardship.

They followed their guide along a nest of corridors, with Lydia desperately trying to keep up with the directions. 'Main sports hall through there. Spectator gallery up those stairs, or there's a lift down that corridor. Any parents or supporters can watch from up there. Space for you courtside of course, Ms Hyland.'

'Right.'

'Practice court down there for your warm-up drills. I'll take my girls to the outside court so you can have free use in there.'

'You have two netball courts?'

'Two inside. Two outside.' She stopped outside a door marked 'Guests'. 'There's a weight and cardio room at the end of the corridor. If you want to use any of the equipment for warm up please do feel free.'

'Thank you.'

Miss Callaghan pointed back at the door. 'And this is you.'

Finally they were deposited in a changing room that was considerably nicer than the one at the gym Lydia gave fifty quid to every month.

The girls, who were normally so full of bravado, looked smaller somehow in these surroundings. Lydia held on to the shard of ice that had hardened in her gut when they arrived. She was not going to have her girls think they didn't deserve to be here. She would not have them think of themselves as lesser.

'All Saints First Team,' she yelled and clapped her hands together. 'Huddle up.'

The girls formed themselves into a loose gaggle around her. It wasn't exactly a circle but it didn't matter. It was good enough. This team was good enough. Now she needed to make them believe that. She allowed herself a deep breath. 'How many matches have we played on the way here?'

The girls shrugged. Damn. Lydia realised she didn't quite know either.

Annie helped her out. 'Twenty-two. Won twenty. Drew two. The best record in the league by an absolute mile.'

'Thank you, Miss Keer. Twenty-two matches. No losses. Is that going to change today?'

There were a couple of murmurs around the huddle. Lydia raised her voice. 'I said, is that going to change today?'

'No, Miss.'

'Like you mean it!'

'No, Miss.'

'That's right. We are going to do exactly what we've done the last twenty-two times. We're going to go out there and warm up on the main court where everyone can see us, they can see what they're up against and then we're going to play a match. And what happens when we play a match?'

'We win, Miss!'

'Again!'

'We win, Miss!'

'And what will we do today?'

'Win. Win. Win.'

'Hands in.'

Seven players. Three subs. Two teachers. Twelve hands swung into the middle of the circle. 'After three,' shouted Lydia. 'One, two, three.'

'Win!' yelled the circle.

Hell, yes.

–

Jane had started to call her mum at eight that morning and then told herself it was too early and cancelled the call. At 9.15 a.m. she started again and then thought that maybe pregnant people got tired so maybe she should wait a bit later yet. At 9.43 a.m. she decided she would definitely call right now, before aborting the whole idea for a third time.

By 10.45 she was in Lydia's car, on a promise to Annie that she'd fill it up with petrol and have it back by night fall, heading towards the M3. The last time she'd driven this route was at Christmas three years ago, after another call from her nan, who'd convinced her that Fey would appreciate having their big sister to visit.

Two hours later she pulled up in front of the big rusty gate that marked the entrance to the family farm, and not just her family, the collection of families, informally adopted family members and general waifs and strays who lived in the farmhouse and outbuildings that the commune had called home for nearly thirty years.

Jane's parents were founder members, and so, in a sense, was Jane, having been two years old when her mum and dad had abandoned their attempt to live a sustainable life in harmony with the planet in a two up, two down terrace in Trowbridge and converted this place into a communal living centre for like-minded souls. Since then many people had come and gone, but Jane's mum and dad, along with the Sams – a lovely couple, entirely coincidentally both called Sam – had stayed.

And it was Big Sam, a hint of grey in his always extravagant beard but otherwise looking just the same as when an eighteen-year-old Jane had walked out of the same gate those years before, who walked out to greet her as she got out of the car. 'Jay!'

She gave him a pointed look. He held up both hands.

'Jay! This is a surprise. A nice one though. You drive on through. I'll get the gate.'

She started to get straight back in her car, but stopped. She quickly skipped around the front of the bonnet and gave Sam a quick hug. 'It's nice to see you too.'

'Ah, don't be daft. I'm a sight for nobody's sore eyes. Your ma'll be right pleased you're here though.'

Jane doubted that rather more. She could still slam the car into reverse and drive away. The thought of explaining herself to her nan kept her moving forward.

There was a constancy to life at the commune that could suck a person in if they weren't wary. Daily needs and individual wants were secondary to the rhythm of the seasons, to what food could be grown and how well it could be preserved or stored. When Jane thought of the early years she remembered different phases. At first of course she was too young to know, but she thought she remembered hunger. Not just the peckish feeling after skipping lunch because someone had to supervise detention, or deal with an accident on the playground, but the gnawing constant companion of real hunger from a belly that hadn't been properly fed for weeks or months.

Then she remembered a golden period, after the commune had grown in size, and they'd worked out how to grow more of what they needed and how to barter for the rest. But that was like a mirage that she could glimpse in her mind for a moment or two before it dissipated into what she really thought of when she thought of her childhood home.

She parked outside the main house, taking care not to drive straight into any of the children or animals playing in the yard. And then she paused. She was here, wasn't she? There was nothing more to do than go inside.

–

Lydia took the netballers through their usual set of practice drills on the main court. The ice in her gut had turned to a less certain knot. The knot that said *you're not supposed to be here. You're going to get in trouble for doing it wrong. You don't know how to behave.* She refused to let the worry show. She told herself they were warming up on the main court because that was good tactics – let the opposition arrive on court after you. Undermine the home advantage by making them walk in on you. And it was what they always did, usually on half the court, while their opponents warmed up at the other end, because what sort of school had four netball courts for goodness' sake?

The tactics thing sounded good though, and Lydia resisted a smile when Miss Callaghan eventually led her team into the main hall and a flash of irritation coloured her perfect face at seeing the All Saints team already in situ.

Lydia took her seat courtside. The first fifteen minutes went well. All Saints finished the quarter leading eleven to seven. The second quarter was more even and by halftime their lead had been cut to two goals. Lydia gathered her team into a huddle. 'Do not take your foot off the gas. Do not let them back into this.'

'They're freaking us out, Miss.'

'How?'

'Like they clap every time we score. It's weird.'

'They're being sporting.'

All Saints' Goal Attack pulled a face. 'Like that's all fair and that but it's a bit much, innit? The keeper keeps patting me on the back. Like I'm a good dog who's done a clever trick or summat.'

Lydia wasn't having that. If they got beat, they got beat, but they weren't going to be patronised. 'Right. Here's what we do…'

Two minutes into the second half Westhall Abbey Ladies' College scored their nineteenth goal in the match. The All Saints team burst into applause and yells of 'Bravo' and 'Good show'. Lydia grinned to herself.

Four minutes later Westhall scored again. This time the volley of cheers was matched by a voice in the viewing gallery. Lydia looked up, and straight into the eyes of the man she'd thrown out of her bed a few hours earlier.

He tilted his head to one side and offered an ever so slightly quizzical smile, before raising his hand in a wave. Lydia looked away. She hadn't seen him. That was the line. She hadn't seen him, so she wasn't ignoring him. It was bad enough when a conquest tried to slide into her DMs. There was no way she was letting one slide into her actual life.

—

> You do not know when to stop.

Emma typed into the private chat window she now seemed to always open as soon as she joined SirWalt's online poker table. Three flashing dots told her that he was typing a reply.

> Well, I've never had any complaints before.

Emma rolled her eyes.

> I meant at the table. You just lost half your chips.
> He clearly had the flush.

> It's only chips.

> But if you think like that what's the point in
> playing? You'll bet on everything.

Pretty much.

She tried to picture him. Was he laughing at her or with her? It was no good. She couldn't visualise him at all. She didn't even know for sure that he was a he, apart from that Walt sounded like a male name. Walt for Walter she guessed.

The next hand was being dealt. Walt tapped out of the table, but didn't leave the chat room. Emma was sitting at the small blind and got an unsuited eight and two. Instant fold.

Not playing any more?

She typed.

Just taking a break. Don't want any attitude from you when I lose the rest.

Emma laughed to herself. She might as well keep the conversation going to pass the time until she was back in.

So how long have you played?

All my life. My dad taught me. He and Mum played before I was born. I think it was a way of keeping a connection to their past life or something. What about you, Queenie?

Didn't play seriously 'til uni though. Assignment on probability.

You not one of those whizz kids who's banned from every casino in Las Vegas, are you?

No!

Emma had never played in a casino. She never played for cash. It was the mental challenge she got her buzz from. It wasn't about beating the system. It was about understanding the probabilities well enough to maximise your chances of winning most of the time.

I don't play for money.

Why not?

Why take the risk?

But what is life without risk?

It wasn't about taking no risks. It was about only taking the right risks, with the highest chance of return, the risks that, when you thought about it, weren't really risks at all.

The flashing dots on the screen told her that Walt was still typing.

What about the rest of life? What about relationships? You have to take risks then.

> Sensible risks.

typed Emma.

> Nope. All in or fold. You can't hedge over everything, Queenie.

> I like to wait until I'm sure.

The dots flashed and then stopped. And then flashed again.

> No. When I'm in, I'm in. When I fall, I fall hard.

I fall hard. Emma stared at the words. It was her turn to say something. Her fingers hovered over the keys.

'Stilts! Do you want to read this again before I send?' Josh called to her from the living room.

> Have to go. Work. Sorry.

–

The yard smelt of manure and soil, but when Jane reached the open front door, another smell hit her – the pot that bubbled constantly on her parents' stove. Officially soup. Actually, little more than vegetable stock, but served up copiously as a remedy for all ills, physical, mental or emotional. Jane took a deep breath in through her mouth and then called out. 'Mum! Dad? Fey?'

'Who is it?' The voice that responded was upstairs, so Jane inched towards the foot of the stairs.

'Mum, is that you?'

'Jane!' Jane winced as her mother bowled down the stairs and wrapped her in a bear hug. 'Did my mother phone you? I knew she would. You didn't have to come all the way down here. It's wonderful that you're here though. Let me look at you.'

She gripped her daughter by the shoulders and stood an arm's length back from her, apparently taking in Jane's appearance. Jane struggled to keep her chin high and her expression bright. She must be a terrible letdown. She'd rejected the values they'd tried so hard to instil but that would not stop her from being proud of who she was, of trying to be proud at least.

And keeping her chin up stopped her from fixating on the very large belly that was filling the gap between them. Her mum wasn't just pregnant. She was really really pregnant.

'Is that big lanky pole of a lad with you?' Her mum got her question in before Jane could ask how far along exactly she was.

Jane shook her head. And that was her way in to the first thing they needed to talk about. Might as well get on with it then. 'We got divorced.'

Her mum tilted her head and stared a second longer at her daughter's face. 'Right you are. Probably for the best. His aura was never quite in harmony with yours.'

Jane stepped out of her mother's grip. 'No. Well, these things happen.'

'And they happen for a reason,' insisted her mother cheerfully. 'Now, will you have some soup? You will, won't you? I insist. Is it lunchtime for your people?'

'My people?'

Jane's mother waved a hand vaguely. 'You know, nine to five people with schedules and such like. I'm eating whenever this one,' she patted her stomach, 'is hungry. And your dad's been out harvesting the beans so he'll have eaten twice already I would think. Fey's out with him. They're growing up so strong. The very spit of your dad, they'll be.'

Annoyingly, after a two-hour drive, Jane did have to concede that it was indeed lunchtime for her people. But, as it happened, it was lunchtime for schedule free holistic farming people too.

'Well, what do we have here then?' Her father peered through at them as he deposited his wellies by the back door.

'Who is it?' Fey was indeed growing into the spit of their dad, but still had a youthful lankiness about them as they shoved through to see who the visitor was, and then launched themselves at their big sister for a cuddle. 'What are you doing here?' Their eyes widened. 'Have you come to share in the blessing?'

'Don't be daft. Jay won't want anything to do with that.' Her father helped himself to soup before taking a seat at the far end of the kitchen table.

'She goes by Jane now,' her mother snapped.

'Sorry, Jane.'

'And you don't know why she's here,' her mother argued. 'She's got news to tell you. She's getting divorced.'

'I got divorced already.' It was years since they'd known what was going on in her life. She wasn't going to feel guilty about not keeping them up to date.

Her dad nodded. 'He wasn't right for you.'

'Apparently not. Wrong aura.'

Only Fey looked sad. 'I'm sorry. I liked Josh. He was sweet.'

'He still is. We're still friends. It's fine.' She smiled to reassure her unworldly younger sibling. 'It's absolutely fine. I promise.'

And that wasn't why she was here.

–

All Saints beat the young heiresses of Westhall Abbey Ladies' College by thirty-two goals to twenty-eight. Lydia was plotting her quickest and most direct route back to the changing room and then the minibus when Miss Callaghan waylaid her with another perfect smile and an outstretched hand. 'Good game. Congratulations, Miss Hyland. Your girls are a credit to you.'

'They're a credit to themselves,' replied Lydia, as she turned to make her escape.

'You're not rushing off? There's a buffet on the viewing gallery. We always offer visiting teams refreshments.'

'Erm… I don't know. We've got to drive back across town and…'

Her objections were quickly drowned out by the sound of the girls running off court and galloping up the stairs with shouts of 'There's free food!'

Lydia took a sharp intake of breath. 'Obviously, we'll stay for a little while. It's very kind of you,' she managed.

She wouldn't be going to join the bun fight though. He was up there so she would have to stay down here. She made a show of busying herself gathering up balls and folding bibs.

'So are you hiding from me or from the massed ranks of the Westhall parents' committee? Because the first is very rude, and the second completely understandable.'

Lydia kept her back to him and concentrated on smoothing out the creases in the Wing Attack's bib.

'You know I can still see you, even when you don't look at me, don't you? You're not an ostrich.'

'That doesn't make any sense.' She turned to face him. 'People can still see the ostrich. That's like the whole point of that saying.'

'So you are an ostrich?'

She laughed despite herself. 'No.'

'So you are avoiding me then?'

Lydia shook her head. 'Didn't even know you were here.'

'Of course you didn't. You didn't look right at me and pretend you hadn't seen me at all.'

Attack was often the best form of defence. 'What are you doing here anyway?'

'Why shouldn't I be here? I don't just pop into existence when you're feeling horny.'

'I mean here specifically. Don't get many thirty-something single blokes at a school netball match.' Oh shit. It was staring her in the face. 'You're not single. You're some lass's dad, aren't you?' Typical. He was probably here with a perfect wife to watch their perfect little Poppy or Annabelle playing in her school netball match. 'You've come down to warn me not to accidentally let anything slip to your wife.'

His easy grin had been replaced by a grim stare. 'No. I'm not anybody's dad. I'm not married. If I was married I would not be the sort of husband who did… well, all the stuff we did.'

The stuff we did. A flash of memory took over Lydia's whole body for a second. Breath against her neck. Fingers digging into her thigh. Flesh against flesh. The heat. The scent of him.

He took a step closer to her and lowered his voice. 'Everyone'll be occupied with their pretty little canapés for a good half hour yet…' He raised one eyebrow.

No. Lydia froze. He was a Saturday night. This was a Sunday afternoon. There could be no overlap.

She stepped back. 'No thank you. I'm at work at the moment.'

He held up his hands in submission. 'Fair enough. I mean, technically I was at work when you dragged me into an alley thirty-five minutes after we met but, sure. You're on the clock.'

'So why are you here?' She determinedly changed the subject back to the here and now, where there was no danger of anyone ripping anyone else's shirt off and licking from their belly button all the way down to… 'If you're not anybody's dad?'

'Sister. The parents are away a lot so I try to come to school stuff if I'm free.' He shrugged. 'Make her feel like someone in the family gives a shit.'

Lydia felt her mood soften slightly. It was kind of him to make an effort. Nobody had ever come to see her matches at school, or her choir recitals, or her plays. 'That's nice of you.'

'Come and get something to eat.'

She shook her head. 'I don't know. You made the parents' committee sound pretty terrifying.'

'I'll protect you.' He held out a hand. 'Seriously, stay close to me and they won't bother you at all. I've been burning bridges here for the last five years. They basically all hate me.'

Lydia allowed herself to be cajoled. 'All right then. But only cos I'm starving. It doesn't mean we're friends or anything.'

He nodded seriously. 'Never thought that it did.'

–

'So anyway, Nana told me your news. Congratulations.'

'Thank you.' Her dad was beaming. 'We're delighted, aren't we?'

'So you did come to share in the blessing?' Fey looked so excited and Jane hated to let them down, but there were some lines that she wouldn't cross.

'No. Sorry. I've borrowed a friend's car. I have to get it back.' Lydia wouldn't care, but the lie softened the refusal for Fey. Jane didn't care what her parents thought. 'But I wanted to see you.' She turned to her mum. 'Make sure you're ok. Make sure you're getting proper medical care.' At your age, she thought.

'Don't be silly. It's my sixth baby, and your dad's delivered four of them, and more lambs than I care to count. I don't need some doctor complicating everything.'

Jane tried again. 'It's just that pregnancy's not always as easy when you're a bit... older. It's fifteen years since you did this the last time.'

Her mum put down her soup spoon. 'I've got everyone around me. I'm not silly. I'll rest when I need to, but you need to relax, Jane. Having a baby is perfectly natural and people have been doing it without poking and prodding since the beginning of time.'

There was no point arguing, so she bit her tongue. 'When's it due?'

Her mum shrugged. 'End of next month. Maybe early the month after. Around the new moon would be wonderful.'

Her dad nodded enthusiastically. 'We were thinking Lunar was a beautiful name.'

Loony Lunar. The nicknames were too easy. They wrote themselves.

Jane finished her soup and made her excuses again, desperate to get back to her nice normal flat, in her nice normal street, and escape the horror that would be the blessing ritual. She could imagine it now – the whole commune gathering to make offerings to her mum's pregnant belly and chant incantations to nature for new life.

'Are you sure you won't stay? Little Sam's going to recite one of her poems.'

Even worse than she'd imagined. 'No. Thank you.'

She left her parents at the kitchen table, but Fey followed her out to the car. 'When will you be back? You'll come to see the baby, won't you?'

She felt bad, but at the same time, this wasn't her place any more. 'I don't know.'

'I miss you. I miss the others too, but at least they send postcards and they call me on my mobile.'

'You've got a phone?'

Fey looked momentarily terrified.

'It's ok. I won't tell.'

'Little little Sam got it for me.' Yes. The Sams had stuck with the naming convention for their eldest child as well. 'She can get anything.'

Jane scrabbled in her handbag for a pen and paper. She scribbled her number down and handed it to Fey. 'There. If you need anything.'

Her younger sibling clutched the slip of paper like it was a precious gift. 'Thank you.'

'I'm sorry.'

'What for?'

She looked around. 'That I can't do more.'

'It's just…' Fey's voice was coloured with anxiety.

'What?'

'Mum. She is quite old to be having a baby, isn't she?'

Jane tried to sound more confident than she felt. 'Well, older than some people, but she's right. She's done this before. I'm sure she'd notice if anything felt wrong.'

Fey didn't look convinced, but what else could she say?

-

The girls were louder and more talkative on the journey home, buoyed by their victory and full of the excitements of the day. Annie let the snippets of conversation from further back in the bus wash over her. She ought to be keeping the girls in order, so Lydia could concentrate on driving, but the will to scold was weak today.

Did you see the tiny Yorkshire puddings? They were like a whole dinner in your hand… They had two swimming pools… Total waste. They should give us one… Don't be stupid. You can't move a swimming pool… You can move the water… But then where would you put it? … Did you hear them say that Goal Defence's dad's a fucking earl…

'Less of the swearing back there please,' called Lydia.

'Sorry, Miss Hyland.'

…But like an earl, that's only one down from a duke… Is Prince Harry a duke?… Yeah… So does the Goal Defence know Prince Harry?

'You're quiet,' Annie said.

'Sorry. Just keeping an ear on what's going on behind.'

Annie looked round. 'I think they're fine. Busy dissecting how the other half live.'

'Them and me both,' muttered Lydia.

Lydia's phone buzzed, and Annie's trilled a second later.

'Oh, new email from the Season,' Annie read from the phone screen. '*Introducing the Season's very first scandal sheet… Scandal sheets were a staple of the Regency season, and the place to go to find out all the news about who was courting whom, and which singletons were attracting the most attention. To read ours, and find out how to tip us off with your very own gossip, click here to download our Scandal of the Season app.*

'*To whet your appetite here's one little titbit to get you started… we couldn't help but notice three very well turned out school mistresses at the first event of the Season. Now there's a rumour that one of them might already have turned a suitor's head, and maybe not for the first time. Will one of our amorous educators be taking a second chance at love or is it true that you can never go back?*'

Annie felt like her chest was tightening. 'That'll be Jane.' She identified the reason for her unease. 'It's a bit off for Josh to use this thing to get her back though, isn't it? I mean, he's writing it.'

Lydia was focused on the road. 'It might not even be about her. We're probably not the only teachers there.'

'The only ones in a group of three where one of them's recently separated from one of the organisers though,' Annie muttered. 'It's fine though. I'm happy for them.'

'Okaaay. Well, download the app. What else does it say?'

Annie tapped the link to download and opened the app as soon as it installed.

Please log in with your Season id number

She tapped back to the email, highlighted her member number, copied, pasted into the app, hit start.

Please enter the two-factor authentication code from the text sent to your registered mobile number.

Seriously?

Finally, she was in. She tapped on:

Scandal Sheet 1 – The Opening Night.

The bit about the three school mistresses was there. She scoured it again, but there was no more detail. There was a plea for attendees to send in their own gossip and their secret wishes for which daters they were desperate to spend more time with, and then the rest of the sheet mentioned the city boys, the legal eagles, and a female attendee for whom hope sprang eternal.

'Oooh! I talked to a girl called Hope. I bet that's her,' suggested Lydia.

Annie read the next section. She clicked her phone off. 'Actually, there isn't much else.'

'You're an awful liar. What does it say?'

'Nothing. Really.'

'Annie, I'm going to get home and read it for myself. You might as well tell me.'

'Are you sure?'

'Yes!'

'Right.' She tapped back to her phone screen. 'I didn't write any of this bit though. I'm just the messenger. Ok?'

'What is it?'

'*And what of our third schoolmistress? The true scandal of the Season comes in the scurrilous rumour that she might be more interested in who's tending the bar than in any of the fine young gentlemen anxious to make her acquaintance. Well, there's no room for snobbery in the pursuit of true love, so perhaps the stories of a below stairs arrangement are true.*'

Lydia didn't reply.

'You said you wanted to know.'

'I'm fine.'

'You're doing the face you do when you've got 9E for double PE.'

'Am not.'

'You definitely are.' Annie put her phone away. 'I'm just going to sit quietly. You can tell me when you're ready to chat again.'

Lydia bit back the urge to protest that she wasn't in a mood and there was no need for Annie to be backing off, because she was in a mood and she didn't want to be chatted to right now. It was a stupid email blast thing. It didn't mean anything. And even if it did, she wasn't embarrassed. She was an adult. He was an adult. They were both consenting – loudly and repeatedly consenting, as she remembered it. She wasn't going to be ashamed of who she got her rocks off with.

But that wasn't it, was it? There was no shade in what Annie had read about that. 'Read it again.'

'What?'

'Read it again.'

'If you're sure… *And what of our third seasonal schoolmistress? The true scandal of the Season comes in the scurrilous rumour that she might be more interested in who's tending the bar than in any of the fine young gentlemen anxious to make her acquaintance. Well, there's no room for snobbery in the pursuit of true love, so perhaps the stories of a below stairs arrangement—*'

There it was. 'Seriously?'

'What?'

'Below stairs? Like he's sodding Cinderella and I'm the stuck-up Prince. Just cos he's doing an honest night's work and I've got me Spanx on and bought something from Zara.'

'Sorry. Josh isn't great at writing stuff like this. He probably meant it as a joke.'

Lydia wasn't laughing.

'I'll be quiet again, I think.' Annie went back to scrolling through her phone in silence, apparently waiting for Lydia's mood to clear.

The whole idea of below stairs and everything it implied was stupid and old-fashioned and everything that Lydia detested. She wouldn't be told that she wasn't good enough, so she wasn't having anyone else told that either.

Although, the hint of unease that had been with her since she'd laid eyes on him watching the netball match from the balcony... how on earth could someone who worked as a barman have a sister who went to a school like that? 'Do you think they have scholarships?'

'What?'

'Do you think that school, Westhall Abbey, has scholarships? Y'know, like free places for the poor of the parish sort of thing?'

Annie shrugged. 'Dunno. Probably. They're all charities aren't they, posh schools? They probably have to.'

A scholarship girl then. That made sense. Poor kid. Probably had it far worse there than if they'd sent her to a regular crappy comprehensive like All Saints.

Chapter Eight

Miss Emma Love
requests your company at a
Garden Party.
To be held on the York Lawn, Regents Park.

The third event of the inaugural Love's Love Social Season was to be a grand garden party where the eligible singletons of the ton would eat from stylish picnic baskets, under elegant gazebos, and potential couples might take a turn around the gardens, in private conversation but still well within public view to ward off any suggestion of scandal or impropriety.

Outdoors was good, Emma thought. Sunshine and flowers and a boating lake packed more of a punch of atmosphere than any function room. *Outdoors is risky*, her mother's voice pointed out in her head; *the weather could ruin it, and it's still not cheap, once you've factored in catering and the gazebos in case it rains. That cloud looks ominous.*

Emma glanced warily upwards. The sun was high in the sky, and the only cloud was white and wispy, providing a hint of shade and taking away the unpleasant stickiness that Emma associated with the idea of summer in the centre of the city. *Lucky* the voice muttered.

And the turnout was good. Emma had set this third event of the Season as the last chance for new members to join. There was a pleasing stream of new clients and the word of mouth they were generating was good enough that they now had nearly twice as many singletons registered as when they started. She told herself, and her mother's sceptical presence inside her brain, for the millionth time that all would be well.

'Is this where I sign up?'

Emma was very confident that she was 100 per cent straight. She'd never had even a sniff of a bi-curious phase during college. But if her preference was ever going to wander, this would be the moment. The woman standing in front of her was very simply the most beautiful human being she had ever seen. She looked like Jessica Rabbit, Scarlet Johansson and Aishwarya Rai had all got together and had a baby. Only hotter. So much hotter.

'Sign up?'

'Yeah. For the Season. I thought people could still sign up today.'

Emma dragged her attention to the second woman standing in front of her. Quick scan through her mental client list. Hope Lucas.

'This is my friend, Charlotte. I told her how much fun it is.'

Why any sane woman would invite this particular friend along to a dating event was beyond Emma. It was like inviting Lionel Messi along to your Sunday pub-league football match and then suggesting he play for the opposition. Nonetheless, turning away a potential dater because they were too attractive seemed counterintuitive.

'Yes. Of course.' She tapped her way to the sign-up screen on her tablet. 'If you could fill in a few details here, and then the payment stuff is on the next screen. Do you have any questions at all?'

'Hope says this was about actually meeting people, getting to know them. Not just sliding into people's DMs and demanding topless photos? Right?'

'Absolutely. We're aiming to bring back the romance and the courtship to modern dating.'

The goddess looked sceptical. Beautifully sceptical, but sceptical nonetheless.

'No unwelcome DM sliding. No dodgy photos. I promise.' Emma scrolled down the tablet screen. 'It's right there in the agreement everyone signs up to.'

The woman read the screen. 'And you can meet men and women? It's not straight only?'

'Absolutely all sexualities, identities and orientations welcome,' Emma assured her.

Hope nodded enthusiastically. 'Come on. What have you got to lose?'

'Is that a polite way of reminding me that my dating life is currently non-existent?'

'I didn't say that,' Hope replied.

'You'd have been right though,' the goddess conceded. 'I guess this can't make it any worse.'

–

Jane hated being late to things. It was an occupational hazard of being friends with Lydia, and she hated falling out with her friends even more than she hated being late. Today Annie was coming straight from her mum's so marshalling Lydia and diverting her from the seven bars they'd passed between the tube and the park, on the grounds that there would be drinks at the garden party and it was twenty-seven degrees so they definitely didn't need a little pre-drink to warm them up, had fallen entirely on Jane.

By the time they stepped through the velvet rope things were already in full swing. Lydia pulled a face beside her. 'Where's the bar?'

'I don't know. We only just got here.'

She was saved from further speculation on the point by her other best friend and her ex-husband bearing down on them. She smiled brightly. Possibly too brightly. The last time she'd seen Josh she'd accused him – quite wrongly – of still being in love with her. She contorted her face with the effort of trying to look effortlessly breezy.

'Where's the bar?' Lydia asked Josh before he had a chance to get out a greeting.

'No bar today. There are drinks in the picnic hampers.'

Jane could see that there were tables and picnic blankets at intervals across the lawn. Some already had guests sitting at them. Others had unopened hampers. 'So we just find ourselves a spot and get stuck in?'

'Well, the idea is that you mingle rather than sitting with the friend you came with. You're supposed to be meeting new people.'

'I'm sorry. There's no bar?' Lydia was still processing the headline information.

'Wine and champers in your hamper though.'

'But no bar? So who serves the drinks?'

Jane frowned. 'I think we serve ourselves, Lyds.'

'So no barmen?'

So that was it. Not like Lydia to be keen to see a shag again though.

Jane glanced at her friend. 'Hoping for some more below—'

'Let's not talk about that,' Annie butted in with uncharacteristic assertiveness.

'Ok.' Jane looked around. 'Look, Lyds. There's a big hamper on the table there. If we sit there, maybe other people will come and join us?' She turned back to Josh. 'Will that satisfy the mingling requirement?'

'I'm sure that will be fine,' Josh conceded. 'I'd better go see if Emma needs me to do anything.'

Which left the three of them. 'So is it true that you and Josh are getting back together? Like that scandal appy thing said?' Lydia asked.

'Absolutely not.'

Annie frowned. 'But it said a second chance at love for a school teacher.'

Jane didn't know what to tell them. 'I read it, but it did not mean me. I assure you. Josh is not interested in me and I am absolutely 100 per cent not interested in him.'

'Protesting much?' sniggered Lydia.

Tension rose in Jane's body. 'Just telling you how things are,' she replied as politely as she could manage.

'But,' Annie took up Lydia's theme. 'You were married. There must still be some feelings.'

'Of friendship. A touch of nostalgia. No attraction.' She tugged at the straps on their hamper. 'Shall we make a start on this then?'

'And Josh is lovely,' Annie would not be distracted.

'He is. Look,' Jane tried again to move the conversation along. 'Individual napkins and cutlery sets.'

'I think she wants to change the subject,' Lydia laughed.

Finally, someone talking sense. Of course, they needed to have the next part of this conversation, but Jane had no intention of having it here, today, in a garden full of strangers.

'I was only asking,' Annie protested.

'It's fine.' Just focus on the hamper and hope they'd let her imaginary reunion with Josh go. 'Look,' she said slightly too brightly. 'Strawberries!'

'But Josh is so lovely. How can you be sure?' asked Annie.

Finally, Jane snapped. 'Because I'm gay.'

–

Sometimes in the midst of any busy social occasion there is a lull in conversation, a moment where for reasons unexplained, conversations across the gathering pause at the selfsame moment. One can only hope that luck will prevent such a moment from coinciding with the unintended yelling of a personal, yet up until this very point still private, disclosure.

The three women stood in silence for what felt like an age before the ripple of conversation around them resumed, at a slightly more animated pitch than that which had preceded Jane's unplanned self-outing. Jane exhaled. If someone had described this moment to her in the abstract she would have expected to be wishing the ground would open up and swallow her. More than that actually, she would have denied the possibility of ever being in this situation. It wasn't her way to lose control and blurt out her personal business.

But here she was.

And she felt lighter.

'Wow.' Lydia's jaw was only just coming up off the floor. 'Why didn't you tell us?'

'I was working up to it.'

'Well, it seems like you got there.' Lydia spread her arms and enveloped Jane in a bear hug. 'Congratulations. Happy coming out day!'

When Lydia released her Jane turned to Annie whose brow was furrowing. 'You were married.'

'Yep.'

'To a man.'

'Yep.' She could see the contradiction.

'Was that a mistake then?'

It wasn't an easy question to answer and she'd answered it already to the only person who had a right to ask. 'Josh wasn't a mistake. I adored him. I still do. But I wasn't being honest about who I am.'

'Does he know?'

'He does.' It was thanks to him that she was standing here in one piece, not that he hadn't been angry and confused and sad, but, despite all that, he'd been kind. 'I am a bit surprised he hasn't told you.'

Annie shook her head. 'He's not the sort to share someone else's secrets.'

'He's a really good guy.'

'But you're not into guys?'

Jane shook her head.

Lydia nodded. 'It's a good thing I put us all down as 'open to anything' on the sign-up form then.'

'You did what?' This time Jane felt her own jaw dropping. *Anything* covered a lot of sexual ground.

'They had boxes to tick.' She looked at her two friends and smiled her most innocent smile, which, Lydia being Lydia, was not very innocent at all. 'I figured neither of you could afford to limit your options.'

'I'm just going to go and…' Annie didn't expand on where precisely she was going, but someone ought to check that Josh was all right. She caught sight of his tall frame at the far side of the garden talking to a petite red head Annie didn't recognise. Annie stopped a few feet away. She probably shouldn't interrupt. Josh was working after all. He might not want to talk about his personal life here. No. Of course he wouldn't. Annie turned away.

But then again, it was never out of order to be a friend, was it? Perhaps he'd welcome the chance to offload his problems. She turned back.

'Oooh, wasn't sure if you were coming or going there!' Col, Colin, Colin Williams caught her elbow as she turned. 'Lovely day for it, don't you think?'

She nodded politely.

'I'm glad to catch you actually. I was wondering,' he continued, 'if you fancied a little meet-up before the next grand event. That's supposed to be the idea, isn't it? We could have a little promenade or some such.'

Annie didn't know what to say. Was he asking her on a date?

'I checked with a lady at the library. She said promenading in the park or along the river was very much the Regency thing. So what do you say? Prepared to pop on your walking shoes?'

'I… er…' Uncertainty made her pause.

'It's just, I think that's what they want us to do isn't it? Meet up between the events, strictly no hanky-panky sort of thing, get to know one another and all that.'

That was what they were supposed to be doing. 'I don't know… I…'

'Right. I see. Not a problem. Of course you don't.' She could hear the hurt behind his upbeat exterior. 'I mean why would you? You're lovely and I'm… well… I'm…'

She couldn't say no now, even if she was sure she wanted to, and she wasn't sure she wanted to. She was open, it seemed, to persuasion. She nodded vigorously to, hopefully, discount her previous hesitancy. 'I'd love to.'

'Really? Oh good show. What about tomorrow then? Strike while the iron's whatnot.'

There was no reason to say no, and Colin was sweet. Perhaps this would be the start of a perfectly acceptable love story. They fixed a time to promenade by the Thames from Westminster along the South Bank towards Tower Bridge.

'Could even pop into one of those places around Borough Market for a tipple or two?' suggested Colin hopefully.

—

If Jane had known the conversational fallout from coming out to her friends would have been done and dusted in five minutes flat she might have bitten the bullet earlier. Perhaps it was the distraction of the tiny cucumber sandwiches and punnets of strawberries – perfect for dropping into a glass of champagne – that had taken up their attention but, within minutes, the subject was changed. The picnic hamper was opened. Mini fruit scones and perfectly round pastel coloured coin-sized macaroons were cooed over. There was something instantly enticing about any foodstuff that had been made miniature. You could eat so many more of them and without it ever feeling excessive. Champagne was poured and then liberally and frequently topped up.

And people joined them at their table. Annie disappeared for a few minutes and came back with that nice Colin chap, and some of his friends, who were soon making jokes and competing for Lydia's attention. Jane would have expected Lydia to be in her element with a gaggle of men trying to outdo one another for her affections, but seemed like she was merely going through the motions.

Jane picked up her glass and decided to take a turn around the lawn to stretch her legs. Groups of potential daters were beginning to split off into pairs here and there. Jane still couldn't picture that being her. She'd only just got out of a marriage. Since then there'd been the single much-regretted one nighter after their evening at the pub, which Annie and Lydia definitely didn't need to know about. Annie would worry that Jane was self-destructing and Lydia would want way more detail than Jane was looking to share.

Ever since she walked out of the commune on the morning of her eighteenth birthday, leaving gifts unopened, and a community to celebrate her coming of age without her, Jane had known what she wanted. She wanted a normal life. She wanted a regular job, a nice apartment, a solid relationship, children. Nothing spectacular, but everything that growing up in her parent's eco bubble had made seem other worldly.

With Josh she'd almost had it all and it had been just as much like she was putting on someone else's clothes as living in the commune had been.

So what did she want now? Not another bloke. If she couldn't love Josh, who was handsome and kind and smart and funny, then clearly that wasn't happening for her.

'Ew!' Something wet and cold erupted down Jane's back. 'What the…?'

'I'm sorry. I'm so sorry.'

Jane turned towards the voice. For a second the world beyond the face she was staring into fell into soft focus.

'I'm so sorry.' The face was talking to her. The woman held up her empty champagne glass, which went some way to explaining the cold, wet, sticky feeling extending down Jane's back. 'Oh, it's you!'

'What?'

'I'm sorry. I didn't see you. I was trying to get away from…' The woman looked behind her. 'Oh God! Shield me!'

She grabbed Jane's hand and swung her around so Jane now had her back to whatever horror the stranger was trying to evade.

'Pretend we're talking.'

'We are talking.'

The woman let out a gale of laughter.

Jane wasn't even beginning to follow what was going on. 'That wasn't a joke.'

Another gale of laughter, this time accompanied by an over familiar squeeze of Jane's arm.

'This is weird now.'

The woman met Jane's gaze. Jane looked away. She was confused enough without the whole soft-focus thing happening again. 'There's a whole gang of rugby blokes who won't leave me alone. I'm sorry. I'm sort of using you as a human shield.'

Jane wasn't sure if she ought to be offended. 'What? Like I'm so gross they won't dare come near me?'

'No! God no. But you did announce that you liked pussy to the whole gathering about half an hour ago.'

That was a fair point. 'You think that will put them off?'

The woman deflated slightly. 'Probably not.'

'Maybe we should walk?'

'Good plan.' The woman took Jane's hand. 'Do you mind?'

Jane smiled through the sensation that her entire physical body was now drifting into soft focus. 'For the sake of the human-shield thing?'

'Of course.'

–

'Did you see that woman?'

It was the third or fourth variation on the same conversation that Emma had walked past today. Her newest sign-up, the supermodel-in-waiting, was the talk of the party, even eclipsing her former sister-in-law's attention-grabbing moment. Emma smiled. This was what the Season needed. People were talking about the scandal sheet as well, whispering about who was interested in who. The whole thing was starting to feel like this was a community with its own atmosphere and internal rhythms, rather than something constructed by a dating agency.

'Everything going well, Miss Love?' one of the park attendants called across to her. Emma looked up. She knew the face. Of course. David McDonald. One of her mother's many success stories.

She made her way over to the velvet rope to chat to him. 'Very well. Thank you.' She noted the garden implements he was carrying. 'The flower beds look amazing. Is that your doing?'

'Well, I thought as you had so many people coming, a little extra weeding and dead-heading wouldn't go amiss.'

'Thank you. It looks glorious.' She smiled. 'I hope you get to take a few flowers home every now and then for...' She checked her memory. 'Angus, isn't it?'

He shook his head quietly. 'Your mum didn't tell you? He passed away last year, so nobody there to appreciate them any more I'm afraid.'

'Oh. I'm sorry.' Emma didn't ask, but she left the silence open, giving him the space to choose to fill it.

'It was cancer. Bugger of a thing.' He cleared his throat. 'He loved flowers. Roses were his favourite. You can't beat a rose.'

'You can't,' Emma agreed.

'When he was ill he did try telling me I should get in touch with your mother again, but I couldn't. And now I'm a bit long in the tooth for starting out with someone new,' David murmured.

'Never too old,' Emma insisted. 'And it sounds like he didn't want you to be lonely.'

'Oh, I know he didn't. Was quite particular about it once he knew he was dying. I wasn't to hide myself away. I was to get out and get on and find someone new. Anyway, I started volunteering here. Give myself something to do, get my hands into the ground, feel connected with the world rather than sit at home and think of him.'

Emma was starting to well up. Her mother had guided David wisely when she'd fixed him up with Angus. It sounded as though they'd had happy years together. She should be immune to the misty-eyed feeling by now, but there was something about hearing people's love stories that got her every time. And her mother was the best of the best when it came to finding people their own personal happy-ever-after. Impossible shoes to fill.

'And then finding someone else never quite happened though.' He shook his head. 'I should let you get back to your guests.'

Emma turned her attention back to the party. Definite couples were starting to form now – people who had danced together repeatedly at the ball, strolling or chatting together now. But a lot of people were still keeping their options open – by choice or circumstance she couldn't tell. There was a lot more matchmaking to be done before the Season closed.

–

Tom hovered on the edge of a group of men chatting and downing champagne. There was one younger guy with an earnest haircut and round wire-rimmed spectacles who would have been just Jack's type. Tom turned to make his oft-repeated joke about Jack's *Doctor Who* obsession and penchant for clever, nerdy, skinny boys. Of course, Jack wasn't there.

He'd promised his mother he'd try. It was only that promise keeping the urge to run away at bay. He stepped closer to the group and listened in for a second. Apparently a ridiculously attractive woman had arrived but was last seen hand in hand with a woman, not just a woman according to the chat, but a woman who'd announced that she was gay in the middle of the party. Tom couldn't help but laugh at the obvious dismay some of the red-trousered chaps seemed to be experiencing at this. He silently wished the now nowhere-to-be-seen pair all the luck in the world.

'Mr Knight?'

He turned towards the voice. There she was. Five foot nothing of pure tenacity. 'Miss Love.'

'I hope you're enjoying the party.'

'I was late. Apparently I've missed the descent of the goddess Venus.'

Emma shrugged. 'Well, you can't win them all.'

Finally he agreed with Miss Emma Love. 'And sometimes you can't win at all.'

'What do you mean?'

He shook his head. 'Nothing. Just being grumpy.' He remembered their run in at the ball. 'And apparently nobody likes that.'

Emma's cheeks coloured slightly. 'Sorry about that.'

'No. You were right. At least my mother would definitely agree.' Maybe he could stay here with Miss Love. She was here in a professional capacity, making her an island of safety in a sea of potential partners. He wasn't above teasing her a little about that professional capacity, though. 'You did, however, promise to guide me to true love and I remain resolutely single. I don't want to cast aspersions on your professional abilities, but here we are.'

Emma narrowed her eyes. 'It's early in the Season yet, Mr Knight. These things can take time.'

Or they could happen in an instant.

'It's only the third event,' she continued. 'Still five more to go and ample time between to further any connections you make.'

'So who would you have me connect with?'

Miss Love looked around. She was actually going to try to fix him up with someone. 'Well, I'd suggest you start by actually talking to some people one to one. Somebody might surprise you.'

Tom relaxed a notch. 'No specific ideas then?'

'It's not just up to me. You are supposed to get involved.' She nodded towards a mixed group of men and women chatting around a hamper a few feet away. 'Look. There's plenty of seats over there. Why not go and see who you click with?'

Tom was frozen to the spot. It was just talking to people. He wasn't declaring undying love, or even agreeing to an actual date. It was sitting in a garden talking. But it was more than that. Everyone here was here with intent. Nearly everyone. 'But I'm having so much fun talking to you, Miss Love.'

If he wasn't mistaken her cheeks turned a tiny bit deeper pink. She didn't meet his gaze. 'I'd be more than happy to make an introduction.' She moved towards the group.

He should follow. It was a beautiful day to be outside, drinking champagne and meeting new people. He just couldn't be the Tom this world wanted him to be. 'I'm sorry, Miss Love.'

He didn't wait to see if she replied. He didn't look to see if she tried to follow. He just ran, past the velvet rope, across the park and away.

–

The goddess didn't let go of Jane's hand until they were well out of sight of the picnicking daters and near the lake at the edge of their cordoned-off area of the park.

'So, I'm Charlotte,' she announced eventually once they were away from the throng of people.

'Jane.'

'Very nice to meet you. So, if you don't mind me asking, what made you want to sign up for this?'

'My friend signed me up. I split up from someone at the start of the year. I think she thinks I need to get back on the horse.'

'You don't agree?'

Jane wasn't sure. 'I don't disagree. I just… I don't think I know what I'm looking for.'

'I do.'

'Really?'

'Absolutely. That's why I'm here. I'm sick of the meat market. I'm sick of "Did you hurt yourself when you fell from heaven?" and "You should be a model" and "Is your name Summer? It should be cos you're so hot." I'm sick of it all.'

Jane took a seat on the grass bank of the lake and watched Charlotte folding her ridiculously long legs underneath herself to do the same. 'I mean, to be fair to them, you are very, very pretty.'

Charlotte pulled a face. 'Don't you start. No. From now on I have three rules for any relationship. I've worked out exactly what I want and I'm not settling for less.'

'Go on.'

'What?'

Jane was genuinely curious. Knowing exactly what you wanted sounded like an impossible dream. 'What are your rules?'

'You'll think they're silly.'

'I won't.'

'You will. And the first one makes me sound kinda arrogant.'

Arrogant was good. Arrogant might distract Jane from the perfect way in which the sun caught the skin on Charlotte's bare shoulder, or the way her hair cascaded down her back. A massive glaring flaw would be super welcome right now. 'Just tell me!'

'Right. Number one: No going out with anyone who says anything physical for the thing they like most about me.'

Jane pulled a face.

'I know. First world problem but I'm sick of it. Rule number two: They have to value the things I can do. And number three. Oh, number three makes me sound either really boring or like I've been a total slag up 'til now.'

Jane laughed. 'Now I'm interested.'

'Monogamy. No wives or husbands or significant others at home. No inviting me back and then producing a partner when we get there and it turning out that I'm the sex doll in some shared fantasy they've got.'

'Ok. Again not an issue I've ever come up against.'

'Well, you said you'd only just split up from someone. You don't know. It's a jungle out there.'

Jane was happy to take her word for it. 'So what do you do?'

'What?'

'You said you wanted someone who valued the things you do, so what do you do?'

Charlotte smiled and the wattage from her smile outshone the afternoon sun. 'I'm nearly a midwife.'

'Nearly?'

'Four more student shifts to get the hours I need and two more births. Then I can register.'

'Wow. Well, nearly congratulations then.'

Another sun-eclipsing smile. 'And nearly thank you. What about you? What do you do?'

Jane leaned back against the grass bank and started to share her own career story, omitting the bit where she ran away from a hippy compound to take her A-levels. That world was in the past. Keeping everything neat and in its own little box – that was the way ahead.

Chapter Nine

9.30 a.m. Sunday morning. Lydia stared at her phone. Nothing. She turned the ringer sound up. Not for any sensible reason. She'd been sitting staring at it since twenty-five past. If anybody had rung she would have seen.

9.31 a.m. She told herself not to panic. It was only a minute. If you had a meeting at half past nine and turned up at thirty-one minutes past you wouldn't even be late. She tapped the screen to stop it dimming to black. She had full signal.

9.32 a.m. Maybe there was something wrong with her phone. She needed someone else to ring her phone so she could check it was working, but then her phone would be engaged if – when – her mum did call.

9.33 a.m. They'd had this system for three years now, since Lydia's mum had taken a kicking so bad it had landed her in surgery and Lydia hadn't heard about it until six weeks later. And in all that time her mum had only missed one call, and that had been because she was locked out of the house after he'd come back half-cut and not noticed, or cared, that Lydia's mum was having a ciggie in the garden when he locked the doors. Aside from that, she'd never been later than 9.32 a.m.

9.40 a.m. Something was definitely wrong. Lydia scrolled through her phone contacts and tapped to call Aunty Jill. She never called her aunt. She sent a birthday card and a Christmas card and a very occasional WhatsApp, but they never phoned. The call was picked up quickly. 'What's wrong?'

'My mum didn't call me this morning. You know our Sunday morning call thing.'

'Shit.'

'When did you last see her?' Lydia asked.

There was a second of silence. 'She asked me to stop going round.'

Lydia's stomach turned over. 'When?'

'Couple of months ago. I saw her in Aldi about three weeks back, though. She said she was fine but she couldn't stop.'

'She called me last week. We talked then for a few minutes. She sounded ok.' Lydia told herself to be hopeful. Her mum's battery could have died, or her credit ran out, or any one of a thousand things that weren't the one she was picturing.

'And she always calls? Every week?'

Lydia knew that her aunt already knew the answer to that. 'Every week.'

'Right. Well, I'd better pop over there then.'

She wanted Jill to take this seriously. Of course she did. It was serious, but her stomach tightened a notch further at her aunt's response. A part of her had been hoping to be told that everything was fine and she was getting anxious over nothing. 'You'll let me know as soon as you know anything?'

'Course I will. Try not to worry. I'll message you soon.'

She was supposed to be meeting Jane and Annie for coffee. *Sorry. Can't make it this morning. I...* What reason could she give? She never talked about her parents. So far as her two closest friends were concerned she had a perfectly normal – if somewhat distant – family life. And what use was staying in the flat? She could stare at her phone just as well in a cafe as she could here.

Jane was already there, sitting at a table in the corner, scrolling through her own phone. Unusually though, Lydia was here before Annie.

'You're not last!' Jane's greeting confirmed the unprecedented nature of her relative punctuality.

'No. Guess not.'

'Have you seen this?' Jane held her phone out under Lydia's nose.

What was she looking at? Stupidly for a second her brain wondered if it was news of Mum. How could it be? It was the gossip email thing from the Season. Lydia must have had one too but she'd been swiping away notifications for anything that wasn't the thing she was waiting for. 'What? No.'

'Listen to this. *The Season has a new undisputed diamond, a beauty so exquisite that this writer has heard talk of little else all this week. Both gentlemen and ladies of the Ton have had their heads turned. But will anyone secure an understanding with such a glittering jewel?* That's about Charlotte, isn't it?'

The cafe door opened again and Annie came through. 'Sorry. I was erm...' She stopped mid-sentence.

'You were...?' Jane prompted.

'I was talking to Josh. Just about the Season and the scandal sheet thing. I said I'd help but then I haven't yet and then the new one arrived and that reminded me so I texted him and then he called me and... well, it was just about that.'

'Ok.' Jane looked as nonplussed as Lydia felt about the extended explanation. 'I assumed you were getting ready for your hot date.'

Lydia checked her phone again. Nothing.

'I'll get us some coffees.' Annie collected their orders and disappeared to the counter.

'She's got a date with that Colin bloke,' Jane said. 'They're going to promenade along the South Bank.'

Lydia's attention was skittering all over the place. Without intending to, she'd gone back to her phone. No messages. No missed calls.

'Are you ok?'

'I'm fine.' She tapped the phone off.

Annie plonked three coffees down in front of them and performed the obligatory *this one's soy milk, this one's got an extra shot, this one's black* hand jive to get them all in front of the right people. 'It's not a hot date,' she said.

A hot what? 'What's not a hot date?'

'She's meeting Colin after this. I told you that already.'

'It's not a *date* date,' Annie clarified. 'It's just a walk. I'm sure he's not expecting anything else.'

'Well, probably not in the middle of the South Bank,' Jane agreed.

Lydia didn't argue, even though there were loads of places down there you could sneak off to get dirty if you felt like it. She didn't have the energy to draw her friend a helpful map.

She checked her phone again. Still nothing. Should she call? No. She couldn't phone her mum. If he answered it would make things a million times worse. Should she call Jill back? What was the point? Jill had said she'd let her know and she would.

Jane and Annie had gone back to looking at the scandal thingy. 'It's just so reductive. Just talking about Charlotte in terms of her looks.'

Lydia's interest was finally piqued. 'So you're on first name terms with the mostly legs woman.'

'She's not mostly legs.'

Lydia conceded the point. 'True. That understates the majesty of her boobs. Those boobs. Did you see her boobs?'

'No.' Jane shook her head. 'And that's a horrid way to talk about someone. She's not just boobs and legs.'

'Ok.' Lydia didn't have the emotional energy to launch into a sermon lauding the heaven-sent nature of the goddess's arse, justified though such a claim might be. 'No need to get all protective.'

'I'm not getting protective.' Jane brought her voice back under control. 'We had a nice chat. That was all.'

Jane's phone trilled on the table between them. Lydia jumped, even though it wasn't her ring tone. She checked her phone one more time.

–

> I don't know anything about you.

> Like what?

Like what? Emma stared at the chat screen for a second and then typed:

> Like how old you are, where you live. I don't even know if you're a man or a woman.

> Man.

And then nothing for a second.

> What if we didn't?

> What do you mean?

> What if we didn't do names and how old we are and where we went to school and what A-levels we got? What if we talked about whatever's on our minds right now?

Emma felt her lips pursing. She liked information. She liked data points. Even the things Josh said she did by instinct – sizing people up and working out who they fit with – were a series of data points. How someone talked, how they dressed, how they wore their hair, what they told you without meaning to. Walt wasn't giving her any of that.

So what is on your mind right now?

she asked.

Honestly?

Was there any point if he wasn't?

Always.

I was thinking about my first girlfriend.

What about her?

Did you have that couple at your school who were both sort of mid-level popular and mid-level sporty and mid-level academic and they got together in about year nine and stayed together right thru and being The Couple was like their whole thing?

Sindhu Khatri and Nate Thomas

Emma remembered them so clearly. Always together. Never on and off. Never at the centre of any drama.

Why?

That was me and Keeley Henson. We were rock solid and then halfway through our first term at uni we just stopped texting or calling each other.

So you split?

That's what I was thinking about. We never officially did. I saw her that Christmas in a club near where her parents lived and she said 'hi' and that was it. But we never broke up. Am I still going out with Keeley Henson?

Emma laughed.

I think you might be.

Shit. I should probably message her or something. At least follow her on Twitter.

It would be polite

agreed Emma.

What about you?

What about me?

> Who was your first?

She thought back.

> Ty. At uni. We were sort of on and off though.

> And how did it end up permanently off?
> Assuming it did and you're not writing this whilst
> listening out for the baby monitor in case Little Ty
> junior wakes up?

> It did.

She paused.

> I introduced him to his wife actually. They run a
> tapas place in Shepherd's Bush.

It was a nice tapas place. She got 10 per cent off by way of an ongoing thank you.

> You introduced him to his wife? Not the love of
> your life then?

> Maybe not. Was Keeley Henson yours?

Silence. Emma waited.

> Shall we rejoin the table?

he replied.

Emma pretended not to notice his evasion and retook her place at the virtual table. Being in the big blind seat forced her to bet despite a nothing hand, and she checked on the flop. Walt raised on the turn. Emma folded. He was far too much of a gambler for her to even try to keep up.

–

Jane tuned out as Annie explained, once again, to Lydia how her date with Colin wasn't a date at all.

> One new message.

She tapped to read.

> Thanks for yesterday. You were a wonderful human shield.

Jane felt herself smiling. She angled her phone away from her friends and typed.

> You're welcome. Let me know if you need me to throw my body between you and an encroaching horde again.

Send.

Breath held. Nothing. She went to put her phone away when it trilled again.

> Well, who can say when the horde might
> descend. Do you offer an on-call service?

Was that an invitation? No. Too vague. But they were flirting, weren't they? Were they? Of course not. The woman was a goddess. Jane put thoughts of romance out of her head. Charlotte was being friendly. She could be friendly in return.

> Sure. Just let me know when you need me.

Send.

That was too much wasn't it? Too eager. Not casual enough.

> Am working crazy shifts this week. Maybe you
> could throw your body against me next weekend?

Throw your body against me? That wasn't friendly. That was definitely flirting. Quite vigorous flirting. She should respond with something equally confident and enticing. Her brain froze.

> Ok

she typed.

It wasn't her best work, but maybe the proposal didn't need much more than clear agreement.

> I'll see you at the casino night then, and we'll fix
> something up.

Jane typed again. She had this flirting thing sorted. Just go along with whatever the object of your desire seemed to be suggesting.

'What are you grinning at?'

'Nothing.' It wasn't nothing. It wasn't anything yet, but it might be the beginning of something. 'That was Charlotte. She asked me out.'

Annie clapped her hands together. Lydia grinned. 'So you're going to get to squeeze that astonishing arse?'

'She's more than just an arse.'

'Yeah, but we already covered her legs and her boobs.'

'What about her face?' Annie chipped in.

'Spectacular,' Lydia confirmed.

'It's probably not even a date. More just a friend thing. Like to say thank you for hanging out with her yesterday.'

'Right. Like Annie's date with Colin isn't a date?' Lydia asked.

'Well, that's different. That's obviously a date. He's totally into her.'

'I don't think he is. He's probably just being kind and maybe he's a little bit lonely and…'

'And Charlotte is really busy so I don't think she's even looking for a relationship, and even if she was, she wouldn't be interested in me, and…'

'…it's just a walk. A walk isn't a date.'

'…we haven't even set a definite time. So it might not even happen. Which is fine…'

'Shut up!' Lydia only raised her voice a fraction. She was the sort of teacher who yelled and chivvied and shouted to motivate and encourage. It was when she went quiet that students quickly found some other place they needed to be. 'You both have dates. Ok?'

Jane nodded mutely. Annie spluttered out an apology. 'Sorry.'

A slightly awkward silence fell between them. Annie filled it. 'So do you think the Season is going to work out then?'

'What do you mean?' asked Jane.

'Well, the whole old-fashioned dating thing. Getting to know people face to face rather than online.' Annie sipped her coffee. 'Do you really think it creates affection?'

Jane thought about it. 'Well, it worked for us.'

Lydia broke her silence. 'What did?'

'Spending time together creates affection.' Jane looked at her two closest friends in the world – Annie, constantly trying to make everyone happy, and Lydia, a coiled spring waiting to explode or implode at any moment. 'Like, we should not be friends, should we? But it works, cos we spent time together and we rubbed along.'

Lydia laughed. 'We spent time together and we rubbed along. What a ringing endorsement.'

'But it is. It really is. We're so different but I love you both.' Jane wasn't normally given to expressions of emotion. Her romantic giddiness was spilling over.

Lydia reached over and lifted Jane's cup to her nose to sniff dramatically. 'What did they put in this?'

'We love you too, don't we, Lyds?' said Annie.

'Course we do,' Lydia conceded. 'Sorry I snapped before.' Her phone chirped and she grabbed it from the table. 'Sorry again. I've got to go.' Lydia was up and halfway towards the door before either of them had time to react.

Annie frowned. 'Do you think she was ok? Maybe I should cancel Colin and check on her?'

Lydia was normally the life and soul of every gathering, but, thinking back, she'd been distracted at the garden party as well as this morning. 'Maybe give her some space? I'll message her later.'

'So you don't think I should cancel Colin?'

Jane shook her head. 'You're not getting out of it that easily.'

The weather that afternoon was bright and warm. Perfect promenading weather by anybody's measure. At Jane's insistence, Annie had her escape route planned — via a scheduled phone call from Jane an hour and a half in. And, with Lydia's firm insistence that this was a date still in her mind, she was to try to approach the whole thing positively. Who was to say that she wasn't The One for Colin?

Her companion was certainly easy company. Colin came fully prepared with an arsenal of anecdotes about his escapades with the rugger boys, the shenanigans at chambers, and the further exploits of his former fiancée.

'So the thing is, she and little brother are now quite the thing. Poor bugger doesn't quite seem to know what hit him. Truth be known, he thought he was getting a knee trembler in an alleyway. Wham, bam and thank you ma'am sort of an arrangement. But then she ends up single and you can guess who was first on her list of rebound calls?'

Annie was finding herself worryingly engaged in the soap opera of Colin's broken engagement. 'So she's still seeing your brother?'

'Well not seeing exactly. He's back on base now. Leave finished. But she's writing to him every day apparently and telling anyone who'll listen that she's an army wife.'

'Right. And are you ok with that?'

Colin was uncharacteristically quiet for a second. 'Well, what you can do? All water under the bridge.' He looked at the river. 'So to speak.'

Their walk took them along the South Bank. Annie loved this part of London. She knew that she shouldn't. It seemed so touristy. A cooler person would have some hidden gem top spot that only the locals knew about, but Annie had always loved touristy places. It gave her a feeling of being on holiday even when she wasn't. And generally, she wasn't. Money for holidays had been short when she was a child, and accommodation that was suitable for Duncan was all but impossible on a limited budget, but she loved the feeling of being on vacation in her own city.

'Do you mind if I have a look at the market? I don't mind if you'd rather carry on.'

'Absolutely fine and dandy by me,' he replied.

They'd reached the BFI and the book market was in full flow. Annie hadn't been here for ages. She remembered discovering it for the first time as a fourteen-year-old, who'd been allowed to ride into town on the Northern Line for the first time. Books were where Annie escaped to and there was something about a second-hand book that felt even more special. You weren't only holding one story, but a fragment of the story of everyone who'd read it before you as well. The very idea was magical.

She wandered among the tables of books, scanning the spines for something a little bit special. She wasn't sure quite what she was looking for. Austen always – a woman could never own too many copies of *Persuasion* – but Heyer as well and really anything else that caught her attention.

And then something did.

He was leaning over a table two rows away from her peering closely at the contents of the box in front of him. The tall frame, the mop of dark hair, the slim face, the particular way his eyebrows knitted together when he was concentrating. Each time she saw him she updated her mental image, but the profile had been stored when they were barely teenagers, when her early sexual awakening had coincided with Josh Love hitting puberty with a chemical intensity that she'd spent the intervening years trying to forget.

She looked left and right, scanning the crowd for Colin. The best thing to do was to get away from here. She didn't want to run into Josh while she was on a date. She didn't want to run into him at all, she reminded herself. And he certainly wouldn't want to run in to her.

She glanced back, hoping that he might have turned away and made off in the other direction. He hadn't. He looked up. He raised a hand in greeting. Annie waved back.

He was coming over. Of course he was coming over. That was what you did wasn't it when you saw an old friend out and about. You came over and said 'hi'. She put her smile on and said 'hi'.

'Fancy meeting you here.' He smiled. 'What are you up to?'

'Oh, you know. Just looking.'

He looked around. 'On your own?'

Of course. He'd be anxious to check if Jane was with her. 'Yes. No. Not exactly. I'm with a friend.'

'Right.' He gestured towards the market. 'Do you remember coming here?'

She nodded. 'Yeah. My mum only let me come into town because you were with me.'

'She didn't trust you on the tube on your own.'

Annie pulled a face. 'You ride all the way round the Circle Line one time and you never live it down.'

They both smiled at the memory. They'd been so engrossed in some ridiculous private joke that they'd missed the stop. And so they'd simply ridden around again.

'You can't do that any more,' said Josh.

'No. Lovestruck kids have to get off at Edgware Road now. Or end up in Hammersmith.' She heard what she'd just said. 'Not that we were lovestruck.'

'Speak for yourself.'

What did that mean?

He moved in closer and lowered his voice. 'So, are you looking for anything in particular?' he asked.

She shook her head.

'Well, there's a whole box of historical romance three tables that way.'

'What sort of thing?'

'I don't know. Women with heaving bosoms on the covers. Brooding men with high collars and cravats.'

She demurred. 'Maybe I was looking for something a bit higher brow.'

He leaned towards her until his lips were inches from her ear. 'Bollocks,' he whispered.

'Well, I might take a quick look.'

He pulled back and smiled. 'I thought you might. And then, maybe we could…'

'So that's where you got to!' Colin bumbled past Josh and stopped at Annie's side. 'Thought I'd lost you to a sea of books.'

Josh stepped back. 'Right. I see. I'll let you get on then.'

'No. Wait. It's not…' It wasn't what? It was – as Lydia had insisted – a date. It was, in fact, exactly what it looked like.

She watched Josh walk away.

'Wasn't that the fellow from the Season? The organiser lady's chap.'

'He's not her chap.' Annie forced her attention back to her actual companion. 'He's her stepbrother. It's a family business.'

'Right. And so you and he are…?'

They were nothing. 'Just old friends. We went to school together.'

'Shall we toodle on?'

They continued their walk as far as Borough market, where Colin suggested stopping for a little tipple. 'Plenty of places along here. Bit chi chi and full of tourists, but I'm game if you are,' Colin said.

He was pleasant company and he became even more amiable as she let the soothing glass of wine he'd bought her carry her along with the flow of his conversation. He didn't have an unkind bone in his body, and genuinely seemed to wish everyone in the world – including his former fiancée – well.

There was absolutely nothing at all to dislike about him. Maybe Annie could be his One.

'So I'll be seeing you again at the next big shindig then?' he asked.

Annie nodded.

'Perhaps we might plan to meet up there?' His enthusiasm was almost infectious.

Perhaps they could. Not everyone got their Captain Wentworth. And you could do a lot worse than polite and kind. Annie hesitated. Maybe she needed to talk to her mum and Jane and Lydia and see what they thought about the whole thing.

'I think that's the idea of the whole affair, isn't it? That people start to form attachments.'

It was, of course. It was what was expected. 'All right then.'

'Really?' His surprise at her acceptance was touching. 'Jolly good. Maybe you'll bring me luck at the gaming tables, old girl.'

Old girl? Old girl didn't feel quite like the start of a romance for the ages to Annie, but not everything was like it was in a romance novel. Some relationships just took a little bit longer to get off the ground.

–

> Been round. Talked to your mum on the doorstep. She wouldn't let me in but she said she was fine and she didn't need any help.

Lydia read the message. Relief. That was the first thing, of course. Her mum was alive and well, physically at least. What she felt next was more complicated. Not quite anger. Frustration. Resentment. Of course she needed help. All she needed to do was ask. She typed back.

> Do you believe her?

Jill replied quickly.

Not really. I couldn't see anything physically wrong, but she was jumpy about me being there.

What can we do?

Lydia already knew the answer to that, but she waited for her aunt to confirm it. Maybe there was something, some new initiative from the police, some charity they hadn't contacted before, someone her mother would accept help from this time.

Jill's response popped onto the screen with a cheerful chirp.

I don't think we can do anything.

Chapter Ten

Miss Emma Love
requests the honour of your company
for an evening of Gaming and Chance.

The fourth event of the Season looked set to go off without a hitch. Everything was laid on by the venue – a rather palatial casino offering private hire of one gaming floor – with the exception of a sudden shortage of bar staff, which Emma had been able to solve with a quick trawl through her contacts and a call to her regular caterer who gave her the number of the bartender who'd worked the previous ball.

With that resolved, all was in hand. Emma mentally ticked off 'something going wrong'. Something always went wrong. Being able to fix it was what mattered. Emma was so certain on this point that something minor going awry and being quickly resolved now made her feel much better about how an event was going to unfold. She could relax a little, knowing the mandatory snafu was out of the way.

It wasn't terribly Regency, of course, to have ladies at the gaming tables, but the oak-lined walls, low lighting and period-appropriate background music gave the feeling that they'd stumbled into a rather fine gentlemen's club. And a gaming night provided an activity that people could engage in together without preventing conversation and flirtation. After the ball, where the dancing had encouraged a certain amount of physical contact, and the garden party, where the interaction had a more languid pace, it was the perfect thing to create a bit of variety and provide a backdrop to form deeper attachments.

Josh was manning the welcome desk, but as the trickle of arrivals turned into a steady stream, Emma went to lend a hand. He was handing a small velvet pouch to Lydia Hyland. 'These are your chips for the night.'

Lydia grinned. 'So what's to stop me just cashing these out and going to the pub?'

'No cash value I'm afraid,' Josh explained. 'Once you've lost them all you're out, but if you win you can use the chips you win through the evening. And then there's a fixed cash prize for the person with the most chips at midnight.'

Emma handed identical pouches to Annie and Jane. 'There are silver chips in there that can be exchanged at the bar for drinks though.'

'I know where I'm heading then.' Lydia marched off in search of refreshment.

These three were all still on Emma's list of unmatched daters. Jane seemed to have hit it off with the impossibly beautiful Charlotte, but that was only one meeting so still lots of potential for things to go wrong. Annie had, according to Josh, been seeing Col, Colin, Colin Williams outside the Season events. On paper that should be a match. They were both clearly the kindest of kind hearts, not a bad bone between them, and Emma had no doubt that Colin would treat any woman he was seeing like an absolute queen. But something felt off. Her matchmaker instincts weren't fully on board. And Lydia. Emma wasn't quite sure why Lydia was even here. She hadn't shown any interest in getting to know potential suitors. Emma's mother wouldn't have let that slide. She'd have been in there giving fate a helping hand. Emma needed to do better.

–

Jane made her way into the room, wandering between the tables without any great sense of purpose. There was poker, blackjack, roulette, and that thing with dice that she was never sure whether it was called crabs or craps. She opened the velvet pouch and tipped the contents into her hand. Aside from the smaller silver drink tokens, she had a nominal £500 in chips. Shame she couldn't cash it out.

She continued around the room. Mani, the sibling who was closest to her in age, had taught her poker years ago after they'd learned it during a summer of parentally sanctioned hostelling when they were only fifteen. Apparently it had been quite the thing to break the ice and pass the evenings. The game here was Texas Hold 'Em.

'I prefer draw poker.'

Jane looked around. She seemed to have achieved an equilibrium where she could now look at Charlotte's face without dizziness setting in. Excellent. That was definitely progress of sorts.

'Do you play?'

Right. Conversation. Looking at the face and making words at the same time. That would be the next step. She dropped her gaze to the floor. 'A bit. I'm not very good though.'

'We used to play during fashion week between shows. I won a Rolex off of Cindy Crawford's daughter.'

'You were a model?' Of course she was a model. Anything to emphasise how far out of Jane's league she was.

'I wasn't very successful.'

Jane finally forced herself to look at Charlotte properly. She had slicked her hair back into a tight bun and created a row of perfectly wound kiss curls across her forehead. She was dressed in a tailored black tuxedo over a black silk shirt. She could easily have walked straight off the catwalk. Jane's dark blue knee length dress felt dowdy and lacking in verve in comparison. 'I don't believe that for one moment.'

'It's true. I hated it and I didn't even make that much money. That's the worst bit. If you're a model, everyone assumes you're flitting from Milan to New York and hanging out with millionaires. But that's like the top 0.0001 per cent. I was very much at the bottom of the ladder.'

'How can you have been? You're...' Jane remembered Charlotte's three rules. 'You're highly skilled in a number of areas, and possibly, but entirely as an afterthought, completely stunning.'

Charlotte shook her head. 'Too curvy for high fashion. Too individual for commercial. Too booby for catalogue. Not girl-next-door enough for TV. Too mainstream for editorial.'

'The wrong sort of stunning?'

'It's all just what's in style that month. And so fake, like they get one size twelve girl so they can say they're inclusive, and she's starving herself down from a sixteen for that, and the rest of us are surviving on lemon water and air so we can claim to wear a six. It'd have driven me crazy if I hadn't quit when I did.' Her companion looked around. 'Anyway, ancient history. I think I might get a drink. Shall we?'

Charlotte ordered herself a single malt, on the grounds that she might as well get the most bang for her free drink buck. Jane ordered a glass of wine. Dowdy again. Predictable. Boring?

'Are you ok?'

'I'm fine.' Jane smiled as broadly as she could manage.

'You seem a bit distracted.'

Distracted by you. 'Sorry.' Jane tried to remember how this was supposed to work. With Josh they'd been out a few times after meeting at a party where he was the friend of her university housemate's brother. And then she'd graduated and he'd suggested moving in and it had all felt like there was a clear path in front of them. All they'd had to do was walk down it.

This didn't feel like that. This felt like standing on the edge of a ten-metre diving board. And soon she would have to either jump or step back.

And she still hadn't said anything. She was supposed to be making conversation. 'I was glad you messaged.' Was that too much? Too keen? Too needy?

'Me too. So I thought maybe tomorrow? We could...'

'I'd bet on you any day, darlin'.' The guy in the shiny grey suit was, obviously, addressing Charlotte. He raised a poker chip to his lips and kissed it. 'What are the odds on you and I hitting the jackpot together?'

Charlotte sighed. 'At what game?'

'What?'

'Well, what game are you proposing we try? The odds on hitting the jackpot are going to vary entirely based on the game.'

The man looked momentarily discombobulated. 'I mean the jackpot of love, honey.'

Jane jumped in. 'But I don't think that's what the chips get you. I think tonight's a fixed prize for the chip leader at midnight. That's what they said on the door.'

Charlotte nodded. 'She's right. I think. We can ask though. Shall we check for you?' She smiled. 'You seem a bit confused about what your chips are worth.'

A smarter man would have walked away at that point. This one wasn't smart though. And now he was also feeling patronised. By two women, one of whom was hot enough to deserve to be stupid and one of whom ought to be grateful for any bloke talking to her at all.

'I'm just trying to be nice. There's no need to have an attitude.'

Charlotte didn't smile. 'You're right. No attitude here. We're just not interested.'

'Fucking stuck-up cow.'

'Is everything all right here?' Josh was standing a few feet away, not close enough to look like he was trying to intimidate anyone, but close enough to be clear that he was involved in the conversation now.

'I think this gentleman was about to move on,' suggested Jane.

The guy turned round. 'Oh mate, you're wasting your time with these two. Frigid, the pair of them.'

'Right.' Josh spoke past the irritant and addressed Jane and Charlotte directly. 'Look, I'm sure you don't need rescuing but we have very clear policies about disrespectful behaviour so...'

Charlotte and Jane exchanged a glance. 'Be our guest,' said Charlotte.

The man wasn't best pleased about being led to the door and encouraged, quite definitely, through it by Josh and the bartender and from the sound of the yelling they heard before Josh smartly shut the door, he was even less pleased to hear that patrons excluded from The Season for a breach of the behaviour policy would not be eligible for any sort of refund.

It wasn't quite the social ignominy that a scoundrel might have suffered in Austen's world, but it was near enough. She turned back to Charlotte. 'Is it always like that for you?'

'Not always.'

'Mostly men ignore me.'

'You're lucky.'

Jane didn't argue.

'I used to try to dress down to avoid it,' Charlotte continued. 'Y'know, shapeless tops and hair scrunched under a baseball cap, no make-up, all that jazz.'

'Basically my weekend uniform.'

'Which is grand if that's...' she paused. 'If that's who you are. But it's not me. I have to wear scrubs or a tunic all week at work. When I'm off duty I want to have fun. The only thing I really liked about modelling was playing dress-up. I want to wear clothes that people notice. I'm five foot ten. I don't want to spend my life not wearing heels and stooping all the damn time. I don't want to make myself smaller to avoid dicks like him.'

Jane sometimes felt like she desperately wanted to be smaller though. She didn't want to have had a life painted on such a broad mad canvas. 'So your true authentic self is spectacular.'

'Why, thank you.'

'I think my true authentic self might be a bit dull.'

'I don't think you're dull.' Charlotte smiled.

Jane was going to jump straight off that diving board, wasn't she?

The casino night did seem to be going well. Not perfectly; Emma's mental list of things she wanted to change or improve was well into double figures, but people were getting to know one another beyond the groups of friends that they'd come with, and definite couples were forming. The gaming aspect was giving those who hadn't yet found the person they wanted to romance for the Season a chance to move from table to table and a focus for starting up conversation.

For the first time in four events Emma allowed herself to relax a little as she walked between the tables. The casino manager, Miles, caught her attention. He must be in his fifties and she'd yet to see him dressed in any way that could be described as anything other than dapper. Tonight he was sporting a dark blue bow-tie above a matching waistcoat. 'Everything to your satisfaction, Miss Love?'

'It's perfect. Thank you.'

'My pleasure. So what is this Season thing?'

She explained as well as she could without drifting too far into sales pitch. His face cracked into a smile. 'You are Emma Love's daughter then? I thought you must be. Your mother fixed my mum up with her second husband. Changed her life. After my dad went, I thought she was just going to fade away. She only had five years with Denis but they were some of the happiest I've seen her.'

'I'll give her your regards.'

'You do that. So you're the boss now?'

Emma nodded.

'And all this is your baby. Dating the old-fashioned way?' He looked delighted with the whole notion. 'It sounds wonderful. I wish I had a moment for meeting people, but working somewhere like this does not allow for normal socialising. Any time anyone wants to take me up the West End I'm inevitably at work.'

Emma's matchmaking instincts twitched slightly but no light bulbs were pinging. 'Is that what you'd go for then, as your perfect date? A night in the West End.'

Miles pulled a face. 'Actually, I can't think of anything worse. I spend all day, every day, under fluorescent lighting in a state of permanent night. I want to see nature. I want to go somewhere where flowers grow and I can see the sky.' He shrugged. 'Not ideal when you live in the middle of the city and work in a casino.'

Emma's light bulb wasn't quite there yet but something in the back of her mind was flickering. 'You like flowers?'

'Love them. My very first job was in a florist's you know. Finished my last O-levels one day, started bunching up chrysanths the next. I loved that job. Do you know, I even thought about getting an allotment for a while, growing my own flowers to sell or just to have about the place? But I don't have the time and do you have any idea what the waiting list is for an allotment in central London?'

Emma did not know, but the light bulb in her brain was finally on full. 'You know what you could do? You could volunteer.'

'Growing flowers?'

'Yes.' She explained about the park where they'd had the garden party and that they had volunteers to keep things tidy and plant the annuals for each season. 'You should go down there.' She smiled. 'You should ask for David. Tell him Miss Love sent you.'

Miles nodded. 'I might do that.'

She hoped he would.

'Now you do something for me.' Miles pulled a handful of chips from his pocket. 'I know it doesn't do for the organiser to win on a night like this but you can't come to a casino night and not have a little flutter on something.'

'I'm working.'

'Everything's in hand.'

Was it? She looked around. 'I promised the bartender I brought in he'd get a break.'

'On my way to cover that right now. Relax. Enjoy yourself. One little game won't hurt.'

--

Jane and Charlotte settled into a booth next to the bar. Charlotte was rolling a poker chip between her fingers. If Jane tried to do that she'd definitely drop it. She took a sip of her wine and tried to remember how conversation worked. 'So you're a midwife now, and a model before that, what about when you were little? Where did you grow up?'

'London. Suburbia. Very normal. I've got a brother. Three years older than me. He's married now, with two kids. I've been living with them while I've been at uni. He's something in finance, so massive house. Like I asked if I could stay, but I could totally have just wandered in and taken over a guest room and he'd never have noticed.' She shrugged. 'Very ordinary childhood. What about you?'

Jane shrugged. 'Oh, you know. What about relationships?' She rushed to change the subject.

'Wow! We're doing that conversation right up front are we?'

That was a bit unfair. 'Well, you did tell me your rules for future dating about twenty minutes after we met.'

Thankfully, Charlotte laughed. 'All right then. There's not much to tell. Nothing that lasted more than about six months. Last relationship was two years ago. I met her during my first placement. She was a junior doctor in obs and gynae, but it fizzled. It's weird dating a person you mostly only call if something's gone horribly wrong with some other woman's vagina.'

'I can imagine it would be.'

'What about you? Relationship wise?'

Right. 'So I was married, to Josh actually, the guy who's helping organise all this.'

'You came to your ex-husband's dating event.'

136

'In my defence my friend signed me up and I did not know he was involved until I got here.'

'So what went wrong?'

'I came out.' It really was that simple. Josh was an excellent husband, but Jane was in want of a wife.

'That would put a dampener on things.' Charlotte twisted in her seat to face Jane properly. 'I noticed you changed the subject when I asked about your family.'

'It's just...' Just what? She didn't talk about where she came from. Where she came from was messy and unusual and made her stand out.

'It's fine. You don't have to tell me if it's too hard. I'm just interested. In you.'

And there it was. That high dive feeling again. She could step off into the abyss or she could run back down to safety. 'I grew up in a commune with four siblings and we got to choose whether we wanted to go to school or not and we had pigs and grew our food and bartered for things we couldn't grow, because my parents don't believe in money or capitalist society.'

'Wow. I have so many questions.' And Charlotte smiled. She didn't look horrified or put off or freaked out. Jane's dive had landed in clear blue water. Tens from the judges all around.

She smiled right back. 'Fire away.'

–

Annie wandered through the casino. She'd never been to one before. Everything she knew about gambling came from either Hollywood or a single, entirely ineffective, attempt by Josh to teach her how to play poker when they were about fourteen. Aside from that her understanding of casinos basically came from James Bond. On which basis, if they all made it through the night without being shot with a poison dart, the whole event would be considered a huge success.

It did mean that she was somewhat out of her element. She had a bag full of chips and no idea what to do with them.

'Blow on them.'

'Excuse me?' She stared at the hand that had been thrust in front of her. Col, Colin, Colin Williams.

'Blow on them.' He shook his hand in front of her. 'It's for luck.'

Annie's brain finally caught up with what she was being asked to do. She leaned forward and blew gently on the pair of dice Colin was holding, and watched as he threw.

A four and a five.

'Is that good?'

'Too soon to say,' he grinned. The dice were passed back to him. 'Blow again.'

'What are we hoping for?'

'Another nine. Failing that, anything but a seven.'

'Ok.' This was much more fun once you got involved. 'I'm thinking of nines.' She blew gently again.

Colin threw the dice the full length of the table sending them bouncing off the raised wall at the end. Annie leaned over to see. A six. And... she realised she was holding her breath as the second dice rolled to its settling place... a two. Eight. She deflated.

The dice were pushed back to Colin. 'It's ok. We can go again so long as we don't get a seven.'

Annie made to step away. She clearly wasn't bringing him luck.

'Where do you think you're going? You can't abandon me mid game.' He held out the dice. 'Come on. One more roll at least. If you go now and I hit a seven it'll be your fault.'

She blew again on the dice and watched the throw.

A three. Again she felt herself holding her breath. Not a four, she murmured to herself. The second dice settled. A six. A six. 'That's nine!' she squealed. 'That's good, right?'

Colin clapped her vigorously on the arm. 'That's very good. Very good indeed.' He glanced at the bag of chips she was clutching. 'You should play, if you want to.'

She did want to, actually. She let him explain how the games worked. Apparently, this was mini-craps, which made Annie giggle, but was also the actual name of the game. The betting and rules seemed inordinately complicated but the basic idea was that somebody threw a pair of dice and tried not to get a seven. Other people around the table bet on the outcome. There was a lot more to it than that, but Annie popped a handful of chips down where Colin suggested and collected a whole lot more from the nice table attendant when she won.

'I won.'

'You did. Do you want to go again?'

She took his betting suggestion a second time, and watched the roll of the dice, and then watched as the attendant swept her chips away. 'I lost?'

'Fraid so. It's just chance with this one though. Some you win. Some you lose.' He nodded at the, now less full, bag in her hand. 'You've still got chips to play with though.' He stepped away from the table. 'Shall we try something different?'

She let Colin induct her in the ways of blackjack and roulette and was almost out of chips when he suggested trying their hands at baccarat. 'It's what James Bond plays.'

'I thought that was poker.'

'In the more recent films, but in the novels he's a baccarat man. Or we could get a drink, if you prefer.'

Annie didn't mind, so she let Colin decide it was time to freshen their glasses. They perched on bar stools with their drinks. Colin was easy company, happy to take the lead without making her feel like she was being bossed around, and apparently keen on her.

'So, thing is, with the whole dating shebangabang, I did wonder whether you and I might, if you will, make this little attachment, as they say, official.'

What?

'I mean we get on rather well, I think.'

That was true.

'And I'd treat you well. You know, wasn't raised to disrespect a lady.'

Well, good.

'And I think, maybe, you don't find me repellent?'

She didn't. She didn't at all. He was very kind, and well-presented, and he seemed serious about finding a relationship.

'So do you think you might want to hook your wagon to mine?'

Well, really what reason was there to say no?

–

Cold air against her skin. His body pressing hard against hers. His fingers digging into her bum through her skirt. Her tongue parting his lips. Lydia revelled in all of the sensations bombarding her and keeping her in the moment. Just focus on how this feels right now. No worries. No past. No future. Just this.

He pulled back. 'I've got to get back to work.'

What? No. Lydia needed more. She pouted at Hot Barman. 'We can be quick.'

'Yeah. I remember.' He looked down the alleyway behind the casino. She'd led him behind the recycling bins, not the actual rubbish so it was, amongst the available options, relatively classy. 'You know I preferred it the time we went back to yours and there was an actual bed.'

'But you don't have time for that.' And after he'd stayed over once and then she'd seen him again the next day, Lydia was already breaking her own hooking-up guidelines by even considering shagging him again. There was no way he was getting anywhere near her flat a second time. She grabbed his waistband and pulled him closer to her so she could tug at his belt. 'Come on. There's nobody around.'

He closed his eyes. 'I'm not saying I'm not tempted.'

She brushed her hand across his groin. He was definitely tempted.

'But seriously? Like there's only so many quickies and one nighters a boy can tolerate before you have to at least take me out to dinner.' He stepped back.

Lydia rolled her eyes. 'There's no need to get all needy,' she muttered.

'I'm sorry. I was working. You're the one who dragged me out here and stuck her tongue down my throat.'

The moment ebbed away from her. She folded her arms. 'Just thought it'd be fun.'

'I'm sure it would.' He stopped a couple of feet away from her. 'Are you ok, Lydia?'

'Yeah. I mean, not as ok as I was hoping to be.' She tried to turn it into a joke.

He didn't let her. 'I mean in general. If you want to, I don't know, talk or anything.'

'I'm fine,' she insisted.

'Ok.' He walked to the end of the alleyway. 'I do need to get back to work though. But, if you wanted to meet up sometime when I'm not working?'

'I don't think that's a good idea.' She wasn't looking for a relationship. She wasn't looking for a friend. All she wanted from him was to feel something right now.

He nodded. And then he was gone.

–

Emma told herself it would be fine to take ten minutes to play the chips Miles had given her. She stepped towards the nearest table. Roulette. Definitely not her preference – a proper game of chance. She would go and find the card tables. Even with blackjack there was a system, a set of mathematical principles, you could apply to shift the odds towards the skilled player over the house.

'Miss Love, you're joining us?'

Emma winced. A client was a client, regardless of whether they were also an immense irritation, and she would never knowingly cause offence to a client.

'Mr Knight, I hope you're having a pleasant evening.'

He gestured at the stack of chips in front of him. 'The only sad thing is that these aren't actually worth anything.'

'Wow. You seem to be having a very pleasant evening indeed.'

'Just dumb luck.'

Well at least he recognised that.

'Do you know how to play?'

'I'm assuming I put my chips on whatever I want to bet on.'

'Yeah. Pick a number.' He indicated the table. 'Or you can bet odds or evens or red or black or you can bet any number in a sector or a column.' He pointed at the relevant squares on the green baize.

'So they're lower risk?'

'And lower reward.'

She watched the next round. She'd never played roulette before, but she realised quickly that with the green zero on the ring, the odds were always ever so slightly tipped in the house's favour. People would think it was fifty-fifty if they bet on red or black, but actually no – that one green number skewed things enough that over the long term the house would always be ahead.

'So what's your lucky number, Miss Love?'

'I don't believe in luck.'

He gave her a disappointed look. 'It doesn't matter whether you believe in it, Miss Love. Luck is what it is. Chance. Fate. Can change a life in a heartbeat.'

'Very poetic, Mr Knight.'

'Call me Tom.'

'You don't call me Emma.'

He tilted his head. 'No. You're definitely Miss Love. There's something arm's length about you somehow.'

She bristled. 'I'm at work.'

'Ok. Let's say it's that.'

She was professional. It wasn't her job to be all touchy feely. It was as much her job to put a curb on people's ill-advised passions as it was to encourage the wiser ones. Of course she had to keep herself a little detached. 'Are we playing then?'

Mr Knight pushed all his chips onto the number eighteen.

'You're going to lose everything.'

'Easy come, easy go.' He grinned. 'Your turn.'

The most sensible thing to do would be to limit her losses and then move on to a game where she could use skill to tip the balance in her favour. But, she didn't want to actually win, did she? It wouldn't look good if the organiser was also the winner.

She picked up her stack of chips.

The table attendant leaned over. 'Are you playing, Miss?'

It wasn't real money and she really ought to get back to work.

'Go on. Pick a lucky number, Miss Love.'

There was no such thing as a lucky number. The best you could do was reduce the chances of having to share your unlikely win. People tended to go for birthdays. She placed her whole stack down on the thirty-two.

Tom raised his glass. 'I'm impressed.'

The croupier spun the wheel and sent the ball rushing counter-ways around the rim. She leaned in to look. Tom was behind her, leaning forward too. 'This is the best bit,' he whispered. 'When it's all still potential. Absolutely anything is possible.'

She didn't reply. She was pretending she didn't know what he meant, that the feeling of floating wasn't threatening to lift her clean away. The anticipation of what might be was kind of wonderful. The ball slowed on its turn around the wheel and slid downwards, bouncing slightly as it settled in a slot on the ring. Emma tried to follow the still spinning wheel with her eyes to make out the winning number.

'Red, thirty-two,' called the attendant.

'Shit,' whispered Tom. 'That's one lucky, lucky number.'

'I won?'

'You won. Play again?' asked Tom.

'Are you?'

'I'm broke.'

The croupier slid a stack over to Emma. She picked a hundred off the top and passed it to Tom.

'Have a go on me,' she offered.

He raised a dark eyebrow halfway up his forehead, and a sexy little grin pulled at the corners of his lips. Emma replayed what she'd just said in her head. 'I didn't mean have a go *on* me. I meant play another round with this chip which I am giving you.'

'And I thought you really were feeling lucky?'

Clients flirted with Emma all the time. It went with the territory. She knew how to handle it. She was friendly up to a point, but she was always professional. It didn't normally make her heartbeat quicken.

She picked up as many of her chips as she could manage in her hands. 'I think I'll leave you to it.'

'What about the rest of your chips?'

'Keep them.' She started to smile, but stopped herself. She was working. She didn't get involved. 'It seems like you need all the help you can get.'

Walking away from the table was the right thing to do. She needed to be focused on work, not on the thrill of taking a chance, of doing something a little bit risky; she had quite enough risk on her hands trying to make the Season a success. From a dating point of view, things were coming together. Couples were forming. People she'd observed gravitating towards one another were now firmly established within each other's orbit. Even her three schoolteachers seemed to be making matches. Well, two of them, at least. Jane was deep in close conversation with the astounding Charlotte, and Annie was just leaving the bar to return to the games, arm in arm with nice Colin Williams.

Across the gaming floor she saw Josh was also watching the action. He frowned slightly before slipping out of a side door that led to the back stairwell. Emma followed.

'What are you doing in here?'

He started slightly at her voice. 'Just taking a minute. It's full-on out there. I think pretty much everyone turned up though.'

That was good. One of Emma's many and various worries was that, as people started to form couples, they would lose interest in the rest of the events, the Season having served its purpose. She really wanted people to stay engaged, to keep up that sense of community and to provide a good example to the more resolutely single attendees.

'You can go and play a bit if you want a break. I've got spare chips.'

'You're all right. Not really in the mood.'

He did have a bit of a face on him. 'What's up?'

He sighed. 'Have you ever thought you were sure about something and then turned out to be completely off beam?'

She wasn't sure what he meant. 'I don't know.'

'Like you think you're on the same page as someone about something big but you've got entirely the wrong idea?'

Of course she hadn't. Emma's instincts about what other people wanted, and needed, were all but infallible. 'Is this to do with Jane?'

He sank down to sitting on the steps. 'Why does everyone keep going on about Jane?'

'Ok. So it's not Jane?'

'No. Well, sort of it is.' He kept his head down, staring at his knuckles, hands clasped in front of him rather than meeting her gaze. 'When I married her I thought it would be forever.'

'Well, everyone thinks that.'

'I mean, I knew it wasn't the most passionate thing but we were close. I thought we understood each other. We seemed to want the same things.'

Emma leaned back against the wall and wrapped her arms across her body against the draught coming down from the roof space. 'So I'm presuming you split because…'

'Of Jane being a lesbian?' Josh helpfully filled in the blank.

They'd never talked specifically about why Josh's marriage ended. He hadn't volunteered any details and Emma hadn't wanted to pry.

'I knew we'd grown apart. I thought I was just working too much. I was almost relieved when I got made redundant. Thought it'd be a chance to reset, you know. Find whatever feelings we used to have or whatever. But, obviously, she didn't want the same.'

Before Jane's rather public coming out, the split was always talked about as being very amicable, entirely mutual, but nothing was ever entirely mutual, was it? One person always wanted out more urgently than the other.

'She said that if I was honest I wasn't in love with her either.' He finally looked up at Emma. 'And I think she was right, but how could I have got that so wrong? How can you not know if you're in love?'

'I don't know.'

'Come on. You're the professional. How do you know if you're in love or not?'

'Honestly?'

'Absolutely.'

She pulled her skirt smooth and sat down as delicately as she could beside him. 'Can I tell you a secret?'

'Sure.'

'This is not for public consumption. My professional reputation wouldn't do well.'

'Ok?'

'I don't think I've ever been in love.'

'Never?'

Emma shook her head. It was preposterous. She was a matchmaker. Her career was love and romance and falling head over heels, but had she ever had that herself? She'd had good relationships, fun relationships with kind and thoughtful men. But had they ever been more than really good mates in the final analysis?

'You've never had that feeling in your gut like the rest of the world is fading away and there's you and that one other person and nothing else can impinge?'

She shook her head again.

'You've never felt like you wanted to go all in? Commit everything to a moment?'

'God, no.' She forced herself to laugh in the hope of hiding the horror in her voice. 'But it sounds like you have. Is that how you felt when you married Jane?'

He frowned. 'No.'

'I don't understand.' It had sounded so totally like he was talking from experience.

'Not Jane.'

The penny dropped. 'Someone else then?' Emma's matchmaker senses finally kicked into gear. 'Somebody now?'

'But how can I be sure? I thought it was it with Jane, and I was wrong. So incredibly wrong.' He laughed a little bitterly.

'But this isn't Jane?'

'No, but it's someone from a long time ago. I thought we had something years back…' He shrugged.

Emma was learning more about her brother's emotional life than she'd ever expected to know. 'This someone hurt you before?' she ventured.

'Yeah.'

She was starting to understand. 'And now she's back?'

He nodded. 'And I still feel exactly the same. And then some.'

'Then you might get hurt again.'

'Great. Great cheerleader for courtship and finding The One, you are.'

She laughed. 'Sorry. But if you feel like that I think you have to go for it.'

'I sort of tried.'

'And?'

'It was like she couldn't hear me. Wouldn't hear me.' He shook his head. 'Unless she was trying to let me down gently.'

'What did you actually say? Did you actually say "Hello, lady. I think I'm in love with you. Do you want to get coffee sometime?"'

He pulled a face at her. 'No. And that's ridiculous. You can't go from in love to coffee. Coffee is like "You're fine. It's worth an hour to consider." Love is dinner, at least.'

Maybe her brother understood the dating business better than he gave himself credit for. 'But did you tell her you liked her and ask her out? Clearly and without room for misinterpretation?'

'Not exactly.'

'Right. Well maybe that's where you need to start.'

He shook his head. 'She's with someone else now, I think. I should have taken a bigger swing when I had the chance.'

Emma's phone trilled in her pocket. 'Sorry. Hold on.'

1 New Message. From Mum.

Emma scanned the contents. It was fine. It was good. Her face, apparently, told a different story.

'What's up?'

'Mum's coming back for a visit. She'll be here for the family day and the final ball.'

'Checking up on us,' he laughed.

No. Not on *us*. This wasn't all Josh's idea. He hadn't been handed the keys to the family empire, thought Emma. She's checking up on *me*.

Emma made her way back into the gaming room. She had nothing to worry about. The Season was going well. The finances were... the finances were going to be fine, she told herself firmly. Everything was under control. She just needed to avoid distractions, stay focused and make sure everything went exactly to her plan.

–

Lydia wandered back inside and studiously avoided the bar area. She'd made the mistake of letting him think they might actually get involved. She saw that now. It was her mistake and she could fix it. From now on she'd keep her distance and concentrate on having fun. She didn't need anybody getting too attached and complicating things.

–

Jane thought this might be the perfect evening. She never would have dared hope, when she'd accepted that she couldn't pretend to be somebody she wasn't any longer, that things might fall into place this easily. Charlotte was spectacular, but the longer they talked the easier it all became. This was what Jane had been waiting for. Her life was falling into place. Everything was simple and nothing was going to mess that up.

–

Annie let Colin take her hand in his again. This was right, wasn't it? This was what the Season was all about – find the right type of person and form an attachment. It was about getting past first impressions, and initial attractions and finding something deeper. It didn't matter that she hadn't been sure of Colin from the outset. He'd persuaded her with his kindness and his good humour, and now here they were.

At the roulette table Tom watched the chips he'd blagged off Emma go up in smoke. It didn't matter. Easy come, easy go, and he was here. He was doing what he'd promised his mum and putting himself out there again. He was working, socialising, creating a semblance of living. He just needed to carry on like this. Across the room all five of them were in perfect accord. Things might have been a little up and down to get to this point, but from now on everything was going to be just right.

Chapter Eleven

> Sorry I ducked out early last night. Lost all my chips so didn't seem much point hanging around.

Jane read the message from Lydia to their group chat while she stood in front of the mirror. It was a welcome distraction.

> That's ok.

She replied.

> What game did you lose at?

There was a second before the screen told her Lydia was typing.

> No. Literally lost my chips. Put the bag down somewhere and never saw it again. You looked like you were having a good night though.

Lydia's comment was followed by a flurry of heart and flower emojis.

> I wasn't the only one.

Jane could see that Annie was reading the chat as well. Attack was definitely the best form of defence.

> Annie and Colin sitting in a tree…

Lydia responded.

> He asked me to be his girlfriend.

Annie's message popped up next.
Lydia replied with a string of laughing emojis.

> You're going steady like in High School Musical or something.

> Well, I'm not the only one.

So the 'attack is the best form of defence' thing could come back at you it turned out.

> True. How is the Goddess this morning?

> I wouldn't know. We're taking things slowly.

Slowly by Lydia's standards anyway, having had two separate conversations and still not slept together.

> We've got our first official date tomorrow.

> That's great. She seems lovely.

Annie could at least be relied on for positivity.

> So today is nothing but waxing and fake tanning then?

Lydia had a more pragmatic world view.

Jane wasn't the waxing type, and Charlotte must spend her work days seeing all sorts of personal topiary. Surely she'd be open minded about the level of cutting back employed.

> I can't imagine going on a date with someone that beautiful. So much to live up to.

Thanks, Annie. That was just what she needed.

Jane took in her own reflection. She looked fine. She looked thirty rather than twenty and she'd never been a gym bunny but she walked places, and went to Pilates when Lydia or Annie reminded her. But, apart from the one night that was never to be spoken of again, nobody, apart from her ex-husband, had seen her naked for over a decade. She turned round and tried to assess the backs of her thighs in the mirror. What was the point? Cellulite couldn't be vanished in twenty-four hours. Some of the rest of this mess could.

> Do they do whole body waxing?

she asked.

Lydia replied straight away.

They do if you pay them enough.

At least she could throw her credit card at one part of the problem.

–

'So legs, underarms and bikini area then. And what are we going for down there? French? Brazilian? Hollywood? Or just a tidy round?' The waxing technician – official title according to the certificate on the wall above Jane's head – hadn't yet peered beneath the towel.

The thought of this random stranger tidying her lady garden was some distance outside Jane's comfort zone. Commune life had been gloriously hairy, so she'd only really discovered hair removal as an adult and she'd tended to confine herself to shaving her legs and armpits in the shower. When she remembered, and never during winter. And Josh had been just old enough that his expectations of female body hair hadn't been skewed irreparably by internet porn at a formative age. Overall pubic hair styling wasn't something she could claim great expertise in.

She tried to remember the snippets Lydia read out from women's magazines in the staff room. 'What's the one where it's just like a strip?'

'Depends. Do you want the hair off all the way round, or just at the front leaving a strip?'

Jane hesitated. 'Does all the way round mean…?'

'It means *all* the way round.'

What would a goddess expect, Jane wondered. 'What's the most popular?'

'Probably Brazilian. Is this your first time though?'

Jane nodded.

'So maybe go French.' She narrowed her eyes. 'It's for a special occasion, yes?'

'Sort of. I've got a date.'

'Better to be hairy than red raw then, I reckon.' The woman nodded. 'And with French you can keep the paper knickers on.'

Jane liked that idea very much indeed.

'You're not on your period are you?'

Jane shook her head. 'Why?'

'Not a problem if you were. Just some people find it makes everything a bit more sensitive down there which isn't great for your first time.'

'I'm not.'

'Right then. You lie back and we'll be done in no time.'

Jane tried to let her mind wander from the hot wax being applied to the tops of her thighs and the edge of her pubic area. At least she wasn't on her period. Wait. It was due, wasn't it? Jane thought back. She knew she'd had a period right at the end of June because, in a rare moment of menstrual cycle complying with her plans, it had started the day after Lydia's birthday spa trip. And it was what now? First week of August. Damn. Hot date with a Goddess and period imminent. She'd better not be going through the agony of her first bikini wax for nobody to see the results.

–

Emma opened her laptop on her knee. SirWalt was already at the virtual poker table. She clicked into the private chat.

> I am on a losing streak.

he typed.

Emma checked Walt's chip stack on the screen. It was way down from the last time they'd played.

> Did you bluff with sod all?

> Might have.

He was worse than Mr Knight. Why was she thinking about Tom Knight? Simply because he hadn't found anyone yet. She'd been thinking about lovely Hope Lucas who was friends with Jane's supermodel, and Lydia Hyland and countless others. That was all. It was her job to think about them. It was her job to find them all the perfect mate. That flirty little smile of challenge at the idea of having à go on her wasn't on her mind at all.

A new hand started. Emma was dealt a pair of threes, and matched the big blind to stay in the hand. Walt folded without seeing the flop. That was unlike him. The first three community cards didn't help Emma's hand. A player with the username BrickBarbie raised hard. The size of the bet led Emma to suspect they were bluffing, but there was a jack, and an eight and a ten on the board so he could easily have a higher pair or even a straight. Not worth the risk. She folded, and typed in the chat.

> Not like you to fold early?

> You must be rubbing off on me.

> Well good. It might save you some money.

> We don't play for money here.

Emma started to reply and then saw the three flashing dots. Walt was still typing.

> Actually, I do have a regular cash game – every Monday. You should come.

That was ridiculous.

> You don't even know if we're in the same country.

> True but you chat in English like a native and you seem to be in the same time zone as me, so I'm guessing UK?

> I could be Irish.

> Are you?

> No.

> Well then. I'm in London.

Emma's shoulders tensed. He was in London. She was in London. She could go. She could meet him, in person. This could be something real. She knew nothing about him, she reminded herself, and, for all Emma did know, he could be married to his first girlfriend from school.

> I'll think about it.

He typed in a place and a time.

> It's invite only. Private game. £500 cap.

Of course she wouldn't go. She didn't play for cash. It was far too dangerous.

> So next Monday?

He continued.

> I'll have to see what I'm doing.

> Scared of me taking all your money?

> I just don't usually play for real.

> You can't hide behind a screen the whole time.

That wasn't what she meant, but she didn't correct him.

> Maybe I like the anonymity.

> It is nice to talk to someone who doesn't know all your business.

It was. Family and work had never been clearly divided for Emma and sharing the house with Josh while he was working for her at the same time, with his ex-wife as a client, was blurring those boundaries more than ever. Playing poker online and chatting to Walt were separate from that entirely.

> Like how you're still holding a torch for Keeley Henson?

She steered them back to the online bubble they'd created.

> Well, nobody in my real life knows that.

Emma smiled.

Walt was still typing.

> You never told me about your first love.

> I did. The uni boyfriend. Ty.

> You said he wasn't The One. So who was?

> You first.

So you're not buying the Keeley Henson thing then?

Should I be?

No. I was married though.

Past tense. Divorced then?

Tell me.

Do you believe in love at first sight?

Not exactly.

What Emma believed in was that it was possible to identify a number of factors relevant to compatibility at first sight. True love required more data.

I didn't. And then it happened. I was gone. Absolutely gone that very first second. You know all those clichés about thunderbolts and electricity?

That was what her clients were after.

I may have heard of them.

Well, it was like the opposite of that. It was like a moment of absolute calm. I've never been so sure of anything in my life.

That sounds incredible.

It was.

Should she ask? They'd said no details. They weren't going to know everything about the other's business.

Was?

Those three dots flashed and dimmed and flashed again.

What's that poem? I thought that love would last forever. I was wrong.

Funeral Blues

typed Emma.

It's Auden.

It's Four Weddings and A Funeral and you can stop getting all clever on me.

Emma laughed.

Walt was still typing.

> Better to have loved and lost though. At least that's what people tell me.

Was it? To be that sure and then to find out you were wrong sounded almost unimaginably awful.

Chapter Twelve

Jane got off the overground at Forest Hill and walked the three minutes to the bar Charlotte had chosen, silently thanking God it wasn't further. Her crotch was dappled in a bright red rash that chafed against her knickers. It was ridiculous. Her preparations for the big date had left her completely incapable of getting down to any sort of hot and heavy date activity, and she was apparently cursed to walk like a cowboy who'd mislaid his horse for the rest of time.

The bar was a quirky little place in a row of shops. It seemed to be a converted bank, or maybe post office. Inside had a faux retro feel with leather banquettes and diner-style booths. Charlotte was already ensconced in one of them sipping on a pint of something that had the look of a serious ale drinker's beer. Jane waved 'hello' and ordered herself a nice safe glass of wine before joining her.

Charlotte raised her pint as Jane sat down. 'They brew this themselves. They've got a micro brewery out the back.'

'I'm not a big beer drinker.'

'I didn't used to be. It's kind of an acquired taste. But I like it.' She took another sip. 'It's a sort of warm happy tipsiness I get with beer. Wine makes me whingey.'

Jane nodded sagely. 'Gin makes me cry.'

'Noted.'

'So…'

'Well…'

Outside the nice safe bubble of the Season things felt strangely more real. They both started to speak at the same time and then stopped and giggled awkwardly but simultaneously. 'You go,' Jane suggested.

'It wasn't anything much. I was going to ask about you. You told me that you grew up in a commune.'

She had. In the cold light of day that felt like too big a disclosure. 'I left a long time ago.'

'Ok. So let's talk about now, what do you do, what's your perfect Sunday, why did you sign up for the Season? All that stuff.'

'Ok. Well, I'm a teacher. Secondary school history.' She fell silent.

'All right… and before that?'

'Erm… Uni in London. I've been here since I was eighteen. Since I moved out of the crazy compound. What about you?' Jane was happy to change the subject before too much more attention fell onto her formative years. 'You're training to be a midwife. Did you always want to do that?'

Charlotte nodded. 'Always wanted to, but it took me a long time to get here. Quit school as soon as I was allowed basically. Then finally came back and started a diploma in health and social care about five years ago, and then got a degree place. Didn't start until I knew I needed to quit modelling though. Wish I'd done it years ago.'

'What tipped you over?' The transition from photoshoot to delivery room was still hard to fathom.

'Honestly? The point where my agency asked if I'd consider a breast reduction.'

'What?'

'Yes. Actual major surgery to make me look more like some random figure that happened to be in fashion that week. And that was on top of a shoot with a particularly sleazy photographer. And the endless diet advice from every angle. *No alcohol.*' She raised her glass at that one. '*No carbs. No sugar. No fat. Lean protein only. If you feel peckish drink half a cup of warm water and visualise an olive to make those hunger pangs go away. It was* ridiculous.' She paused. 'Man. I'm hungry just talking about it. Do you want to get food? I want to get food. I'll get us some menus.'

Jane's phone rang while Charlotte was collecting menus from the bar. Unknown number. Jane didn't normally answer those but she tapped the green button out of curiosity.

'Jay?'

'Fey?'

Something in her sibling's voice wasn't right. There was tension there. 'What's wrong?'

'It's Mum. She's having contractions but she said she had another month. And she won't let me call for an ambulance or a doctor or anything, but it's too soon, isn't it?'

'I'm not sure. Hold on.'

Charlotte was sliding back into her seat on the other side of the booth.

'Erm… odd question. Professional question. How early is too early in a pregnancy to go into labour?'

Charlotte looked her up and down. 'Why?'

'It's my sibling on the phone. My mum's pregnant. She's a bit…' Jane never knew what to say. 'Well, she hasn't seen a doctor or anything and she didn't think she was due for another month or so. But it's her sixth baby, so she must know what she's doing. Mustn't she?'

'They're on the phone now?'

Jane nodded.

'Put them on speaker.'

Jane did as she was told. 'Fey, this is my friend, Charlotte. Charlotte, this is Fey.'

'Hi Fey. Your mum's having a baby?'

'Yeah.'

'And she's in labour now?'

'I think so.'

'Ok. How far apart are the contractions?'

'I dunno. It seems to go up and down. Maybe eight or ten minutes. Sometimes less.'

'Ok. That sounds like it could be Braxton Hicks. How long has it been going on?'

They heard Fey shouting to somebody else in the house.

'She says her waters broke during the night.'

'Right. Who else is there with you?'

'Everyone's here.'

'Who's everyone?'

'That'll be the rest of the community,' Jane clarified.

Charlotte raised an eyebrow. 'Ok.'

'So what should I do?' That was Fey again. 'I'm scared. Can you come, Jay? She won't let me call anyone else.'

Jane shook her head. 'I can't. I'm half an hour away from home. I don't have a car. I borrowed one last time.' What could she do? There was no way she'd get to her parents' home in any sort of useful time.

'I'll drive,' said Charlotte.

'It's two hours away.'

Charlotte was already standing up. 'It's fine. I've hardly started my pint and my place is only round the corner. Come on.'

Jane clicked the phone off speaker and put it to her ear. 'Did you hear that? We're on our way.'

'Thank you. What do I do 'til then?'

'Just keep an eye on her. And… wait.' She ran to catch up with Charlotte. 'How will Fey know if the baby's coming?'

'Put them back on speaker.' Jane did as she was told. 'Listen to me, Fey. If she's bleeding – like fresh blood, more than a few drops, or if she starts wanting to push, or if you can see the baby's head or the cord at all, even if you're not quite sure, you phone an ambulance. Do you understand?'

'She doesn't want me to.'

'If she's bleeding, if she wants to push, if you can see the baby or the cord, what do you do?' Charlotte's voice brooked no argument.

166

'Call an ambulance.'

'That's right. And don't panic, Fey. Everything's going to be ok. Jane and I are on our way.'

Jane followed Charlotte's long-legged stride along the street and down two side roads into a residential avenue of large semi-detached houses. Charlotte stopped at the bottom of a driveway. 'My brother's house. I've been renting his spare room while I was doing my training.'

Jane was distracted by something else entirely. The car on the driveway – the car Charlotte was now striding towards – was a silver Porsche.

The last time she'd driven to see her family it was in Lydia's twelve-year-old Clio. 'Is this your car?'

'I'm a student midwife. What do you think?'

Student midwife slash supermodel, thought Jane.

'It's my brother's mid-life crisis car. Gorgeous house. Successful career. Bright, brilliant, glorious wife. Three ridiculously precocious children. So obviously he's taken up hot yoga and bought a Porsche.'

'Will he mind you taking it?'

Charlotte threw open the driver's door. 'He never drives it. They've got a big family estate thing for actually going places.'

Fey phoned three times more as they bombed their way along the M3, first to say that the contractions seemed to have settled at seven or eight minutes apart, which Charlotte said was good and fine and no need to panic yet. The second call was to say that their mum had decided to make jam and had made it as far as the kitchen and was now pouring sugar into the biggest pan she could find in between waves of clutching a wooden spoon between her teeth and breathing hard, and was that normal? Charlotte confirmed that it was not entirely normal but nothing to be worried about. 'Physically at least,' she added as Jane ended the call. Finally, as they were making their way along the country roads that led to the commune, Fey called to say that Little Sam wanted to bless the birthing room with sage and was that all right for the baby? Jane dealt with that one. 'Fey, if blessing the birthing room with sage, or burning incense or dancing round a fucking scented candle was bad for babies neither of us would have made it this far, would we?'

Two hours after running out of the pub they were pulling up in front of the entranceway. Twice in a fortnight was the most Jane had visited in twelve years. She jumped out and opened the gate for Charlotte and then hopped back in the car for the drive up to the buildings.

'Look, I know you said the commune, hippy, off-grid thing sounded cool, but like, remember that I moved out. Ok?'

'Now I'm even more intrigued.'

Jane pointed at the farmhouse that dominated one side of the yard. 'They'll be in there.'

–

Annie had said she was busy. Jane had her Big Date. And Lydia was remembering why she hated the summer holidays. So much time. Big acres of it stretching out in every direction. The enormity of the empty space horrified her. She needed to be productive, busy, surrounded by people. When she was on her own she...

Lydia picked up her phone and opened a clothes resale app. She scrolled through pages of dresses she'd never wear, and dresses almost identical to ones she already owned. She put a scarlet-red racer-back bodycon dress into her basket. If she wore it with heels and straightened her hair and slicked it back and did black eyeliner and lashings of mascara with bright red lipstick she'd look like one of those women from a 1980s pop video. She'd look like someone else. She clicked 'Buy' before she could change her mind and smiled for a second at the idea of the new Lydia she might become.

The fizz of possibility didn't last long. The dress almost certainly wouldn't fit the way she pictured it. She wouldn't look cool and retro. She'd look like she was trying too hard. She opened Rightmove and picked a location. South coast today. She often looked for places by the sea or in tiny villages in the middle of rolling countryside. Always somewhere different from where she was right now. She scoured floor plans and photos of houseboats and sea-view apartments on Brighton marina, and tried to picture herself living by the ocean, cycling or jogging along the seafront. Maybe that Lydia would be content.

She considered puppies she could adopt from her local rehoming centre. Would Lydia like a dog? She tried to imagine herself walking a dog on Wanstead Flats, nodding hello to the other dog walkers. That Lydia would have wellies and a cheerfully coloured waterproof and a rosy outdoorsy sort of complexion. Maybe she should buy some wellingtons.

She watched YouTube for a bit, and then turned on the TV and flicked between channels. Nothing held her attention. She needed to get out of the flat. She pulled on her running gear, turned her music up loud to quiet her thoughts and set off to pound along the pavements.

–

They found Jane's mum sitting at the bottom of the stairs in her dressing gown. She glared at Jane. 'I told Fey there was no need to call you.'

Jane took in the scene. Her mum looked exhausted. Little Sam was wafting what smelt like a bunch of sage around on the stairs above them. Big Sam was sitting cross-legged in the hallway with his eyes closed and his hands pressed together in prayer position. Fey was at the foot of the stairs, alongside their mum, clutching their phone and staring at the screen intently.

'Where's Dad?'

'Camping in the far field,' snapped her mother. 'He's connecting with the land before the coming of new life.'

Jane opened her mouth to say that he ought to be here and that they all ought to be in hospital, but Charlotte spoke first.

'How far apart are the contractions now?' Her tone was bright and businesslike.

'Who's this?'

'This is my friend...' Jane's voice was overpowered by a sudden shriek from her mother.

Fey turned their phone screen towards the newcomers to show the timer screen. 'Three minutes. They're three minutes apart now.'

'Ok. And do you feel like pushing, Mrs...'

Fey and Jane both froze.

'Mrs and Miss are both remnants of a dysfunctional gender binary that subjugates those outside of a narrow form of masculinity,' shrieked Jane's mother.

'Good point. Well made.' Charlotte didn't flinch. 'What shall I call you then?'

'Today I am Storm.'

'Marvellous. So do you feel like pushing yet, Storm?'

'Soon,' whispered Jane's mother.

'Ok.' Charlotte still seemed perfectly calm. 'Do you mind if I have a little feel of your belly, just to see how things are going there?'

Jane's mother frowned. 'You're not a doctor, are you? I don't trust hospitals.'

'Absolutely not.' Charlotte squatted down in front of her. 'I'm a midwife. I practise totally mother-led birthing. And I'm Jane's friend. I'm only here because she needed a lift, but, as I am here, why not indulge me?'

'You're Jane's friend?' Jane's mum's face softened a little before she squealed with another contraction. 'I want to push,' she panted.

Jane felt sick. She'd managed to avoid the births of the rest of her siblings, between being too young to notice or understand, or through actively hiding in the attic when Fey came along.

'Jane!' Charlotte's voice cut through her horror. 'Jane, can you get some towels or sheets or something? Something we can wrap the baby in? And something to put on the floor?'

'Shouldn't we get her in bed?'

Charlotte turned back to her mum. 'Do you want to get into bed?'

'Nooooooo!'

Charlotte nodded. 'I think we're good here. Towels. Sheets. Go!'

Jane did as she was told. Towels would be upstairs and she couldn't exactly climb over her mum to get them. She nudged Big Sam out of his meditation with her foot. 'Can we get towels from your place?'

'My place is your place, Jay. You know that.'

She ran across the courtyard and into one of the converted stable blocks that now served as home to the Sams. There was a stack of laundry on the table in the kitchen. Jane grabbed it all.

When she got back everything was quiet. Her mum was panting gently and Charlotte was bent over reaching between her mother's legs. Everyone else was silent. 'What's wrong?'

Charlotte looked up. 'The cord is round baby's neck, but that's ok.'

'That's not ok.' There was a cold feeling reaching up from Jane's stomach and into her throat. 'That's really bad.'

'It's all right,' insisted Charlotte.

'I want to push again.'

'Great. I'm going to hold baby's head.' Charlotte's attention was back on the baby. 'Go for it. Exactly like you did before.'

Jane turned away and stared out of the door into the yard as her mother screamed and pushed behind her. She'd run away from this place. She'd run away from a world where people gave birth on stairways with sage blessings and meditation and not a doctor or an epidural in sight. Everything fell quiet again. It shouldn't be this quiet, should it? On TV there was a lot of screaming and pushing and then a baby cried. Why wasn't there a baby crying?

She wouldn't look. If she didn't look she could still be miles away. She could be in her flat in London where everything was clean and neat and just as it ought to be. She couldn't stop herself hearing though.

'Ok. Baby's not moving. Fey, I want you to call an ambulance.'

'No.' That was Jane's mother.

Charlotte's voice was level and calm but still definite. 'Just to be on the safe side. This is perfectly normal though. It happens all the time. Fey, do it.'

Fey pushed past Jane in the doorway and ran out into the yard clutching their phone. Jane watched them tap the phone screen three times and hold it to their ear. It was going to be all right, she told herself. Charlotte knew what to do. The ambulance would be here soon. Everything was going to be ok.

'Next time you push I'm going to hold baby's head and together we're going to see if we can get baby to do a little somersault to loosen the cord.' Charlotte was still talking in her calm but insistent tone.

For the first time Jane didn't hear her mother argue with Charlotte's intervention. Jane forced herself to turn and look. Her mother was still on the stairs, sitting up with her feet pulled up one step below her bum. Charlotte was kneeling between her legs. Jane concentrated on her mum's face. She was quiet and still for a moment but Jane could see that underneath the sweat and the defiance she was afraid.

Then her mum screamed.

'Ok. One more push,' shouted Charlotte. 'Push!'

Another scream. And then quiet. And then finally, all reedy and thin, the sound of a baby's cry.

–

Emma closed the poker app and opened her mammoth spreadsheet. The next event was a formal dinner and that meant she needed a seating plan. Emma was a devotee of a largely paperless office, but some things were best done the old-fashioned way. Twenty minutes later, her clients' names, neatly printed onto individual slips of paper, were spread across the dining table. There were still plenty of people who hadn't yet formed a firm attachment, and the sit-down dinner was Emma's best opportunity to put a hand on the scales and weight things in true love's favour.

She was toiling over her matchmaking jigsaw when she heard the doorbell ring. She let Josh, who'd just returned from the gym, get it, and heard him tell whoever was arriving that he just needed to jump in the shower.

'What are you doing?'

Emma jumped in her seat as she turned towards the voice. 'Annie?'

'Sorry.' Annie was standing in the doorway. 'Josh asked me to help with the scandal sheet, but I'm a bit early. I should have waited outside. I'm sorry. I can come back later, or not. I don't mind. I don't want to get in the way.'

'It's fine. I just didn't realise you were here.' Emma gestured towards her matchmaking jigsaw. 'I'm working out the seating plan for next week. Trying to sort out who goes next to who.' She picked up two names. 'Like you'll be with Colin, obviously.'

Another thought struck Emma on that topic. 'Will you be putting yourself in the scandal sheet?' News of matches made was just what was needed to get people thinking that it was time to stop treating the Season as a series of fun nights out and start getting serious about homing in on a long-term prospect.

'Oh. Maybe. I don't think anyone's interested in me.'

'We all love a love story though,' Emma insisted.

Annie was quiet. Maybe not a love story quite yet then? Emma filed that alongside her previous uncertainty about the match but didn't say anything out loud. Sowing doubt amongst people who'd already paired off wasn't part of her plan.

'Anyway, I'd better get on with this. Make yourself at home. I should warn you that Josh takes forever in the shower.'

Annie pulled out a dining chair and sat down. 'Can I help?'

Emma's jaw twitched slightly. She didn't need help, but Josh apparently did need help with the scandal sheet, so she could hardly send Annie away. 'Of course you can.'

'Who's on which pile?'

Emma had already started dividing her slips of paper into two piles. 'So these ones are people who are already either definitely coupled up, or heading in that direction.' She spread the second pile across the table. 'And these are the still singles. The challenge is to work out who to put them with so they'll have the best possible chance of hitting it off with someone.'

Annie leaned over. 'She's not still single,' she said, picking up a slip of paper. 'She was holding hands with…' She scanned for a second slip. 'With him at the end of the casino night.'

Emma looked at the two slips. She was a university administrator. Twenty-seven. Single for the last eighteen months. Organised, calm, little bit shy. He was more outgoing. Worked as a counsellor though, so good at listening presumably and emotionally intelligent enough to be able to resist dominating the conversation. How had she missed that potential match? 'Good spot.' She moved them to the couples pile and picked up another slip. 'Ok then. What about him?'

Annie frowned. 'I don't know if I've met him.'

'Tall Asian guy, longish black hair.'

'The fireman?'

'Former firefighter,' Emma corrected.

Annie nodded. 'Oh, he's lovely. How is he still single?'

Emma thought about it. 'I think people want to take care of him. Did he tell you why he left the fire brigade?'

Annie shook her head.

'He got injured. He has scarring all up his arm and one hand is partly paralysed now. I think women try to look after him and that's not what he wants. Or needs.'

'He's straight?'

Emma nodded.

'Ok.' Annie scanned the names still spread out across the table. 'What about her?'

Emma read the name on the slip. The woman was a student at the moment but she'd gone back to university after leaving the Navy and she still had something of that military no-nonsense approach to her. She'd be more likely to compare war wounds than to try to mother him and the fact that they were both starting second phases in their lives was a nice bit of serendipity. Emma paper clipped the two slips together. 'You've got an instinct for this.'

'Hardly.'

Emma didn't let her reject the compliment. 'Seriously, if you're ever thinking of a change of career, let me know.' Not that Emma could afford to take on an assistant. She wasn't technically paying either herself or Josh a salary at the moment, so hiring another person was a long way out of the question.

Annie blushed slightly. 'Oh, well. Thank you.'

'You're welcome.' Emma turned back to the table. 'Now, who else do you think would go well together?'

–

Jane was reduced to a spectator, as her newest sibling was wrapped in a towel – I brought those, she wanted to yell – and placed in mum's arms. Big Sam was dispatched to tell Jane's dad that he was a father again. Little Sam took Fey into the kitchen and set about laundering the piles of towels and sheets Charlotte had spread across the stairs and making cups of herbal tea for everyone involved. And then the sound of sirens arriving drew Charlotte into the yard to update the paramedics on a safe delivery.

And Jane and her mother were alone. 'Do you want to hold them?'

Jane shook her head. She liked babies when they were cleaned up and sleeping peacefully. This baby still had vagina gunk on its little purple head and, Jane's stomach turned over at this thought, it was still connected to her mum's insides. Charlotte had agreed that there was no need to cut the cord yet. Jane wasn't sure about that. She'd seen births on telly. Everything got cleaned up and covered up much more briskly than this.

'So who was that anyway? Didn't get so much as an introduction before she had her head in my vulva.'

'My friend. Charlotte. She's a midwife.'

Her mum stroked her newest child's cheek. 'And she's just a friend?'

Jane nodded. 'What else would she be?'

'I just wondered. To drive all that way to help out with something like this. She must be a good friend.'

'I only met her last week.'

Her mother smiled. 'Some friend then?'

They fell silent for a second.

'I know you pride yourself on not being like us...' her mother started.

'It's not that.'

'It is. And it's ok, but you do know that all we've ever wanted is for you to find your own way, don't you? A way that's right for you?'

'Even if that's not the same as your way?'

Her mum patted Jane's arm. Jane did her absolute best not to wince at the stickiness of her touch. 'It's your life. You've got to live it as yourself.'

Charlotte came back in with the paramedic. 'I know you don't want to go to hospital, Storm, so is it ok if Jenny here checks over baby and then we call out the community midwife? She'll be able to deliver the placenta and make sure everything's ok.'

'Ah, the placenta'll be fine. It'll come away when it's ready and then we'll bury it and plant a new tree in the front field.'

Jane winced. There were currently four trees in the small copse at the foot of the front field. As the eldest, her own afterbirth had missed out on that honour on account of her being born before her parents went crazy and moved off the grid. 'Mum, you should see the midwife. I mean at your age...'

'I'm perfectly healthy,' her mother snapped.

Charlotte tilted her head. 'Humour us, Storm. Let the midwife come and then Jane and Fey can stop fretting and we can all piss off and leave you alone.'

Eventually Jane's mother nodded. 'If she comes she won't try to make me go into hospital?'

Charlotte shook her head. 'Not unless it's absolutely necessary and there's nothing to make me think it will be.'

'All right then.' She glared at Jane. 'But only to stop this one going on at me.'

The community midwife was a brisk but kind woman with a bosom that entered the room a good fifteen seconds before she did. Fortunately, Jane's dad had returned so Jane was all too happy to be shooed out of the way while the midwife cut the cord, checked the baby over and delivered the placenta.

Fey wandered over to the Sams' place, leaving Jane and Charlotte standing awkwardly in the yard.

'Sorry,' seemed like all Jane could offer.

'What for?'

'All this. Not the date you were planning.' Jane hesitated. 'I mean afternoon. Drink. Not date date. I didn't mean.'

'Right.' Charlotte stared down at the floor.

'Anyway, I'm sorry. That we ended up here. And thank you. Thank you for everything. You were amazing.'

Charlotte smiled. 'Just doing my job. I guess that was unofficially my first delivery as a fully qualified midwife.'

'Really? You got your last two?'

'Yeah.'

'Congratulations!' Jane moved to hug her and managed to trap Charlotte's arm between them, and of course Charlotte was so tall she could barely reach up. She gave her an awkward pat on the shoulder and stepped back sharply.

The silence between them was horrible. Charlotte broke it. 'I'll go check how things are going, I think.'

Jane let her go and so found herself alone in the yard. Of course she wasn't alone. The life of the commune was continuing around her. The pigs were snuffling in their pen at the side of the buildings and there were voices in the front field behind the old farmhouse.

'Did Storm have her baby?'

The girl running towards her had long straggly braids pulled back into a band at the nape of her neck and henna marks across her hand and up her arm. Jane nodded.

'That's amazing. Blessings on them both.' The stranger smiled. 'Are you thinking of joining the community?'

Jane shook her head. 'Been there, bought the T-shirt.'

The girl frowned. 'What do you mean?'

'I grew up here. Long time ago.'

'That must have been amazing.' The girl smiled brightly. 'I can't imagine ever leaving here. I've never felt freer than since I arrived.'

Jane nodded politely. She didn't associate this place with feeling free. She associated it with feeling trapped in a life she hadn't chosen. She'd been in constant search of an escape to normality.

Her dad appeared in the doorway to the farmhouse. 'All cleaned up now if you want to meet your newest brethren properly.'

'Excuse me.' Jane made her way back into the house.

Her mother was ensconced on the old tatty settee in the main room now, with a hand crocheted blanket across her legs and her new baby clutched to her breast. Her still bare breast. Jane didn't know where to look.

Her mother glanced up and laughed. 'Don't be such a prude. Skin on skin contact is good for the baby isn't it?' She looked to the community midwife for confirmation, apparently happy to have a professional in attendance if she was going to back up her argument. 'Your dad's getting some bread and soup for everyone. You'll eat with us, won't you?'

The midwife made her excuses and left with promises to visit again in due course. Jane made to follow her, readying her explanation that they needed to drive back to London before it got too late.

'Your friend's already through in the kitchen. I think she must have been famished.'

Clearly her mother was correct. Charlotte was sat at the kitchen table, chatting happily to Jane's dad and to Little Sam, gulping down soup and cooing over the delights of the homemade bread.

'So we don't believe in gender roles or constraints,' her dad was explaining. 'All the kids can find their own identity when they feel ready. And we let them choose between getting the bus to traditional school or being schooled in the community here.'

Charlotte was nodding approvingly.

'And generally, we try to be as self-sufficient as possible, so everything gets re-used. Most of us are vegetarian but for those who aren't we insist on using every last part of the animal. We have goats for milk, a few sheep, pigs, and they'll eat any scraps you can't persuade a human to try. And we have chickens. Fey is setting up new bee hives at the moment...'

'It sounds incredible.'

This was all wrong. Charlotte belonged in Jane's London compartment. She was part of the Season. She was part of the nice, safe, polite world that Jane had built for herself. They'd been forced to come here by circumstances, and that was one thing, but someone like Charlotte wasn't supposed to fit in here. Jane never had.

Jane marched back into the front room. 'We can't stay long,' she told her mother.

'That's up to you, darling. You'll hold the little one before you go though, won't you?'

The baby was all clean and fresh looking now, so Jane conceded, and perched herself on the arm of the sofa next to her mum, and let her pass the baby into Jane's arms. 'There,' said her mum. 'This one looks just like you did when you were little. All the others took more after your father, but you and Lunar here look more like me.'

'You're sticking with Lunar?' Jane turned to look at her mum. She could feel the weight of the baby in her arms but something was stopping her from turning her full gaze to the little one.

'I think so. I know they came in the daytime and it's not new moon 'til next week but I'm sort of fixed on it now.' She patted Jane's arm. 'I'm going to go and have a wash while you're getting to know this one.'

Once they were alone Jane slid tentatively onto the seat of the chair next to the sofa and forced herself to look at the sleeping babe in her arms. 'Hello, Lu,' she murmured. 'Welcome to the madhouse. I'm your big sister.' Then she stopped. 'You might not see me that often but you'll see Fey and they've got my number so if you need anything from the outside world you tell Fey to let me know.'

She fell silent. There was nothing she could say to protect this tiny little person from the world. There was no way to know whether they'd thrive or shrivel in the bubble their parents had created. There was no way of knowing whether they'd be clever or funny or beautiful or kind. Or mean, come to think of it. How could anyone be expected to shepherd a tiny life like this to adulthood without getting everything terribly wrong? Her parents had got it terribly wrong. Surely, Jane running away proved that. If she ever had a child of her own she would do everything differently. They'd have the stability and order she'd craved.

The baby wriggled and mewed in her arms. Jane sat stock still, desperate not to wake the sleeping babe. She couldn't do this. She couldn't be here. She couldn't play happy families and cuddle this baby and still be Miss Woods who taught History and was going out with the overwhelmingly capable midwife. It was too much. It wouldn't all fit together.

'Aren't they gorgeous?' Fey bounced into the room. 'Flora is making pasta for everyone, like literally everyone, for this evening, and we're going to have a whole community meal to celebrate. You'll stay, won't you?'

'Take the baby.'

'What?'

Jane thrust the precious bundle towards Fey. 'Just take it.'

'Are you ok?'

She passed Lunar to Fey and ran through the hallway and out into the yard.

She heard the footsteps behind her but she didn't slow down. Jane kept running, across the yard, past Big Sam, ignoring his greeting, past the Porsche, up to the gate. She fumbled with the stupid piece of rope that held the gate closed.

'Jane! Jane!'

She didn't turn around.

'Jane! Where are you going?'

It was Charlotte. 'I need to get out of here.'

'Ok. Well, we'll head back soon.'

'Right now.'

Charlotte took a step back. 'I haven't finished my lunch.'

'I don't care.'

'Well, I do. Your family have offered us food and I'm partway through mine and it would be rude to leave now.'

Jane heard herself laugh. 'You don't want to be rude? You drove for two hours to deliver her baby cos she's too stubborn to go to a hospital like a normal person. And they'll keep feeding you soup until you're ready to burst and you know what? You'll never finish the soup. There aren't enough people in the world to ever finish that bottomless cauldron of slop.'

Charlotte folded her arms but didn't reply.

Jane hadn't finished. 'And it won't stop this place being completely insane. I ran away once. I can run away again.'

Charlotte sighed. 'I'm not leaving in the middle of a meal.'

'Fine.'

'Fine.'

They stood opposite one another for a moment in silence. Jane broke first. 'Sorry.'

'What for?'

'You've been amazing and I'm yelling at you.'

'It's ok.' Charlotte stepped towards her.

How could she explain her behaviour? 'I don't have the easiest relationship with my parents.'

'I got that. I'm sorry if I waded into the middle of something without thinking.'

'No.' Jane wasn't having that. 'You've done nothing but help.'

'With the baby, sure. But after that, I didn't think about how weird it all must have been for you.'

'So we're still friends?' Jane asked hopefully.

Was there a tiny hesitation? 'Friends? If that's what you want.' Charlotte took another step closer.

Jane shook her head. Friends wasn't what she wanted. She also hadn't wanted their very first kiss to be in a rundown farmyard, but she could close her eyes and imagine they were at her flat or in a nice normal bar somewhere in town. She leaned forward and pressed her lips to Charlotte's, and, just as she hoped, everything around them fell away. There was her and Charlotte and that was all that mattered. Simple.

Chapter Thirteen

Miss Emma Love
requests the honour of your company
for an evening of fine dining and intimate
conversation.

They were back at the Guild of Underwriters. That didn't
sound right. Company of Underwirers? Whatever. Emma liked
coming back to venues she'd used before. Much less margin for
error when she'd already made sure everything worked to her
liking once.

And, in this case, it meant she got to catch up with Harriet
and get all the details on another budding romance. In the event
she didn't even have to ask.

Harriet ran into her, almost the second Emma was through
the door of the function room, emitting what could only be
described as a squeal. An actual squeal coming out of an adult
human woman. 'He's perfect. He's met my parents already, and
my mother adores him, and even my dad – my dad has never
liked anyone I've been out with – my dad said he seemed like
a decent chap, which is basically the highest praise he can give.'

Emma took Harriet's hands. 'And what about you? Are you
happy?'

Harriet nodded. 'So happy. Thank you. Oh, and speak of
the devil!'

Robbie Martin strode into the function room. 'Sorry, Miss
Love. I'm guessing I'm not supposed to see behind the curtain
while you're still setting up.'

Emma smiled. 'I think we can make an exception.'

He entwined his fingers with Harriet's. 'I did want to thank you. Harri told me you had a hand in persuading her to make a move.'

'All part of the service.' With that in mind, she knew she had a couple of members not attending tonight, and the meals were already paid for… if she moved that person so they were nearer to… and then she could put him there… and that would leave an empty space at Robbie Martin's table. 'If you'd like to come along tonight, Harriet, I can make space.'

'Well, I'm supposed to be keeping an eye on things.'

Perfect. 'You can keep an eye on things while you have dinner.'

So what if Harriet wasn't a client? Mr Martin was, so that was a big tick in her spreadsheet – another perfect pair matched up successfully.

'Ok, but I'll knock my meal off the invoice. I am supposed to be working.'

Even better.

Robbie Martin was looking thoughtful. 'I haven't seen much publicity about all this, apart from the initial flyer and newspaper piece.'

Emma tensed slightly. 'Well, I've been quite busy actually making all this happen.'

'Not criticising. Just wondering who does your PR?'

'Well, me.' Obviously. Other people didn't do things the way Emma wanted.

He pulled a business card from his pocket. 'Well, if you want any advice or if there's anything I can do to help, more than happy.' He squeezed Harriet's hand. 'I owe you. Anyway,' he turned to Harriet. 'I will see you both tonight?'

They said their goodbyes. Another very happy couple that Emma could tick off, but there were still so many to go. No time to rest on her laurels. 'So, anyway, is everything looking good for this evening?' she asked.

Harriet pulled her attention back from gazing at the space Robbie Martin had just vacated. 'Everything's on schedule. We need to put the place cards out.'

'Good.' Everything did look to be in hand. 'You got the seating plan?'

Harriet walked her over to the beautifully elegant list of tables and placings. 'How long did you spend on this?'

Emma demurred. One never showed one's working, but, even with Annie's unexpectedly insightful assistance, the seating plan had been many hours of labour. She'd encapsulated everything she'd observed from the previous four events. She'd ensured that the couples-in-waiting who needed a final push were seated together. She'd placed those who really needed to admit to themselves that the object of their affections was not interested at all as far away as possible from the person they were hung up on, surrounded by better and more suitable options. And, of course, she'd flung a few people together who she didn't think had met one another yet, but who she absolutely believed would be perfect together, once the ice had been broken.

She scanned the list and quickly indicated the changes that needed to be made to accommodate Harriet's attendance. Everyone else was already perfectly placed. Almost everyone else. There was, unfortunately, one square peg for whom she simply couldn't find a matching hole. Mr Tom Knight. She'd put him with Annie and her friends, which was a bit of a cop out, because Annie was with Colin, and Jane and Charlotte were taken. Which just left Lydia Hyland. Could she see him with Lydia?

The problem was that she couldn't see him with anyone. Every potential match she tried to imagine jarred. He needed someone who wouldn't indulge his sour moods, but someone who could have a laugh as well. She told herself that Lydia might be that person if she could resist the urge to sneak off for a fumble with the bartender when she thought nobody was paying attention.

It was possible that Lydia and Mr Knight were beyond even Emma's help, but she was so close to completing the perfect Season at the first attempt. It was not impossible that at the end of the final ball every single person who had signed up would have someone on their arm. Emma's mother had always told her that no matchmaker was perfect. Even the best failed occasionally. Emma almost dared to imagine proving her wrong.

–

Lydia looked at the pile of clothes on her bed. She had high-street dresses. She had online haul finds. She had kooky charity shop vintage gems. She had bodycon. She had floaty chiffon. She had long dresses. She had short dresses. She had 3 a.m. purchases from random websites that shipped from China. And none of them were quite right. She pulled off the long black body-hugging dress she was wearing and tossed it on the bed. Jane would be here soon.

Jane would pick something random from the pile and tell Lydia she looked fine. But it wouldn't be right. Nothing ever was. She dragged a pink, fifties style dress out of her wardrobe and tried that instead. In front of her mirror, she tried to be objective. The colour didn't make her look stupidly pale. The floaty, flippy skirt hid her cyclist's thighs. It was a halter. The overall effect put her in mind of a pink version of that white Marilyn Monroe dress from *Some Like It Hot*. Only without Marilyn's face or figure or perfect blonde hair. Maybe she could take that as an inspiration though. She could scrape her hair back into some sort of bouffanty thing and go for a matt foundation, black winged eyeliner, lashings of mascara and a bright red lip. Maybe she'd look sexy and retro and classic.

Although obviously her hair wouldn't do that. Her hair would frizz and send curls sticking out in whatever direction they wanted to go. She pulled it into a high bun and decided that was as good as it was going to get. But then that didn't work with the outfit, did it?

Maybe if she went back to the black dress?

The buzzer rang. That was ok. She still had time to get changed one more time before Jane got pissed off and started buzzing Lydia's neighbours to let her in. Another buzz. Or maybe she didn't. She ran over and pressed the button to open the main door downstairs.

Fine. She'd have to stick with this dress and hope she could do her make-up well enough to look all right. She clicked her door open so Jane could come straight in and sat down on the floor in front of the full-length mirror. Her hand was shaking as she started trying to do her eyeliner. She took a deep breath and looked at the face in the mirror. You are good enough, she told herself. You are enough.

The mantra was all very well, but the woman in the mirror didn't look as though she was entirely buying it. Why had she signed up for this whole Season thing anyway? It was the sort of thing fun, up-for-anything Lydia did, but she knew she didn't belong at fancy events with fancy people. You could take the girl out of the hell she grew up in, but…

'So how many times are you gonna get changed before you're ready?'

Jane was in a simple long rust-coloured jersey dress that skimmed the tops of her feet and had a deep plunge into her cleavage. 'You look really elegant,' Lydia said.

'Thank you. How about you? Come on. Stand up. Let me see.'

Lydia did as she was told. 'I look a mess.'

'You look phenomenal.'

Lydia turned back to the mirror. 'I look a mess.' She picked up a red mini dress from the mound of clothes on the bed. 'Do you think this would be better?'

Jane rolled her eyes. 'You would also look phenomenal in that. Come on though. No time to get changed. This is beautiful, and…' She checked her phone. 'Our Uber is three minutes away and I've got a five-star rating to protect.'

'Ok. Ok. Mascara, lipstick and then we can go.' Lydia painted her lips red and her lashes darkest black. It wasn't great. It was never going to be great, but she would have to do.

–

It was the same venue they'd come to for the ball. The Guild of Smotherers, or the Assembly of Free Wardrobe Wranglers, or some such, Lydia thought. One of those things that sounded fancy and a bit medieval. The Liveried Company of Alchemists. That kind of jazz. Tonight the room was set up for a banquet with circular tables for six or eight. There was a string quartet playing in one corner and flower arrangements at the centre of each table. It was, she guessed, supposed to create an atmosphere of relaxed sophistication. It was making Lydia feel anything but relaxed. So long as there wasn't a seating plan, she told herself it would be fine. She could find the table nearest the exit and skive off at the earliest opportunity for a stiff vodka to calm her nerves.

Annie bowled into them in the doorway. 'We're all sitting together,' she trilled. 'Charlotte's already here. She's with us too.' She stared at Jane. 'She's very very pretty, isn't she? And tall.'

Jane nodded. 'Yes. Pretty and tall, amongst many, many other qualities.'

'Where's the bar?' Lydia could feel the clamminess starting in her hands. 'One of you could get me a drink.' An additional challenge for the evening – how to keep enough alcohol flowing to take the edge of the panic rising in her gut without having to talk to Hot Barman.

'No bar tonight. All waiter service. It's super fancy.' Annie seemed to have taken on the role of chief cheerleader for the whole endeavour. 'Come on. I'll show you where we're sitting. Colin's with us as well. So that's lovely.'

She led the way to a table right at the very centre of the room, the very furthest Lydia could possibly be from the exit, the toilets, or even the fire escape. She was seated with her back to the main entrance. She could ask to swap, but she could see that Annie and Colin were opposite her and she supposed they'd want to sit together. She could cope. It was one evening. The table was laid for six. Herself, Annie, Colin, Charlotte and Jane. Charlotte was between Jane and Lydia and on the other side of Lydia who? She peered at the name card laid at the top of the place setting. Mr Thomas Knight.

Well, Mr Thomas Knight, she thought, I hope you're hot and I hope you're not looking for anything serious at all.

–

Mr Thomas Knight, pleasingly, was hot. Tousled dark brown hair, dark eyes, tall, slim, wearing a tuxedo in the style of a someone who was imagining it was a leather jacket. He was very much the sort of welcome distraction that Lydia would go for. Maybe the evening wouldn't be a write-off after all. She could be sexy Lydia. She could flirt outrageously and then bundle him out the door.

She caught him glancing at her name plate as he sat down. 'Miss Hyland?'

'Lydia.'

'Hello Lydia.' He grinned. She grinned back. Game on.

She'd established that he didn't follow football but did have surprisingly strong views on the last season of *Game of Thrones*, and was about to absolutely floor him with a strangely racy Night's King joke when an arm slid over her left shoulder.

'Your fig and goat's cheese tartlet, Madam.'

The voice was ice. Cool, precise, clipped. It wasn't the tone she was used to hearing in that voice. She turned in her seat. So bartenders could also wait tables. She supposed that made sense.

'I trust that's to your liking. Chef's vegetarian cooking is very highly thought of.'

She met his eye. She refused to be bowed. She wasn't doing anything wrong. 'I'm sure it will be delicious.'

'Excellent. Do let me know if there's anything else.' He moved away.

Tom's plate looked quite different to hers. A carnivore then. 'What's yours?'

'I think it's duck.' He placed his fork on the edge of his plate and picked up the menu card from the centre of the table. 'It's a duck and orange filo parcel.'

'Fancy.'

'Not your style then?'

Lydia shrugged.

'Tell me then, what would your perfect dinner be?'

'Chip butty. Loads of vinegar on the chips. Can of Dr Pepper.' It was true. It was the taste of home, in the best possible way, in that it wasn't actually the taste of home. It was the taste of a couple of half-remembered moments when things were calm and they were out on the front to see the illuminations, behaving like a normal family. It was the taste of the childhood she should have had.

'Classy.'

Something in Lydia's shoulders tensed ever so slightly.

'I haven't had Dr Pepper for years though,' he continued. 'Can you even still get it?'

'You can.' She turned her whole body towards him. She could suggest taking a walk and hunting down a can. It would get her out of here and she knew how to behave with a guy she'd just met on their own at the end of a night. That was easy.

–

'Excuse me.' Tom pushed his chair back and stood. There was a sudden rash of sweat around his collar and a feeling as if the room was shifting around him. He all but ran to the hallway and then down the stairs, two at a time, and out onto the street. He gulped the muggy London evening air into his lungs.

For a moment his life – no, not his life, his future – had flashed in front of his eyes. Drunk Lydia was flirting and, just for a moment, he'd been flirting back, and at some point she was going to suggest getting out of there and, if he kept flirting, then he'd probably agree and they'd end up back at her place, or his place, or wherever and then he'd be having sex with someone, and then what?

He'd be moving on.

–

Lydia pushed her tartlet around the plate. He'd be back, she assumed.

'Lydia's the absolute queen when it comes to discipline.'

The sound of her name pulled her back into the conversation. Annie was seated on the other side of Tom's now empty chair, and then Colin and Jane brought you all the way around to Charlotte right next to Lydia.

Charlotte raised an eyebrow. 'Discipline? Really?'

'In the school sense, not the naughty sense,' Jane clarified.

'Well, never say never,' Lydia deadpanned. Charlotte was obviously off limits. Lydia wouldn't go near someone else's partner. It was a hard and fast rule. Well, maybe not hard and fast. A wife at home was a sure-fire way of ensuring blokes didn't overstay their welcome. But a friend's lover was definitely off limits. She rifled back through the mental Rolodex of one-night stands. No friend's partners. No friend's exes. One guy a friend was interested in, but he was a dick and the friend was better off knowing that. Lydia's moral codes involved a lot of shades of grey but there were some lines even she wouldn't cross. And knowing that made Charlotte safe. She could flirt without risk.

Only she couldn't flirt that much. It was abundantly clear the couple only had eyes for one another. Lydia was a total third wheel.

Tom finally returned from the bathroom, or wherever it was he'd disappeared off to. Thank goodness. Lydia filled her glass and put on her best smile. The second course was risotto for the vegetarians and beef wellington for everyone else. Lydia leaned towards Tom's plate and wondered aloud at how snug the beef was all wrapped up in the flaky pastry. She thought there was some sort of snuggling up metaphor in there but she couldn't quite get to it. He nodded politely. She went to fill his glass, but found it blocked with his hand. 'Early start,' he explained.

That was fine. That was good. It would mean he wouldn't hang around too long in the morning. 'Well, you don't mind if I do?' she smiled, filling her own glass.

But then the bottle was empty. She held it up. They needed more wine. Jane leaned across the table. 'Don't wave the bottle around.'

Lydia dropped her arm like it had been slapped. Of course don't wave the bottle around. She was getting everything wrong.

A white cotton-clad arm appeared over her shoulder and lifted the empty bottle away, replacing it with a full one. She didn't need to look behind her. She recognised the scent of him. Oh for goodness' sake, she did not go around learning how people smelled. That was not who she was.

She turned her attention back to Tom. 'Hoping we might get something special for dessert?' she simpered.

'Chocolate delice with summer berries,' he read off the menu card.

'But for afters.' Lydia dipped her finger in her wine glass and sucked the liquid from the end.

'Actually, I do have an early start tomorrow. And the main course was very rich. I'm not sure I need anything else.' He stood and nodded at the group as a whole. 'Enjoy the rest of the evening.'

Lydia had crashed and burned before. She was sure she had. Well, crashed at least but never quite burned because it was usually more of a 'You'll do' situation, rather than a sitting next to someone for an hour and then getting blown off position. She poured another glass of wine.

Chapter Fourteen

'You're leaving us early, Mr Knight.' Emma caught up with him on the stairwell. She knew he was likely to make a dash for it at some point, so she'd been keeping an eye out. It was time for some tough love for Mr Knight. 'You know if you don't commit and put the time in you're not very likely to find The One.'

He turned back to face her. 'Well thank you for your concern, Miss Love, but I think I'm about as likely to find The One in there as I am to win the lottery tomorrow.'

'Well, you might win the lottery,' she snapped back. She didn't believe herself. The chances of winning a meaningful amount on the lottery were vanishingly small.

'I doubt it. I don't buy a ticket any more.'

He set off again.

Emma carried on after him. 'But you did buy a membership for the Season, so there must have been some reason, some hope there.'

'You think I chose to buy a membership for this?'

'Well, I know you did.'

'I'm doing this because I promised someone I would. So I turn up and make chit-chat and then I go home. All of this is ridiculous.' He was balling his hand into a fist at his side. 'You can't guide people to fall for the right person. We love who we love.'

Emma stopped in her tracks. 'Well of course we all want that spark.'

'I'll tell you about falling in love,' he continued. 'It's messy and it's inconvenient and it's brilliant. And you're lucky if you get one real shot at it in your life.'

'In my experience...' Emma started.

'What experience?' He stepped back up so he was one step below her, his face now level with hers. 'I've never heard mention of a Mr Love.'

Emma sighed. 'So you can't be a cardiologist if you've never had a heart attack? I help my clients to find the perfect partner for them. I help them learn not to settle for second best, so what sort of message would I be sending if I didn't wait for true love for myself?'

It was a well-rehearsed answer and it was true. She was waiting for that perfect person, the one where she would know absolutely and without question that he was the one for her.

'True love?'

'You have a problem with that?'

He was quieter now. 'I...' He swallowed back the crack that had crept into his tone. 'No.'

'So why so sceptical?'

For a second she thought he was going to walk away without a reply, but he turned back. His voice was lower. 'Because love isn't all this crap, is it? Love hurts. Love makes you think it's forever and then...' His voice faltered.

'Love makes people happy.'

'You know nothing about love, Miss Love.'

'So you're resigned to being alone?'

He shook his head. 'I find being alone more tolerable than the alternative right now.' He stepped back and down the stair. 'Goodnight, Miss Love. You've got a room full of people who want to find The One. Don't waste your time on me.'

–

The dessert and coffee section of the evening was a blur. Lydia thought she'd been poured a coffee, against her will, but she hadn't drunk it. She had had more wine. She'd crashed and burned with the bloke with the stick up his arse, but she could still be fun, kooky night-out Lydia. People liked her. She was a bit outrageous, said things other people wouldn't dare say.

Sometime during coffee Josh came and said 'hi', and then left to check on things with Emma. *Ooooh, the boss calls* Lydia had shouted. And then she'd made a sort of whip-crack noise and action. Was funny, wasn't it? Cos his sister was his boss.

Then Annie came and sat next to her and talked to her in a very quiet voice which was nice and calm for a while but ultimately boring. 'Can we go on somewhere?'

Annie hesitated. 'I'm supposed to be here with Colin.'

So boring. Lydia turned to Charlotte and Jane. 'You'll come out with me, won't you? Somewhere with a bit of life.' She had an actual bona fide brainwave. 'Somewhere with dancing!'

Charlotte put a perfect hand on Lydia's shoulder. 'I think you might be best off heading to your bed.'

Lydia raised an eyebrow. 'Is that an offer? Cos your girlfriend is like, right there.'

Jane jumped in. 'I think she meant alone, Lyds. Come on. I think you've had enough tonight.'

Jane was looking at her the way her and Annie always ended up looking at Lydia at the end of a night out. They were good friends though. She was lucky to have them. 'You're my best friend,' Lydia announced. Then she grabbed Annie by the arm. 'You're my best friend too.'

'I know, honey. Come on. Let's find you a cab.'

Lydia shook her head. 'Get tube. No money for cab.'

Annie put her arm around Lydia. 'I'll lend you it.'

She was tired. Maybe going home was the best idea. She wrapped her arms around her best friends' shoulders, one on either side of her, and they hopped and skipped – with just one tiny little fall – down the stairs. She jumped in the taxi, clutching the forty quid Annie had pressed into her hand.

'You'll be ok?'

Lydia nodded. She'd be great. She was going to go home and go to bed. Everything would be better in the morning. Ten minutes into the journey she decided she was far too wide awake to go home. She didn't need her friends to go out. She had cash now. She leaned forward. 'Can you take me back into town, mate?'

–

Annie followed Jane back up to the grand dining room. 'Do you think she'll be all right?'

'Yeah.' Jane didn't sound as definite as she usually did. 'Once she's slept it off she'll be ok. I'll message her tomorrow.'

'Your evening seems to be going well.'

Jane beamed. 'Charlotte is incredible. It all feels so easy and at the same time... incredible.'

What were the chances she'd be Jane's bridesmaid twice before she was a bride herself, Annie wondered.

Josh had reappeared at their table and was chatting easily to Charlotte. He was one of the few men here who was taller than her, and his classic tall, dark and handsome looks as he leaned towards her gave them the look of a perfect couple on the cover of a romance novel.

Annie took her seat next to Colin. He reached across and took her hand. That was nice. 'So I was having a little think about after this whole thing is done. I thought we could pop off somewhere. Maybe a weekend, or maybe when you have half term. Nice hotel. Cotswolds maybe? Or down to the South Coast?'

'Whatever you think.' Josh was still chatting animatedly to Charlotte and Jane.

'No. I want to pick somewhere you'll enjoy. Where would you like to go?'

Annie really didn't mind.

'Or we don't have to go away. If you're not sure, just say.'

Josh was standing up and heading over to the next table. The host with the most. He stopped and turned back. 'Just wanted to say thanks, Annie, for all your help.' He grinned. 'I know Emma won't have said thanks, cos that would involve her acknowledging that somebody else helped, but thank you.'

'That's ok.'

'I'm trying to work out where to take this one for a weekend away,' Colin told him.

'Alton Towers,' Josh answered immediately.

'I didn't see you as an adrenaline junkie,' Colin laughed.

'She won't tell you she is, but I don't think I've ever seen anyone happier than Annie at the top of a rollercoaster.'

They'd never been to Alton Towers, but they'd done Thorpe Park twice, once as teenagers bundled into the back of Josh's dad's car and once when he was married to Jane, who, it turned out, was not a fan of rollercoasters at all, so had been stuck holding bags and coats while Annie and Josh went on everything. Annie didn't think about that day, but apparently Josh did.

He moved on to work his charm on other guests on other tables. 'So is that what you'd like to do?' asked Colin.

'I really don't mind.'

'You say that a lot.'

'What?'

'That you don't mind.' He turned in his seat to face her fully. 'What do you really want, Annie?'

What did that mean? She wanted all sorts of things at different times.

'I would like to keep getting to know you better and to spend an awful lot more time together and then, down the line a bit, I want to settle down, get married, have kids. That whole shooting match.'

She giggled slightly nervously. 'I thought we were just talking about a weekend away.'

'Well, I was,' he replied. 'But I want that to lead to something. To at least have the potential of leading to something.'

She nodded. 'If that's what you want.'

'Well, if that's what *we* want. I know it's early but do you think I might be someone you'd want to be with, you know, for the old long haul?'

And there it was. How was she supposed to know? How could you know that you would like someone now and still like them in a year's time or ten years' time or twenty? At the next table a guest laughed at something Josh was saying to them.

'Right. Well, I see then.' Colin pushed his chair back.

'What? I haven't answered.'

He nodded his head towards Josh. 'You didn't need to. Your face said it all.'

He thought she was... He actually imagined that she was carrying a torch for... 'I'm not. Josh and I are just friends.'

Colin stood up. 'And is that what you want to be? Friends?'

Finally she knew the answer. It was right there in front of her, just like it always had been. She shook her head.

He nodded. 'Understood. Message received. No harm done. Better to get these things out in the open and all. Maybe best to see how that works out before jumping in with the next chap though.'

–

Lydia's taxi pulled up right where it had picked her up. She thrust half her money at the taxi man and staggered back onto the pavement. Pavement. Paaaavement. It was a fun word. Lydia was sitting on the pavement. She giggled. Funny, funny pavement.

'What are you doing back here?'

She looked up at the voice. 'Hot Barman!' she yelled.

'Will.'

'Will I what?'

'My name is Will. Still. What are you doing sitting on the ground?'

Lydia wasn't sure. She should get up. She had a little think about how to do that. She went onto all fours and then one foot and then the other foot and then hands off the ground and…'I'm up!'

'Well done.'

No. Not well done. Standing up made the world all swirly and it made her stomach all clenchy. 'Gonna puke.'

'Right. Er…' He grabbed her hand and pulled her to the kerbside. 'Aim for the drain, I guess?'

No. The feeling had passed. 'Not going to puke,' she announced. 'So, what are you up to? Wanna come back to mine?'

He shook his head. 'I don't think you're in any fit state right now.'

'You saying I can't take my drink?'

'Well, fifteen seconds ago you were threatening to puke in a gutter.'

'But I didn't.'

'But you nearly did. Anyway I thought you had other interests tonight.'

Well, so what if she did? 'I don't have any other interests right now.'

'Weirdly, second choice after three bottles of wine isn't my idea of romance.'

'Who said anything about romance?' She closed the gap between them and leaned in to whisper in his ear. 'I don't need hearts and flowers. I just want to fuck you.'

And she meant it. Only… no… wait. 'I am gonna puke.' She managed to turn away from him at least, before the contents of her stomach spread themselves over the flagstones in front of her.

Oh God. She was pathetic. She wasn't fun wild Lydia. She wasn't impressing anyone. She was an imposter. She was faking fitting in and everybody knew it.

'Shit. Are you crying?'

Was she? All she could think about was the burn of bile in the back of her throat and the humiliation of how public her failure was. 'Probably. I should go home.'

'On your own?'

'What? You still fancy it?'

'I meant will you be ok on your own?'

She didn't have enough cash left for a taxi. She could get the tube though. That would be fine. She could not throw up on the tube. She'd not thrown up on the tube loads of times.

'Look. My place is nearer. Why don't you come back with me?'

She wasn't sure.

'Not for sex. You can have a shower and sleep it off and I'll sleep on the floor or something. And then maybe in the morning I'll make you some toast and walk you to the bus stop.'

She gave in. 'Thank you.'

'Come on then. Are you warm enough?'

She shook her head and let him take his jacket off and wrap it round her shoulders. This was her lowest moment. It wasn't that she'd crashed and burned in front of all her friends with some idiot she didn't even fancy. It wasn't that she'd had to scrounge cash off Annie to get home and then hadn't even gone home. It wasn't that she'd thrown up in the street in front of someone who, apparently, was trying to be kind to her. It was the kindness. It was the fact that she was letting someone, some man, look after her. This was the lowest she could possibly fall and she didn't even have the fight in her to resist.

—

'So...' Charlotte stopped at the entrance to the tube. 'I should...' She gestured towards the steps.

'I'm on the bus.'

'Yeah.'

The silence hung between them. Since The Kiss in her parents' yard, Charlotte had messaged or called every single day.

She'd hung off Jane's every word at dinner. Their fingers had brushed one another's arms, and hands, and thighs.

But Jane still wasn't sure. Nobody had said out loud what this was. Charlotte had implied more than friends before she'd kissed her but what precisely? Friends with benefits? In which case the whole thing had been low on 'benefits' beyond that one world-stopping kiss. Or something more than that?

'I was wondering…'

'We could…'

They both spoke and stopped.

'After you,' Charlotte demurred.

Great. Jane would have much preferred Charlotte to go first. How far out on this limb was she prepared to climb? 'We could maybe meet up sometime. You know, if you're not busy. Or not if you…' It was too long since she'd done this, and she'd never done any of this with anyone like Charlotte. She'd never felt like her heart might stop beating the second the person she was next to walked away. Nothing had ever felt so perfectly right or so utterly terrifying.

'Meet up? Sure.' Charlotte nodded.

'Ok. Great. What were you going to…?'

'I was going to ask if you wanted to come back to mine.'

Right. 'Like for coffee?'

Charlotte's perfectly painted red lips spread into a smile. 'Well, I was thinking for sex.'

'I've never… With a woman.' Did she need to tell her that? Charlotte already knew about Josh, so would she assume? Or would she be expecting Jane to have been out every night exploring her new sexual freedom?

'We don't have to. No pressure.' Charlotte stepped back. 'Entirely up to you. Your pace. Whatever you want.'

What Jane wanted was to gorge herself on Charlotte's closeness. She wanted to kiss, lick, touch, explore and be explored. 'Your place then,' she whispered.

'Sorry it's a shithole.' He unlocked the door to a terraced house on a street of identical terraced houses. 'It's a share, so I'm in here.' He led her into what would presumably have been a sitting room in some more palatial past when this had been a family home, but was now converted into a bedroom for one.

'It's a single bed.'

'Yeah. I'll sleep on the floor. You can have the bed.'

'I can do the floor.'

He shook his head. 'You're fine. I'd just lie awake all night feeling guilty. And it's not that good a bed, so you're not really winning.'

'Thank you.'

'Right. Well, bathroom's the first door at the top of the stairs. Can you manage to get upstairs ok?'

She nodded. The combination of throwing up and walking from the bus stop had sobered her up a notch.

In the bathroom, she found toothpaste to spread on her finger and did the best approximation of brushing her teeth she could manage. Then she gulped water straight from the tap into her mouth and tried to gargle away the vomit taste from her throat. Finally she faced up to looking in the mirror. Mascara was halfway down her cheeks, which was a blessing in some ways because the black patches hid some of the blotchiness.

She looked the woman in the mirror in the eye. Never again, she promised herself. Tomorrow she'd go home; she'd hide in her flat for twenty-four hours and then she'd do better in future. She'd drink less. She'd buy vegetables. She'd do yoga every morning and she wouldn't end up in front of some random bloke's bathroom mirror picking vomit chunks out of her hair ever again.

Back in the bedroom he handed her an oversized T-shirt. 'You can sleep in this if you want to get out of those clothes for a bit?'

'Thank you.'

'I'm gonna go brush my teeth and then I might sit up and read for a bit in the kitchen, so you can get changed. I've put a bowl by the bed, just in case. And a glass of water. Drink it.'

'Thank you,' she muttered again. She should try to say something else. 'I'm sorry.'

'Don't be. Everyone gets a bit fucked-up once in a while.'

'I seem to do it more often than most.'

He shrugged. 'No judgement here. Get some sleep. Everything always seems better in the morning.'

Chapter Fifteen

Things didn't seem entirely better in the morning. On the one hand, she'd managed to sleep and she hadn't thrown up again, so that was two big wins. On the other hand, her tongue seemed to be made of sandpaper, she was only wearing a T-shirt, she was in a random bed in a random house in who knew what part of London and the noises that were permeating through the building were reminding her that this wasn't just a random guy's house. It was a houseshare. At some point she was going to have to emerge from the cocoon of safety of this bedroom and engage with the rest of the household.

Lydia sat up in bed and closed her eyes as a wave of nausea rolled over her. Hot Barman was nowhere to be seen. Maybe she didn't have to engage with the rest of the household. She swung her legs off the bed. Her tights from last night were balled up on the floor. She didn't need them. She pulled the T-shirt she seemed to be wearing off and yanked her dress from last night back on. If only she had another pair of shoes with her. Skyscraper heels left little doubt that this was a walk of shame outfit.

Not that she had a lot of choice in the matter.

She picked up her shoes and tiptoed into the hallway.

It was a classic houseshare hallway – half blocked by someone's bike, with a ledge above the radiator where unwanted post seemed to gather to die. He'd been kind to her last night. Maybe sneaking out was too rude.

There was a slightly chewed biro next to the mail stack. She grabbed it and the top envelope and wrote.

Sorry to sneak out. Things to do. People to see. Thanks for last night.

Now where to leave it so that he'd see it? She looked around. The second envelope in the pile caught her attention. It had been redirected at least twice, the original address scribbled out, but the name was still visible.

Viscount March.

Lydia bit back a snigger. Hot Barman shared a house with a viscount? That didn't seem very likely.

Should she sneak back into his bedroom to leave the note? That was probably the best chance of him seeing it, but also more chance of getting caught. She didn't have time for this. She'd just leave it here on top of the pile. Surely, somebody would spot it sooner or later.

She was opening the front door when she heard the footsteps behind her.

'Not even saying goodbye?'

She stopped. 'I left a note. I've got stuff to do. So…' She picked up the envelope and waved it at him. 'See. Said goodbye. And thank you.'

Now she looked she saw that this one had been redirected too. *Viscount March* again. She pointed at it. 'You must have fancy housemates.'

He didn't quite meet her eye. 'Yeah. Well, you know, I take people as I find them.'

Weird reaction. Lydia didn't care. She just wanted out of there. 'I'll be off.'

'Sure you don't want a coffee?'

Of course she wanted a coffee, but there was coffee at her place and in coffee shops and all sorts of other places that didn't require her to spend time one to one with him. Needing rescuing one time did not mean they were involved.

She was halfway out of the door when the penny that had been dangling in the air since she'd picked up the envelope finally dropped. He'd been at that stupid posh school, hadn't he? To watch his sister play? Fury replaced the need to get the hell out of there.

'You're a fucking viscount?'

'What?'

She picked up the whole pile of envelopes and brandished them. 'This is you, isn't it? Viscount March.'

'Not exactly.'

'And what does that mean?'

'It means I'm not a proper viscount. It's a courtesy title.'

'Right. Well in that case I'm the Duchess of bloody Narnia.'

'No. I mean it's because my dad's an earl and so...' He sighed. 'It's not really me. I'm just Will.'

'Ok, just Will, what was I then? Social experiment? Shag a commoner week?'

He shook his head. 'I thought you were adamant this didn't mean anything anyway.'

'I was. I am.'

'Then why are you so angry?'

It was a fair question. She had no right to be pissed off with him. She hadn't asked if he happened to be a member of the landed gentry. She hadn't actually asked his name. But every nerve ending in her body was alert, feeling some unnamed danger, ready to fight or run away. 'I don't know.'

She'd had enough. He might have been kind to her last night, but maybe that was just another sightseeing trip into life with the normal people. She marched through the front door and down the pavement. Or at least onto the pavement, where the soles of her feet reminded her that she was in London and gravel was ouchy and the streets were lined with God knows what. He caught up with her while she was balancing awkwardly on one leg trying to put her shoes back on.

'Let me buy you breakfast.'

'I don't need charity, thank you very much, milord.'

'Ok. Let me sit opposite you while you buy yourself breakfast.' He pulled something out of his pocket and held it towards her. 'I was going to use this anyway.'

She frowned at the crumpled twenty pound note he was proffering.

'It's yours. You tried to give it to me last night as payment for lending you my jacket.'

She sort of vaguely remembered. She also remembered that she'd scrounged it off Annie earlier in the evening.

'So you can buy your own breakfast.'

'But you'll be there too.'

'I feel like I owe you an explanation of the whole viscount thing.'

'It's fine. Really. I get it. You're on some posh-boy gap year to see how the common people live.'

'It's not like that.'

She didn't care. 'Fine. I'm happy to eat a bacon sandwich while you tell me how your family aren't that posh really.'

'Oh God no,' he grinned. 'My family are incredibly posh.'

Sitting with an all-day breakfast sandwich in front of her – bacon, sausage, fried egg, on a white barm cake with lashings of brown sauce – her antipathy toward him was starting to ebb slightly, enough to acquiesce to his insistence on paying anyway.

'I thought you were vegetarian.'

'I mostly am. My hangovers aren't.' She'd been vegetarian since she was nineteen, when she'd moved into her second year uni shared house and found herself with one vegan, two vegetarians and one gluten-free pescatarian. Eating steak wasn't how you fitted in. 'So tell me about viscounting Viscount Viscountson.'

'Like I said, it's a courtesy title.'

'I don't know what that means,' she muttered.

'Well, I'm my father's eldest son, only son actually – he keeps trying for a spare but after me it's nothing but girls so far as the eye can see – so I'm entitled to use one of his lesser titles.'

'Lesser titles?' How many titles did one person get?

'My father is the Earl of Hanborough, but he's also Viscount March, and earl trumps viscount so he's the Earl and the viscountcy is sort of going spare.'

'For you to pick up.'

'Well, for people to use, whether I choose to or not.'

She stared at him. 'Why wouldn't you?' It was the ultimate safety net, wasn't it? A title meant you were someone and it couldn't be taken away from you. It meant you didn't have to scrape or fight or try to fit. It meant everything else had to fit around you.

'Because it's not who I am. It's not even who my father is. He inherited it from his dad, who inherited from his all the way back. None of them earned it until you get to some guy who was mates with Nelson or Wellington or William the Conqueror or whoever and got given a big bit of Oxfordshire to look after. I didn't ask for any of it.'

'But it's still yours.'

He cupped his mug of tea in his hands. 'Whether I want it or not.'

'What time is it?' Where was her watch? She probably hadn't worn it last night, had she? It was a big bulky thing with a heart-rate monitor and a stop watch and an interval timer. It didn't go with the elegant dressing for dinner vibe.

'Half nine.'

Shit. She pulled her phone out of her bag. He'd lied. It was 9.29 a.m. She exhaled. 9.30 a.m. Nothing. She stared at her phone. Still nothing.

'Are you ok?'

She couldn't reply. She realised she was holding her breath again. She stared at her phone. Still nothing.

'Seriously, what's wrong?'

Then it rang. Once. Twice. Three times. And then nothing. She exhaled. Her mum was safe, but she couldn't talk right now. That was ok. Well not ok. It was what it was. She stuffed her phone back into her clutch bag.

'Are you like, a spy or something?'

'What?'

'What was that? That was like some kind of code or something.' He leaned back. 'I mean it's fine if you are. I think my Great-Uncle Simon was a spy. I don't know. The family don't really talk about him.'

'I'm not a spy.'

'PE teacher would be an unusual cover story.'

The silence sat for a moment. Lydia wasn't going to break it.

'So the silent call thing?'

'My mum.' Why had she said that? She never talked about home. Not to Annie or Jane. Not to anyone. 'She rings me every Sunday.'

'And you don't talk to her?'

He had no right asking questions about her life. He had no clue. Poor little rich boy slumming it because he could, free to run back home whenever he felt like it. 'Sometimes she can't talk. If my dad's there she can't talk in case he gets one of his moods on about her talking to me and beats her up.'

She stuck her chin out, challenging him to dare to sympathise.

'So she rings and rings off and you know she's ok? That's clever.'

'Yeah. Well, it's the best I can do.'

'She won't leave?'

Lydia shook her head. She'd tried. She'd fought. As soon as she was big enough to make a stand she'd stood, but her mum always had an explanation. He was trying to change. He was better when he wasn't drinking. It had been hard since he lost his job. Things were always about to get better. They never quite did.

'What are you doing for the rest of the day?'

'Going home. On my own.'

He grabbed his chest like he'd been shot through the heart. 'Fine. If that's what you want. But I just thought, I'm not working today. And it's August so I'm guessing you're not working, so maybe we could be not working together. As friends. No strings.'

'I don't really do friends.'

'That's not true. I saw those two trying to make sure you got home ok.'

'Girlfriends are different.'

'Then think of me as a weird stubbly girl you've had sex with.'

'Ew.'

'I'll let you choose what we do.'

It was pure curiosity that made her agree. Not that she wanted to spend the day with him at all. It was just nosiness. 'I want you to show me where you grew up. Your like – what do they call it – family seat.'

He shook his head. 'It's miles away. I haven't got a car.'

'I have.'

'Seriously?'

She nodded. She wanted him to show her how the other half lived.

–

Emma's laptop was calling to her, but for some reason, her usual workaholic instincts were in retreat. She told herself she'd been working very hard and a day off was in order. She'd earned it. She wasn't just putting off the inevitable pain of going through the pile of invoices in her inbox.

Josh was standing in the hallway holding an envelope when she came downstairs. 'Did you see anyone delivering this?' he asked.

'No. What is it?'

'It'll be from Mum. My mum. But she must have delivered it herself.' Josh was still in somewhat irregular contact with his mum, despite her moving out of the family home when he was a toddler. He bought her a present and went to visit on Boxing Day and she called or emailed sporadically through the year.

Emma checked the date in her head. 'It's not your birthday.' Then she remembered. Trevor. He would have been sixty-five today. 'I'm sorry. I completely forgot.'

Josh ripped the envelope open. The card had a picture of flowers on the front. He turned it round so Emma could read the note.

Thinking of you today, love Caroline (mum).

'Brackets mum?'

Josh shrugged. 'She is who she is.'

'So are you doing anything to mark the date?'

'I don't know. Are you free? I was thinking about his last birthday.'

Josh's dad's last birthday had been just before he started chemo, after the cancer diagnosis. He'd been in good spirits, refusing to entertain any negativity, determined that the treatment would do its job. The whole family had gone to Richmond Park and taken a picnic. Trevor and mum, Josh and Jane, and Emma. 'That was a fun day.'

'So what do you think? It's nice weather. Head to the park, think about old times. I think he'd prefer that to us doing something dreary?'

Emma agreed. And it gave her something to do on her day off that wasn't spending all day playing poker online and chatting with someone she'd never met, and then feeling guilty and giving up on leisure and just getting on with work. And now she was thinking about work.

'Did you talk to that Tom Knight last night?'

Josh nodded. 'Only briefly. Lyds was sort of monopolising him.'

'In a good way?'

'In a drunk way.'

Emma couldn't claim to be surprised. She'd known that wasn't a love match from the conversation she'd had with Mr Knight at the end of the evening but she'd hoped there might at least have been a hint of the beginnings of a spark.

'You can't wave your magic wand over everyone, Stilts.'

'Doesn't mean I can't try.'

'I'm well aware. But love doesn't always happen to order. Sometimes it's really inconvenient.'

Not on Emma's watch it wasn't. 'Not the point. Mr Knight is paying us to find his special someone. Even if he is a miserable bugger.'

Josh laughed. 'Next event I will make identifying a potential match for Mr Knight my number one priority. So what do you reckon then? Picnic in the park and raise a glass to Dad?'

'Let's do it.'

An hour later, laden with far more food than they were likely to consume, they were sitting on a blanket in Richmond Park. Josh was quiet.

'Thinking about your dad?' Emma asked.

'Thinking about him and Big Emma.'

'Don't call me that!' They both chorused Emma's mum's invariable response to Josh's attempt to distinguish between the Emma Loves. Emma Love senior's refusal to be known as Big Emma was one of the main reasons that younger Emma had got stuck with Stilts for so long.

'What about them?'

'Just how right they were together.'

He was right.

'And also I was thinking about how she made it all happen.'

'Very unethically if you ask me.' Trevor had been a client. He'd come to Emma's mum looking to find someone. It was ten years since his first wife had left and Josh was getting more independent and Trevor had thought he was due a bit of Trevor time.

'There's no rule against dating clients.'

'Well, not a rule as such, but…'

'And I think she gave him a refund.'

Emma knew her mother better than that. 'I bet she didn't. I bet she charged him more for finding such a perfect match.'

'Have you ever done that?'

'Done what?'

'Dipped your hand in the work cookie jar?'

Of course she hadn't. Emma was a professional.

'You must have scrolled down your client list for the best options?' he insisted.

'Absolutely not. That would be like…' What would it be like? 'It would be like a hairdresser using their clients' hair for wigs.'

'I think that is a thing though. You can sell your hair, can't you?'

'Fair point. Bad example. Dentists nicking their patients' teeth then.'

Josh looked appalled. 'Keeping teeth is more serial killer territory.'

'See. Bad idea.'

He shrugged. 'It worked for Dad and Emma. And look at us. A divorced thirty something who's moved back in to his parents' house and a matchmaker who's never been in love. Maybe we need to be a bit braver about putting a hand on the scales and tipping things in our favour.'

She was starting to regret telling him she'd never been in love. 'I've had perfectly good relationships,' she pointed out.

'And when was the last one?'

'I don't know. I've been busy with work.'

Josh was not in the mood to be distracted. 'Seriously, when was the last time you had a boyfriend, Stilts?'

Emma thought back over the men she'd dated. There was Ty. She met him in Freshers' Week and they'd dated on and off until just before finals but they'd never talked about staying together after uni.

And then she'd worked for a year as a PA in a big bank in the city. She'd dated Mark for five months. He was an insurance broker she'd met through work and he was great – actually he'd arranged her mum's insurance for moving to Spain. And then she'd been single for a year or so, started working for Love's Love, and met Anthony through Mum's friend, June. That had been great too, but he'd always been planning to travel so they'd said an entirely amicable goodbye when he'd saved enough money to head off to Cambodia.

And then Joe. Joe had worked in the coffee shop at her gym. He was a sweetheart. Probably the closest she'd ever come to moving in with someone but actually when they talked about it they'd both realised that they worked better as mates. And the girl who worked reception was so obviously perfect for him. Emma could totally see it. She was godmother to their twins.

And since then…

'Well, like I say, I've been busy with work.'

'For how long?'

She wasn't sure. Joe's twins were what? Eighteen months old now. And he'd been married for six months maybe before they announced that Shelley was pregnant. So… no. It couldn't be. 'It might be a couple of years.'

'A couple?'

'Maybe three or four.' Five. It was five the voice in her head told her. Five years since she broke up with Joe and nobody had made it past the three-date mark. That couldn't be right. She racked her brains. There must have been someone. At some point.

'Stilts, you'll seal up down there. You'll be like a born-again virgin.'

'I don't think that's how it works.'

'But do you want to risk finding out?'

Emma gave her brother her best 'don't push it' look. 'I'm focused on work at the moment. And we tell our clients not to settle, don't we? That everyone deserves true love. I'm setting a good example.'

'And your mum told me to keep an eye on you when she went away.'

'So this is brotherly keeping an eye on me? Making sure I find the right person?'

'I'm not so fussed about you finding the right person,' her brother replied. 'I just don't want the sexual frustration to boil over into collecting commemorative teaspoons or something.'

'You think that's what women do if they're not getting enough?'

Josh grinned. 'I'm just saying it's a danger.'

'Well, I promise to let you know if the urge to buy silverware becomes too strong.'

'Thank you.'

'Now can we change the subject please?'

They did and the afternoon passed in a haze of gin and snacks and memories of Trevor and the little bolted together family he'd helped create.

–

Despite Will's continued objections Lydia got him back to her place and changed quickly into yoga pants and a T-shirt. She had no intention of sleeping with him again, so there was zero need, for once, to dress to impress. And then she bundled him into the car.

'We could do something nearer,' he suggested. 'It's two hours' drive.'

'That's fine.'

'What about the zoo? Everyone likes the zoo.'

'No. They don't. Animals in cages.' She shuddered. 'We're not going to the zoo.'

'Or we could find a pub by the river somewhere?'

'You're going to show me your family estate, Viscount March. No getting out of it.'

He looked a little uncertainly at the gaffer tape that was holding the knob on the end of the gear lever. 'Are you sure this thing will even get there?'

She nodded. 'Cleo has never let me down.'

'Your car is called Cleo?'

'Yep. Cleo with an e. And she is a Clio with an i.'

He patted the dashboard gingerly. 'Come on then, Cleo with an e. We believe in you.'

She spent the next two hours peppering him with questions. 'Did you have servants?'

'No. Well, there was an estate manager. And a housekeeper. And cleaners, obviously.'

'Servants then,' said Lydia.

'Well, we didn't really call them that.'

'Doesn't change what they were though.'

'Did you have television?'

'Yes.'

'An Xbox?'

'No.'

'A pony?'

'Two,' he muttered.

'You're super posh!'

'And you didn't get that from the viscount thing?' he deadpanned. 'Turn left here.'

'Where?'

'At the junction you just missed.'

'Well why didn't you say earlier?'

'Because last time you said I warned you too early and we ended up trying to drive into someone's house.'

'Well you said next left.'

'I wasn't including driveways.'

Eventually they arrived outside the elaborate iron gates that marked the entrance to Witford Hall, the formal family seat of the Earls of Hanborough. 'Oh Jesus,' Will murmured.

'What's wrong?'

'It's an open day.'

'A what?'

'The house is open to the public.'

'Is that a problem?'

He shrugged. 'It rather rules out us quietly sneaking in.'

'Rather,' she mimicked. 'Well, you know I don't just want the five-pound tour, don't you? I expect to get to go the other side of the velvet rope.'

He nodded. 'I'd kind of assumed that. Go on then. Straight up the drive.'

Lydia followed the wide driveway as far as a fork where a bored-looking lad in a high-vis jacket was directing cars to the left, towards a field marked out for parking. Will shook his head. 'Stay right.'

The lad stepped in front of them. Lydia wound down her window.

'Visitor parking on the left, Miss.'

'We're not exactly visitors. Well, I am,' Lydia clarified. 'He lives here.'

The lad laughed. 'Nice one, Miss. To the left please.'

Will seemed to be shrinking further and further into his seat. 'I don't live here, but my parents do,' he muttered.

The high-vis boy laughed again. A little less certainly this time. By now another older gentleman, who'd rejected the high-vis in favour of a more classic wax jacket, was making his way over. 'What seems to be the problem?'

He peered into the car. 'William! Viscount March, welcome.' The man's vowels were plummier than a plum pudding. 'I'm afraid we weren't expecting you.'

'It was an impulse thing. My erm...' Will looked at Lydia. 'My friend was keen to see the old place.'

Lydia frowned. It was subtle but Will's voice had changed too – his words were a little bit more clipped somehow.

'Very good. Well welcome...' The wax jacket's voice trailed away.

'Miss Hyland, may I present James Hargreaves. My father's estate manager.'

'Miss Hyland, it's an honour.'

She nodded uncertainly. She didn't think meeting her was that exciting. 'Thank you,' she offered.

'So can we go through?' Will gestured towards the right-hand path.

'Of course. Shall I let the kitchen know you'll be dining with us?'

Will shook his head. 'Let me surprise her.'

'She'll be delighted to see you.'

Lydia made to close the window. Will leaned across. 'One more thing. My father?'

'The Earl and the Countess are currently residing in their Dubai apartments.'

Will gave a short curt nod. 'Probably best.'

Lydia followed Will's directions down the right-hand path.

'This'll take us to the back of the house. We can park by the kitchen and go in that way rather than with everyone else.'

'Ok.' She drove in silence for a moment. 'You really didn't want to see your dad then?'

'Easier not to.'

'How come?'

He shrugged. 'How long have you got?'

Not long enough it turned out, as seconds later he was directing her to park in a gravelled area at the back of Witford Hall. She gasped as she got out of the car. Even from the back the Hall was breathtaking. It was a large, handsome, stone building, standing proudly on rising ground. 'It's huge.'

'Yes.'

'How many bedrooms does it have?'

'Hard to say.' He grabbed her hand and pulled her back to the lawn so they could see the whole width of the building. 'You can't see from the back, but it's a U-shape. So there's the central house and then an east and a west wing.'

She giggled at the ridiculousness of it all.

'The east wing hasn't really been used since, I don't know, before I can remember, so that's all closed up. The family apartments are in the west wing. That's where my room was, and where my dad and his wife live when they're here. And then the middle section is basically a museum. That's the bit people get to tour round.'

'We used to come to places like this on school trips. But real normal people do not actually live in houses like this.'

'No. Real normal people don't.' He took a deep breath. 'Come on. Hopefully there'll be someone in here who's pleased to see me.'

She let him lead her by the hand through a door into a cool stone corridor. As soon as they were inside she could hear voices, people shouting and talking. One voice rose above the others. 'Where's that next batch of fruit scones? How many are in the oven now? Come on.'

She was picturing a kitchen with marble worktops and old-fashioned copper pans hanging from the ceiling. Food would be cooked on a huge range oven, or even over an open fire in the stove. The reality was quite different. Stainless steel units, commercial ovens, kitchen assistants in white tunics and blue hairnets.

The source of the loudest voice was instantly clear. The woman at the centre of the swirl of activity was wearing chef's whites over dark blue baggy jeans turned up to show cherry red Doc Martens. Her hair was covered under a red-and-white polka-dot bandana. She turned as Will and Lydia came into the room. A curl of greying hair and a crinkle at the corner of her lips suggested she was older than the energy she was pouring out into the room implied. 'William March, what have I told you about coming into my kitchen without washing your hands and covering your hair?'

Will grinned. 'I think you told me I could get away with it because I was so adorable.'

She shook her head. 'Well I must have been soft in the head then.' She pointed at the doorway. 'Into the scullery, boy. I'll bring you a scone.'

'Come on.' Will pulled Lydia along with him. 'You don't argue with Aggie when she's in head chef mode.'

The room across the corridor from the main kitchen was more like a slightly modernised version of the kitchen Lydia had been picturing. Massive range cooker – check. Pots and pans hanging from the ceiling – check. Marble worktops – check. Island unit with stools for breakfast – less in keeping with her vision.

A moment later, the chef reappeared carrying two massive scones and a pot of tea. 'Warm from the oven. These are £3.69 if you go round to the tearoom.'

'Thank you.' As the scent of freshly baked scone hit Lydia's senses her bacon butty suddenly seemed to have been a very long time ago.

The woman, Aggie, Will had called her, pulled a stool out and sat herself down opposite them. 'So now then? What brings you back here? And who is the beautiful girl you've brought with you?'

Will leaned forward. 'You know she can hear you?'

'I don't mind. She called me beautiful and gave me a scone. She can talk about me as much as she likes.'

Aggie laughed, long and loud and deep, right from the belly. 'I like her. What's she pissing about with a wastrel like you for?'

'We're just friends,' Lydia replied before Will could have a say.

'Very sensible.' Her face crumpled into a broad smile. 'I'm joking. This one was the sweetest, most generous-hearted boy in the world when he was little. I have never heard an unkind word from him in my life.' Aggie turned her attention back to Will. 'Now, before your head gets too inflated, what are you doing here today?'

'Just showing Lydia around.'

'I see.' She gave Lydia a conspiratorial look. 'You want to watch yourself. He's not brought a girl back here in thirty years.'

'Honestly, we're just friends.'

'So you keep saying.' Aggie sighed. 'Right. Bus-loads of folks coming to gawp at us today and the cafe won't stock itself. Back to work for me. You two have a nice time. Come and say goodbye before you disappear off again though.'

Will promised that they would and then they were left alone.

'You're different here.'

'What do you mean?'

'Quieter. And you talk different.'

'No. I don't.' He stood up briskly. 'Come on. What do you want to see?'

'Family apartments. Show me where you actually grew up. And then we can do the public bits.'

'All right then.' He led the way back along the stone corridor and up some stairs to a door marked Private, where he stopped.

'What's wrong?'

'I haven't been here for a really long time.'

'Will any of your family be here?'

He shook his head. 'Not if Father's not here. Libby's staying at school, or visiting friends, all summer. She prefers that to coming here on her own or carting herself out to Dubai. Georgie's the youngest. She'll be with the parents. The others are all married with their own houses and families to worry about.'

'How many sisters have you got?'

'Seven. Basically every time there's a new wife he has a couple of goes at getting another son.'

'And only makes girls.'

Will nodded. 'So many girls. Hordes of them.'

Lydia reached past him and pushed the door open. 'So there's no one here. It's just rooms. Rooms can't hurt you.'

And it was just rooms. There was a musty uninhabited feel, but beyond that so much was normal. Sofas and coffee tables and ring stains where someone had forgotten to use a coaster. Family photos covered a table next to the fireplace in what she took to be the main living room. Lydia homed in on those and picked out a snap of a young boy – no more than twelve or thirteen – on top of a massive chestnut brown horse. 'Is this you?'

Will nodded.

Lydia looked again. 'It's the only one.'

Will took the photo from her hand and studied it. 'I think this was the morning of my first hunt. And my last hunt. It wasn't very long before the ban and I cried when the hounds got the fox. This was before that though.' He set it down. 'Probably why it's still out. Probably the last time he was proud of me.'

Lydia opened her mouth to tell him she was sure that wasn't true, but stopped herself. She'd tried years ago to tell friends what her dad had been like and they'd assured her that things couldn't be that bad. It hadn't helped.

She turned her attention to the fireplace itself. 'This is so fancy.'

'Georgian, I think.'

Lydia nodded like she understood the architectural implications. She turned her gaze up to the high ceiling. 'How do you clean the lights?'

'With a stepladder. Or a feather duster on a sort of extendable pole thing.'

'You mean you've actually cleaned them?'

He grimaced slightly. 'I've seen it done.'

'Show me your bedroom.'

'It's a guest room now, I think.'

'Don't care. Want to see.' Why did she want to see? Why was she gorging herself on a life so remote from her own? It wasn't like she was ever going to live somewhere like this.

'All right.' He led her down the hallway and up to the top floor. 'These rooms would have been servants' quarters, but Aggie and James have converted one of the barns and nobody else has lived in for years, so these ended up as children's rooms.'

223

Right at the end of the corridor he stopped. 'Right then. In for a penny.' He pushed the door open and held it for Lydia to walk past him.

What she walked into was a beautiful room – the full width of the wing, at the very end of the building so the roof came down on three sides, with sky lights cut into each. It lacked the grandeur of the rooms downstairs and was painted plain magnolia with a dull beige carpet and a cream duvet set. It looked like a room in a million forgettable budget hotels. But it could so easily be stunning. This was the sort of room you would dream of as a master bedroom. You could turn one of the smaller rooms next door into an en suite and...

'Wow.' It was Will who broke the silence.

'What?'

He came into the room and sat down on the bed. 'I mean, Libby told me they'd cleared my stuff out, but I thought there might be something. Like a hint that I existed.'

'I'm sorry.'

'It's not your fault.'

'No. I mean sorry for making you come here. I didn't think.' How sad could a viscount's life be, she'd thought. 'I don't always think.'

'I could have said no. You can't make people do stuff if they really don't want to.' He looked around. 'You know you said I was different here?'

'Yeah.'

'You're right. I think sometimes I'm different everywhere I go.' He stopped. 'I can't explain it.'

Lydia could. The constant feeling of knowing that you weren't right and that you were about to be found out. She sat down next to him. 'Like you're always putting on a new costume to try to fit in?'

'Exactly that.'

They were both still staring straight ahead, sitting on the end of the bed in this strange characterless room that could be anywhere. Her fingers gripped the duvet next to her leg. He was close to her. She could feel the warmth of him. She stretched out her little finger ever so slightly towards him and found his hand mirroring her own. The touch of her finger against his filled her senses. The room around her receded. The sound of the birds outside the window faded into quiet. There was nothing but the burn of the line of skin on the side of her hand that he was touching.

She could turn now and pull him to her, and they would fall back onto the bed in a tangle of limbs and lust and need. Why didn't she do that? It would be good sex. They'd done it enough times to know that. But neither of them moved, apart from their two hands touching, stroking, entangling silently between them.

It was slow. Agonisingly, lusciously slow. When she finally turned to him it wasn't a choice, it was an inescapable certainty that they were going to kiss. Lydia turned her body, closed her eyes, and moved her lips to his, savouring every exquisite moment of nearness, of imminence, of anticipation of him, before they kissed. And then her senses were overwhelmed entirely by the taste of Will on her mouth. It was delicious and languorous, as though they could spend the rest of their days captured inside the moment of this kiss.

She had to have him. She hadn't planned to. She'd been adamant that if they were going to hang out then the sex part of their dalliance was definitely over, but she didn't care any more. She needed him. She pulled her lips away. 'Fuck me,' she whispered.

'Ok.'

She jumped off the bed and went to close the blinds.

'Wait.'

'What?'

'I want to see you.'

Chapter Sixteen

Lydia shook her head. She had rules for sex. Not rules as such, but habits, preferences. It happened in the dark. Or somewhere nobody would expect or require her to get naked. And she closed her eyes.

'Why not? I've seen it all before.'

'No. You haven't.'

She watched him think about it. 'You're right. I haven't. It's up to you, but I'd like to see you,' he said. 'Without a costume on.'

Lydia let the cord for the blind drop away from her hand. 'You as well then.'

He nodded. She watched him stand up and reach down for the hem of his T-shirt. He took it off slowly, one inch at a time, and then threw it aside. 'Your turn.'

She was wearing a bralet under her T-shirt so that was ok. She'd wear a crop top and leggings at the gym. But this wasn't just anyone looking at her. This was Will and he wasn't merely looking. He was actually seeing her. She forced a deep breath into her chest and lifted her T-shirt over her head. 'You again.'

She watched him pull his shoes and socks off and swiftly followed suit. And then she watched him unbutton the fly on his shorts and let them drop to the floor. 'Now you,' he whispered. 'If you're sure you want to.'

She nodded and bent down to peel her yoga pants away. 'No real sexy way to do this,' she giggled, standing on one leg to pull her foot through.

'I disagree.'

And so there she was. Down to her underwear. Her bralet, which wasn't too bad, and knickers that were on the practical end of things. 'Not very sexy,' she apologised.

'Again, I disagree.' He hooked his fingers over the waistband of his boxers. 'Wanna keep going?'

She met his gaze, looking him straight in the eye. 'I do.'

'Go on then.'

'You first.'

He pulled his boxers down his legs and stepped out of them. She looked at him. Naked in front of her. Every atom of her being was aching to touch him. But not yet. He wanted to see her first. She wanted to be seen. She pulled her bralet off first over her head and then, quickly, before she had too much time to think about it and without looking at him, she yanked her knickers down and kicked them away. Every instinct was to turn her body away or pull her arms around herself in protection. She fought the need and raised her chin.

'You're beautiful.'

She let herself look properly at him. He was staring at her, but not with hostility or disgust. 'So are you,' she whispered.

And then she closed the gap between them, pressing her body urgently against his, and claiming his lips. They tumbled onto the bed. Lydia arched her back and he planted kisses all the way down her chest and across her stomach and then down to her thigh. She spread her legs wider for him to kiss her, and lay back as he slid his tongue into her.

She was entirely exposed, around him, underneath him, naked with him. She closed her eyes and let the waves of pleasure roll through her body.

And then she felt him move above her. 'Look at me,' he whispered.

She opened her eyes and took him in. He looked perfect.

'Have you got anything? A condom?'

'Shit. Yeah. I think so.' He grabbed his shorts from the floor and found one in the back of his wallet.

'Excellent boy-scouting,' she quipped.

He shook his head. 'No making a joke of it. We've come this far.' He held up the condom. 'You're sure?'

She nodded. Right then, she was sure.

–

Annie was settled in the one good chair in Duncan's room, sitting by his bed, while their mum took herself off for a bath. Annie was three years and three weeks old when Duncan was born, and three years and four weeks old when her useless dad – as he was inevitably termed even in her own imagination after years of listening to her mum – had decided that he couldn't hack it any longer.

Ever since she was little, she'd come and tell Duncan about her day at school or college. Her mum had taught her that even when he couldn't react, Duncan was still listening. Today her head was full of only one thing. Colin had told her, hadn't he, that she needed to work out what she felt for Josh before she jumped in with some other chap. He was right. Of course.

–

The second time Annie Keer met Joshua Love was a brief yet perfect interlude in the young Miss Keer's life. It was the momentous day of her graduation as a scholar of English, and Miss Keer was upon the town.

Annie had made her way to meet her university classmates with the intent of sharing one last hurrah. At least it was the last hurrah for her companions. Annie herself had found little time for revelry during her college years. Unfortunately, on this final occasion, a failure in communication left Miss Keer separated from her friends but, as luck would have it, she was, once more, in the vicinity of Mr Joshua Love.

And from that chance meeting, in the rather less than salubrious surroundings of Club DanceTonic, the former intimates reignited their

acquaintance. Several times. With passion, tenderness and an assured-
ness of mutual devotion that would surely mean this chapter in their
story would end, not in further estrangement, but rather in the sort of
long-term union promised every time we read the words 'happily ever
after'.

–

Annie remembered that weekend as if it were a chapter from a novel. First read long ago, but subsequently pored over for new nuances of meaning, before finally being put aside as nothing more than a childish fairy tale. Those two days had been everything. They'd talked about moving in together. Josh already had a job and a rented flat. It was a poky one-bed, barely more than a studio, but what did they need space for? It had all sounded so easy when she was lying in his arms.

But then what? She'd told her friends from college, and her mum, and Duncan and reality had started to make little tiny cracks in her certainty. She'd have teaching placements coming up and she didn't know where yet. And she was still young, not quite twenty-one, and she hadn't seen Josh for years. How could she be sure after just two days?

That was what her mum had asked her. *Are you sure?*

A braver woman than Annie would have talked to him about her worries, looked him in the eye and suggested they take their time. A braver woman still would have trusted her heart and entertained no sneaking doubts. Annie had texted. It wasn't fair to keep him hanging on when there was no way, she had thought, she could be sure of her heart. And clearly he was well over it now.

'I'm in love with Josh.' The words were out of her mouth before her brain had a chance to examine them and hide them away.

Duncan's eyes were open. He blinked once.

'Are you saying yes?'

She pursed her lips at her brother. 'You didn't know that. I didn't know that.' It was hopeless anyway. 'I'm not going to do anything about it, of course. He's Jane's ex and even though she's not into him any more you can't get it on with a friend's ex. You just can't. Lydia would say it broke some sort of code.' So that was that. She wiped Duncan's chin. 'So anyway that's what's happening with me. I'm in love.'

'Course you are, sweetheart.' Her mum was standing in the doorway. 'You've been in love with that Love boy since you were five years old.'

'Don't be silly.'

'I'm not. I remember him traipsing round after you like a lovesick puppy from when he was knee high. You always led the way in those days.' Annie's mum's face clouded for a second.

'What's wrong?'

'Nothing, sweetheart. But things change, don't they?'

Annie knew what she meant. Being in love with a boy in the playground when you were five was not the same as declaring love for your best mate's ex at thirty-one.

She checked her watch. 'Do you want a hand with Dunc?'

'Please.'

The two of them fell into a well-practised routine of helping Duncan out of his pjs and washing and powdering his skin so he'd be comfortable in the fresh pair. When they'd finished Annie's mum stroked her boy's hair. 'Annie, you know that me and Duncan are all right, don't you? I've got my carers' group and there's Hilly and the day centre and the new GP is wonderful.'

'What do you mean?'

'I mean that we love that you come round so much. You're always welcome, but you can't put your own life on hold.'

Annie bristled. She wasn't. This was her life. She was living it exactly as she was supposed to.

Her mum hadn't finished. 'I hate to see you not making the most of yourself. You had such big dreams.'

Annie shook her head. She didn't have any dreams. She was perfectly content with her life the way it was. 'I'm fine.'

'Annie, sweetheart, think. What did you want to do when you were at school?'

She thought about it. She remembered being a good student. It wouldn't have been fair to play up and bring more stress home to Mum. So she listened. She did her homework, usually late in the evening, after Duncan had had his night time feed and medications. She hung out with Josh and a couple of other friends she'd lost touch with now. She didn't drink very often. She'd had marijuana once when she was in sixth form and talked for a long time to a portly red-suited man who might, with hindsight, have been a post box. She'd gone to university. She'd got a good job near enough to Mum and Duncan to get their shopping and come over and help out when she was needed.

'You were such a determined little girl. And so full of ideas.'

Was she? She looked at her mum. 'I don't remember.'

'Always with your nose in a book. You used to get so cross if you thought the wrong ones had got together.'

And then she did remember. At least parts of it. She remembered making Josh play dress-up when they were seven or eight where she was a princess and he was the king. And she remembered walking back to the tube from the book market telling him how Jane Eyre should never have gone back to Mr Rochester or why Linton deserved better than Cathy.

And she remembered how he'd listen, and how sure of herself that had made her feel. Anyone who could command the full attention of Joshua Love must be somebody who mattered.

'But you didn't think I should be with Josh. You didn't want me to move in with him.'

Her mother looked blank.

'After graduation, you convinced me—'

'I wanted you to get your qualifications. I didn't mean for you to put your life on hold. I thought you'd go out with him and maybe move in together later.'

231

That wasn't right. 'You persuaded me…'

'I just wanted you to be sure,' her mum whispered.

–

Afterwards, Lydia ran a finger across his torso and stopped at a long silver line across his shoulder. 'What did you do here?'

'Oh, I was in a car crash when I was a kid.'

'Shit. I'm sorry.'

He ran a finger over the line of the scar. 'They told me I was lucky. Just cuts and bruises. I was tiny. The child seat did its job I guess.'

Lydia waited. She had a terrible feeling there was more.

'My mum was driving. She was killed.'

She'd thought the scar thing might be cute. She was sure she'd read it in books and the stories were always adorable childhood anecdotes. She lifted her head up and rested on her elbow. 'I'm sorry.'

'I don't remember her to be honest. I have flashes of memory of the actual accident but I was three and a half. I don't have any sense of her as a person, apart from what Aggie told me when I was older.'

He reached out and gently touched the run of three circular red scars on the top of her arm. 'Are those cigarette burns?'

She nodded.

'Your dad?'

Another slow silent nod. There wasn't much else to say.

'I'm sorry. I'm glad you got away.'

'Me too.'

'Why do you hide who you are?' he asked.

'What do you mean?'

'The costume thing. Why do you do it?'

And this was where they were different. This was the ocean that couldn't be bridged. 'No choice. Left home. Couldn't go back. Had to adapt to fit in. And I'm not rich or connected, so you either fade into the background and watch everyone else

232

and copy what they're doing, or you get loud and in people's faces and let them think you're the mad one, the one who's up for anything.' The light outside was beginning to turn mottled. 'Come on. We should get home.'

'We could stay – go back tomorrow. It's school holidays. I'm not working 'til tomorrow night. We can nab some leftovers from the kitchen and bring them back up here. We don't have to see anyone else.' He pulled her hand to his lips and kissed the back of it. 'I'd prefer to not see anyone else.'

She pulled away. 'I have to get back.'

'Why?'

'Because.' He was the son of Lord Who-knows-whattington and she was nothing from nowhere. And she didn't do relationships. She didn't let her guard down.

She remembered the feel of his gaze on her skin. She remembered the feeling of being seen without any walls up at all. And she shut it down. She didn't let her guard down twice.

'Why do we have to go back?' he asked again.

'Because none of this is real.' She stood up and collected her clothes from the room, pulling them on quickly without looking at him. 'You can't live in a fantasy because it makes you feel good.'

'What part of this was a fantasy?'

She ignored the question. 'I'm heading back. If you want a lift, be by the car in five minutes.'

She marched out of the room and down the stairs. Sex was sex. How she felt didn't matter because feelings weren't to be trusted. It didn't matter how much you wanted someone to be a certain way, you couldn't make it happen by wanting it.

She stormed through the private apartments and down to the kitchen level on the ground floor.

'Are you lost, sweetie?' Aggie was coming the other way along the hall.

'No. Just heading off.'

'Will not with you?'

'He's coming. I think. I don't know. He might stay over.'

Aggie laughed at that. 'When hell freezes over maybe. He's not spent a night here since he was seventeen. Until today he's only walked through the door to see his little sisters.' She looked hard into Lydia's face. 'And he's never brought a friend here. Not one. Not even a mate from school.'

Lydia fought to hold on to the piece of ice she was wrapping around her heart. 'Well, going home can be complicated.'

Aggie nodded. 'I'm glad he's found someone who understands that.'

'It wouldn't work though, would it?'

'What wouldn't?'

The woman was a stranger. What did it matter? 'I'm from nowhere. I was in care half the time as a kid cos... well, I just was.' She looked around. 'All this. It's like a different world.'

Aggie shrugged. 'I was two years old when I came here with my mother from Jamaica. And I'm married to an estate manager on an English country estate. It's all one world, love. And no relationship is easy. It comes down to how much you want to make it work.'

Lydia nodded politely, even though Aggie was wrong. You could want things to work all you liked. It didn't make any difference.

The door to the stairwell behind her swung open and slammed closed. She looked round to see Will still pulling his T-shirt down. Aggie smirked. 'I thought it was the house you were giving the private tour of?'

The look Will gave her must have echoed the one on Lydia's face because Aggie stopped smiling in an instant. 'Well, if you're heading off, let me give you some food for the journey.'

'It's only a couple of hours. We're fine.' Lydia was keen to get out of there and get back to normality.

'Don't bother.' Will stepped close behind her. 'If Aggie's decided you need feeding, you're getting fed. It's quicker to accept it.'

Aggie loaded them up with scones, sandwiches, drinks, crisps and flapjacks, and then she pulled Will into a hug. 'Don't stay away so long this time. This is your home too. Not just his.'

Will shook his head. 'It doesn't feel like home.'

'But one day it will be. Whether you want it or not. I'm not asking you to make peace with your father, just with yourself.'

—

They drove back without talking until they were well into the city. 'Where do you want me to drop you?'

'Anywhere near a tube is fine.'

'I can take you home.' She wasn't sure why but there was a gnawing feeling in her stomach that she needed to somehow make something up to him.

'Fine.' She followed his directions past the pub they'd been to that morning. The Crafty Fox. That bacon sandwich felt like a long time ago.

'Here will do.'

She slowed to a stop, checking there was nothing behind her. There was no space to pull in.

'Right then,' he muttered.

'Maybe I'll see you around,' she offered.

'Is that what you want?'

'I mean sure. We had fun, didn't we?'

He shook his head in apparent disbelief. 'You know what most people do when they meet someone and they get on and have fun, as we're apparently calling it? They swap numbers. They arrange to meet up. They choose to spend time together.'

Lydia could feel her hands tensing around the steering wheel. What did he want her to say? That wasn't who she was. And she wasn't going to change for some bloke.

'Fine. Well ok then. Maybe we'll see each other around.'

The car shook with the force of Will slamming the door. Lydia let go of the wheel and rubbed her eyes. She wasn't crying. She wasn't going to cry.

A car horn sounded behind her.

She flipped her middle finger in the direction of the impatient driver and set off towards home.

–

After her day off with Josh, Emma resolved that she would definitely get on top of the Season finances on Monday. She was going to sit down and update all the income and expenditure in her finance spreadsheet and then she'd know, finally and for definite, what commitments she'd made and whether she could honour them.

Of course, planning for the next event came first. That was urgent. Then she dealt with her emails and reread the latest scandal sheet. It was evening before she finally forced herself to look at the numbers. Extra champagne at basically every event. A couple of breakages from the first ball. Nothing major but here and there were little things she hadn't planned for and they all added up. They all added up on top of an idea that was already eye-wateringly expensive to begin with. The numbers swam in front of her eyes. She closed the spreadsheet and logged into the poker site instead.

Walt wasn't playing on their regular table. Of course. His real-life cash game was on a Monday night, wasn't it? She scrolled back through the chat. She could walk to the station right now and be in town in an hour. He'd asked her enough times. Why not?

She pulled her trainers on and grabbed her jacket from the hook by the door. It was a £500 buy in. That was what he'd said. She really couldn't afford that but if his friends bet anything like Walt did she'd come home richer than she set out. And if not, £500 was a drop in the Season's rapidly deepening financial ocean.

The walk to the station took twenty minutes. It would be fun. She'd play some cards, meet her virtual buddy in real life, take some of his money and come home again. No big deal. Just a nice evening out.

She turned the corner at the end of her street and walked along the main road.

Of course it was possible that it would be more than a laugh. She'd got on better with Walt online than with any bloke she'd met in the real world for years. Maybe there was something there. She reminded herself that she was being ridiculous. He was probably forty years older than her. She wasn't even sure he was single.

Emma stopped at the pedestrian crossing and waited for the green man. As she crossed the street the voice in her head got louder. It wasn't just a card game, was it? It was something bigger than that. It was Schrödinger checking how the cat was feeling. It was Eve deciding whether she fancied an apple. Walt was a good thing, but what if he was only a good thing as he was? At the moment he was safely compartmentalised into his chat box and virtual table. What if bringing him into real life broke the spell?

She turned down the final side street towards the station. This was stupid. Meeting Walt could only break something if there was something there to break. And there wasn't. They were mates. Barely even mates. They'd chatted a bit online. She was fooling herself if she thought there was anything more to it than that.

She strode up to the ticket machine and bought a return into town. She'd get cash when she got there, play a few hands, meet a few people and come home. That was it.

Five minutes until the train arrived. She took a seat on the platform. What would walking into that room be like? Would she recognise him? Would he be pleased to see her? The idea of a stranger pulling her into his arms swam through her senses. The idea that she would walk in and they'd be drawn to one another, overcome by passion, by need, by – what had he said? – that he'd never been so sure of anything in his life. That wasn't what she was expecting. Of course it wasn't. And who would ever get to feel like that twice in their lives? And, having felt it once, whoever would settle for less the second time around?

The train pulled into the station. Emma crumpled her ticket into a ball in her pocket and set off to walk back home.

Chapter Seventeen

Miss Emma Love
requests the honour of your company
at a dance lesson for the young ladies and
gentlemen of the Ton.

'Mum! It's me,' Tom called out as soon as he was through the front door, knowing full well that if he didn't his mum would send the carer, Hilly, running down three flights to see who it was. He'd told his mother a thousand times that if she sold this place she could buy a flat or a bungalow somewhere with a warden and have money left over, but she was adamant. This was her home. This was the house that Tom's father had bought as a home for their family. The fact that that family hadn't come until she was nearly fifty and the fact that Tom's dad had passed on a few years later didn't change that. Her every hope and dream and memory and regret was in these walls. It was where they'd lived their family life and it was where she intended to stay.

And who was Tom to argue? His father had left her well provided for and the carers who came in each day and night saw that everything she might need was attended to, and, though her body was tiring, her mind was still whip smart.

Hilly was placing a tray with soup and a bread roll in front of Tom's mum when he made his way in. His mother waved her spoon at him. 'Arriving at a meal time, I see? Is there any left, Hilly?'

'I'm fine. I slept in. I've only just had breakfast.'

He pulled a seat up opposite his mother. She narrowed her eyes as she stared at him. 'You're different.'

'Am I?'

'Well, you said you slept in.'

That was true. He had. 'Well, it's all these parties and God knows what you've got me going to. It's exhausting.'

'Nonsense. You're young. You should be out every night. What's different is that you're sleeping.'

'Yeah. Well, last night, at least.' He thought back. He did have to concede that insomnia was a less frequent visitor than it had been a few months, or even weeks ago.

'And you've got your smile back.'

'I always smile when I come to see you,' he joked.

'You do, but it doesn't always make you look happy. You've got a bit more life about you.'

There was no point arguing with her. 'If you say so.'

'I do say so.' She sipped delicately from her soup spoon. 'This isn't terrible. I do think Hilly might be improving in the kitchen.'

'She'll hear you.'

His mother nodded. 'I should hope so. And I'm being nice. I said she was improving.'

'If you upset Hilly I am not finding you a new carer,' Tom warned, only half joking.

'Oh, you'd leave your poor mother to suffer alone, would you?'

He grinned. 'With not so much as a second thought.'

'See. You're making jokes again. So who are they?' his mother asked.

'Who's who?'

She put down her spoon and caught him in the full beam of her stare. 'Whoever's put the spring back in your step.'

Hilly reappeared from the kitchen. 'Who's got a spring back in their step?'

'Tom. He's got a new paramour. I'm sure of it.'

'A paramour?' Hilly raised her eyebrow at Tom. 'You can probably get an ointment for that.'

His mother shook her head. 'It means he's seeing someone. A special someone.'

'I didn't say that.'

'So tell us all about them then?' said Hilly.

Tom turned back to his mother. There was a brightness in her eyes that wasn't always there any more. 'He's clearly smitten,' she insisted.

What did it matter really? In a few weeks he could just tell them it hadn't worked out. That was the way things went sometimes. His mother would still be happy to believe that he was dating again. What the hell? 'Yeah. She's really cool.'

His mother nodded. 'So it's a she?'

'Yep. Yep.' Apparently so, thought Tom. That was fine. His imaginary significant other could be whatever he decided. He told himself he wasn't picturing anybody in particular. 'She's sparky. Likes to be in charge, you know.'

'Just what you need,' his mother declared. 'So when do we get to meet her?'

You don't, he thought. 'She's very busy. With work.'

'Too busy to meet her boyfriend's dying mother?'

'You're not dying,' he pointed out. 'And it's about your seventh dying wish. When you're actually dying you'll have no more cards to play. You'll be the boy who cried wolf.'

'The old woman who cried dying,' confirmed Hilly.

'Well, who's to say I'll not be gone tomorrow?' She peered at Tom over the top of her spectacles. 'And then how would you feel?'

'Devastated, of course,' he replied smiling broadly.

'But she won't die tomorrow,' Hilly added. 'Not with the excitement of meeting this new girlfriend to keep her going.'

Any other carer would have felt the sharp edge his mother's tongue for that, but Hilly had somehow been admitted to the very select group of people from whom Mrs Knight would accept familiarities and even, in rare circumstances, teasing.

'So tell me about her properly. What's this job that keeps her so busy?'

Tom held up his hands in protest. 'Hey. It's early days. Maybe give me a chance to get to know her properly first?'

'I married your father three months to the day after the first time I met him.'

'I'm well aware.'

'I'm just saying. All this "early days" business is nonsense, isn't it? When you know you know, and you deserve to find happiness again after... well, you know.'

He did know very well.

His mother patted his hand. 'It's good that you're not shutting yourself away. That's all. Anyway, I need to know when I'm going to get to meet this girl.'

'I don't know. Not 'til after this Season thing. We're supposed to be courting.' Wasn't that the whole idea?

'You're doing the Season?' The edge of disbelief in Hilly's voice was palpable.

'Not my idea,' he clarified with a sharp look towards his mother.

'I bet it wasn't.' Hilly laughed. 'But then that's easy, isn't it? She'll meet her next week.'

'What?'

'The sister of a lad I do afternoons with is doing that. Part of it's that you get to introduce your para-wotnots to your nearest and dearest. They're having a family lunch thing.'

Were they? He thought quickly. 'Well, you know Mum doesn't like going out so much?'

'Well, if it was to meet your young lady...'

'I can bring her,' said Hilly.

He shot Hilly a very definite look. 'Is it on one of your days?'

'I'm sure we can work that out.' She turned back to his mum. 'You'd like to go to the family day, wouldn't you? Meet Tom's new girlfriend.'

'I absolutely would, Hilly. Thank you so much for offering to take me.' There was a hint of laughter in her eyes as she turned back to her son. 'Well, hasn't this all turned out wonderfully? Say thank you to Hilly.'

'Thanks a lot, Hilly.'

—

'Regency dancing!' Annie was practically beside herself with excitement as Lydia let her friends into the flat.

Jane was too busy staring at Lydia to express an opinion on the dancing. 'You're ready?'

Lydia nodded. 'It said long skirts.' She was wearing a maxi dress she'd bought on a whim last summer. It was bright pink with beading around the neck. She didn't think it was really her but how was she supposed to tell? 'This is all right, isn't it?'

Jane nodded. 'It's great. Only usually you… Are you feeling ok?'

'I'm fine.' Of course she was fine. Why wouldn't she be fine?

'Right. I guess we're going to be early then.'

Lydia grabbed her handbag and stood up.

'I mean not this early. I haven't even ordered an Uber yet.'

Annie swirled in front of the mirror in her own attempt at a long-skirted Regency dancing look. 'Isn't it romantic?'

Lydia couldn't be doing with that. 'Well, let's get on with it. The weather's nice. We can wait outside.' She wanted out of the flat. She wasn't sure why. She wanted something to change. She wanted the itchy feeling on her skin, like it was too tight somehow, to fade away. She couldn't outrun her own skin, but maybe she could leave the feeling at home.

—

'Two lines, please.' The woman who appeared to be in charge of them was a generously built sixty something, whose spectacles sat on top of her head. Nothing about her flowing linen top or

243

greying messy bun rationally accounted for her rather military command of the situation. But when she clapped her hands and repeated, 'Two lines, people!' the group damn well organised themselves into two lines.

'This,' the dance mistress announced, 'is a longways set. The predominant form of dancing in Austen's time was English country dance and the longways set is the backbone of English country dance. Later on we will practise square sets, but if the call is for longways, or "as long as you will" this is how you begin. Do we all understand?'

The group nodded uncertainly.

Jane was opposite Charlotte and Lydia was opposite Annie. Any convention of men in one line and ladies in the other had been brushed aside by the inclusive nature of the Season. The instruction was simply to line up opposite one's partner, and Lydia and Annie were partnerless. Jane was yet to hear the full story of the demise of Colin Williams, but if she could see that Annie was just sort of going along with things, then presumably it hadn't taken very long for him to notice too.

Looking down the line she was starting to recognise some of the other daters. As well as Colin, there was Charlotte's friend, Hope. There was the nice ex-army lady who was lined up opposite the charming firefighter. Everyone looked like they were having a good time. Jane stole a glance across at Charlotte, and knew, without doubt, that possibly for the first time in her life, Jane was having the best time.

She listened to the next set of instructions. Within the longways set they were to be divided into shorter sets of three couples, or 'triples' as Sergeant Major Dance termed them. They would dance within those triples in a combination of turns and steps and reels. And somehow everyone was in the same boat. Nobody knew what they were doing. Clearly, every single person in the room was winging it. Looking around, Lydia seemed to be winning at Regency dancing. She was fit enough to not go pink in the face after three rounds of skipping with her partner along the length of the set and back again, which was giving her a definite edge, and she seemed to have been born with a basic sense of rhythm.

Jane placed herself roughly mid-table. She could count to three and to four and generally remember which count went with which tune. Charlotte, on the other hand, was terrible. Wonderfully, beautifully, magnificently and gloriously terrible. She turned the wrong way. She crashed into Jane and into the people on either side of her.

After four dances in the longways set, their instructor called a break. Emma grabbed the microphone and invited them to help themselves to refreshments. There was punch and canapés on the table at the back of the room, and half an hour for mingling and getting to know one's partner a little better.

'How are you following this?' Charlotte gasped.

'I don't know. How are you not?'

'It's impossible,' she laughed. 'Why do you look so pleased?'

'Just delighted to have found your Achilles heel. I've sort of been assuming you must have a secret drug habit or be into something really weird.' It was the truth. The only fly in the ointment of Jane's perfect romance was the niggling suspicion that it was too perfect. Finding Charlotte's weakness was a relief. Terrible at traditional country dancing – Jane could comfortably live with that.

–

Help yourself, had been the instruction. That, presumably, meant no bar staff. Lydia told herself she wasn't looking but she did spot two white shirts by the buffet table. She stood on tiptoes to see if Will was there.

He was not.

She slid round the side of the crowd heading for the punch-bowl and waved to attract the waitress's attention. 'Do you know Will? He usually does the bar at these things.'

The girl nodded. 'I'm being him.'

'What?'

'Just got a call to come cover for him.' She shrugged. 'Heavy night, last night, I guess.'

'Right. Thanks.' Couldn't face it?

A shrill ring tinkled from inside her bag. She ran out into the hallway, delving in her bag for the phone. 'Hello?'

'Lydia?'

No. It couldn't be.

'It's your Aunty Jill.'

Everything around Lydia stopped. The noise from the dance studio receded. Her own breathing magnified to fill the void. Why would Jill be phoning her? All the things she could imagine that could be wrong ran through her head. It was her mum. It had to be her mum. He'd finally done it, hadn't he? 'What's happened?'

'It's your mam, pet.'

She'd always known this phone call would come one day, whether it was Jill, or a neighbour, or the police. One day the phone would ring and the hope that something might change would die forever.

'She's in hospital.'

'She's alive?'

'Oh God, yes. Sorry. Yes. She's in hospital. She's not in a great way but she's going to be all right.'

Oh, thank goodness. Lydia should go there. She couldn't go there. He'd be there. She'd promised herself that she would never go back. She'd determined to become whoever she needed to be to never have to go back to that place again.

'There's something else, pet. Your dad.'

'I don't care about him.'

'No. Quite right, but he is your dad. He's been arrested. I can't get any detail but it sounds like they're going to charge him with assault and they were talking about attempted murder.'

Attempted murder? That would mean prison. Proper prison. Not in for twenty-eight days and out again prison. 'What did he do?'

'Attacked her with a knife, pet. I'm sorry.'

'It's not the first time.'

'I know.'

Of course they both knew. They'd both tried to help. They'd both called the police, women's aid, anyone else who would listen and Lydia's mam had always said the same thing – that she fell, that it was an accident, that she'd brought it on herself, that she didn't need any help, thank you very much.

'She won't give evidence.'

'It were in the back garden. The next-door woman videoed it on her phone, so she might not have to. And I talked to her for a minute while we were waiting for the doctor to come round. She was conscious and asking if she could come stay with me for a bit.' Her aunt hesitated. 'She was talking about not wanting to be in the house with him.'

Lydia sat down heavily on the bench in the corridor. It was one of those long wooden ones you got in primary school gyms. It was far too low for her but it was sit down or fall over. There were too many emotions to process. He'd tried to kill her mum. Her mum had nearly died. Her mum hadn't died. Her mum had survived. He might go to prison. Something might finally change. 'Should I come up there?'

'Oh, that's up to you, pet. There's always a space for you on my sofa if you want it though.'

'They're starting again in a minute.' Jane stuck her head around the doorway to the dance room.

Lydia told Jill she'd call her back and hung up the phone. She needed to stand up and go back into the dance practice. That was what she was doing today. All of the stuff Jill had told her was somewhere else. She didn't move.

'What's wrong?'

'My mum's in hospital.'

'Oh God. I'm sorry.' Jane came and sat down next to her. 'What's happened?'

'Someone stabbed her.'

'Shit.'

'My dad stabbed her.'

'You're missing the…' Annie skipped into the corridor and stopped. 'What happened?'

'Lydia's dad stabbed her mum.'

'Oh my God.' Annie sat down at Lydia's other side.

Lydia took a deep breath in and wiped the back of her hand across her cheeks. Weeping in corridors was not the Lydia way. 'It's the sort of thing he does though. And she's going to be fine.' She started to get up to go back and join the practice.

'Wait. Wait.' Jane's hand on her arm stopped her. 'There's a lot I'm still getting my head around there. Your dad stabbed your mum?'

Lydia nodded.

'Is that why you never talk about home?'

Lydia shrugged. 'It's boring, isn't it? Nobody likes a sob story.'

Annie looked stricken. 'But we're your friends. We care about you. We want to hear everything.'

'I'm not the heart on sleeve type.'

'But maybe we could do something. We could help,' Annie argued.

'There's nothing you can do.'

'My parents are mad hippies who live in a commune and called me Jay 'til I was eighteen because they don't believe in gendering their children.' Jane's words came out in a single breath, rushing over one another into the world.

Now it was Lydia's turn to be overwhelmed with new information. 'Why do I not know this?'

'I guess I'm not the heart on the sleeve type either. At least I wasn't, but actually I took Charlotte there to see them all in the maddest circumstances and after I'd got over myself it was kind of liberating. They're just people and secrets sort of get bigger the longer you keep them. And it's like the bigger they get the heavier they are and the harder it is to carry them alone.'

Maybe she was right. Lydia took a breath and forced herself to tell a fraction of her story out loud. 'My dad beats my mum up. I got taken into care a few times but she always said it was accidents and things so I went back and then got taken away again and it was crap. So, as soon as I could, I left.'

'See. Saying it wasn't so bad was it?'

Jane was right. It pissed Lydia off immensely to admit it but saying it out loud did make it instantly smaller. It was still her baggage. She still had to carry it, but the shame she carried alongside it might, at least, get a little lighter.

'Every school I went to it felt like people were looking down on me, pitying me. I don't want to be pitied. I don't want to be treated like I'm a charity case.'

'You're kidding?' Annie jumped in. 'You're the least pitiable person I know. Do you know where All Saints finished in the netball or hockey or athletics leagues the year before you arrived?'

She shook her head. She ought to know that but she didn't remember ever being told. Annie would know, of course.

'Nowhere, because we didn't have teams until you set them up. We didn't have a bus to get to events until you charmed that lovely pastor bloke into donating one. You're a force of nature.'

'I'm always trying so hard to fit in.'

Jane shook her head. 'Fitting in is fine, but you don't need to. You don't fit in with the world, Lydia. You bend the world to fit around you.'

That couldn't work, could it? She'd get found out. One day someone would look at her and see her and they'd know. *Look at her and see her.* She looked at her two best friends, Annie squeezing her left hand like life itself depended on it and Jane, not as tactile, but still here in this moment alongside her. 'Thank you,' she whispered.

They shared a moment of silence. Only a moment. Lydia's need to fill the thinking space hadn't vanished in a single heart to heart. She needed to shift the focus.

'So I presume hippy commune parents are cool with the lesbian thing?'

Jane nodded.

'That's brilliant.' Lydia could very easily imagine her own father's reaction if she told him she was gay. It would have been the same as his reaction to anything else that fell outside his horribly narrow comfort zone of pub, tea on the table and then back to the pub. 'I'd love to be a lesbian.'

Jane laughed. 'Well, there's no limit on numbers. You're very welcome.'

'Nah. I really like cock.' Lydia's tension eased a fraction as she made her friends laugh. 'Think of the practical benefits though. Going out with someone you could send to buy tampons without having to draw them a diagram and still ending up with incontinence pads instead because they got overwhelmed and panicked in front of all the lady things.'

'It's the dream,' Jane confirmed.

The earlier disclosures still hung in the air. Lydia pushed them away. 'So what about you, Annie? What happened with nice-but-dull Colin?'

'He wasn't dull!'

Jane pulled a face. 'He was a little bit. What did happen?'

'It's not important.'

'Of course it is,' Lydia insisted. 'You just did a whole speech about how we're friends and we care about what's happening to each other. If I have to tell mine, you have to tell yours.'

There really wasn't very much to tell. 'He wanted someone who was a bit keener I think.'

'So you weren't keen?' asked Jane.

Annie shrugged. 'He's very nice.'

'But he doesn't set your heart alight?'

–

Did he? Annie hadn't really thought about it. He was kind and personable and wanted to make her happy. Shouldn't that be enough? 'Not really,' she admitted.

'So who does?' Lydia nudged her in the ribs. 'There must be someone who sends you all giddy in your downstairs area.'

'Or who you find emotionally and mentally stimulating?' suggested Jane.

Annie ignored Lydia's theatrical yawn.

'Maybe that doesn't happen for everyone.' Annie had read all the love stories. She wasn't Lizzie Bennet. She wasn't Emma Woodhouse. She wasn't even Anne Elliot. She wasn't the heroine. She was the quiet sister, the fortuneless friend who would be lucky to make any match at all. 'I would have settled for Colin,' she whispered. 'But he wouldn't settle for me.'

'Nobody should be settling for anyone.' Jane was strident now. 'I did that for years. It wasn't fair on either of us.'

How could anyone see Josh as settling? Well, obviously someone who wasn't into men. 'Josh is perfect though.'

She heard it at the same time as her friends. She said it before her brain had time to squash the thought down and pack it away.

'Well, this is awkward.' Lydia was looking from Annie to Jane and back again.

'You like Josh?' Jane asked. 'You never said. All those years. You never so much as hinted.'

'I didn't know.' It was partially true. 'He was marrying you. I didn't let myself think it… I'd never have…'

Jane nodded briskly. 'I know you wouldn't.'

'And I won't now. I mean, he's not into me and he's your ex and it's weird and I'm probably better off on my own and I'm sure he's not into me.'

'You already said that. About him not being into you,' said Lydia.

'How do you know he's not?' Jane asked.

'It doesn't matter. It's too weird anyway.' There were a thousand reasons this was a terrible idea. Annie was busy. Her mum and Duncan needed her. He was Jane's ex.

'It is a bit weird, but I left him.' Jane shrugged. 'I can't object to him getting it on with anyone he fancies.'

'He doesn't fancy me!' Annie raised her voice. She never raised her voice. It was sort of exciting. 'He might have years ago but I messed it up and he's moved on and it's over.'

She didn't need to look over at them to picture the look Lydia and Jane were exchanging.

'I think you need to tell us about years ago.'

Annie shook her head.

'Told you I grew up on a commune,' Jane muttered.

'And I'm distressed,' Lydia added. 'You have to do what I want.'

Annie took the deepest of breaths. 'Well, you know I knew Josh at school?'

They both nodded.

'Well, that's not the whole story.' And she told them about the perfect weekend they'd spent together and how she'd been persuaded that the timing was wrong and that she was too young to be sure. 'And then the next time I saw him,' she turned to Jane. 'He was your fiancé.'

'Oh my God!' Jane was wide mouthed.

'What?'

'You're the girl.'

'What girl?'

'The girl who broke his heart! He told me about you. He said there was someone he thought was like The One, but she didn't feel the same. Oh my God! You gave him serious trust issues.'

Annie shook her head. 'It was a long time ago. I don't think he even remembers.'

Jane almost laughed. 'Seriously? You're the girl!'

'But he's your ex, and he's not even interested any more...'

Lydia stood up. 'Stop it.'

'Sorry. I...' Annie was being insufferable, wasn't she? Going on about her own life when there was real big important stuff happening to Lydia.

'Just stop doing yourself down. Why wouldn't he still be interested? He's single. You're single. You know he fancied you before. Why the hell wouldn't he now? If you want him, you need to sodding well go and get him.'

Annie was too stunned to speak.

'And you,' Lydia turned her attention to Jane. 'So what if you grew up in a commune? Who gives a fuck? Did your parents love you? Did they try to do their best?'

Jane nodded silently.

'Well then, why are you hiding that?'

'I just wanted to be normal.'

'Well don't we all? Look. It sounds like we've all got stuff in our pasts, but we have to carry on, don't we? Here and now.'

Lydia was right. Of course she was right and what she was dealing with was a million times worse than simply having loved someone and let them go. But it also wasn't the same, Annie realised. The mess Annie was in was of her own making. She'd hurt somebody who cared for her. She was the one to blame.

Lydia took a deep breath in. 'I have to go home, don't I? See my mum.'

Jane nodded. 'I think so.'

'Right.' Lydia picked up her bag and took a step back towards the dance studio and then stopped and turned around and stopped again.

Annie went over to her. 'Home first. Pack a bag. I'll come with you, if you want.'

'No. You need to do your shit. Gotta put yourself first.'

'I will.' Annie tried to believe herself. 'Putting you first for a little bit right now though.'

–

The dance rehearsal had been an excellent idea. Emma pursed her lips ever so slightly as she remembered that it had been Josh's suggestion, but letting people have a go at the dances without pressure to get them right and without the strangeness

253

of Regency dress and a full band playing, was huge fun, as well as being useful preparation for the final event, which was now only two weeks away. The family day and then the ball and then the first Love's Love Season would officially be at a close.

'Miss Love?'

Emma sighed. Into every well-laid plan, some piece of grit must always fall, but she'd thought this particular irritation was absent today. From his flushed expression and the fact that he was still wearing a jacket she gleaned that he had, very possibly, just that second run through the door.

'A little late joining us today, Mr Knight.'

'Sorry. Late night.'

What sort of person spent hundreds of pounds on something and then overslept and didn't bother to turn up? Two more events and then Mr Knight would no longer be her problem. Right now though, he was one of the remaining single people on her list, and very much her concern.

'We're about to finish up.' In fact the dance instructor was right that moment turning off her music and thanking the students for their time and their attention.

'Sorry, again. Dancing though, how hard can it be? Hold on to a body and sway, right?'

'One does not hold onto anyone's body in Regency dance.'

He was still loitering.

'Mr Knight. What can I do for you?'

'This next event…'

'The family lunch?'

'Yeah. You're letting people's families come?'

'Not letting. Encouraging. A proper Regency season would have been chaperoned throughout, and part of forming a long-term bond is introducing that person to your nearest and dearest. Don't you agree?'

His discomfort was obvious.

'I mean it's not compulsory. We know some people don't have that sort of relationship with their family.'

'It's not that…'

Curiosity got the better of her. 'What then?'

'Is there any way you could not let certain people's families come?'

'No.' Obviously not.

'No. Right. Didn't think so. Could you possibly tell one particular family that they can't come?'

'Your family?'

'My mother.'

Emma sighed. She had no intention of getting in the middle of whatever was going on with Mr Knight and his mother. 'If you don't want her to come, why did you tell her about it?'

'Long story.'

'Tell me.'

'It's not your problem.'

'If it's getting in the way of you finding your one true love, Mr Knight, then it's very much my problem.'

He made no attempt to hide his incredulity. 'My one true love?'

'As I keep reminding you, that is what we're all here for.'

'Apart from you?'

She bristled. 'I'm working.'

'You must get comments though?'

'What do you mean?'

'About being a single matchmaker. You know, physician heal thyself and all that.'

'Only from idiots.' Her voice was ice.

–

Tom hesitated. The idea that was growing in the back of his mind was crazy, but all he'd had when he'd arrived here was 'persuade her not to do the family thing', which was, it seemed, a non-starter. And he'd clearly hit a nerve with the single match-maker jibe.

He'd still need to convince her that the insane notion he was cultivating would help her out too. He hadn't banked enough goodwill points with Miss Emma Love to persuade her to help him out of the kindness of her heart. 'It might get some of those idiots off your back if they thought you were seeing someone.'

'But I'm not.' She started to walk away from him, picking chairs from around the room and piling them three high.

He jumped ahead of her to assist. Looking helpful couldn't hurt his play, could it?

'But imagine if people thought you were, but in a way that meant you didn't actually have to go through any of the troublesome bits of being in a relationship?'

She straightened the pile of chairs he'd just stacked. 'You find being in a relationship troublesome?'

'Don't you? Honestly, Miss Love?'

'Forgive me for asking for the seventy-eighth time, why did you sign up for The Season again?'

Ok. So self-interest wasn't quite cutting it, but she hadn't walked away. He needed a new approach. There was always honesty. 'My mum wanted me to sign up.'

'Seriously? How old are you?'

'Twenty-eight.'

'And your mum chooses your social engagements for you?'

He shook his head. 'It's not like that. I signed myself up, obviously. You were there. But my mum is desperate for me to find someone. I promised her I'd try.'

Emma stacked the last lone chair on top of a stack of three and folded her arms. 'So here's a crazy idea – why don't you try?'

'Yeah. That would have been potentially helpful if a) I actually wanted to find a partner and b) I'd started six weeks ago. Now it's a week away from her coming along to meet the new love of my life and I've got nobody to show her.'

'So tell her you haven't met anybody yet? Maybe she'll be able to help you make a match. That's what mothers would have done if this was a real Regency season.'

Selective honesty hadn't got him there. It was time to go nuclear. It was time for total honesty.

'I already told her I met someone. She's delighted. I need a fake girlfriend for next week. Please will you help?'

Emma didn't even bother to try to hide the fact that she was laughing at him. 'You want me to pretend to be your imaginary girlfriend.'

'No. I want you to pretend to be my real girlfriend.'

'But you don't have a real girlfriend.'

She was being purposefully obtuse now. 'And that's the problem.'

She gathered up her bag and keys. He had one more shot. 'My mum is so desperate for me to find someone, and she saw this thing in the paper and so I signed up and she was so pleased I was coming. And yeah, I told her I'd met someone. It made her happy. It was a little white lie and then she heard about this family day thing and now she's expecting to meet her.'

'I don't see how this is my problem.'

'It's not. But you'd be helping me out and it would get people off your back too, wouldn't it? If you had a boyfriend?'

She didn't answer.

'Go on. One lunch and then you're off the hook?'

She shook her head. Damn.

'One day doesn't work for me.'

'What?'

'Well, if I'm supposed to be the queen of hearts…'

Something caught in his throat. 'The what?'

'You know the queen of romance and matchmaking. Having one date and then the guy running for the hills isn't the image I'm trying to project, is it?'

Hold on. She wasn't saying no. She was negotiating. 'What would work for you then?'

'It would have to look like a proper relationship. People would have to believe it had been going on quietly for a while and it has to last to the end of the Season. Being single is bad

257

enough. I definitely can't be recently dumped. I can't spend the evening with people looking at me sympathetically and asking what went wrong.'

That was only one more event after the family lunch. 'Ok. So 'til the end of the Season.'

She nodded. 'And then we have to agree how we're breaking up. I should dump you.'

'Why?' He could be the dumper. That was every bit as believable.

'Because then your mum can't have a go at you for throwing a good thing away and I'm not the poor little matchmaker who couldn't hold on to her man.'

Annoyingly, she was right. 'Fine. We stay together until the Season is over and then you dump me.' He held out his hand to shake on the deal.

She moved to take his hand and then pulled back. 'Wait. We'll need to put some work into this. If we're going to convince your mother that we're madly in love I need to know more about you than your name.'

'All right. So we need to revise.'

'When?'

They could hole up somewhere, right now, buy a couple of beers and share their life stories. That sounded like an actual date. And anyway, he glanced at the clock, he had other places to be. 'Can't tonight. What about tomorrow? We could meet for coffee and go over our CVs.'

'Deal.' They finally sealed it with a handshake, an exchange of mobile numbers and an agreement to meet at the Caffè Nero near Waterloo station, which met Tom's requirements of being both convenient and resolutely unromantic. And just like that he had the perfect girlfriend – one who required nothing from him.

–

Emma watched Tom jog down the street to the bus stop.

'Is he your young man then?'

The dance teacher followed her out of the studio and set about locking up. Emma started to shake her head and then remembered herself. 'Yes actually. Well, you know, early days but yeah.'

The woman nodded appreciatively. 'Lucky. He's got a lovely bum. Nice strong glutes for a gavotte.'

Emma obviously had zero interest in either Tom's bum or his abilities in relation to whatever a gavotte was... Some sort of fancy cake perhaps?

The woman handed her an envelope. 'My invoice. You don't need to deal with it now.'

Emma ripped the envelope open. Better to know how much deeper into the pit this afternoon had sent her. She scanned the contents. 'This isn't right.'

'I think it is, dear.'

Emma read again. The caterer was invoicing her separately, so this bill covered the studio time and the teacher's fee. The total came to £50.

'My girl's coming in to clean before my classes tomorrow, and I have to pay her.'

'Yeah. Of course, but what about the rest?'

The dance teacher gave a little smile. 'Well, you're Emma Love's daughter, aren't you?'

'Yeah.'

'Met my Richard through your mother.' She pulled her phone out of her pocket and showed Emma the lock screen. It was a family photo with generations of children and grandchildren leaning into the frame. 'Four kids. Nine grandchildren now. Two step-grandchildren, and one of them's pregnant. I keep telling them I'm far too young to be a great grandma. Anyway, I owe your mother far more than a dance lesson.'

Emma was supposed to be doing this on her own. Even from the other side of the continent, her mum was bailing her out.

'Thank you. I really appreciate it. I'll give your regards to my mum.'

'Do that. I owe her my whole life.'

Chapter Eighteen

Emma set off home. Josh was out so she would have the house to herself for the evening. She made her mental plan. Takeaway. Glass of wine. Log on. Don't think about the Season finances.

She rang in her delivery order as she strolled back from the station. It was a routine she had honed to well-practised perfection, so she was home, make-up cleaned off, work suit hung in the wardrobe, her lounging uniform of yoga pants and T-shirt on, laptop fired up, and poker site logged in, just in time to answer the door to her lemon chicken and special fried rice.

She set her dinner out next to her computer, poured a massive glass of wine, and clicked to take a virtual seat at the private table.

All right, Queenie.

Hello, Walt

She typed back.

Two cards appeared on the screen in front of her. Paired kings. She grinned. The evening was looking rosy.

The flop gave a nine, a six and a two. Someone with seven and eight would have an open route to a straight. She checked. Walt raised. Her instinct was to fold, but she had paired kings. She saw his bet.

A five on the turn. That would make the straight if he was sitting on a seven and eight. He checked. She did the same. The rest of the table followed the same pattern.

The river was a king. Trip kings. So there was no chance of an opponent having three aces. Only the straight could beat her. Walt went all in. She should fold. The risk was too high. She checked their chip totals. All in for him was two million. She was sitting on eight. She could see his bet. Her finger hovered over the fold button. It wasn't even real money. There was no risk. That wasn't the point. If you took that attitude you bet on anything and never won a game. She should fold.

But... he was a bluffer. She knew that. He was the sort who'd bet on raindrops running down a window pane. She matched his bet and closed her eyes.

The rest of the table folded immediately. And he had... she braced herself for the seven, eight and the straight. He had... the seven, but his second card was a three. Nothing. He had nothing.

> Well played. I thought you were going to wimp out.

She smiled to herself.

> Maybe you don't know me as well as you think.

> Or maybe you've changed? Maybe you don't hate taking chances as much as you say.

She shook her head. Ridiculous.

> Or perhaps I've learned to read you.

262

> You didn't come on Monday.

He called her bluff.

Should she tell him?

> I nearly did.

> What stopped you?

It was just words she was throwing out into the ether. If she couldn't tell the truth here, where could she?

> I didn't want to spoil this.

Because this was something. This was the only place where she wasn't Miss Love, or Emma Love's daughter, or Josh's little sister, or the person who was supposed to be in control.

> You think meeting me would spoil something?

> Maybe.

> Maybe it would improve it.

But it would change things, she thought.

> It's a risk though.

So you folded instead of taking the chance?

Pretty much.

He didn't reply for minute. Emma wondered if he'd logged off altogether. The three little dots reappeared.

I don't know if you can live without taking risks.

Says the man with no chips left

she typed back.

And if you'd folded you wouldn't be sitting on that stack right now.

Poker isn't life.

Of course not. The rewards in life are bigger.

Emma's stomach churned with the horrid out-of-control feeling she'd always hated.

I like chatting like this. I didn't want to mess it up.

Another long pause before he answered.

> Maybe you're right. Maybe this is safer.

That's what she'd concluded. She couldn't be disappointed if he felt the same. Could she?

Walt was typing again.

> Tell me about your day.

Ah. A brisk subject change to ease the awkwardness. Exactly what Emma would have done herself.

> I thought we didn't do that.

> Let's live a little.

> Not much to tell. Been at work. One very annoying customer with a very mad idea, but apart from that, same old, same old.

> A very mad idea?

She started to type the story of the infuriating Mr Knight and his need for a fake date and then she stopped and tapped back to delete what she'd written. She didn't want to tell Walt about her dating life, even her pretend dating life.

> It's nothing

she typed.

He didn't reply.

> How was your day?

she tried.

> Not too bad. Went to see my mum. Gotta keep
> my status as her golden boy in place.

> Is it under threat?

> Never! I'm offended at the suggestion. I'm the
> perfect son.

She added 'loves his mum' to the very slim list of things she knew about SirWalt.

She realised that she hadn't played the next hand and his chip stack was down to zero, thanks to her. They were just chatting.

> You're not mad with me for the no-show?

> Only for a second.

He clearly wasn't that disappointed that she hadn't turned up. For the best really. She didn't even know what he looked like. She might have walked past him in the street a hundred times and not looked twice. This wasn't a relationship. It was better to keep it that way.

She started typing.

> I've got to go. Got…

How should she describe it?

> some work to do for tomorrow.

> Tomorrow's Sunday.

> Busy, busy, busy.

she typed.

Chapter Nineteen

Tom ran into the cafe nine and a half minutes after their agreed meeting time. She was already there. Of course she was already there. He'd have guessed she was the punctual type.

'Waiting long?'

'Long enough.'

He grinned. 'Less than ten minutes isn't late. It's within the general "on time" bracket.'

'No. It's not.'

He looked at what she had spread across the table. Tablet, upright on its stand ready, he guessed, for note-taking. Ring binder, bright blue, apparently brand new and with coloured dividers. 'Got a meeting after this?' he asked hopefully.

She shook her head. Right. He excused himself to grab a coffee with an extra shot.

'So what's all this?' he asked, fearing he already knew the answer, as he took the seat opposite her.

'Revision materials. All the things you need to know if anyone is going to believe that you're my boyfriend.'

'It's my mother we're trying to fool. She's never met you. She's not exactly going to set an exam, is she?'

'Your mother is the main focus, sure. But my stepbrother and my mum are going to be there and I don't see any way that I can be acting all loved up with you without them noticing, so you need to be convincing too. Otherwise the whole thing falls apart.'

She had a point. He wished she didn't, but she did.

'Your mum's going to be there?'

'Yeah. She's still a company director. She wants to come and see how it's all going.' There was an edge of something in her voice.

'And it matters what she thinks?'

She nodded silently.

'Because?'

'Because I promised her this would work,' she whispered.

'All right then.' He lifted the folder towards him. 'Best get stuck in then.'

He opened to the first section.

Birth & Childhood

'Why do I need to know that you were seven pounds precisely at birth? When did you ever kick off a first date by telling someone your birth weight?'

'I like to be thorough.'

He patted the ring binder, which he now realised was actually a lever arch file. 'I can see that.'

'So what about you?'

'Sorry. What?'

'What have you prepared for me?'

'I thought we'd just sort of chat.'

She stared at him. 'We have one morning to pull this together and you've done no preparation.'

He shrugged. 'I know all about myself though. I'm a walking revision guide. Seriously, ask me anything.'

'What was your weight at birth then?'

'I have no idea.'

'I'll ask your mum.'

He shook his head. 'Please don't. I was adopted. There. That's a thing a serious girlfriend would probably know.'

'So she's your adoptive mum.'

'She's my mum.' He could hear the tension in his own voice. He swallowed. She was helping him out. There was no reason

269

to be snippy. 'I came to my parents when I was nearly two. I don't remember anything before that and I've never been in contact with my birth family.'

She nodded. 'Ok. So brothers and sisters?'

He shook his head. 'I think they would have wanted to adopt again but my dad got ill when I was five or six, and he died when I was nine, so no. Only child.'

'I'm sorry.'

He turned the page in the grand folder of Emma and laughed. 'You put school photos in!' There she was, hair pulled back into two pigtails and a middle tooth missing. 'How old is this?'

'Year three, so I was seven.'

'Well, you were adorable.'

'Thank you.'

'So what about you? Brothers and sisters?'

'One brother, three years older than me. You'll have seen him at the events.'

'Tall dark-haired guy?'

'That's him. Stepbrother really. My mum married his dad when I was twelve and Josh was nearly fifteen.'

'Ok. Now we're getting somewhere. One stepbrother who works for you. Mum who's a director of your business. So family's important to you?'

She nodded.

'But we're going to be lying to them?'

Emma hadn't quite thought about it that way. She'd thought that it would be good for business if it seemed like she was in a successful relationship. She'd thought that it would stop Josh teasing her. She'd thought that it would help Tom out without any real downside for her. But what if her mum adored him and three weeks later she had to tell her it hadn't worked out? She thought through the plan. Mum was mainly coming back to check on the business. Tom could be introduced as a new suitor and then he could quietly be dropped from conversation over the next few weeks. 'It'll be fine. I'm sure you're not so charming that they won't be able to get over you.'

He laughed. 'You haven't seen me turn it on.'

Her brain served her an unwelcome flash of that grin at the casino night. Just a look. Not even really a moment at all. She shook her head. 'I think we'll be ok.' She tapped the folder in front of him. 'You've got work to do and all I know about you is that you're adopted. I need more information.'

'Fine.' He flicked through another few pages. Emma felt her lips pursing. She was quite sure he wasn't taking in the names of her primary school teachers and classmates at all. He stopped. 'All right. So you went to university in Exeter?'

She nodded. 'What about you?'

'Royal Academy of Music.'

'Don't be silly.'

'Piano and composition.'

'You're a pianist? Like as a job?'

'Amongst other things.'

She tapped 'Pianist' into her notes, and another memory came to the surface. She'd seen him before the first ball when he said he'd been working. She remembered seeing 'a recital of chamber music' on the events board and assuming that couldn't be him. Emma wasn't used to sizing someone up and getting them wrong. 'So are you in an orchestra or a band or something?'

He shook his head. 'I sometimes play with an ensemble – classical stuff. Mostly I play session music for bands and TV and adverts and anything else that needs it to pay the rent. And I compose a bit for jingles and stuff like that.' He paused. 'And I play—'

'Ok. So you're a pianist and I'm a matchmaker. What else? What do you like to do for fun?'

He fell silent, sipping on his coffee and not meeting her eye. 'What's wrong?' she asked him.

'Nothing.'

'Ok. So what do you do for fun?'

'Not much.'

He was definitely avoiding the question. He was into something dodgy, wasn't he? 'I need to know if we're going to make this believable.'

He rubbed the base of his thumb under his eye. 'I… I used to like to travel and swim and dive and I loved the beach.'

'Used to?'

'I don't know. Do we want to tell each other our sad stories?'

'Do we need to?' She paused. 'I mean for the fake romance thing.'

He nodded. 'Right. Yeah. For the fake romance thing. So, I was married before.'

'You're divorced?'

He shook his head.

'I'm sorry.'

'We were on holiday. We rented a boat to go snorkelling. We always used to go out together so we could keep an eye on one another, but I didn't feel very well. He said he'd stay near the boat and not go out of view. I was watching him. I only looked away for a minute.' He rubbed away tears from both cheeks. 'He was a good swimmer and he was a dancer so he was in really good shape. I don't even know exactly what happened.'

Emma could feel her own eyes getting moist. She blinked the tears back. This wasn't her place to cry. This wasn't her tragedy. 'How long ago?'

'Two years.'

'I'm so sorry.'

He nodded. 'I think my mum worries that I'll never find anyone else.'

'Do you want to find someone else?'

'I don't know. I loved him. He loved me. We were in paradise and it all fell apart in an instant. It feels like nothing is constant. So I don't know. I don't know what falling in love again would even feel like.'

She was supposed to be an expert in these things. She'd worked with widows and widowers before. She tried to think about it as her professional self. A second chance at love. Wasn't that what everyone in that situation wanted? 'Tell me about him.'

'Isn't going on about your beloved partner bad first date etiquette?'

She smiled. 'Maybe but this isn't a proper first date. But only if you want to talk about him.'

'So he was a dancer, like I said. He was assistant choreographer on a show at the Palace Theatre. I was playing piano for the auditions. That's how we met.'

'Love at first sight?'

'Everything at first sight,' Tom whispered. He took a big gulp of coffee. 'Sorry. This isn't what you came here for. Let me write down my inside leg measurement for you.'

She laughed lightly, letting him know that she would go along with his choice to lighten the mood. 'So, sorry, to clarify – you said *he*?'

'Yeah. I'm bi. Well, pan, but people don't know what that means sometimes.'

She nodded and typed pansexual into her notes.

'You're ok with that?'

'Is your fake girlfriend ok with you also liking men?' She smiled at the ridiculousness of the question but she answered anyway for the avoidance of doubt. 'Yes. Of course, I'm fine with that.'

'Cool. Good.' He looked serious again. 'And if this was for real?'

'Yeah. I mean people who are going to be tempted elsewhere, are going to be tempted. It's nothing to do with sexuality.'

'Ok. That's not me, for the record,' he added. 'If I'm with someone, I'm with them. All in.'

'It's that simple?' she asked.

'With the right someone I think it is. Yeah.'

She held his gaze a moment longer than she needed to. 'But you're not looking for anyone at the moment anyway.'

'And neither are you.'

'No.' Of course not. This was an entirely unromantic mutually beneficial arrangement. Emma looked back at her notes. 'So, sorry, your husband's name was?'

'Jack.' Hold on. He pulled his phone from his pocket and tapped the screen on before he held it out towards her. The lock-screen image was two men – Tom and she presumed, Jack – arms wrapped around one another, cocktails in hand, faces tanned, smiles broad.

'You look happy.'

'We were.' He paused for a second, staring at the screen before he put his phone, face down, on the table. 'Onward. What about the basics? Where do you live?'

'Richmond. I'm supposed to be getting my mum's house ready to sell, but mostly I seem to just be living in it. What about you?'

'Herne Hill at the moment. I've moved a few times recently though. Had a place in Walthamstow with Jack but since he died I can't quite seem to settle.'

'I'm sorry.'

He shook his head. 'Anyway, what about your dating history?'

She pointed at the folder. 'Purple section.'

–

Three days after the dance lesson, Jane was in her bathroom. She set the timer countdown on her phone for three minutes.

Three minutes.

It had been Lydia's stupid joke about lesbians buying sanitary protection that had made her think. She hadn't bought any since she'd been seeing Charlotte. Had she? She'd done the count back in her head, then she'd done it again on her calendar and then she'd ignored her own conclusion for two days thinking that maybe her period would just appear and this was nothing more than her stupid overanxious brain turning nothing into something.

Two minutes, twenty seconds.

The one-minute test had only been £1.49 more expensive. She cursed herself for being such a cheapskate.

Two minutes, eight seconds.

She thought of Lunar. The idea of a whole life appearing in front of her – a whole person who wasn't there one moment and was the next. A new life with endless possibilities.

One minute, fifty seconds.

It would be negative. Of course it would be negative. Lots of things could make a period late. Stress. Stress was definitely one of them. Two visits to her parents would probably be enough. And before that it had been the end of term and that was always busy. And she'd only recently got divorced. And she'd come out to her friends. By any measure there'd been a lot going on.

One minute, twenty-six seconds.

And then she thought about Charlotte. Who was she kidding? She always thought about Charlotte. It was so right. Everything she'd thought would be weird or difficult about a new relationship had just fallen into place. Things felt easy, natural and as though they were both reading from the same script. It wasn't even that she'd been starting to imagine a future for them. It was as though that future was already written and everything was simply slotting into place. And now, in one stupid night, her body might have torn up the script.

One minute precisely.

All she'd ever wanted, through the years growing up in mess and goat shit and madness, through the years of being married and feeling as though she was playing a role she didn't know the words for, was for things to be straightforward. She wanted a simple life.

Thirty-eight seconds.

And now she was on the brink of that. Work was crazy but it had structure and she was good at it and it suited her well. Her flat was small but perfectly ordered. And Charlotte was everything she'd never dared to hope for. There wasn't space for a baby. A baby wasn't in the plan. Babies were messy, loud and unpredictable and she'd run away from all of that once already.

Nine seconds.

It didn't matter, of course. It was going to be negative. Nothing was going to throw Jane's second chance at happiness into chaos.

The timer on her phone bleeped insistently.

Zero seconds left.

She picked up the pregnancy test and turned it over.

–

Emma took the last plate out of the dishwasher, put the whole stack into the cupboard and then stood back and scanned the kitchen. There was a place for everything, and it looked as though everything was in its place.

She made her way to the hallway. The phone and message pad were on the table next to the door. She'd moved Josh's hoodie off the bottom of the bannister and put it in his room. She'd vacuumed. She'd cleaned the window in the front door.

Living room. Nothing, so far as she could see, was out of place. Her mum would find something though and if there was nothing to find she'd make something up.

Josh's car pulling up outside meant it was time. Emma ran to the kitchen and filled the kettle. They had the nice Lady Grey tea bags from Waitrose and posh biscuits. If her mother was going to find something amiss she was going to have to work for it at least.

'We're back,' Josh yelled from the hallway.

Emma rushed through. Her mum's signature skirt suit and neat chignon were gone. Of course they were. She'd been retired for months now. She let her mother wrap her in a hug. 'Shall I put the kettle on?' Emma asked.

'Oh, don't be so English. I think the sun is well over the yardarm.'

Emma's mother never drank on a week night and never more than one glass with dinner at the weekend. 'Ok. I think there's some rosé in the fridge.'

'Lovely.'

'I'll get drinks,' Josh offered.

Emma followed her mum into the sitting room.

'Oh.' There was a note of disappointment in the exclamation. Here it came. Mrs Love's checklist of all the things that weren't quite up to scratch. 'You haven't changed much, dear.'

'I didn't think you'd want me to.'

Her mother shrugged expansively. 'It's no bother to me, is it? I don't live here any more. Shall we sit in the garden?'

Over wine and kettle chips her mother filled them in on her new yoga class, the watercolour painting group that Judy from downstairs was setting up, the book club and her Spanish lessons.

And Emma realised something. 'You're not coming back, are you?'

Her mother ran her fingers up and down the stem of her glass. 'I don't think so sweetheart.' She looked around. 'There's something missing here now, you know?'

They fell quiet for a moment. It was strange. Emma didn't feel her stepdad's absence usually; it was as if her brain had drawn him in next to her mum in Emma's mental picture of life in Spain, but now her mum was here the gap alongside her was palpable.

Chapter Twenty

The Love Family
request the honour of the company of Mr Tom
Knight,
accompanied by his closest family, for luncheon.

'I haven't done a seating plan.' Emma pointed the elegant calligraphy sign inviting people to mingle and take a seat wherever they chose, out to her mother, and waited for the explanation of why she ought to have arranged the seating herself.

Her mother nodded. 'Informal. Very nice.'

'I mean I could have done a seating plan, but it's a friends and family day so I don't have definite final numbers. Which would have made things a little bit tricky.'

'Yes. Of course. I understand.' Her mother leaned over one of the tables to smell the flower arrangement. 'These are beautiful.'

'You don't think flowers are a bit of a cliché for a dating event? You're not worried about allergies?'

'Oh, I'm sure people can take an antihistamine if they need to. It looks lovely.' Her mother looked around the room. 'I'll pop myself in the corner there. I know you two have got work to do.'

'Don't you want to check the buffet? They might be putting vegetarian options on the same platters as the meat.'

'I'm sure you've got it all in hand.'

'What are you doing?' Josh put a hand on her shoulder as their mum walked away. 'Why are you goading her into finding something wrong?'

She couldn't explain. It was how things had always been. Her mum was the queen bee. What she said was the final word on any subject.

'You've been mental ever since she arrived.'

'I have not. I mean there's loads she'd normally pick up on.' She pointed to a pair of tables towards the back of the room. 'Those tables have different cloths to the rest.'

'Do they?'

'Yeah. There's a motif thing round the edges.' She turned a full three-sixty to assess the rest of the set-up. 'Do you think the quartet will have covers for their music stands?'

'Nobody will be looking.'

'I'll be looking. And Mum. She might not be saying but she will be noticing.'

Josh shook his head.

'And I've got something else to tell her.' Why on earth had Emma agreed to this? 'Well, to tell you both.'

'What?'

Her mum was now sitting at a table in the corner of the room checking her phone. Emma could see the difference in her. She was tanned. Her hair was hanging loose around her face. She looked relaxed rather than full of pent-up energy.

'Stilts!'

'What?'

'What else do you have to tell us? You're making me nervous.'

'Right.' If she was going to sell this lie she might as well start now. 'I'm seeing someone. He's coming today.'

'Who? Not one of the daters?'

She nodded.

'What happened to not shitting where you eat?'

'What?'

'You made a big deal about it being unprofessional.'

'And you said it was fine,' she reminded her brother. 'He came along wanting to meet someone and he met someone. Everybody's happy.'

'Yeah. You really look happy.' He prodded the side of her forehead. 'You've got a vein here that's gone all twitchy.'

'I just don't want it to be a whole big thing, you know. His mum's coming and our mum can be…' Emma didn't know how to end that sentence. 'Well, you know.'

'So you want me to run interference?'

'Yeah. If you could get together with someone entirely unobjectionable in the next twenty minutes that would be perfect.'

'Does that imply that she might find your chap objectionable?'

'No.' She thought about it. Her experience of Tom to date was that he was scruffy, rarely punctual and often grumpy. 'Maybe,' she conceded, but the picture of the relaxed smiling man with his arms wrapped around his partner was still there in her memory. The person she'd met only gave the briefest of glimpses of the person in that photograph. 'I don't know.'

'So which one is he?' Josh frowned. 'I'm trying to remember who's still single.'

'Mr Knight.'

'You call your boyfriend Mr Knight?'

'Tom.'

Josh shook his head. 'Not that miserable bugger you stuck Lydia with at the dinner?'

'He's not miserable.' Emma bristled slightly on behalf of her imaginary beau. 'You said Lydia was all over him. He was probably trying to escape without being rude.'

'And he was trying to escape because he was already seeing someone?'

That seemed to make sense. More sense than the actual truth anyway. 'Yeah. Obviously.'

'Didn't you tell me to prioritise finding a match for him?'

Damn. She had, hadn't she? Time to bluff. 'I don't think so.'

'You did.'

She shook her head as definitely as she could manage. 'You must have misunderstood. Now will you go and keep Mum company while I sort these tablecloths out?'

'You're serious about the tablecloths?'

Emma didn't dignify the question with a reply. If a person couldn't see that simply swapping one of the two different cloths with another from the other side of the room would make the whole thing look more like intentional variety rather than tasteless accident, then she really didn't have time to explain.

–

Finally, the room was set up to her satisfaction. Today's event was different to anything they'd tried before, but it was essential to the Season idea. It wasn't so much about making sure families approved as seeing how the person fit into your real life. The Season was a bubble, a beautiful, charming romantic bubble, but a bubble nonetheless. And in a week's time everyone would be back in reality trying to make their Season romance translate into something with longevity. Today was about bridging that gap.

She watched the guests arrive. The daters were getting a little bit blasé about the pretty table settings and the champagne on tap. She needed to remember that for the final ball. The venue was spectacular but everything else was going to need to be perfect if she was going to elevate things further still. The newcomers though, were stopping to coo and whisper over the beautiful flowers and were giggling with delight as they picked up their glasses of champagne.

She watched the waiting staff making their rounds with trays of drinks. Her caterer's regular bar manager had cried off for the last three events, but whoever had replaced him seemed to have things in hand and everything was going smoothly. She turned her smile up to eleven and set off to make her rounds.

First stop Jane and Charlotte, who had already taken seats at a table in the corner nearest to the buffet. An older woman with her hair wrapped in a bright purple scarf was next to Jane. She had a tiny baby in a papoose at her chest. On Jane's other side was Charlotte and then a rather more conventionally dressed couple. Emma smiled. 'Welcome to The Season.'

'Thank you.' The older woman looked up from the baby at her breast. 'Oh, you're Joshie's sister, aren't you? I remember you from the wedding.'

Of course.

The woman grabbed Charlotte's hand. 'You'll not mind us mentioning it, will you? They were all wrong for each other. Not like you two.'

Jane interrupted. 'This is my mum.'

Emma nodded. 'Welcome.'

'And this is Charlotte's brother, Evan, and his wife, Sanjita.'

Emma smiled across the table.

'It's their first time out without their youngest, you know?' Jane's mother interrupted. 'I've suggested coconut oil for her nipples, haven't I?'

Sanjita nodded with an expression of disbelief. 'Yes. Yes. You have.'

'Mum!' Jane's face was turning an ever-deeper red.

'Oh, don't be embarrassed, love. She'll thank me when her nipples aren't sore any more.'

Emma moved on. Colin Williams. Her heart sank a little. Still on his own but joined now by a rather glamorous woman in what looked like Roland Mouret. 'Colin, how are you?' Emma dipped her head to kiss his cheek.

'Tickety boo. This is my mother. Big bro couldn't make it – all tied up with wedding preparations.'

Emma had heard snippets of the saga of Colin and his brother's intersecting love lives. She decided on discretion rather than questioning further. She turned to his mother. You would not have laid bets on this woman raising this son. Colin was a bit over-eager but that over-eagerness was rooted in his deep wish to make people happy. This woman was the opposite. She was cool in the very best and worst senses of the word. Emma smiled regardless. 'Welcome. Colin has been quite the star of the Season. I don't think there's a person here who's not at least a bit in love with him.'

She saw Colin grow an inch under her praise.

'But nobody quite ready to commit so far as I can see?'

Colin shrank back down again.

'Sometimes these things are a marathon rather than a sprint, Mrs Williams.'

'Ms Delaney. I got shot of that wastrel's name the same day I got shot of him.'

'Apologies. Ms Delaney.' Emma left them to their mutual disappointment, more determined than ever to find Colin his much sought happy-ever-after. He needed someone caring, someone who'd be kind to him and see the good heart under the bluster, but also, she realised, someone with the backbone to stand up to his mother. And someone who wouldn't shag his brother. That, she hoped, was a given in any of the matches she made.

Annie was standing by the entrance. Emma joined her. 'Do you have anyone coming?'

'I told Mum about it, but she's busy with Duncan and his regular carer couldn't come today so…' Annie shrugged. 'I don't think so.'

She was squeezing her hand so tightly into a fist that her knuckles had whitened. 'I'm sure she'd be here if she could.'

'Of course she would.' Annie was smiling but the wobble in her voice was clear. Emma searched for the right thing to say.

'Hilly!' exclaimed Annie.

'What?'

'Hilly's here, the carer. That must be why she couldn't sit with Dunc.'

Emma followed her gaze. A tall athletic woman in a bright pink tunic top was pushing a lady in a wheelchair through the lift doors and directly towards them.

Emma let Annie move past her to greet them. She hugged the carer and the two started a chatter of why they were both there and… Emma couldn't listen. She couldn't concentrate on what they were saying, or what was happening in the party, or what anyone might be saying to her. The room fell away and there was only one thing left. The man coming out of the lift behind them. No scruffy floppy hair, no leather jacket, no scowl.

Thomas Knight was wearing a dark blue linen suit over a collarless white shirt. His hair was brushed and gelled away from his face. He smiled.

She smiled back.

And for a second that was all there was.

And then the moment broke. Sounds crashed in. Tom was moving towards her. This was it then. Showtime.

–

The way she was staring at him almost made him stop where he was and run back to the lift and out of the building. No. She was only doing what he'd asked. She was playing the part of the adoring girlfriend in the loved-up heyday of a new romance. It wasn't the way she was looking at him that was the problem; it was the way he felt when she looked at him like that.

It was too late now. 'Em!' He walked right up to her and kissed her cheek. Just her cheek. Your mother is right there, he told himself, quieting the other voice that said if he was really her boyfriend surely he could steal a kiss on the lips.

Actually, although he'd been tasked with memorising the names of her seventeen favourite childhood toys, they hadn't talked about whether they were going to kiss or hold hands or anything like that and he didn't want to disrespect whatever boundaries she wanted to keep in place. Maybe they could get away with acting like they were a little uncomfortable in front of family.

'So, Emma, this is my mum.'

Emma stepped forward and grasped his mother's hand. 'Mrs Knight?'

'Gloria. You can call me Gloria.'

He stood back and watched as Emma was introduced to Hilly. She had grace. He had to give her that. She was polite and friendly but not too much, and she was attentive to the people she was meeting, listening intently to what they were telling her. The perfect matchmaker, he supposed.

'And Tom, this is Josh, my brother.'

Tom shook hands with the tall man who'd joined them while Emma was meeting Hilly. Jeez that was a firm handshake. Ah, the overprotective big brother thing. Tom kept the wince off his face and slapped Josh cheerfully on the arm, pretending everything was peachy. This fake boyfriend thing was so much easier than the real deal. If he was really Emma's partner he might have been upset by Josh's alpha male act. Relationships were easier when you took the feelings out of them.

–

'You come and sit with me dear.' Tom's mother directed her carer towards an empty table in the middle of the room. 'I want to hear all about you.'

'Emma's working, Mum. I told you she wouldn't be able to sit and chat the whole time.'

'Oh pish. I'm sure she's got time to keep an old woman company for a few minutes, haven't you, dear?'

'Of course. Can I get you a drink or something to eat first though?'

'I'll get those,' said Hilly. 'I'll never hear the end of it if you get waylaid.' She leaned over her charge. 'No interrogations. Remember? Don't scare her off.'

'As if I would.' She turned her attention onto Emma. It was like being caught in the full beam of a spotlight. 'So, tell me all about yourself.'

What to say? What would Tom already have told her? Not much, Emma suspected. Although Gloria Knight seemed like a person who would have a way of getting whatever information she wanted, even from a son who was used to dodging her queries. Sticking close to the truth was their agreed approach. It seemed the least likely to cause anyone to slip up. 'Well, I'm a matchmaker. Seeing Tom is a bit naughty actually. There's a sort of unwritten rule.'

'Do you break the rules a lot?'

Emma floundered. 'Well, no, of course not. Never had so much as a speeding ticket. And the dating thing is more of a guideline.' She looked into the older woman's face. 'And you're joking?'

'Of course I am. My son,' she raised her voice to ensure she was heard as Tom approached their table, 'may think I'm a humourless old woman.'

'I do not.'

'He speaks very highly of you,' squeaked Emma.

'I'm sure.' Gloria beamed. 'Don't worry, dear. My only reservation is that any fool can see you're far too good for him.'

'Mum!'

Gloria looked around the room. 'She did all this?'

Emma nodded.

'It reminds me of the tea parties we used to put on when his father was alive.'

Now Emma was genuinely interested. 'Tea parties?'

'We were caterers. We went everywhere before this one came along. I once made crêpes suzette on a yacht for the Sultan of Brunei.'

'She didn't.' Tom was shaking his head.

Gloria caught Emma's eye. 'Parents are always dull old people in their children's eyes,' she explained. She tapped the arm of her chair. 'Before motherhood and wasting muscles I had quite the life.'

Emma grinned. 'It's not over yet.'

'You think there's a young man here to put a spring in my step?'

Tom looked entirely mortified.

'Well, maybe not here but I will check my books when I get back.'

Gloria smiled. 'You're sweet. But I'm not on the market. I have my puzzles and Hilly's nearly good enough at cards now that I don't win every time. I'm doing very nicely as I am.'

Tom moved to take the seat next to Emma, twisting in his chair so that they were both facing his mum. That put him slightly behind Emma. She was aware of his presence without looking around. She could lean back a little and her body would be against his arm. His lips would be alongside her cheek. His hand might... She straightened her back and perched, bolt upright, on the edge of her chair.

'So, tell me where else you've prepared crêpes suzette?'

The older woman's eyes gleamed. 'No shifting the spotlight, dear.' Gloria looked around the room. 'You have done a marvellous job here.'

'Thank you.'

'Hasn't she, Tom?'

She turned to see his reaction. 'Yeah.' He looked around. 'It looks amazing.'

'Now go and see where Hilly is with that food, dear.'

'And leave Emma unguarded?'

'She'll be fine. I don't bite.'

'It's ok.' Emma squeezed Tom's hand in what she hoped would look like a casual gesture of affection. Did it look like that? It didn't feel like that. It felt like a moment of radiance in the darkness. And then she couldn't remember how to let go. How did you let go of a lover's hand casually? What was she supposed to do with her fingers? How did fingers work? Why fingers? Why? She dropped his hand like it had scalded her. Cool cool cool. This was all fine.

He gave her the weirdest look as he stood to check on Hilly. Probably wondering when she'd gone completely mad and forgotten how to operate her own limbs.

'I can see right through him you know?'

That couldn't be good. 'What do you mean?'

Gloria rested her hands on her lap in front of her. 'When Jack went he was devastated. I know what that's like but with his father he'd been ill for a long time before. We knew it was coming. I got to say goodbye, but for someone to be there all full of life and then…' She paused. 'Well, it seems impossible, doesn't it? That it could all go away like…' She raised a hand and clicked her fingers. 'It changed him. He guards how he feels now. But I'm his mother. I see it.'

'What do you mean?'

'I see how he looks at you, dear.'

She'd promised she'd play along but she could hear how much Gloria had invested in Tom being happy. 'It's really early days still.'

'I know. I know. But he's all in. I can see that even if he can't. Silly boy.' She looked around, apparently checking whether her son was on his way back. 'It never leaves you, wanting to be able to scoop your children up and make everything better. It's the hardest thing knowing you have to let them deal with all the pain of the world, so I won't say any more than this. Please don't hurt him, Emma. I know you can't promise. But do say you'll try. He's taken so long to put himself back together. I don't think either of us would manage if he had to do it again.'

Emma nodded silently. She was wrong, of course. Tom thought of her as a crazy woman with an over-fondness for ring binders. But Gloria was a lovely lady. She didn't want Gloria to think badly of her. 'It is early days, but of course I don't want to cause him any pain.'

She could see Tom making his way back to the table.

'I should get back to work. I'll try to come by again a bit later.' She headed in the opposite direction as briskly as she could.

Those at the rest of the tables seemed to be enjoying the party. There was a good ripple of conversation around the room and nobody, that she could spot, was glaring wordlessly at their son or daughter's new beau.

Hilly had stopped by where Annie and Josh were standing in the doorway. Emma made her way over.

'You escaped then?'

Emma nodded.

'And you've still got all your limbs. So you must have passed muster?'

'I think so. She's sweet.'

Hilly laughed from her belly. 'She definitely likes you then. Took about six months of working there before I got a smile out of her.'

'But you persevered?'

'Of course. People don't always like having to have a stranger in to look after them. They want independence. It's natural that it takes a while to adapt.'

The beginnings of an idea were brewing in Emma's head. 'So have you ever had a patient you couldn't win over?'

'Not yet. Why?'

'And you're single?'

'Yeah. Split up with someone just before Christmas.' There was a wariness in her voice now. 'Why?'

Josh interjected. 'She's in matchmaker mode. It's easier to go along with it.'

'I'm not sure I want to be matchmade.'

Josh shrugged. 'She's really good. You'll almost certainly like them.'

Emma was on a mission now. 'And do you date men or women or either?'

'Men.'

'Great.' The next bit was trickier. 'And what's your priority? You know, looks versus personality?'

'I dunno. Personality I guess.'

Emma ran through her requirements. Caring – tick. Not a pushover – tick. Would she see Colin for the catch Emma was convinced he was?

'Why did you break up with your last boyfriend? Sorry.' She pulled what she hoped was a suitably apologetic face to defuse the potentially awkward question.

'Seriously?'

Emma nodded.

'It wasn't any one thing. I don't know. It seemed like he was more bothered about being cool than being happy or kind.'

Bingo. She threaded her arm through Hilly's. 'Then I have someone I'd absolutely love you to meet.'

–

Tom came up from behind her. 'Is it your family's turn then?'

She supposed it had to be. Her mother didn't know about the whole boyfriend thing yet, but Josh would tell her and then there'd be an outrage that she hadn't had an introduction. She gave Tom a quick once-over. He scrubbed up well. Very well. Would it be enough for her mum? 'Once more into the breach then.'

He laced his fingers through hers. 'Is that ok?'

She nodded. She nodded because she couldn't exactly remember how to make words. Everything in her consciousness was the touch of his hand against hers, the warmth of skin on skin, the strange urge to turn to him and run her other hand across his chest. 'Yep,' she managed.

Her mother was still sitting in her corner, apparently contentedly watching the world spin around her. It was a front. Emma knew that. Inside, she'd be mentally ticking off all the things she would have done better.

'Mum, there's someone I want you to meet. This is Tom.'

She watched her mother take in the clasped hands and the nervy tone in her daughter's voice.

'Tom, lovely to meet you. I'm Emma.'

'Emma as well?'

She nodded. 'Well, men do it all the time, don't they? John and John junior and all that nonsense, so why not?'

Tom took a seat next to Mrs Love. 'Why not indeed? Emma said you lived near Malaga?'

Emma was impressed. It sounded like he'd done his homework reading after all.

'Torre del Mar. Do you know that part of Spain?'

'A little bit. We stayed near Nerja for a couple of weeks a few years ago.'

'We?'

Tom glanced to the floor. 'I was married before. My partner died.'

'Oh, I'm sorry. You'll know I lost my Trevor.'

Tom nodded. 'Emma said.'

'Moving on's the right thing. It doesn't mean you've forgotten them.'

What the actual? Tom looked like he might be starting to well up. Emma's mum was not the heart-warming moment type. Emma jumped in. 'Tom's a pianist.'

'That's right. And I play—'

'Oh. I always wished I'd learned an instrument.'

'Well, it's never too late.'

Mrs Love laughed. 'I'm already learning to paint. I don't know how I ever had the time to work, you know. Retirement takes up all my time.'

Tom grinned. 'I think I'd be good at being retired. Being able to do the things you love without worrying about whether they're bringing in enough money to pay the bills sounds blissful.'

'It's not bad. I think back now, and I think I worked too hard. All those years with Trev, you always think there's more ahead of you. What would I have done differently if I'd known?'

'What would you have done differently?' Tom asked.

'I'd have stopped more. Taken holidays. Gone places with him.'

Emma was a spare part. Tom had got more out of her mother about her actual feelings about the world in five minutes than Emma had in the last ten years. She took a deep breath. 'I'll leave you two to it. Lots to do,' she said and strode away without pausing to see if either of them raised an objection.

–

Lydia found Annie sitting alone in the sea of happy, and some statistically inevitable less happy, families. 'You're on your lonesome too?'

'My mum's got Duncan, so...' Annie shrugged.

Lydia knew Annie's brother was disabled but she'd never asked any more than that. She should have. It was a problem with keeping your own past under wraps. It discouraged you from asking about other people's for fear of the question coming back to you.

'Does he need someone all the time?'

Annie nodded. 'It's hard, but Mum won't think about residential care while she can still manage at home. Did you see your mum?'

Lydia nodded. She'd visited while her mum was still in hospital, expecting to be disappointed, convinced that, once again, her mother's bruises would fade and cuts would heal and she'd say that it had been little more than an accident. Instead, it was as though something inside her mother – the wall that had allowed her to keep what was really happening tightly locked away behind her insistence that everything was all right – had shattered. Between tears she met Lydia with a stream of apology, regret and resolutions to never go back. Then Lydia had gone to the police station and talked to a nice PC who had promised to check through records and make sure that the statements Lydia had given before she ran away were appended to the current file, and given Lydia a phone number for victim support and contact details for the domestic violence worker who'd been allocated to her mum's case. 'It's going to take a while for me to believe that she's really not going back, you know?'

'That's understandable.'

Lydia looked around. 'So are we each other's family for the day?'

'Not just for today.'

Lydia turned away to wipe the tear that was threatening to fall from her eye. 'No need to get all touchy-feely on me.'

'Sorry! So, apart from me and Jane, who would you have here if you could?'

'Well, Mum and Aunty Jill.'

'Who else?'

Lydia thought. There was only one answer. 'Think I've got to go.'

'You only just sat down.'

If she waited, she'd get cold feet. 'I know who I wish was here and I have to go and tell him.'

Annie's eyes widened. 'Who? Is it your hot barman?'

For goodness' sake, you couldn't go around referring to someone as Hot Barman. What was Annie thinking? 'His name is Will,' Lydia informed her.

–

Tom's mum squeezed his hand conspiratorially before she got into the waiting taxi. 'You've got a good one there.'

'Early days, Mum.'

'That's what she said.'

'Anyway, why aren't you quizzing this one about spending her whole afternoon chatting up some bloke?' He threw Hilly an apologetic look for diverting the fire in her direction.

'I was not chatting him up.'

'Really?'

'Really. He was chatting me up and very welcome it was too.'

He waved them off, hopeful that Hilly's new romance would be distraction enough from Emma to stop his mum phoning him for updates every hour on the hour for the foreseeable future.

'So, you and Stilts?'

He turned to find his pretend girlfriend's big brother standing on the pavement behind him. 'Stilts?'

'Cos she's so tall.'

'But she's like five foot nothing…' He got it. 'And that's the joke. Very funny.'

'No. It's not. It's stupid, but I've called her that since I was fifteen so…' Josh shrugged at the immutability of family nicknames. 'You're not her type.'

Tom felt himself bristle a little. 'And what is her type?'

'I don't know. More forgettable, I guess.'

'I don't know what to say to that.'

Josh shrugged. 'Just don't screw her over. Ok?'

'I won't.'

'Cos I'm shit at the big brother thing but I would totally have a go at beating you up if I had to.'

'You would?'

Josh didn't look sure. 'Yeah. Maybe. But I'd definitely rather not, so don't cheat on her or lie to her or any of that.'

Tom nodded. He could get on board with that. 'I can assure you that Emma and I are 100 per cent honest with each other.'

'Good.'

Annie came down the wide stone steps behind them and onto the pavement. 'Emma says you're allowed to eat the leftovers now.'

'She doesn't let you eat?'

'Oh God no. Not until the guests have all been round.'

Another taxi pulled up in front of them. A short, stout woman got out and carefully counted out her coins to pay the driver.

Annie gasped. 'Mum!'

'Am I too late?'

'No. You're here. What about Duncan?'

'Mrs Eveley from downstairs is sitting with him. She's got all the numbers to ring if there's a problem.'

'You left Duncan with Mrs Eveley?'

The older woman nodded. 'Well, you said this was important to you.'

Tears were glistening in Annie's eyes.

'No need for crying, sweetheart. Now where's this buffet?'

–

Annie led her mother back inside and listened to her coo over the fancy building and the beautiful flowers and the still plentiful buffet. It wasn't until they were settled in a corner of the room that her mother turned her attention to Annie. 'I've missed a lot of your things over the years, haven't I?'

'It doesn't matter. You were busy.'

Her mother shushed her. 'Let me finish now. I was busy but I have two children. You were so bright and so definite about your place in the world. I think I let myself think you didn't need me as much.' She chewed her Vietnamese pork ball. 'But I'm still your mum too.'

'Of course you are.' All Annie's instincts were to reassure her mother and make her feel better. 'You were a great mum.'

'I did do my best but I know it must have felt like Dunc was more important some times. He just, he needed me all the time.'

'I know.' Annie really did understand.

'I never meant you to feel like you were in second place.'

She should say that she didn't feel that. The words wouldn't come out.

'You were always every bit as important,' her mum continued.

Annie couldn't reply.

'Right. Anyway...' Her mum looked around the room. 'Where's that Joshua boy got to? I need to give him a piece of my mind.'

'You really don't.'

'Well, what's he thinking of not falling over himself to win you back? Silly feller.'

That wasn't fair. 'It was me who ended it last time.'

Her mum narrowed her eyes. 'But you've let him know you're interested?'

Annie shook her head. 'Do you think I should?'

Her mother opened her mouth and then stopped. 'I think that has to be your decision, love.'

–

Tom stood on the pavement for a long time. He knew he ought to go back in, say thank you to Emma, plan their next step, arrange a time to work out how they were going to extricate themselves from this whole situation. And yet, he found he was in no rush to go back to that reality. In this moment he was Tom Knight who had had a lovely afternoon with his mum and his new girlfriend, who was beginning to break the ice with her scary brother. He was Tom Knight who had a life.

And as soon as the thought took hold, he tensed himself for the wave of guilt to come. The guilt that said, why are you still here? How can you think about being happy? How can you bear the slow but sure way that the burden of that day and that loss was starting to lessen? It wasn't fair. That's what his guilt told him. He had no right to be here, and no right at all to be happy.

And that voice was still there. But it was quieter. It didn't hit him with the force that he'd come to expect.

He turned to head back inside, where he took the lazy option and pressed the button for the lift rather than jogging up three flights of stairs. The door opened almost too quickly so his brain couldn't make the connection between the button press and the arrival of the elevator. And there, as the doors opened, was Emma.

'Hi.'

'Hi,' she replied.

He stepped back to let her come out of the lift.

She shook her head. 'I was looking for you.'

'Right. I was heading back up.'

'Ok then.'

He stepped in beside her and pressed the button for the third floor. The doors didn't close immediately. He heard himself laugh, the weird awkward laugh of escaping tension. He pressed the button again.

'So I think it went all right,' she said.

'Yeah. My mum loves you. And your brother did the "don't mess with my little sister" talk.'

She laughed. 'Did he pull it off?'

'Not entirely. He didn't seem totally confident on the whole beating me up part.'

'He's a nerd. He could probably hack your Instagram and make you look like a dick or something.'

'Which, to be fair, is a much more twenty-first-century threat.'

He pressed the door close button again. Finally the lift decided to play along. The doors juddered shut.

'Thank you for today. It meant a lot to see Mum happy.'

He turned towards her. Her. Him. An enclosed space. Think unsexy thoughts, he told himself.

It didn't help.

She stepped towards him. 'It was fun actually. And you were right. It was good not to have to do the single matchmaker explanation at every turn.'

He stepped towards her. 'I'm glad it worked out. So you thought it was fun?'

'What do you mean?'

Another half a step closer. 'Well, maybe we should do this again sometime?' What was he doing?

'Pretend to be a couple?'

Another step. His body was inches – less – away from hers now. He could feel the warmth she was radiating. He was a tiny fleck of dust in her orbit. He realised for the first time what his body already knew. He wanted to kiss her. He was going to kiss her.

She moved another inch. Her breast brushed his chest. He dipped his head to her lips.

Third floor.

He jumped three feet backwards as the door opened.

Emma stood stock-still staring up at him. 'I need to... I...'

'The party?'

She nodded.

'You should go.'

'Right.'

–

She walked out of the lift. What just happened? Nothing had happened. What had happened was that she hadn't kissed him. She hadn't pulled him close to her. She hadn't run her fingers through his hair. She hadn't slid her fingers into his belt buckle. She hadn't wrapped her legs around his waist as he... She hadn't done any of that.

There were still a few guests in the function room. She should check in on the people she hadn't talked to yet. And she would. In a minute. She diverted to the ladies' to give herself a moment to process what hadn't happened in the lift. The bathrooms at the Guild of Seamstresses, or whatever this place called itself, were seriously plush. You walked in to an anteroom with basins and a whole wall of mirrors with little ledges in front of them and chairs for sitting down and doing your make-up. And then there was a wide archway through to the actual cubicles.

Emma glanced through. One cubicle occupied. She took a seat in front of one of the gold-framed mirrors and inhaled deeply, counting to four as she did, and then exhaled counting slowly – one, two, three, four, five, six – in her head. And then again. In for four. Out for six. Nothing had happened in the lift.

But you wanted it to, the voice in her head insisted.

Nothing happened.

And you're upset about that.

Emma shook her head. And breathed in and out again. She wasn't looking for a boyfriend. She was very busy with work. She was focusing on her career right now.

And then there was Walt. Nothing had happened with Walt either. She hadn't even met him in real life, but she found herself logging on more and more often in the hope that he'd be around, and she had the sense that, just maybe, he was doing the same.

Nothing had happened with Walt. Nothing had happened with Tom and they'd clearly agreed that nothing would. So why did she feel like she was cheating on them both?

'Oh!'

She'd been too preoccupied to hear the cubicle door open and the person come through to the anteroom. 'Mum! I didn't realise you were in here.'

Her mother's face was flushed, her eyes slightly damp.

'Are you ok?'

'I'm very well.' Her mother washed her hands efficiently and thoroughly.

'Are you sure?'

'Of course.'

The armour was there. It had gone for a moment when she was talking to Tom but now it was back. What had he done that Emma couldn't? 'You must miss Trevor.'

Her mum turned off the tap and rested her damp hands on the side of the basin. 'It's harder at something like this. I keep catching myself wanting to take charge and say "Trevor, can you get those tablecloths swapped over?"'

Of course she'd noticed the tablecloths.

'But he's not here. This is your show and it's all wonderful. You don't need me interfering.'

'I miss you interfering.' The truth was out of her mouth before she could stop it. 'I know it was only because you cared.'

And that was it. Getting things just so was how her mother showed she cared.

'I'm blown away, you know.' Her mother's voice was cracking slightly and she wasn't looking straight at her daughter. 'By you doing all of this on your own. It's really something.'

'Thanks.'

'You don't need me looking over your shoulder.'

Emma swallowed back her own tears. 'What if I do?'

'You know you don't. And I'm sorry. I can't. It's too hard. Sometimes I wonder if I ran away to Spain. I wonder if I ran away from the memories, because when I'm here it's overwhelming. My whole life – the family and the business – was tied up with him. Without him I don't know how to be when I'm back here. Does that make sense?'

Emma almost wished it did. The idea that you could love someone so much that their absence felt like the loss of part of yourself was incredible to Emma.

'Over there, I don't expect to see him every time I walk into a room. Here, his absence is all I can think about. In Spain I can remember his presence.'

Grown-up Emma understood, but for the little girl inside her, her mum's fussing and picking had been one of life's constants. 'I miss you sometimes.'

Her mother looked at her for the first time in the conversation. 'I've hidden away a bit, haven't I?'

'I understand why. I do.'

'I didn't mean to. I needed some time to work out who I am on my own. I'm still your mum.'

This was the moment to nod, give her mum a quick hug and get back to work.

'What's on your mind?'

'Nothing. I'm fine,' Emma replied automatically.

'Something's on your mind. Or someone? That nice young man maybe?'

Was it? Her brain was increasingly resistant to maintaining the pretence that she wasn't attracted to him, but she barely knew him. It was a crush. Nothing more. She had bigger problems. 'I don't know if I can do this without your help.'

'You are doing it without my help! It all looks wonderful.'

But that was just the thing. 'I'm not. We're barely solvent, and that's only because people you set up keep giving me discounts. And half the people are still single.' Emma buried her face in her hands. 'Oh my God! What if they all ask for refunds?'

Her mother took a sharp inward breath. 'Right. I'll be bossy Emma for the next ten minutes and then you're on your own.'

Ten minutes was not going to be enough.

'Firstly, you inherited a business. If people are giving you discounts because of things I did that's just goodwill towards the business, where you've worked for the last five years, so you've earned it. Don't look a gift horse in the mouth. If people are giving you money off because we found them the love of their life, then make the most of that. Who else have we fixed up who might help out?'

Emma wasn't sure. Wait. She thought back over the last eight weeks. An idea was forming.

'Secondly,' her mother continued. 'Half of them are not still single. I reckon fifteen or twenty at most. And some of them are well on the road.'

Emma shook her head. 'Hardly. Look at Colin! I practically threw a random stranger at him.'

'Which ones were they?'

'Colin with the scary mother.'

'And the tall lass. Well, they hit it off. Good work. So what if it was late in the day? Who else?'

'I don't know. Lydia Hyland. She's Jane's friend. I'm not sure she's even here.'

'Well, I don't see how I can help with her then. Who else?'

'Annie. It looked like her and Colin were getting together but then she dropped him.'

Her mother frowned. 'Joshie's Annie?'

'She's not Joshie's Annie.'

Her mother laughed. 'Oh darling, maybe you do need my help after all.'

–

Lydia made it as far as the street before her resolve started to weaken slightly. The late afternoon air was hot and muggy, she didn't have enough money for a cab and actually she wasn't entirely sure she'd know where to send it anyway. That was a problem. Think, Lydia. They'd been to the pub. She remembered the pub. *The Crafty Fox*. She googled:

Crafty Fox pub London

There were three. She clicked onto the map view. Three pubs but only one south of the river. She could do this.

She had to do this. And she had to do it right now before she had time to change her mind. She ran to the tube and didn't let herself slow down. Once she was on the train out of Victoria she started to think. What was she going to say to him if she even found him? What did she want from him? What was she even hoping for? What made her think he'd be prepared to even talk to her after the way she'd behaved the last time they fu— her brain stumbled over the word – after they made love?

Who even was this new Lydia? Was she going to be the sort of person who made love rather than properly shagging?

She emerged from the station and followed the directions to the pub, hoping that once she was there the streets would start to look familiar and she'd be able to navigate her way back to the green front door he lived behind. And the streets did look familiar. Unfortunately, they also all looked the same.

She stopped outside the first green door that fit the bill. Terraced house, middle of a row, short path down to the street, messy front garden, parked cars lining the road. Was she actually going to walk up to the door and knock? Just walk up and say, 'Hi. Sorry I binned you off. I think I might love you.'

Even the idea of it was ridiculous. He was an actual bona fide lord. She'd said she wouldn't be looked down on but he was so far up the social ladder he could probably barely even see her anyway.

But he had seen her. She'd felt it.

Yesterday's Lydia would probably have walked away right now. Last week's Lydia wouldn't have got on the train. Last month's Lydia wouldn't even have dared to think of standing here. How much further could she go?

She opened the rickety metal gate, walked to the door, and raised her hand. The door swung open before she made contact.

'I didn't think you were going to make it for a minute there.'

He looked tired. There was a weariness in his eyes and his skin was pale. The thought that she'd got it all wrong hit her. Maybe he hadn't given her a second thought. Maybe he just hadn't been at work for these last two events because he was sick.

'You were watching me?'

He nodded. 'What are you doing here?'

'I'm being brave.'

'Ok.'

'Can I come in?'

He hesitated for a moment before he stood aside and let her pass.

She stood in his bedroom with her back to the window, willing him to come over to her, or to sit on the bed and invite her to join him. He stayed at the far side of the room near the door, arms folded, watching her. 'What do you want, Lydia?'

She'd come this far. She would not let her fear take charge now. 'I wanted to say thank you.'

'For what?'

For all of it. 'For seeing me. For not running away.'

He grimaced. 'Shame I can't say the same to you.'

'And sorry as well then, I guess.'

'You guess?'

'Sorry I freaked out.'

His expression softened a little. 'Then why did you?'

'All of it. You're rich.'

'My father is rich.'

'And you went to some ridiculous school I'm guessing and you definitely seem like you'd know which fork to use, and I didn't and I don't and I'm crap at pretending.' She stopped. That wasn't quite true. 'Actually, I'm really good at pretending, but it's knackering. I'm so tired all the time. I'm so tired of trying not to slip up.' She fought to keep the sob out of her voice. 'It's exhausting.'

He looked at her, really looked at her, and nodded. 'I know.'

'Do you?'

'I didn't ask to be a viscount any more than you asked for your life. And I know it's not the same but I know what it's like to feel different and to feel like you have to divide yourself up into pieces depending who you're with or where you are.'

'Why don't you ever go home?'

'I went home with you.'

'You know what I mean. Before that. Aggie said you hadn't been for years.'

He leaned back against the wall. 'When did you last go home?'

'Yesterday.'

His eyes widened. 'Shit. What happened?'

'Lots of things. My mum's fine. I think things might be going to change.'

His lip twitched up at the corner. 'I'm glad.'

'Me too. I'd like to tell you all about it sometime.'

He shook his head. 'Maybe.'

She wanted to tell him everything but not here and now. Right now was just about him and her. 'I asked about you, though. Why don't you go home?'

'Not such different reasons from you probably.'

She couldn't picture that. Of course he was different. Everything was different. 'But home for you is beautiful.'

'Aggie's beautiful. And James. I miss them but I send them cards at Christmas and birthdays and all that.' He took a deep breath. 'I don't go back because every single inch of that place is a bad memory.' He looked right at her again. 'The cupboard I used to hide in if my father was looking for me. The bedroom he shut me in to calm down after I made a scene by crying at my own mother's funeral. The room where I helped three different stepmothers pack when he decided to move on to someone else.'

'He sounds like a bastard.'

'He is. I mean, he's not violent but he's not kind. He's who he is, and who he is and who I wanted to be didn't fit together.'

'Do you think you can choose who you want to be?'

He shrugged. 'I don't know. I don't know if you decide who you are or if you just are who you are. But I know how much it takes out of you always trying to be someone else.'

They fell into silence.

'Why are you here, Lydia? You've said thank you and sorry. Was that it?'

That couldn't be it. She didn't dash across London to say thank you, however much she needed to say that to him. There was something else, something she hadn't said out loud to anyone before, something she'd learned was a weakness to be buried away.

Her mouth went dry. Her throat tightened like her whole body was trying to hold the words in. She wouldn't let it. She was going to be her true self and if that wasn't enough she'd... She didn't know what she'd do. The thought was terrible.

'Why are you here, Lydia?'

'Because I don't know who I am and I feel like you might.'

'I don't think that's something I can tell you.'

She could see him closing back in on himself, pulling up the barrier. She only had one more thing to offer. 'I don't let people get to know me. Ever. I don't let people see me.'

'I know.'

She turned and pulled the scratty, stained curtain behind her closed. What was coming up was a private show. She reached down, grabbed the fabric of her dress and pulled it up to take it off.

'Lydia.' There was an edge of warning in his voice.

'What?' Her heart rate jumped up.

'You don't have to do this.'

'Do you want me to stop?'

He shook his head. 'I want to know why you're doing it.'

She had nothing left to offer but the truth. Her own unadulterated absolute truth. 'Because I love you.'

No silence has ever been bigger than the silence right after you've told somebody you love them and they haven't responded. Lydia let her dress drop back down over her calves. 'Right. Well, I understand. I'm sorry.'

'You ran away.' His voice stopped her from running again. 'After we slept together at my dad's house you ran away.'

That was unfair. 'I drove you home.'

'You ran away,' he insisted.

She nodded.

He closed his eyes for a moment. 'I think I need you to go.'

'I understand.' She tried to walk out with as much dignity as she could muster, promising herself she wouldn't cry while he could see her. She paused in the doorway. 'I was going to ask if you wanted to come to the ball tomorrow. Whole big Regency costume thing. Never mind. Stupid idea.'

–

After walking her mum back to the tube, Annie found herself at a loose end. Jane and Charlotte had headed off together and Lydia had left mid-conversation in a flurry of sudden urgency. Annie should go home. Instead, she wandered back towards the lunch venue. Everyone would have gone by now.

Maybe not quite everyone. If she happened to be just passing when Emma and Josh came out then maybe they'd… maybe he'd notice her and maybe they could get a quick drink, or something, for old times' sake.

This was pathetic. It was like waiting in the corridor outside the lesson of a boy you fancied so you could 'accidentally' run into them. Annie had never done that. At school Josh had always sought her out. He'd never for one second made her feel like he was settling for spending time with her. She'd never been his fallback option. When she'd been with Josh, as a kid and over that one glorious weekend, she'd felt like she was right at the centre of the story.

And she hadn't afforded him the same respect. She'd told herself that she couldn't say anything because he was with Jane. And then she'd told herself that he was Jane's ex so he was off limits. Those were excuses, weren't they? Good excuses. Moral excuses. But still excuses for not looking into her own heart and taking the risk of going after the thing she wanted more than anything in the world.

Jane had called her 'the girl who broke his heart' and, if that was true, she was also 'the girl who'd never said sorry'. It was time to ball up her courage and do something. She made it as far as the doorway to the function room. There were a couple of waiting staff still clearing tables and Emma was talking to Josh's stepmum at the farthest end of the room. She could march over there and ask if they knew where he was. That would be the most direct approach. Or she could call him. Or email. Email was good. That would give her time to think about what she wanted to say.

'Did you forget something?' Not email then. Annie turned towards his voice. Joshua Love.

'No.' Actually... 'Yes. Sort of. Not forgot exactly.' This wasn't going right. She took a deep breath to settle herself.

'I was looking for you, actually.' That was what she wanted to say, but she hadn't spoken. That was Josh. He was looking for her. 'I went outside. I thought you'd already gone.'

'I walked my mum to the tube. You must have missed me. I came up in the lift.'

'I did the stairs.'

'I don't really like lifts. I prefer escalators,' she added. Why was she talking about escalators?

'Right. I don't really mind.'

He fell silent. Annie determined to grasp the moment. 'I was looking for you, too.'

'What for?'

'I wanted to tell you I was sorry.'

He didn't ask what for.

'I let people persuade me it wasn't right, when I knew it was right.' Tears were coming. 'And since then nothing has been right again. I faded away cos I was pretending that the biggest part of me didn't exist.' Tears were streaming. 'That's the part that's in love with you. I just pretended it wasn't there and without it...' She couldn't find the words. Without it she'd been less than herself.

He stepped towards her, reaching a hand towards her face. She let him rub the tears from her cheek with his thumb. 'Thank you. For saying sorry.'

'That's ok.' She stepped back. It was a load off her shoulders. She'd admitted what she'd been carrying all these years. Maybe now she could start to heal.

'Where are you going?'

She stopped.

'I haven't told you why I was looking for you.'

Presumably to ask her something for the next scandal sheet or to thank her again for helping Emma with the seating plan.

'I've got something for you.' He pulled his phone from his pocket, unlocked the screen and handed it to her. She was looking at the scandal sheet app, but this wasn't content she'd seen before.

'What's this?'

'Just read it.'

> The chance of former love reborn was the talk of the Ton at the commencement of the Season, but it seems that some readers may have misconstrued our meaning when we shared the story of this starry-eyed schoolmistress. This is no jaded Jane or lovelorn Lydia.

Annie looked up. Josh had moved away and was leaning on the bannister rail, gaze fixed on the stairwell below him. She read on.

> This is a story of young sweethearts grown apart and hearts bruised by experience. A story that has unfolded over many years.

Annie's hand was shaking as she scrolled down the screen. It was all here. The child determined to marry their best friend from school. The nerdy awkward teenager thriving in the light of their soul mate's attention. The perfect weekend and the heartbreak of the pledges made coming to naught. And then the part she'd never known.

> The third time Mr Joshua Love made the acquaintance of Miss Anne Keer, after a period of extended estrangement, was aged twenty-six at a work Christmas party where he

attended as the guest of his betrothed, one Miss Jane Woods.

Of course, all was quite well and proper with this arrangement. It was some years since the young Master Love had first been promised to Miss Keer so it would have been quite dishonourable for him to acknowledge even the smallest pang of regret, and Miss Woods knew nothing of this prior attachment, beyond a cursory acknowledgement of a former childhood acquaintance. Which was as it ought to be. There was no benefit in raking over such distant history. And so when Miss Woods proposed Miss Keer as her bridesmaid, what cause for objection could there possibly be?

Imagine the pain of standing at the front of one's own wedding knowing absolutely and with immovable certainty that the wrong woman is walking down the aisle towards you.

It was the story of Annie and Josh retold, as she'd retold it to herself a million times. But these weren't her feelings. They were his.

She read the final line.

After all of that, would it be too much to hope that on this fourth time of meeting, Miss Keer might be persuaded to give one who is sure of his heart a final chance?

And there he was standing right in front of her, fear etched on his face. 'You read it?'

'I did.'

Josh moved so he was only inches away from her. 'Say something.'

'I'm scared.'

'What of?'

'What if you change your mind?'

He pulled back. 'What if *I* change *my* mind? You do remember what happened last time?'

'My mum thought I shouldn't settle down so young. And there was Duncan, and my course and my career.'

'I didn't ask your mum to move in with me.'

He didn't. She could explain it a thousand ways. She could explain that it hadn't been the sensible thing to do. She could explain that she'd let other people convince her she didn't know her own mind. She could come up with a million reasons for how she'd let him down, but none of them were the truth. 'I was frightened.'

'You broke my heart,' said Josh.

'I'm sorry.'

'So I need you to tell me if there's still any chance at all for us. Because if there isn't I deserve to know. This half agony, half hope business is torture.'

How could he doubt for a second her feelings for him? Because she had given him cause for doubt again and again and again. She'd stood back and smiled supportively while he married someone else. She'd promised herself to him, body and soul, and then run away. She'd chosen fear, and the life she knew, over the life she wanted. She'd failed to be true, to him or to her own heart. 'I'm yours,' she whispered.

She heard him inhale. 'Truly?'

Annie raised her chin to look him directly in the eye. 'Truly.'

'And what about when you talk to your mum or Lydia or whoever and they say it's a stupid idea, or that it's too soon after Jane, or that it would be sensible to take things slow or whatever it is that they'll say?'

'It won't matter.' This was what certainty felt like. 'I have made my choice.'

And finally, they kissed.

–

He'd run away. Tom couldn't pretend otherwise. He should have followed Emma out of the lift and waited until the end of the afternoon and had a conversation with her like an adult.

He should have apologised. He should have explained that he'd been distracted by the emotion of the afternoon. He should have reassured her that nothing like that would ever happen again.

Instead he'd run. Because his old friend the guilt was back in abundance. Pretending to care for someone for the greater good wasn't a betrayal. He could justify that, but wanting her, letting his mind be full of only her, was like cheating on someone who would never get mad with him again.

He went straight home. He had no interest in bars or clubs or being anywhere at all where other people were. He grabbed his tablet, opened the poker app and slumped onto the sofa. He'd play a couple of hands online for tokens. Just to keep his mind busy.

He joined an open table and lost half his chips in one hand betting recklessly on a pair of fours when there was a king and a jack on the flop.

The next hand he had a route to a straight on the river and shoved all in. Some anonymous player in some other living room in some other world saw his bet and the straight didn't materialise. Of course it didn't. It had been a stupid unnecessary bet. He'd made a lot of those recently.

He had forty quid sitting on his account. He could replenish his chips and play again. He came out of the open table and clicked 'view players' on his regular private room. No Queen of Hearts.

Probably best. He'd almost made a fool of himself with one imaginary girlfriend today. Flirting online – because he had been flirting, he couldn't kid himself otherwise any more – with someone who didn't even want to meet him would be sinking further into his own mess.

–

'That went well, I think?' Charlotte was making herself at home, opening all of Jane's kitchen cupboards in search of a snack.

'Well, my mother adores you. Likes you more than me,' Jane conceded. 'Your brother's not convinced though.'

'Meh. He's just a bit buttoned up. I think Storm terrified him into silence.'

'She can have that effect.'

Charlotte dropped a bowl of crisps on the table and passed Jane an open bottle of beer. She raised it to her lips. And stopped. 'I might not have a drink actually.'

'Are you ok?'

'Yeah. Just a bit tired.'

Charlotte took the bottle from her and lined it up next to her own. 'You don't mind if I do?'

'Course not. I'll get some water.' She left Charlotte snuggled on the sofa with her pjs on and a beer in her hand. She tried to take a picture of the moment in her head to store it for the months ahead. This was everything Jane wanted. Maybe she could hold on to it for another day or two, another week, another month perhaps. At some point the bomb underneath them was going to explode though. Nothing Jane could do would stop that. 'I've got something I need to tell you,' she said.

Charlotte listened in silence as Jane explained about the blond guy and the instantly regretted one-nighter at a very confused time and while Jane explained that she was going to keep the baby. The depth of that conviction had stunned her. Holding newborn Lunar had terrified her. Thinking about it in the abstract she would probably have said she'd definitely consider ending the pregnancy, but when she saw the positive test something shifted. This wasn't just a baby. It was her baby and she was going to give this child every part of her. Just like her own mum, Jane now realised, had tried to do. 'And that's why I think it's better that we stop this now. I need to concentrate on the baby.'

'You're pregnant?'

Jane nodded.

'And you're breaking up with me?'

She was breaking her own heart to do it, but it was the right thing. It wasn't just what Jane wanted any more. A baby would change everything. Motherhood would be messy and overwhelming. It would dominate her life for years to come and she feared it was all she could manage. She couldn't expect Charlotte to share that chaos with her. 'I'm sorry,' was all she could offer.

Chapter Twenty-One

Miss Emma Love
requests the pleasure of your company
at a Grand Ball
to mark the close of this season of love.

The final event. The big finish. Emma patted her head to check her ringlets were still secure. Regency hair was hard. Literally in places, considering the amount of hairspray she'd had to apply. But everything had to be perfect. Not a single hair out of place would be tolerated tonight.

Somerset House. Actual Somerset House. Former home of the Royal Academy – a place where the great and good of the Regency era would have come to view exhibitions, to see and be seen. The thrill of knowing that they were walking where the real diamonds of the ton in years gone by would have walked was impossible to deny.

Josh was checking his phone. 'No rain forecast for the next seventy-two hours. You must have been born lucky, Stilts.'

Luck had nothing to do with it. She'd spent hours poring over average rainfall charts for London in August for the last thirty years. Of course there was an element of uncertainty, but she'd mitigated that by negotiating an option of moving to the Seaman's Hall if the worst happened. There was no space for luck in tonight's plans.

Venue staff were running around setting up seating, and the staging and audio for the band. Everything looked to be in hand. Emma checked her schedule. Time to get ready herself.

'We should get dressed,' she said to Josh. 'They've set up a room for us. Our outfits are in there already.'

'Great.' Josh wasn't even pretending to be down with the period dress part of the final ball.

Emma ignored his tone. 'It is great, isn't it?'

The room she'd commandeered was off the main courtyard and down a corridor. It was a general dumping ground for all the things that had, at some point, been used for events, meetings or exhibitions. She grabbed the garment bag her dress had come in and found a handy display board to get changed behind. She ought to have stays and a chemise and stockings, but it was the twenty-first century and the middle of summer so she'd opted for bare legs and a strapless bra under her petticoat and dress. She pulled the petticoat over her head and then stepped into the dress. It buttoned at the back. 'Can you do me up, Josh?'

'If you'll explain what I'm supposed to do with these bits…'

She peered out from behind her display board. Josh had got his Regency gentleman shirt on over his boxers and was waving the long tails at her.

'Yeah. I think you're supposed to sort of tuck them in under your wotnot, between your legs.'

'Why?'

'I think it was instead of pants.'

He dropped the shirt tails. 'Ew. So you'd have a skiddy shirt?'

'The phrase "skiddy shirt" is not part of any woman's Mr Darcy fantasy. Ok? Never say those words again.' She turned her back to him. 'Now button me in please.'

He did as he was told and then set about the rest of his outfit with frequent interjections from Emma about what to tuck into where and how to tie his neckcloth, which Emma, of course, redid for him. Eventually they stood back and assessed each other.

'How do I look?' she asked.

'Ridiculous, Stilts. We both look completely insane.'

316

Her worry about things going well must have cracked onto her face for a second because he changed tone. 'You look fantastic. I'm so proud of everything you've done to make this work.'

'Did I do ok?'

He squeezed her hand. 'Better than ok. Mum and Dad would both be so proud if they could see all this.'

Emma grimaced. Her instinct was to argue, to say that Mum would be going around correcting everything, but she had to let that idea go. 'Yeah. I think they would.'

'Especially with tonight's late additions.'

Emma glanced at the time. 'And he'll be here soon. One of us ought to be out front to catch him. You've got the list he sent over.'

Josh nodded. 'It's all in hand. Relax. You've got this.'

Emma took a deep breath. 'Right then. Let's get this show on the road.'

She barked instructions at him as they made their way back to the courtyard. She would liaise with the venue and the caterers. He was on reception duty looking out specifically for the musicians who were due to arrive – a swift check of the watch – in fifteen 'Fifteen – one five, Josh, one five' minutes, and for Emma's newly listed special guests.

'I thought you'd want to schmooze them yourself.'

'I will, but in case I miss them. There's a lot to think about tonight.'

He headed off to the main gate to look out for his charges. Emma allowed herself a small sigh of relief.

–

He should have got changed when he got there, Tom realised, as he nodded politely at yet another stranger who stared as he went past.

He was learning a lot on his journey to Temple station about the demographics of Londoners by how they reacted to a man in full Regency dress sitting down opposite them. Women, he discovered, had no complaints at all. In fact, had he appreciated the depth of collective womanhood's Mr Darcy complex sooner he might have dressed this way more often. A few men were also enthusiastic – something about breeches seemed to be acting as a sort of hyper-focused gaydar. Generally though, the blokier blokes seemed less keen. Individually they just sidled away and pretended they hadn't noticed him. He was hoping to make it to his destination without coming across a group of lads who'd already had a few beers. It was a feeling he associated with being part of a couple with Jack – like they were always visible, always slightly aware that they might hold hands and exchange a kiss in front of the wrong person.

By the time he got to Temple and out onto the street he was trying to enjoy the attention. Most of it was amused or interested rather than anything more intimidating.

Josh was hovering by the gate. 'Nice get up,' he grinned.

'You don't brush up so bad yourself. I promised Emma I'd be here early.'

Josh nodded. 'I'm not sure where she is. Look out for waiters running away in terror and track back from there.'

As it happened he didn't have to follow the sounds of the cries of reprimanded workers, Emma was right there, standing in the middle of the courtyard. She seemed to have her eyes closed and be entirely absorbed in her own world.

Her tightly coiled hair was catching the glow of the low sun. Her skin was kissed with light. Something caught in Tom's throat. There was an air of contentment and stillness about her he wasn't used to seeing and he found he was reluctant to interrupt the moment.

–

Emma opened her eyes at the sound of footsteps. Tom was a few feet away, dressed, as instructed, in tail coat, high collar, neck cloth and breeches. He was next to the line of fountains that ran along the centre of the court. For a second she had a flash of an image in her head. The fountains firing, Tom reaching for her and pulling her under the shower, hair swept back from his face, water running down his neck and onto his shirt, wet lips searching for hers...

'Are you ok?' he asked.

'I'm fine.' Of course she was fine. His hand against her cheek, his lips... Emma shook her head. She was here for work. 'How long have you been there?'

'Only just arrived. What were you doing with your eyes closed?'

She looked down to the ground. 'It's silly.'

'Tell me.'

'I was trying to imagine what it would have been like to come to a ball somewhere like this for real.' At least that was what she'd been imagining before her mind was filled with Thomas Knight. 'In an actual Season with chaperones and lords and ladies, everyone trying to make the best match for their social advancement and status and to keep body and soul together.'

'Not for love?'

She shook her head. 'Well, that's the storybook version, but not unless you were very lucky, I don't think.'

'I wanted to... before people got here...' Tom hesitated. 'I wanted to say something about what happened in the lift.'

She didn't have time for this. 'Nothing happened in the lift.'

'Well, technically but...'

'But nothing.'

'Emma, we nearly kissed.'

'Which is just another way of saying that we didn't kiss.' She stepped backwards, out of his orbit. 'Do you like how it all looks?'

Emma followed his gaze and tried to look at the space through a newcomer's eyes. The edges of the courtyard were lined with tall lamps, flames dancing in glass cylinders to provide light as the evening went on. The musicians had clearly got the dress code briefing, as had the waiters and the bar staff. The main courtyard was circled by seating and small tables, and then at either side of the centre there were two long dancefloors, perfect he presumed, for dancing two longways sets, and right in the centre the feature that gave the courtyard its name – the strip of fountains that rose up from the floor. The sun was still shining brightly on the cool pale stone of the buildings.

'It looks incredible,' he said.

'Thank you.'

'Won't people get very wet?'

'It's not going to rain.'

'I meant the fountain.' He pointed down at the water point beneath his feet. 'Should we even be standing here?'

'They won't fire until the very end of the night.' She looked away over his shoulder, trying to get the image that was playing on a loop in her mind to stop. 'Well, unless someone really pisses me off before then.'

'I'll make sure I play nicely then.'

'Thank you for doing this. I know it doesn't matter to you apart from your mum thinking you're with someone, but a matchmaker getting dumped just before her big night doesn't look great for me.' She should tell him about the rest.

'It's fine. I'm trusting that you're going to have enough time to dance with me.'

'With the guy who skived the dance lesson?'

'Fully caught up on YouTube,' he promised. 'I can reel and promenade with the best of them, I assure you.'

'Well, I suppose a dance or two would make it all more convincing. I need to talk to you about…'

Josh jogged over to them. 'One minute to seven. Are we ready for doors open?'

Emma nodded. The other things would have to wait.

'Robbie is at the bar with Harriet,' Josh added. 'Both ready and willing to schmooze their little hearts out on your behalf.'

Tom frowned. 'Who's Robbie?'

'I'll explain later.' She would. She really would. Emma turned slightly away from him and addressed Josh. 'Let's do it then. Doors open.'

–

Annie had insisted that all three of them should arrive at the final event of the Season together. They'd started together, so they should finish together. Walking through the gates to the vast Fountain Court though, she was somewhat underwhelmed with her companions' levels of enthusiasm. 'What is up with you two? You were both completely silent in the cab.'

Neither of her friends responded. She turned on Lydia first. 'You shot out of the thing on Saturday like you were on a mission. Where's your get up and go got up and gone to?'

Lydia stared at the floor. 'I went to see someone. It didn't go very well.'

That wasn't really an answer. 'You went to see your hot barman?'

'Will.' She folded her arms. 'It didn't work out. What else is there to say?'

Now Annie felt bad. Lydia had been so full of life a couple of days before. 'I'm sorry.'

'I shot and I missed,' she muttered. 'Apparently it happens.'

Annie turned to Jane. 'What about you? Just upset we made you spend half an hour with us rather than Charlotte?'

'Actually, we broke up.'

Now Annie and Lydia were both paying attention. 'When?'

'Why?'

'Things got complicated.'

Annie wrapped an arm around both of her friends. 'I'm really sorry.'

'It's ok,' Lydia reassured her. 'We can be three single old maids together.'

Josh was heading in their direction. Right. 'About that…' Annie started.

'Nothing wrong with being single anyway,' Jane chipped in.

'Absolutely not,' agreed Lydia. 'Single women live longer. I read that somewhere.'

Annie extricated herself from the three-way hug. 'I need to tell you…'

Josh was almost upon them.

'Live longer. Probably have less stress,' Jane suggested.

'Definitely.'

'It's just that…' Annie tried one more time but it was too late. Josh was here. *Don't kiss me.* Unfortunately, Annie's psychic communication skills were no better than her verbal ones.

He bent and planted a kiss on her lips, before greeting the others with a cheery lack of awareness of the social dynamic he was walking into. 'Presume Annie's told you all about…' He gestured towards himself and his now-girlfriend.

Lydia and Jane shook their heads in unison.

'I was trying to.' Annie looked at her friends. 'Honestly, I was.' She turned back to Josh. 'And it's a bit awkward because they're both single now.'

He frowned at Jane. 'What happened with Charlotte? I thought you two were about twenty minutes away from running off to Gretna Green.'

'We broke up. I don't think she's even coming tonight.'

Josh was looking past them all towards the gate. 'I think she's already here.'

–

The woman making her way into the court wasn't the dazzling Charlotte that Jane had met at the garden party or the impeccable statuesque goddess she'd flirted with at the casino night. She wasn't even warm comfy Charlotte who'd been snuggled up on Jane's couch twenty-four hours before or the brisk capable

Charlotte that had delivered Lunar halfway up the farmhouse stairs.

This Charlotte was in Regency dress, but a Regency dress that looked like it had been screwed up in the bottom of a gym bag for the last three months. Her hair was half tied back in a messy bun, but not a stylish Hot Girl messy bun just a messy-messy bun. What looked like yesterday's mascara was smudged down her cheeks.

Jane rushed over before she could consider whether that was a good idea. 'Are you ok?'

'No.'

'Right.' It wasn't the biggest issue but Jane had to ask. 'What happened to your dress?'

Charlotte tried to smooth it down. 'Decided I wasn't coming so I scrunched it up in the bottom of the laundry basket so I didn't have to look at the stupid thing hanging on the wardrobe. Then I thought, why shouldn't I come? So I picked it out again.'

'I'm sorry. About everything.' It was all she could say. It wasn't enough.

The ball was starting to get going around them. At the microphone Emma stepped up and invited people to take to the floor for the first dance. Jane took Charlotte's arm and steered her to a quieter corner.

'I really am sorry.'

'You said.'

'It's for the best.' Why couldn't she see that? 'You don't want the mess of me with hormones running riot and then a new baby to deal with.'

'How do you know?'

Well, obviously she knew. Charlotte was perfect. Everything about her was just right. Jane and her new baby were not going to fit into Charlotte's put-together world.

'When you said you were pregnant, do you know what I thought?'

'How you were going to get out of there without causing offence?'

Charlotte folded her arms. 'No. That's what you thought. I thought that's brilliant. And I knew that was a mad thought, cos we've only known each other a few weeks, but when you said you were having a baby I, straight away, thought I was going to be part of that. Because it might only be a few weeks but I already cannot think about a future that you're not part of.'

'I just assumed…'

'Well don't assume.'

No. This was insanity. 'There's an order to things. Relationship. Home. Children,' Jane explained.

'I don't think the baby knows that. It's coming whether we're ready or not.'

'But it's not your baby.'

'I didn't think I was the father.' Charlotte raised a hint of a smile. It vanished as quickly as it came. 'I just thought we were an Us. You know?'

Jane reeled. 'We can't have a baby together. We haven't even said I love you. My flat isn't big enough for two people and a baby and you don't even have a place and…'

'I love you.'

'What?'

'I love you,' she repeated. 'We can probably sort the flat thing out later. Babies are really little anyway. Just like shove it in a drawer or something.'

'Is that your professional opinion?' Jane's joke didn't get a laugh in response. 'What's wrong?'

'I said, I love you, Jane.'

That. Of course. It wasn't simple. Not really. Love didn't make everything else straightforward but maybe you could start from love and deal with the madness from there. Jane took her partner's hand. 'I love you, too.'

–

The bar was working well. No queues. The circulating waiters were covering the whole plaza and not just feeding the same corner again and again. Robbie was holding court with Harriet at his side. Emma still needed to go and press the flesh there but to do that she needed Tom.

And there he was.

Perfectly on cue. A knight in shining armour. Or at least a fake boyfriend in breeches, which was good enough right now.

'Emma,' he kissed her cheek.

She caught herself just before she raised her hand to her cheek to touch the spot his lips had grazed. 'Tom! Right. I need to talk to you about…'

He shook his head. 'I was promised a dance.'

'Ok, but…'

'Dance first. Talk later.'

Why not? They took their places facing one another and the announcer declared that this song would be a courtesy start. 'What's that mean?' Tom hissed.

'I thought you said you were all caught up.'

'I thought I was.'

'A courtesy start means that each group of six within the set only joins in the dance when the first couple reach their mini set.'

Tom and Emma were at the farthest end of the dance floor. 'So what are we supposed to do until then?'

'Well, at a Regency ball this was when a lot of the actual courting took place. You're far enough away from the chaperones that they can't listen to every word but you're not so out of breath from dancing that you can't actually hold a conversation.' She smiled. 'So this is the bit where you can actually woo and seduce your intended partner.'

He raised a lazy eyebrow. 'Ok, but what are *we* supposed to do?'

She shrugged. 'Tell me something I don't know about you.'

'I don't know. You know about Jack. And you know that I'm an insufferable mother's boy. There's not much else.'

'And you play piano.'

'And I play...'

A squeal from the set on the other half of the dance floor distracted Emma for a second. She turned to make sure no horrid misfortune had befallen anybody and deduced that the sound was Hilly recovering from a rather enthusiastic spin Colin had launched her into. Still, they both seemed to be enjoying themselves. Emma gave herself a mental pat on the back for seeing the potential in that match and for sneaking Colin a guest pass for tonight's grand finale.

She turned back to Tom. 'Sorry? I missed that.'

He shook his head. 'Nothing major. What about you? What don't I know about you?'

'Well, nothing if you read the revision materials I gave you.'

'Let's imagine for a moment that I might not have entirely finished them. What one thing should I know? What's the essence of Emma Love?'

The essence? That was a crazy idea. You couldn't distil a person down to one thing. But if you could... she thought about it. Annie would be romantic. Josh would be protective. Jane was conventional with a rebellious heart fighting to get out. Lydia was wild. Emma was... 'I'm scared.'

Her words were blown away on the volley of music that accompanied the first couple promenading to the head of their set. Tom held out his hand. 'Don't be scared. I've got you.'

She placed her hand in his. It was a dance neither of them knew how to do, thanks to her being in work mode right through the practice session and him having tried to make up for his lack of caring via the internet. But somehow that seemed not to matter. They copied the moves of the others in the set and when she turned completely the wrong way and crashed right into him, rather than following him round in a semi-circle, he smiled and slid his arms around her waist to balance her.

It was just four repeated steps. A walk forward toward one another, two steps around to reach the opposite side of the set, drop hands and turn hand to hand down the side of the step, and then walk forward again in your new position to take hands again and restart the series. And somehow, if everyone remembered which way they were supposed to be facing, you moved up and down the set as it went along.

There was something hypnotic about the movement of the people around them and the waves of coming together and stepping apart. And each time she reached for his hand she was more confident, more comfortable, more sure that they'd found their rhythm.

The music stopped. The spell ought to have broken. Emma started to pull her hand away.

'Stay.'

She turned her face towards him. 'What?'

–

Good question. He'd said stay. What did he mean? Stay here and have another dance? Stay in this moment? Stay with me?

You can't live life with the handbrake on. He couldn't, anyway. Not any more. 'Come with me.'

'Where to?'

'I don't know.' He loosened his hold on her hand a little to give her the chance to pull away. She didn't. 'Somewhere quiet.'

'There's nobody in the Seaman's Hall.'

He let her lead him past the stage and through the double doors at the back of the courtyard. That brought them into a huge marble-floored room, lined with white columns and then through that room and out the other side onto a terrace overlooking the Thames.

'Quiet enough?' she asked.

The terrace was huge with views across the river. They were completely alone right in the beating heart of London.

He faced her, still holding her hand in his. 'I wanted to talk to you about the fake boyfriend thing.'

'Right. Yes.' Her tone was businesslike.

'We never talked properly about how or when we were going to end it.'

He felt her grip on his hand tense.

'And so what I was thinking,' he continued. 'Was what if we didn't?'

'What are you saying?'

'Stay with me.'

As they left his lips the words took on a weight and a solidity that felt absolutely right. He'd been telling himself he was still him. He was telling himself he wasn't hiding because he was still out there, even though he was sleepwalking through life. He'd told himself he was still the same risk-taker he'd always been but he hadn't risked anything that mattered. He'd told himself he didn't believe in love any more but that wasn't the man he truly was.

He said it again with a certainty he hadn't let himself feel before. 'This feels right. At least it does to me, so what do you think? I think we should stay together.'

'You mean we could go on a real date or something?'

'Sure. We could. Or we could go to a casino and gamble 'til we've got nothing left beyond the clothes we stand up in. Or we could jump out of an aeroplane together. Or go to Vegas and get married tomorrow.'

She started to pull away.

'Why not?'

'We barely know each other.'

That was where she was wrong. 'I know your weight at birth. I know what schools you went to. I've met your brother. You've had the seal of approval from my mother. I know that you love to be in control and not being terrifies you. You know that I lost someone and it almost broke me and so I do not say any of this lightly, but I want to be happy. And I want to see you happy. And I think we might be happy together.'

She was hesitating. She wasn't saying no, but something was holding her back.

'What is it?'

'Are you… I mean… would you be…?'

He stepped back slightly. 'Are you worrying that I'll go off with a bloke?'

'No!' He watched her try to put her unease into words. 'It's not men. It's one man.' She didn't meet his eye. 'What if you're not ready? After Jack. It's so obvious how much you loved him.'

'I did. I do. But.' This was hard to put into words but he had to try. 'It's not even about whether I'm ready. Life is moving on whether I'm ready or not. The universe, for whatever reason, put us on each other's paths. Walking away and saying it's just bad timing would be less scary right now, but what about tomorrow? Or next week, or next month? I don't want to wake up in a year's time and regret not grabbing hold of this moment.'

–

This wasn't part of Emma's plan. Emma's plan was the business. She still had so much to do before it would be the right time for fitting somebody else into her life. This was a risk she hadn't assessed. 'What if it doesn't work out?'

He grinned. 'But what if it does?'

'You can't just jump into things like that.'

'Sure you can.'

Maybe he could, but it wasn't her way. She thought things through. Her relationships were amicable but not impulsive or passionate. He moved closer to her.

Her body reacted to his closeness. He lifted a hand to her cheek. 'So you don't want me to jump right in and kiss you then?'

This was her chance to step away. This was the moment to say that probably it would be better if they stuck to their arrangement and then went their separate ways.

His fingertip traced a line across her cheek and down her neck. 'Please, say if you want me to stop.'

She should say something. 'Don't…'
He lifted his hand. 'Don't?'
'Don't stop,' she whispered.

Chapter Twenty-Two

And then he kissed her, hard and deep and passionate and she met his passion with her own. Something felt as though it had been unleashed inside her that she'd kept under tight control until now. Emma knew everything there was to know about love and relationships, and right now everything she knew was wrong. There was no professional opinion that could have told her how this would feel.

Eventually she pulled herself away, on the cusp of the moment where her body would have overruled any attempt her brain made to call a temporary halt. 'I'm supposed to be at work,' she gasped.

He stood back breathing deeply. 'We're going to pick this up later though, aren't we?'

'The second the last client walks out of those gates,' she promised.

'I'll hold you to that.'

'Good.'

They wandered back through the hall hand in hand and emerged into the courtyard.

'Emma!' The voice was coming from Robbie Martin who strode over to greet them. 'And this must be the mysterious Mr Knight?'

'Tom.'

'Tom Knight, Mr Right.' He smiled. 'That's not a bad line actually. Anyway, I've got so many people for you to meet.'

'I was trying to tell you…' Emma hissed, but it was too late. Robbie was already making introductions. There were journalists. There were influencers. There were YouTubers. All gathered, at Emma's request, to help provide a PR shot that would help take the Season from one-off experiment to long-term business.

'They're going to talk about the Season aren't they? Not just my love life?' she whispered to Robbie.

'Of course, but it's such a great angle. Matchmaker meets her match at her own event.' He smiled. 'And that's what you're selling, isn't it? The chance to find true love. Seriously,' he lowered his voice. 'If you hadn't found Tom I'd have told you to find someone and fake it.'

Emma felt the hand that was holding hers let go.

–

Charlotte and Jane seemed to have reconciled. Annie was hanging off Josh's arm. Lydia was the last of the three spinsters of the parish still standing. She was trying to tell herself that admitting she had feelings for Will was personal growth and that his response didn't change that.

Love was, quite literally, all around her though, and while she hadn't joined the Season intending to find her soul mate it was a little depressing to be one of the only people still alone as things were drawing to a close.

'Madam.' A white-gloved waiter held a tray with a single glass of champagne in front of her.

She shook her head. She suspected she'd had far too much already.

'It's from the gentleman at the bar.'

Lydia took the glass and looked around. There weren't any single guys, or groups of guys, anywhere near the bar. 'Sorry. From who?'

The waiter pointed more directly this time. 'The gentleman at the bar.'

And there he was, leaning on the bar, tiny smile tugging at his lips. She walked over slowly, determined not to give herself away by sprinting directly into his arms. 'I didn't expect you to be here.'

He leaned towards her. 'Work. You know.'

'And you couldn't get out of it?'

'Oh, I could have. This is the first recorded case of somebody bribing a colleague to let them come and do an extra shift.'

Lydia frowned. 'You could have come as my guest. I invited you.'

'Yeah, but I'm an idiot. I thought you might have changed your mind and this way I could pretend I had to be here and it was nothing to do with you at all.'

She wanted to be cross and make him work for the sleepless night he'd put her through, but she could feel the smile cracking across her face. 'But it has got something to do with me?'

'Yeah. I freaked out when you came round. I got scared, cos you were being so brave and brilliant and I didn't think I could live up to you so I chickened out and didn't try.'

'I understand. I did the same. You were right. About when we went to your dad's…' she couldn't say house, '…massive, fuck-off mansion. I ran away.'

'So we're even now?' He carried on before she could answer. 'I should have just said the thing I've been wanting to say since the first night I met you.'

'What?'

'What I should have said is that I love you. Of course I love you. How could anybody not?'

'Plenty of people don't. I'm a mess.'

'Yeah, but you're a really hot mess.'

And he was a really hot barman.

–

Emma finally managed to pull herself away from the crowd of interviewers, with promises that there'd be lots of chances to take pictures and video of the fountains later, and genuine hope that all the people Robbie had brought along were genuinely impressed by the whole idea. Tom had vanished long before she'd been able to get away. She found him by the gates.

'You're going?'

He shook his head. 'No. Yeah. I think so.'

'I'm really sorry about all that. I meant to tell you.'

'What are pretend boyfriends for if not the PR opportunities? All part of the service.'

'No.' This was all messed up. 'I really was going to warn you.'

'It's fine. You don't owe a fake boyfriend any explanation.'

There it was again. 'I thought it wasn't fake.'

His shoulders seemed to relax a notch. 'I'm sorry. One of the bloggers was asking about my past relationships, like she wanted the full sad story. It was just a bit much.'

'I'm so sorry. I didn't think it would be anything like that. I was really going to brief you, but then we got...' How to describe the kiss, the feeling of his lips on hers, the way the world faded away? 'We got distracted.'

'Is that what the kids are calling it?' He raised an eyebrow.

'I am sorry, though.'

'I know. It's just talking about Jack to promote your thing... it feels a bit like we're using him or something.'

He was right. Of course. She should have thought. 'Just stay to the end of the ball? Let me make it up to you.'

He shook his head. 'I don't feel very partyish, I'm afraid.'

She stepped back. 'Where will you go?' The thought of him being alone with his hurt cut her up. 'I could come with you.'

'You're busy. I get it,' said Tom. 'I do have another thing I was supposed to be at tonight. It doesn't seem that important now, though.' He reached a fingertip to brush her hand. 'Just give me some time.'

Emma went back to the ball. She ought to be doing something. The caterer would need reminding to bring more canapés. She looked around. Waiters were circulating. Nobody was fainting from hunger during the break from the dancing. Then the musicians. They'd need reminding to come back from their break. She headed towards the stage. Josh was shepherding the dance caller back to her microphone. Drinks. They would be bound to have run out of something. She went that way instead. Annie was behind the bar. She smiled as Emma came closer. 'Just brought another case of fizz down.'

'Right. Thanks.' So everything was in hand. She turned away.

'Are you all right?' Annie was scurrying after her.

'Yeah. I'm fine.'

'Only I saw Tom leaving.'

'Right. Yeah. It's complicated. He's widowed. There's a lot of emotion to deal with.' The knot in her stomach tightened. Her fear was right. She couldn't compete with a ghost, could she?

Annie flung her arms around Emma who found herself in the midst of a ringletty cuddle whether she chose to be or not. 'I'm sorry. You two seemed so right, you know?' Annie stood back. 'You know that feeling when you see two people and you just know it's going to work out for them?'

'Yeah. I do. Obviously.' But her mother had warned her; nobody got it right every time.

'This is an amazing party!' Lydia Hyland barrelled into them dragging a young man Emma recognised, but didn't remember from the sign-up list, behind her.

'I'm glad you're enjoying yourself.'

The young man nodded. 'She is. We are. She's very drunk.'

Lydia nodded happily. 'I am, but I'm happy drunk, and Will has instructions to cut me off if I've had too much.' She slapped a hand to her face. 'I haven't introduced you!'

'You really don't have to.' There was a gentle warning tone in his voice.

'I'll do it the way that doesn't embarrass you. Aaaaaanie, this is Will.'

They exchanged greetings.

'And Emma, this is Will. See,' hissed Lydia. 'I didn't tell them you were a viscount.'

He rolled his eyes. 'I think they might have heard.'

'But not from me,' she shot back.

Emma finally worked out where she knew Will from. 'You work the bar for us.'

'Guilty as charged.'

'And you're a viscount?'

'Shhhhh.' Lydia held a finger up to her lips. 'He doesn't like people knowing that.'

Will rolled his eyes. 'I'm going to get you a glass of water.'

Lydia nodded seriously and the three women watched him walk away.

'I've got a viscount working behind the bar?' Some of the bloggers would love that. Emma filed it away under 'Not her story to tell'.

'Not just a viscount,' Lydia corrected. 'A hot viscount.'

'Ok.' Emma had many, many more questions but none of them seemed likely to get an answer more detailed than 'Hot viscount.'

'How much have you had to drink, Lyds?' asked Annie.

'Too much. I drink too much when I'm nervous, you know.'

'I know,' replied her friend.

'Lot of fancy people at this thing. Makes me nervous.' She was quiet for a moment. 'Less nervous now. He says he loves me.'

'Quite right too,' replied Annie.

'What are we talking about?' Jane and Charlotte joined the group.

'About the hot viscount who loves Lydia,' explained Emma.

Jane nodded. 'We met him. I don't think he wanted us all to know he was a viscount.'

Lydia laughed. 'Well sod it. I'm in love with a viscount and I'm not ashamed of how posh he is, cos it's not his fault, is it?'

'I guess not.'

'If you marry him,' asked Jane, 'will you be a viscountess?'

'Yeah.' Lydia's eyes were wide. 'Is that a thing? He's gonna be an earl when he grows up. Do they have earlesses?'

Emma left the friends together and found Josh at the edge of the dance floor. 'We did this,' she said.

'You did this,' he corrected.

'You helped and I know I'm not easy to help.'

'You do tend to like things a certain way.'

'Well, sometimes there's a right way.'

'And sometimes it doesn't matter so long as shit gets done.' He laughed. 'And it got done. You made all this happen.'

Only just. 'The casino and the dance woman gave us discounts,' she admitted. 'And Robbie is doing all this PR for nothing.'

'I know.'

'How?'

'I looked at your precious spreadsheet.'

How dare he?

'And there's a solid business there,' Josh continued. 'If you'd used Dad's life insurance money as starting capital like Mum suggested you wouldn't have ended up so stressed out.'

'I wanted to do it all on my own,' she whispered.

'I know.' He looked around. 'But all this is huge. Finance and event planning and PR and sales and admin and that's before you even get to the actual matchmaking. You're brilliant, Stilts. You don't have to be perfect.'

She was furious for the intrusion and flattered by the opinion.

'And I have a proposition for you,' he said. 'I have about six grand left from my redundancy. I'll put that in to cover our outstanding bills, but after that, equal partners. I can do all our IT and a lot of the finance stuff.'

He held his hand out for her to shake.

Partners? Not being entirely in control. Josh would do things differently. Not her way. Not her mother's way. It was a risk. Emma waited for the feeling of dread to come. It wasn't there.

She shook his hand. 'Deal.'

'You were totally right about the main thing.'

'About what?'

'Finding love in person,' he replied. 'People have to show who they really are. It's too easy to hide yourself online.'

Chapter Twenty-Three

Tom watched Ted deal the next hand. Having arrived late, Tom was pretty even in the game so far. He'd lost a bit and won a bit but nothing big, nothing that made him feel like he was living on the edge of his skill level.

Ted made a half-hearted quip about Tom having lost his nerve.

'I'm dressed like a fucking extra from *Pride and Prejudice* and it's my poker playing you're taking the piss out of?'

Ted shrugged. 'What do I know about your young person clothes?'

The deal gave Tom nines in the hole swiftly followed by another nine on the flop, alongside a two and the queen of spades. He bet cautiously, not so much as to spook anyone sitting on a pair. The turn didn't help him. He checked and watched his opponents do the same. The queen of hearts. Of course. What else would it be? Full house.

He felt like he hadn't had a hand this good for months. His dad had always said the cards have no memory but Tom had to admit he'd started to feel like the fug in his soul was infecting the random fall of cards at the table. At least this proved him wrong. His head was all over the place and the queen of hearts came to save him. He caught himself glancing towards the door. She'd come to save his poker hand anyway. Across the table, Ted shoved all in. The next player folded. Tom shoved without hesitation and kidded himself that he saw Ted's face tense ever so slightly behind his dark glasses before he revealed a third queen in his hand. Trip queens. Decent hand. Not decent enough.

It was a good pot to win. Normally a win like that would send a little thrill through Tom's body. Today he collected up his winnings and stepped away.

'You can't pack in now, mate?' Ted was not impressed.

'This is way less than you've taken off me recently,' Tom shot back. He shuffled the pile of notes into a wad and rolled them tightly to stuff in his back pocket. 'Always a pleasure.'

'Then why don't you sound like you're having fun, lad?'

Ted had known him since he was a kid. This game had been Tom's dad's game back in the day. Ted knew more of Tom's secrets that most. He could tell him. Tom shook his head. 'A story for another time. I'm gonna head off now.'

He might as well. The Queen of Hearts was never going to appear and if she did what would he say? *Lovely to meet you. I think I've fallen in love with someone else?* That was going to be tough to sell as an opener, but his heart was elsewhere. He'd had a chance to take a real risk, one that mattered, not one that was just a turn of a card, and he'd bottled it. He'd folded the one time he needed to hold his nerve.

–

If she'd been told eight weeks ago that she'd be all set to walk out of the final ball, Regency dress still on, and stride off down the Strand an hour before the party ended, Emma Love would have said you were insane. Aside from the fact that at the ball was exactly where she wanted to be, it was also where she needed to be. Nobody else could be trusted to ensure that everything ran to time, that the dancers were cleared to the edge of the floor before the fountains fired and that everyone had champagne in hand for the final moments of the Season.

But of course someone else could. Someone else would. The new Chief Finance Officer of the Season and his very enthusiastic girlfriend, and would-be matchmaking consultant, were more than capable of ensuring things were brought to a close with sufficient finesse.

And Emma had somewhere else she wanted to be. She'd planned the Season to end on the final bank holiday of the summer, which meant it was Monday night. Monday night was when SirWalt played his regular game. And Emma was an idiot. Of course she was an idiot who might still be entirely wrong. This whole notion that she couldn't shake from her head was like a house of cards that she'd built up but which could be blown away in a second. It was easy to hide yourself online, Josh had said. But people could just as easily give themselves away.

So what if his dad had taught him poker?

So what if he loved a game of chance?

So what if he'd lived in Walthamstow?

So what if he'd made a joke about being a knight the first time they'd met?

So what if he'd kept trying to tell her he played something other than piano?

So what if his mother had described him as 'all in'?

So what if he had somewhere else to be tonight?

Those things could apply to anyone. But she had to know. She had to take the chance. She had to embrace the fact that if she was wrong she was gloriously and hopefully and romantically wrong.

She strode towards the main gate, only to have her momentum stalled in an instant. Tom was here, standing in the entranceway. He wasn't across town playing poker. Of course he wasn't. Why would he be?

'I thought you'd gone—'

'Where are you going—'

They talked over one another in a volley of confusion.

'I was looking for you,' he offered.

'Me too. I mean I was looking for you.'

They stopped and stared for a moment. One of them needed to speak. Emma took a breath. 'I thought I knew where to look for you because I had this stupid idea that you might be…' She ran out of steam. 'It's complicated.'

'Tell me.'

'Do you play poker?'

'Yeah.'

She couldn't still be right. 'Did you head off to go and play in a private cash game?'

'How did you know that?'

She was right. She was actually right. Emma almost laughed at the obviousness of it once you knew. 'I hoped it was you,' she said. 'I didn't believe it could be.'

'What? But?' He shook his head. 'What do you mean?'

She took a step towards him. 'Think about it. If you were a matchmaker what username would you pick?'

His jaw opened a little. 'You?'

She nodded.

'The Queen of Hearts?'

'Walt?'

He nodded. 'I was still living in Walthamstow when I set the account up. It was not long after Jack. I couldn't face going out and playing tournaments.'

Emma balled up her courage again. 'Why did you come back, Tom?'

'Because I know I messed up. I used them asking about Jack as an excuse to freak out and run away. And I'm furious with myself for that. Not half as furious as he'd have been, though.'

She mustn't cry. She was still at work. She couldn't go back to the party with mascara halfway down her face. It was too late. Tears spilled from her eyes. 'Can I ask you something about him?'

'You can ask me anything.'

'Would he, would Jack have liked me, do you think?'

Tom nodded. 'He'd have loved you. I'll always be sad that I lost him, but he treated life like a grand adventure. He'd hate the idea that I couldn't keep going. And there is nobody else I want to share the next adventure with. It's you.'

It was that simple. She was it for Tom, and he was it for her, regardless of timing or planning or what her spreadsheet said. 'I'm glad. Cos it's you for me too.'

He stepped forward and pulled her into his arms. 'So what is the next adventure?'

'This.' She reached her fingertip to his cheek and ran it down to his neck where his shirt was open to the chest. And she leaned towards him and pressed her lips to his. When she finally pulled away she remembered something else. 'They're about to fire the fountains.'

'And?'

'And do you wanna come and dance with me in the rain?'

He kissed her very lightly once again before he answered. 'Always, Miss Love. Always.'

Epilogue

Happily ever after

Later, when the dancers had danced their final reel, and the last of the champagne had been poured, Emma looked around the denizens of the Season.

People had found one another. They'd found those connections she'd hoped for. All around her she saw arms around bodies, hands clasped together, heads resting on shoulders. All around her she saw love blossoming in the late summer warmth.

There was Col, Colin, Colin Williams, whose hopeful heart had finally been met with kindness. There was Annie and Josh, arm in arm, whispering about their plans for the lives they'd put on hold. There was Jane, hand in hand with Charlotte, on the brink of beginning their own unique family. There was Lydia – could she really be the next Countess of Hanborough? Why ever not? Love, Emma realised, did seem determined to find a way.

Tom slid his arm around her waist and she leaned back into the warmth of his body. 'So what next?' he whispered. 'Vegas? Gretna Green?'

She laughed. 'I'm embracing risk. I'm not insane.'

'So what do you want?'

She looked around. Hope Lucas was standing alone at the edge of the dance floor. 'I want to do this again. At Christmas time. But better. Anyone who didn't make a match this time will get a discount.'

'And when you're not at work?'

'I want to come to your cash game and clean you out,' she joked.

'I thought you didn't play for real money.'

She turned to look him in the eye. 'I guess right now I'm feeling lucky.'

'Me too,' he whispered. 'And I'd bet on us any day.'

'So would I.'

'All in?' he asked.

'All in,' she confirmed.

A letter from Ally

Hello!

Thank you so much for joining me for the social season. I'm delighted to have you here with me for my first book with Hera and our first adventure with Emma, Tom, Josh and all our fabulous daters.

I started writing this book during the winter lockdown at the start of 2021 and being able to disappear into this wonderful world of romance and friendship was an absolute tonic during a difficult time. My biggest hope is that *A Season for Love* might provide the same bubble of positivity and joy for readers, as it did for me when I was writing it.

I'd love to hear your thoughts on all our budding romances, and which couples really won your hearts?

You can get in touch on:

Instagram: @msallysinclair

TikTok: @msallysinclair

Twitter: @MsAllySinclair

Facebook: facebook.com/allysinclairauthor/

And on my website: allysinclair.com

Or you can email allysinclairauthor@gmail.com

Thank you so much for reading *A Season for Love*. I can't wait to welcome you back, along with Emma and our next group of hopeful romantics, for the Christmas Season!

Lots of love,

Ally

Acknowledgements

Huge thanks first of all to everyone at Hera, especially Keshini Naidoo and Jennie Ayres, for seeing the potential in this story and for working so hard to make the finished book as fabulous as possible. Thank you in particular for guiding me through the structural edit to end all structural edits so beautifully – the book is a million times better as a result.

Thanks as well to Julia Silk and everyone at Greyhound Literary Agents. Every author will tell you that their agent is The Best, but mine actually is The Best. Huge thanks, as always, Julia.

The part of writing a book before it gets as far as an agent or editor is an incredibly solitary process. I'm not sure I'd ever get through it without the best crew of writer buddies in the world. Annie O'Neil, Daisy Tate, Imogen Howson, Janet Gover, Jeevani Charika, Jessica Thorne, Kate Johnson, Rhoda Baxter, Ruth Long and Sheila McClure – thank you, just in general, for being there.

This book is as much about friendship as it is about love, so this one's for all of you.

And finally, much gratitude to EngineerBoy, the most excellent emotional support human for an over-stressed author that there ever has been.